Death Brand

Scott C. Ristau

PublishAmerica

Baltimore

First printing

ISBN: 1-4137-7300-1
PUBLISHED BY PUBLISHAMERICA, LLLP
www.publishamerica.com
Baltimore

Printed in the United States of America

This book is dedicated to my family in gratitude for their love, guidance, and forgiving patience.

Chapter 1
Ascension

Last night, Torrin Murgleys fell asleep to the sound of thunder. It was a sleep plagued by nightmares, a torment he suffered all too often. He dreamed of a boiling blood-red sea churned by cavorting demons, splashing and playing in the foul water. But like the night, the storm was over and the dream a fading, inconsequential memory.

The day's dark cycle ended with the rising flood of light delivered with the coming of dawn. The sun's brightening rays penetrated the morning air, as did the pounding of a fist against an oaken door, the clamor of arguing voices, and the explosion of pottery breaking against an unyielding stone wall.

Prodded by these familiar intrusions upon his slumber, Torrin awoke to a day initially similar to virtually every other he had known in his young life. From the other room Torrin heard the coarse, ugly voice of his father, loud and cursing. Although he couldn't clearly discern all her words, Torrin's mother could also be heard. But his bed was warm and his pillow soft, so Torrin shut his eyes and rolled over, wrapping the covers more tightly around him. He was too tired to care. Besides, it was nothing new; he had heard it all before.

But as the mental fog between sleep and full awakening evaporated, Torrin's mind came alive with remembrance that he had with great impatience longed for this day, believing it to be the crucial first step by which he would reshape his life so as to become a person with value and one capable of making a significant difference in the world. And that belief would prove true, but not in the manner by which Torrin had hoped.

Kicking legs and flailing arms against the restraining blankets, Torrin was now in a great hurry to be up and moving. But with movements confused by an eager anticipation to leave his bed, Torrin became entangled in his covers and crashed to the floor, nearly knocking himself unconscious. Cursing his fumble-footed nature and thankful that no one had witnessed this most recent exhibition of it, Torrin rose and dressed with less speed and more deliberate concentration. He selected a pair of tan pants and a cranberry colored tunic of a thick quilted material. Once dressed, Torrin stood for a moment admiring his reflection in a full-length cheval mirror. The mirror's oval frame had been carved from richly grained walnut in the design of a serpent engaged in the immortal act of devouring its tail, its coiled body encircling the smooth surface of the glass plane. A pair of bright, multifaceted crystal orbs were inset within the graven, brooding sockets of the serpent's eyes and chips of ivory, pointed and white, were inlaid as fangs. Despite that its intended purpose was to flatter the vanity of people, the mirror itself was an impressive work of art, a finely crafted piece of ornamental furniture.

"Not bad," Torrin reassured himself, scrutinizing the familiar image reflected by the mirror. In truth, Torrin's physical appearance was generally unremarkable. He was of average height and build with sandy-brown hair and eyes that were an imperfect shade of blue. His nose was a bit broad but not too pronounced. He had a young face which was unscarred and unblemished. In short, his looks were quite ordinary, unmarked by any particularly handsome or hideous distinction.

Torrin tilted his head from side to side, studying his profile in the mirror, then looked his reflection over from head to toe. Overall, he considered himself a rather handsome seventeen-year-old man. But he worried that few, if any, seemed to share this opinion. His mind moved in the all too common dance between concern over how others saw him and adamant protests that he did not care, that for him their opinions lacked significance.

Why should I care what people think? Most are half-witted fools anyway, thought Torrin. *Just because I don't have girls hanging all over me, telling me how smart and good-looking I am, doesn't mean it isn't true.* The image of these girls lingered and Torrin smiled, fantasizing for a moment about the idea of such female admirers. Unfortunately, it was doubt that really hung on him. *But what is beauty or wisdom without someone to appreciate it,* he wondered, *someone to recognize the quality in question but who is removed from the object under evaluation.*

Unable to resolve this minor dilemma, Torrin pivoted from the mirror, turning his attention away from the worth of his character.

Today marked the anniversary of Torrin's birth, his natal day. But this was only indirectly the cause for his excitement. Something was about to happen today which Torrin believed possessed a greater importance to his life than recalling the occasion of its inception. The direction of his future would depend upon the outcome of today's events. So his birthday was a trivial affair compared to the test Torrin would soon face. Nor did he have much interest in the noise to which he had awakened. The commotion was undoubtedly some new or continuing dispute within his family in the adjoining room.

Being a nobleman, Torrin had a private bed chamber high within Castle Gairloch. The door to his chamber led to an attached great room that he shared with his parents and older brother for meals and leisure. They also had adjoining bed chambers of their own. But it was at times like these when Torrin would have preferred to avoid his immediate family and their myriad problems that he wished for a more private way out of his room.

It is said that only a mule denies his family. Torrin Murgleys felt, at times, quite mulish indeed.

For Torrin, a person credited nothing from his ancestry, not blame or praise. Instead, he considered the value of a person to be solely contained within the individual. You inherit only your own past and produce only your own future. Although holding tremendous promise for the synergistic benefit of its members, in practice the random construct of a family often proved to be a ruinous institution. Individuals are typically too different for peaceful cohabitation, so compelled by their tenuous kinship. One's immediate family might well be the quintessence of familiarity and although familiarity may not always breed contempt, if this lack of respect does exist, a family is merely a house of fools doomed to perish. Family places power in the hands of those whom we did not necessarily choose to entrust it. In a disharmonious family, half the time the individual worries that the others know too much about him, know too well how he may be hurt. The other half of the time, they seem not to understand him at all. And there is injury in that ignorance, the apparent apathy, as well. Family creates an environment that allows for abuse free from the scrutiny of the public eye, not to imply that society's vision is always objective or rationally interpreted. Torrin did love his family. He could not deny that truth, painful though it may be at times, but it was a love not without its challenges.

They're not all that bad, Torrin mentally confessed. *Mostly we just leave each other alone. Still, claiming that things could be worse does not justify a bad situation nor excuse destructive behavior. I don't know why we can't get along. It would probably be best if we stopped trying altogether. But then perhaps the World Spirit uses one's family to test us, for if we cannot learn to understand and accept our relatives, how can we ever learn to tolerate one another as a society?*

Having shored up his courage, and with little other choice as it was the only way out, Torrin opened his door.

The room on the other side of the doorway was large and brightened by the amber-hued light of the early morning sun drifting through the windows in broad bands of soft golden radiance. A tall ceiling capped the room, at least twelve feet in height. A wainscoting of blonde wooden panels lined the lower one-third of the walls. The walls themselves were made of slate gray stone and decorated with tapestries rich in color and imagery. A heavy carpet of corded cloth covered much of the floor. Elegant furnishings tenanted the room; chairs, tables, candle sconces, glazed pottery, and display cabinets stacked with figurines. A few pieces of cut wood burned in the fireplace, keeping the morning chill at bay. The room was both warm and lavish. And the scene being played out upon this stage was a familiar one.

Torrin's father, Devin, had apparently just returned from another night of drinking and associated entertainment. Torrin's mother, Marketa, in a vain attempt to teach Devin that such intemperate behavior was unacceptable, had locked him out. But it was an empty threat. Only a little physical abuse to the door and a few harsh words were required for Devin to be allowed access to his home.

The battle between his parents had lost its initial fury and was winding down as Torrin entered the great room. Devin slouched in a settee, nestled between the couch's embracing arms of elaborately carved wood and against padded cushions sheathed in a velvety fabric of blended beige and forest green. One hand cradled his forehead above a face set with irritation and the discomfort one experiences between the glow of drunkenness and the onset of a hangover. Torrin recognized the familiar look but without much sympathy. Marketa continued her attack on Devin but in a more subdued manner than before; her devotion to the quarrel had already begun to wane. Meanwhile Aragon, Torrin's older brother, sat at the table reading. He seemed completely uninterested in his surroundings, as if he were alone with his book.

Torrin joined his brother at the table and asked, "Have I missed breakfast?"
No response.

"Aragon, have I missed breakfast?" Torrin repeated, his voice carefully raised.

"Hm. What? No not yet. Now keep quiet; can't you see I'm busy?" Aragon grumbled, distracted and annoyed at the interruption of his study for the purpose of such frivolous dialogue.

As if on cue, and perfumed with the scent of freshly baked bread, Dora entered with their morning meal. Dora was a servant who Torrin had known much of his life. She was friendly to him and Torrin had always liked her. Somewhere in her late thirties, Dora was a mature woman but with a shapely hourglass figure that was well displayed by her light cotton, low-cut dress and snugly fitted bodice. Lustrous short black hair surrounded her smiling, gentle face. Unlike the conceit or haughtiness present in so many physically attractive women, Dora managed to express her beauty while preserving an endearing impression of modesty.

Moving around upon the table, Dora unintentionally brushed against Torrin. And in setting out the plates of food, she bent low enough to afford him a delightful view of her upper anatomy, a brief but bewitching glimpse of a magnificent bosom immodestly revealed by her arousing décolletage. Furtively, Torrin studied the soft lines of Dora's face. She had large soulful eyes, clear and seemingly untroubled by dark emotions. Her pale-pink lips were wide and glistened with a hint of lingering moisture. Torrin's gaze slipped to her shoulders, then glided over the fullness of her breasts, down the fine inward curve of her waist and across the rounded sweep of her hips.

Recently, Torrin had begun to appreciate Dora in a fashion much different from his early childhood when she would tell him bedtime stories while supervising him in his parents' absence. Torrin was not a child any longer and he now looked at Dora with curiosity about what it might be like to lay with her, or to couple with any woman for that matter. To his acute frustration, Torrin was still a virgin and increasingly impatient about altering that facet of his character. He felt more than ready to learn the full pleasures of the flesh and Dora appeared well equipped to teach him these much-desired lessons in carnal knowledge. Regrettably, however, these pleasant musings were brought to an abrupt halt by the slight cuff of his father's hand to the back of Torrin's head.

"Pick your tongue off the floor, boy," jeered Devin while scrutinizing Dora himself. "She's too much woman for you, Torrin. And unfortunately not quite good enough for me, at least not anymore." Now looking with bloodshot eyes directly and meaningfully at his son, Devin finished by mocking, "Besides, I thought you aspired to be my mother's catamite and were saving yourself for just that purpose. Isn't that right, you little pervert? Don't you wish you could be Grandma's plaything?"

Torrin flushed with rage and embarrassment at his father's derision, his generous dispersal of ridicule that gave insult to Torrin, Dora, Marketa, and even the queen all at once. His throat tightened and his blood ran hot. But Torrin was impotent to reply other than to stare at his plate with all the hate and disgust he felt for his father.

Had he been able to look at her, Torrin would have been impressed that to all outward appearances Dora was unabashed by Devin's choler and lubricity, the hostile indecency of his behavior. It was as if she had not heard him at all. Devin's obscene mockery rolled off her like rain from a steepled roof.

Dora completed her duties with a dignified equanimity that never faltered, bringing a wondrously calm and steady grace to the chore. Maintaining this proud bearing, she left without a word, pausing only to place a gentle hand on Torrin's shoulder in commiseration, a tender touch that told him she would hold nothing his father said against him. But that small bit of sympathy only flamed Torrin's anger and embarrassment. A man wants to be admired by women, not pitied.

By the time Torrin had choked down his breakfast, which his anger had given an acrid flavor, Devin had passed out and Aragon had left. Marketa too was preparing to leave for a colloquy she planned to attend in another part of the castle. It seemed she was always involved in some lecture or similar group activity, most of which Torrin regarded as peculiar in nature. Although her studies were unconventional and involved the exploration of eccentric ideas, she seemed to think it was essential to continue these allegedly enriching pursuits. She often remarked that a life without learning and one devoid of self-examination is an empty existence. One seeking knowledge cannot be thwarted even by death. Through the pursuit of greater awareness, life goes on.

Whatever the hell that's supposed to mean, thought Torrin. *And why*, he wondered, *if my mother considers education to be of such value and importance, does she seem so apathetic to her own sons' academic development? She didn't care when Aragon left the Prelature and she never asks about my schooling.* With this unanswered question, Torrin also took his leave and, as he walked through the castle's chilly stone corridors, turned his mental attention to his father.

Devin was the eldest son of the castle's monarch, High Queen Bryana. But Devin, as well as everyone else, knew he had no hope of inheriting the throne. That honor and distinction would likely go to Devin's considerably younger brother, who like the queen had been born with the power of magic. Though it had skipped their father, Torrin and Aragon had also inherited magical ability, a condition that galled Devin's pride rather than enriched it. It seemed to Devin that within his family those with magic surrounded him while he had been cheated of the ability. He resented that others had power he was denied, both in terms of magic and of the throne. This resentment had matured over the years into intimate contempt. He had dug a well of bitterness from which he often drank.

Like his father, Torrin's mother was also mundane, without magic. And sometimes it seemed that this was all his parents shared in common. Although Torrin believed that at one time his parents must have been in love with each other, he also acknowledged the possibility that Devin had married Marketa merely to spite the queen. Queen Bryana never cared for Marketa and made it clear that she believed her son should have married better.

Long ago, Torrin had given up attempting to understand his parents' relationship and the hope that they might still be in love. This realization was finally accepted several years ago when Torrin overheard a confrontation between his parents similar to the one that occurred this morning. Devin had taken one of Marketa's friends as his lover. Marketa soon learned of Devin's indiscreet paramour and confronted him. During the confrontation, Marketa was screaming at him that, among other things, she no longer wanted to be his wife. She wasn't going to put up with his affairs any longer. If he loved her, he'd stop and if he didn't, she would leave him. Devin tried unsuccessfully to placate her by swearing that he was sorry, that he loved her, and that he would never again be unfaithful to Marketa. But they were the same tired, empty promises. Marketa wanted more from Devin to convince her that he would truly change. Seeing that Marketa was unwilling to forgive him, Devin's tender pleading voice turned suddenly cold as he abruptly changed his tactic. Torrin's father explained in a frighteningly dispassionate monotone that without his consent his mother, the queen, would never permit a legal dissolution of their marriage and that if Marketa left him he would kill her and their children. The icy sound of his voice left little doubt that he meant what he said. So with that, the discussion terminated. Devin's laconic statement, coldly unemotional, may not have prevented future arguments but it did establish an underlying boundary for their domestic disputes.

Having reached his first intended destination, Torrin stood collecting his thoughts before the home of the woman he loved. A girl actually, being a few months younger than Torrin himself. And much to his unexpected delight, she returned his love with love of her own.

They had been completely devoted to one another for nearly a year. Having no real magic, she had nonetheless cast a spell over Torrin that bound him to her. For the first time since he was a very young boy, he felt not alone. He felt like someone genuinely cared about him, was interested in his feelings, and wanted to understand him. Torrin still found it difficult to believe that someone like Lenore could be in love with him. And because of his shaky confidence, Torrin would periodically be struck with the irrational fear that this shining aspect of his life would somehow be taken from him.

Responding to his knock, Lenore opened the door.

"Good morning. I hope I didn't wake you?" Torrin inquired and immediately regretted it. *Why do I always say such stupid things*, he wondered.

It was obvious that she had not just left her bed. Her light brown hair was perfectly combed and clean, shimmering with a golden light, a refulgent sheen that was warm and inviting. The lush mane draped over her supple shoulders where it embraced an immaculate emerald gown covering her from nape to ankle, its simple elegance made beautiful by her strong and slender form. A gold chain designed of fluid interlocking lines encircled Lenore's fair neck and dangled enviably in her petite bosom. Her gown accentuated the cool green color of her eyes, eyes that sparkled with alert intelligence. The sight of her lovely visage and her perfumed lavender fragrance caused Torrin's pulse to quicken and his mind to flounder.

"No, I've been up for some time now," Lenore answered with an understanding smile. "Happy birthday! I have a present for you; wait here and I'll get it."

With the fluid grace of youth, Lenore spun quickly around and stepped back inside. Torrin waited eagerly for her return, for the corridor was suddenly drab and lonely in her absence.

After a minute or two, she came back carrying an eloquently crafted battle axe. Attached to its dark hardwood handle, the steel axe head was constructed with a leaf-shaped pike at the top and two curved blades, one half as long as the other.

Leaning in close to kiss his cheek, Lenore pressed the axe into Torrin's hands.

"It's wonderful!" Torrin was thrilled with the gift and enthusiastically tested the feel and balance of the axe. "Thank you," he said, still admiring the weapon. "It's fantastic; is it enchanted?"

"Only with my love," said Lenore.

"Powerful magic indeed, with this I shall be invincible!" Torrin boasted lightheartedly. "Thank you so very much. Not just for this, but for everything. I'd be lost without you; you mean the world to me. This has been the happiest year of my life. I love you." And they kissed as young lovers will.

They complimented one another, providing a near perfect balance for their individual strengths and weaknesses. Lenore was not given to excessive sentimentality or effusive displays of affection as Torrin was known to indulge in, at least with her. But like Torrin, she was intelligent, although with a common sense that he sometimes lacked. Lenore was a practical, no-nonsense girl with a strong will to which Torrin would generally acquiesce. Yet she seldom took unfair advantage of Torrin's submissiveness to her, being also thoughtful and fair. Where Torrin was idealistic, Lenore was firmly rooted in reality. They needed each other and seemed to realize it. But more importantly, they respected and cherished one another.

Parting from their kiss, Torrin gazed longingly at Lenore. "You look gorgeous. You wouldn't by chance be leaving to meet another man behind my back?"

Her appearance and Torrin's unwarranted jealousy were not topics Lenore enjoyed discussing. She liked compliments but was embarrassed by them. So she quickly changed the subject by asking if he was going to combat training today.

"Yes. In fact, I'm on my way there now," answered Torrin.

"My parents wanted to know if you could stop by tonight. We would like to have a little celebration in honor of your birthday," invited Lenore.

"I can't tonight, you know that. I'll be at the convocation of the wizard Prelature for the First Rite of Ascension ceremony. The World Spirit willing, tonight I will finally be ordained a prelate. I'm sorry, but since I'm not sure how long the ceremony will last, I can't really make any other plans," Torrin explained with returning excitement and anxiety. "Besides, if I fail the test and the queen chooses not to make me a prelate, I'm not going to feel much like celebrating."

"That's fine about dinner and don't worry so much! I'm sure that you'll be made a prelate and an excellent one at that. Certainly no one deserves it more than you. You've worked for it with more dedication and diligence than anyone else I've ever known," she said, slightly jealous of the time Torrin devoted to his studies rather than to her. "And besides, the queen *is* your grandmother after all." She made the last comment in lighthearted sarcasm, playfully implying that his heritage would assure success.

Torrin failed to catch the humor of Lenore's joke.

"The High Queen would never show favoritism to me! She is a noble and just leader, both as queen and as archprelate, and would never debase herself with such gross injustice. She is the savior of our people, the living embodiment of virtue and integrity. It's ridiculous to think that she would promote me within the Prelature simply because we are related by blood," exclaimed Torrin indignantly.

"Torrin, I was only teasing." The muscles of Lenore's face tightened to form a pinched, yet pretty, scowl. "Lighten up. For crying out loud, you take everything much too seriously; you're too tense. I agree with your adulation of Queen Bryana. She is a great monarch and deserves your praise. I'm proud that you are her grandson and I understand that you are too," Lenore replied with a slight moue, again feeling moderately jealous of Torrin's divided affections.

"Don't say that!" Torrin snapped. "You know I don't believe it, that I can't believe it. If I take pride in the accomplishments of my grandmother, then I must also share the shame of that satiric sot, that drunken womanizer I'm forced to call my father. I am no more and no less than what I am. My value does not extend to my family," insisted Torrin angrily.

"All right, all right. I'm sorry I said anything at all; I certainly didn't mean to offend you. Please, let's change the subject," urged Lenore. "How about if we have a dual celebration dinner tomorrow for both your birthday and ascension to prelate? Not that I'm sure you deserve it after the dreadful way you've treated me today."

Torrin reddened slightly, realizing that he had overreacted. Upon swift reflection, he felt guilty for his outburst and a bit foolish for his hasty words.

"I'm sorry," said Torrin, trying to calm himself. "It's just that everything has me a bit on edge these days—my family, the Prelature. Dinner tomorrow would be wonderful. I'll see you then, if you're still willing."

They embraced and kissed again. Separating from the prolonged union of their lips, Torrin left for combat practice after reminding Lenore of his love for her and asking that she extend his greeting to her parents.

After Torrin left, it took Lenore a moment to regain her own composure, a composure that was seldom flustered. But Torrin's excessive glorification of the queen and bitter attitude toward the rest of his family troubled her. Regardless of what he said, Lenore knew that Torrin's faith in the queen did in large part preserve his faith in the world and in himself. He depended upon the queen as an example of righteousness to support his belief that such qualities existed in the world and could be cultivated within himself. The other examples that his family afforded Torrin caused Lenore concern over what kind of a husband and father Torrin might one day prove to be. *No*, she reminded herself, *I love Torrin and know him to be of good character.* It wasn't fair to question him. He had never hurt her nor been unkind in any way, and she had no justifiable reason to suspect that he would change.

So Lenore resolved to continue her day as planned. She was on her way to Torrin's home to invite his family to join her own at tomorrow's celebration dinner for Torrin. However, she was admittedly a little apprehensive about going alone to see Torrin's family, in consideration of what he had told her about them.

Her own experience with the Murgleys family was rather limited. Lenore thought Aragon to be rude, if not down right mean, for he seemed always to be quietly brooding, his features perpetually drawn in a scowl that could hardly be considered friendly. Whenever she encountered Aragon, he appeared angry over something he considered her too witless to comprehend. Although their styles were different, Aragon could be as arrogant as his father. On the other hand, Marketa's mode of behavior was sociable and she was generally eager to engage in amiable conversation with virtually anyone. However, even though Marketa was friendly enough, she still made Lenore uncomfortable in that Marketa's ideas and associations were strange to Lenore's staid perspective. And then there was Torrin's father. Lenore had seen Devin about the castle many times but had been introduced to him only once. Torrin had proudly presented her to his father at a party but Devin scarcely acknowledged her, being preoccupied with the interest of another woman. It was an awkward moment, to say the least. Lenore had felt bad for Torrin, for he had been obviously hurt by his father's indifference and embarrassed by Devin's open impropriety.

All things considered, Lenore hoped Marketa would be the one to receive her call. So she was disappointed when at the second beat of the ponderously large brass knocker, Devin answered the door.

"Good morning my lord. I'm sorry to disturb you, but I was wondering if I could speak with you *and* your wife," inquired Lenore hopefully.

"My wife? She's not at home and I'm afraid I'm in need of my rest. Come back some other time," replied Devin as he began to close the door.

Putting her hand against the door to forestall its closure, Lenore hastily added. "I'm Torrin's girlfriend, and it will only take a moment."

The door came back open. Beneath an arched eyebrow, Devin's

expression now appeared more interested and alert as he invited Lenore in. Once he had her inside, Devin closed the door and eyed Lenore appraisingly.

Devin was a tall, well muscled and handsome man with strong, rugged features. His hair was black, short and neatly trimmed, like his beard. His eyes were dark and penetrating, often bearing an aspect that could make your skin glaze over in an icy sweat caused by the uncomfortable sensation of loathing and power that emanated from his gaze. Aragon had inherited that look, but not Devin's disarming smile. It relaxed the intimidating pressure of Devin's stare, making those graced by it feel both relieved and privileged. Though his family had discovered the lie camouflaged by that smile and developed a resistance to it, the endearing expression still captivated others. Devin was confident, wild, and crass. Men admired him, women desired him. If he treated them as a friend, most people felt better about themselves. Or maybe they just felt safer. Devin could identify and prey upon a person's most sensitive areas with the precision and ferocity of a predatory hawk locating from above a mouse in a wide grassy field. With this ability he could deliver insults that would strike a person to the very center of his soul. Devin would use this power in varying degrees depending on his mood, and often followed it with a jovial remark that made his victim unsure if he should laugh or be enraged. Nonetheless, Devin was generally well liked by the castle's soldiers. They considered him a good companion in both battle and carousal. His appearance, boldness, and ardent pursuit of merriment made him popular with men and women alike. But even his friends knew better than to trust him.

Devin moved uncomfortably nearer to Lenore. "So, you're Torrin's girlfriend? Tell me, why would such a lovely young girl be interested in my son? If it is wealth or power you're after, you won't find it through him and certainly more handsome men are available to you," smirked Devin with a lewd, conspiratorial wink.

Lenore did not like the sound of that nor the direction this encounter seemed to be taking. Nervously, she stepped back from Devin's advance.

"I love your son for what he is, and I've come to ask you to do something for him," said Lenore in a voice that quavered only slightly.

But Devin interrupted her by again moving forward, positioning her between himself and the wall. Devin's smile unfolded with flourish, which to Lenore was in no way endearing but rather a reflection of his tumid ego, licentious designs, his inflated self-image and immoral intensions.

"A most touching sentiment, but wouldn't you prefer a more erudite lover, one better schooled in the art?" Devin invited.

Holding her with his intent gaze, Devin gently slipped his hand around the base of her neck, slowly lifting Lenore's soft golden-brown hair above her delicate shoulders.

"You should wear your hair up, my dear, to better display your lovely neck. In fact, your beauty would be much enhanced if you revealed more of your silky flesh in other areas as well."

He let his hand fall back to her neck; her hair fell with it in a cascade of fine shimmering filaments. His callused hand was rough against her skin. Even if she were not afraid to turn her gaze, she could not look away from his eyes. They were hypnotic, captivating, and she felt trapped by them. Slowly, deliberately, Devin's other arm enwrapped her slender waist in a snug embrace. A titillating shiver danced up her spine in reaction to the feel of Devin's hand. It glided lower and his palm cupped the firm, sweet meat of Lenore's buttock.

A galaxy of emotions whirled within her. She flushed, her heartbeat frenzied from a strange mixture of fear, revulsion, and the unexpected stirring of arousal.

Devin drew her toward him, his mouth approaching hers. Lenore felt too weak to move, too stunned to think. She pulled back. He moved with her, and their lips met. Devin's kiss was greedy, as if the act were a craving that had gone too long unsatisfied. With expert skill, he tried to stimulate the same need in Lenore, strove to animate her latent lust.

Instinctively, she wanted to kick, scratch, and scream at him. *Don't let him touch you*, came the cry of her panicked thoughts, falling over one another in a mad tumble. *He's a pig, and he's Torrin's father! Have you forgotten about Torrin?* But at a deeper, more primitive level, she wanted something else, wanted what Devin offered.

He was unlike any man she had ever kissed before. In terms of looks alone, he was the kind of man most women desired. If unaware or uncaring of his true character, Devin was undeniably attractive. Her pulse pounded with the rhythm of a runaway horse. She knew this was wrong, but her body rebelled against restraint, responding to Devin's passionate urging. Preparing an attempt to push away, her small hands closed over Devin's upper arms. The biceps were large, the muscles taut.

She struggled to regain control of her senses and of the situation. But it was another who ultimately decided the battle's outcome.

The door latch rattled. A quiet squeal issued from metal hinges as the door swung open, the sound serving as a catalyst for Devin to disengage from their kiss. But, unwilling to yield completely, he kept his hold on her in a relaxed embrace.

It was Aragon at the door. He stared at them with initial surprise that quickly melted into characteristic apathy.

Lenore pulled away, making abruptly for the exit.

Devin called after her in smug sarcasm, "Wait my dear, you did not get what you came for."

She slammed the door behind her and moved rapidly down the hall, feeling scared and saddened for a strange mix of reasons. She was ashamed, but even her remorse was tainted by a whispering hint of disappointment. Still, Lenore felt enormously grateful that Aragon had, in essence, rescued her. But this carried with it the unpleasant impression of indebtedness to someone with whom she shared a mutual dislike. One could only hope that Aragon would have sense enough to keep quiet about this until she could figure out what she was going to tell Torrin.

Torrin moved swiftly through the familiar corridors of the castle in which his entire life had been spent. His boots thudded and scrapped against the floor, producing a hollow, lonely sound that echoed back memories of his past. He thought of years gone by and wondered if perhaps he judged his father too harshly. In reality, not all of Torrin's memories of him were unpleasant.

When Torrin was much younger, the two of them frequently went on long horseback rides together through the surrounding countryside. In his early youth, he would sit in the saddle in front of his father and listen to Devin's stories and patient responses to Torrin's incessant questions about the land they rode through and the things they saw. Later, Devin had taught Torrin how to ride a horse of his own and like his father he had become a skillful rider. Torrin had loved their wildly exhilarating cross-country horseback races, laughing and shouting as they thundered through the trees and across the plains. But those pleasant times together had ended not long ago when Torrin, for the first time, bested his father in such a race. Torrin had been all smiles at first, immensely proud of himself and certain that his father would be too. But when he saw his father's reaction, Torrin's joy quickly died. Anger lined his father's face as he left Torrin and rode away in an embittered silence. Devin held that silence for over a week, refusing to speak even a single word to Torrin, and he never again went riding with him. Despite his father's irrational behavior, Torrin missed those times and felt guilty for precipitating their end by upsetting his father.

When Torrin arrived at the practice arena, he realized he was late. Other students were already engaged in mock combat while their instructor evaluated their performance, shouting orders and offering advice when needed. The harsh clamor of clashing arms filled the arena with a chaotic din. The air was ripe with the sour smell of perspiration. Now and again, students cried out in victory or shouted with pain. Most of the practice weapons were made of wood rather than steel, and those that were not had blunted edges to keep the combatants from actually killing a fellow student. Nevertheless, bruises, cuts, and other injuries were quite common.

After donning his practice armor, Torrin went to the arms instructor and apologized for being late.

Tyrus regarded him coolly. He stood nearly six feet tall, and weighed approximately one hundred and eighty pounds. His dark, sun-bronzed complexion resembled tanned leather more than it did human skin. Tyrus had a narrow face with sharp, hawk-like features. Standing tall and straight, his posture seemed comfortably relaxed, yet at the same time an impression of constant preparedness surrounded him, as if he were poised to counter an attack at any given moment. Tyrus was a battle proven fighter and it showed in stark evidence.

"Don't let it happen again," Tyrus growled. Then smiling, "After all, what does it matter how good a soldier is if he arrives after the battle?"

Torrin grinned back and apologized again. He liked Tyrus. Having known him longer than the other students in his charge, Torrin was able to learn there was more to Tyrus than suggested by his usual gruff demeanor.

Torrin was by no means Tyrus' most competent student, in fact the opposite was more likely true. Despite his speed, courage, and ample physical power, Torrin remained in the beginners arms class while most others of his age had progressed to more advanced training. Despite this, Tyrus had become fond of Torrin, impressed by the boy's temerity, his indomitable spirit in the face of repeated defeat. Torrin took a beating, yet willingly came back to fight again. Tyrus could appreciate such a brand of courage.

Torrin was still being trained in the use of mundane weapons, those without magical enchantment. It was required that a student become proficient in their use before advancing to magically enhanced weaponry. This proficiency was demonstrated by winning tournaments using mundane arms. This requirement was imposed so as to ensure that a soldier was competent and not dependent on the magic contained in the weapon. It was also done to make sure that the soldier possessed sufficient ability to control the enchanted weapon rather than be overwhelmed by its power.

Torrin accepted the logic of this system and believed it extended to his own inherent magical ability, that he should be able to effectively use mundane weapons without drawing on his own magic. However, during combat this restraint required a conscious effort that frequently caused Torrin enough distraction to permit his opponents to beat him. Torrin's skill had greatly improved over the years but he never won any tournaments. Tyrus understood the nature of Torrin's shortcoming but did not agree with his rationale for its continuance. Few wizards were also soldiers, but those that were typically were the best, not sharing Torrin's theories on restraint of personal magic.

"You need work on mass weapons," Tyrus told Torrin. "Grab a mace and shield and pair off with Logan over there."

After practicing for a few hours, Torrin washed and changed into what he considered his most flattering set of clothes: black trousers and a billowy white shirt covered by a green vest made of split leather with a soft, supple finish. The vest was trimmed in black around the v-shaped neckline and shoulder rolls. About his waist he buckled a wide brown belt. As Torrin pulled on his boots preparing to leave, Tyrus approached him.

"You did well today, Torrin. You're getting a lot better; I have a strong feeling you'll win your next tournament. You're a good fighter, don't doubt it. You have attained a high level of skill, but you still need to learn to relax and let it flow."

In many ways, Tyrus had become a father figure to Torrin, and his generous comment meant much to him. "Thanks, I'll try harder," said Torrin.

"No, Torrin. You're missing my point. You don't need to try anymore, just let go, let it happen, naturally," said Tyrus. "Don't hold back in a fight; you've got the experience, you know what to do. If you keep second guessing your every move, you'll never land a blow. And remember, the real weapon is not what you hold in your hand, be it a sword, a mace, an axe, or whatever. The true weapon is the warrior himself. And even his skill can be ultimately worthless if he does not have the will and release necessary to effectively employ himself *as* a weapon."

Torrin nodded, silently grateful for the encouragement and advice.

Tyrus gave Torrin a hardy slap on the shoulder. "Don't be late for practice again though. You're still my student and I won't tolerate tardiness," Tyrus commented over his shoulder as he turned to leave.

The sweat Torrin had worked up in combat practice was gone but not the appetite which had accompanied it. Knowing hunger was an enemy he could defeat, Torrin began working his way through the castle toward the kitchens. The walk there was a pleasant one, despite the fact that Torrin's body, sensitive to recently received abuse, complained with aching muscles and throbbing bruises. But Torrin's mind considered these sensations a reward for his exercise and a symbol of his developing strength.

He loved this castle, a love that carried with it a complex mix of attitudes. It was the only home Torrin had ever known. He felt loyal to the castle and its inhabitants, as if he belonged to them or owed them gratitude and service. But he also experienced a deep pride and sense of ownership, that any attack on the castle would be an attack on him personally and that he was morally justified in determining what was in the castle's best interest. However, at a more conscious level he realized that in truth that responsibility was ultimately the Queen's.

Every part of the castle held a special significance for Torrin. Every room, wall, window, and walkway was in some manner a part of Torrin's personal history. For seventeen years Castle Gairloch had been the theater upon which the drama of his life had been played, its walls and occupants an ever present, if not an always supportive, audience to his continuing performance, witnesses to all his great joys and sorrows and everything in between. It was as if his experiences had left an emotional residue upon the castle's physical structure or as if the rooms were really chambers of memory and just by entering he could experience old emotions thought consigned to the past. Likewise, his hopes and dreams were linked to this place and its people.

On his way to the kitchens, he chose a seldom used but well lit passage. He walked through a long, straight, empty stone corridor that seemed to impart a feeling of strong resolve and purposeful direction, like that which Torrin was trying to create within himself. But so much of his life seemed to be spent hoping for something more, waiting for something wondrous that was forever just out of reach. For some inexplicable reason, he knew that he was special and destined for greatness. He knew that one day he would find and fulfill some transcendent purpose that would lift him above other people and make him an object of their love and respect.

Even the lower regions of Castle Gairloch appealed to Torrin despite the fact that they were essentially abandoned, occupied only by insects, vermin, and an occasional derelict or adventure-seeking young boy. In his earlier youth and against the orders of his parents, Torrin had frequently explored these lower regions.

Once, before he had developed the power of illumination by magic, Torrin ventured alone into a newly discovered dungeon, a maze of deserted rooms and hallways deep within the castle. And on that occasion his torch had gone out, leaving Torrin lost within absolute darkness. At first he felt claustrophobic, as if the castle would at any moment crush him beneath its unimaginable weight. He screamed and cried in terror, but when no help came his perspective began to alter. His claustrophobia changed into the sensation of floating in an endless sightless void, completely alone and unconnected in the world, a sensation that still inspired fear but fear of a different nature.

He had been afraid to move, but equally afraid not to. Torrin attempted to retrace his steps in the perfect blackness in which he was now entombed, slowly feeling along the stone wall. The catacombs had been uncomplicated before being plunged into a life or death struggle for escape. Now he seemed hopelessly lost. Head and body quickly became badly bruised from collisions with unseen obstacles. After a while, Torrin got down on all fours, crawling like an animal. Hours passed and the only evidence of his having moved at all was the damage inflicted upon himself. As Torrin groped his way forward in the utter darkness, the palms of his hands tore open and began to bleed. His hands and knees were soon smeared with the cold, fleshy remains of crushed slugs, that unlike the snakes and other creatures of this dungeon had been too slow to avoid Torrin's blind advance. Lacy spider webs, broken skeins made of sticky gossamer threads, clung to his face. Roaches fell in his hair. Centipedes marched across his skin. The unmitigated dark served to enhance the silence of his prison, so that the slightest sound was loud and threatening. Water dripped with a pounding echo. The movement of unknown horrors thundered through the cavernous chambers. He heard unpleasant scratching, the tiny, quick claws of rats skittering across the stone. There were other noises too, sounds his racing imagination could not explain; which were more, rather than less, menacing as a result of their indefinable nature. His sense of smell also seemed to become more acute, more perceptive now that sight was gone. The strong sent of fetid mildew and animal waste that the light had held at bay now assaulted Torrin's nostrils en masse, causing him to retch. In his blind search for escape, Torrin's probing hands continued to encounter other disquieting substances that were undoubtedly best left unseen and uncontemplated.

There was no way to measure time, but after what seemed like days, Torrin finally saw a torch advancing toward him. Initially he felt overwhelming relief, then fear that this person lurking in the bowels of the castle may be a madman or criminal.

Finally, he saw that it was his mother coming toward him and, although relieved at his rescue, Torrin became afraid of what potential punishment was about to befall him. But his mother was alone and she did not scold him, punish him, or even reveal Torrin's crime to his father. She simply led him out of his prison to the sanctuary of Castle Gairloch's populated regions. What is more, she told him that the next time he went exploring to pay closer attention to his surroundings and rely on all his senses, not merely that of sight, to form a mental map of his whereabouts.

The next time, Torrin thought with wonder, unable to believe his ears. Not only was she not angry at his disobedience, she anticipated his repetition of it and gave him good advice for when he did. Torrin was amazed that his mother could venture into the dark and forbidding labyrinth from which they had emerged. Furthermore, she had done it alone. She proved herself to be courageous as well as caring. This was one of Torrin's better memories of his mother.

He could smell the kitchens now and hear the raucous activity of those about their work. The varied aroma and clamor of the kitchens contained elements both repellent and inviting. Thoughts of hunger quickly replaced those of his misadventures in youth.

Once inside the pell-mell of the kitchens and seeing how busy everyone appeared, Torrin was reluctant to disturb any of the cooks or scullery servants. Then he recognized someone whom he thought might not mind an interruption, a cook named Mangus, his cerise face reddened by his close proximity to the hot cooking fire. Mangus appeared old but was probably younger than suggested by his sweat-covered features, aged more by labor than by time. His frame was taller than Torrin's but stooped. Mangus was generally an affable sort of fellow, good natured and quick to laugh. Torrin hoped he would find him in such a mood today, for regardless of status, Torrin did not like to impose on people.

Attempting humor, Torrin spoke with obvious sarcasm. "Are they still letting you prepare meals after those three people died of apparent food poisoning? Tell me, is there anything worth eating in here that won't kill me?"

"Not a thing," replied Mangus, continuing the jest. "All we have today is pig slop and horse dung. Care for some?"

Torrin laughed back. "Sure. Double helpings of both, please."

Mangus paused from his work and let a young apprentice take over the hog that was being carefully roasted. Mangus walked away but quickly returned with a plate of baked chicken, beans, roll, and a cup of weak ale for Torrin.

"Here you go lad. Eat up." Mangus cocked his head, regarding Torrin more closely. "Hey, I know you; you're Marketa Murgleys' boy, aren't you?"

Torrin nodded as he ate. The food was quite delicious.

"That's a damn fine woman, your mother. She really helped me and my wife. Yes sir! You see, the misses and me weren't getting along too great. Got to the point we couldn't hardly stand being in the same room with each other. We were fighting all the time and she wasn't fulfilling her duties around the house, if you know what I mean. Then one day, your mother happens to see me and she asked me about how I was doing, like we were friends or something. Well I told her and once I did she really showed an interest and we talked for a long time about my problems. She said she learned some things from her counselor that might help my wife and me. Told us to try and remember why we fell in love with each other and got married in the first place. I said it was b'cause I got her pregnant. Well, Marketa said that yes, the welfare of our children was an important motive for my wife and me to get along better, but that there must have been something more between us in order for us to have had children in the first place. That got me thinking and talking about how it used to be with my wife, how we would talk for hours and how sweet she was back then. I also started thinking about all the two of us had been through; the fire, the miscarriage, and her parents' death. Well, by the time I got done talking with your mother, I had fallen in love with my wife all over again. Can you believe that? That night, I cooked my wife the best meal I ever have, and that's saying a lot mind you, and I spent all we had saved to buy her the grandest gown I could find. I wanted to make her feel royal, because thinking of our old love made me feel like a king. Let me tell you, she was as happy as a pig in shit, and so was I. Things have been a lot better between my wife and me since I had that little chat with your mother. She's a miracle worker, no doubt about it. I still can't get over how a woman of high standing like her would bother to take the time to help someone like me, but she sure did. You're damn lucky to be her kin. When you see her, tell her ol' Mangus says hello."

Old Mangus' prattle about his mother was making it difficult for Torrin to digest his food. Meals had become decidedly less appetizing lately.

Torrin thought it ironic that his mother should be giving advice on marriage and the dynamics of proper family relations. Torrin hardly considered her qualified. People inclined to help others who were emotionally distressed often were the worst choice from whom to receive such help. Meaning, these do-gooders were frequently unbalanced themselves and looked for comfort in the problems of others. The blind leading the blind is seldom very therapeutic.

Torrin also did not hold in very high esteem the counselors whom his mother claimed were essential for preserving her mental and emotional well-being. He considered them charlatans who stole money in exchange for providing the patient with excuses to feel sorry for themselves and rationalizations for their sins and shortcomings. Blame was assigned to others, freeing the patient from the burden of taking accountability for his own life. Torrin believed that those people, like his mother, who blamed their problems on others or their environment were weak and willing victims of life's abuse.

Torrin completed his meal and thanked Mangus. "The food was most delicious, and I'll be certain to extend your salutations to my mother. She will be pleased to know that you considered her helpful."

Dusk began to settle as Torrin walked nervously and hopefully through the portico leading to the assembly hall of the wizard Prelature. The coppery light of the setting sun cast long shadows over the walls and paved walkways. The night was cool and buffeted by the shifting currents of a capricious breeze. It tugged at the folds of Torrin's dark blue robe, the garment that signified his membership in the Prelature. But as yet, no colored sash adorned his robe, indicating that Torrin was still merely an acolyte and not yet a prelate.

Other robed figures were also making their way into the hall for the ceremony of the First Rite of Ascension, a kind of graduation ceremony for wizards in training. Along with several other acolytes, Torrin had at last proven himself to the senior members, demonstrated that he was worthy to be ordained a prelate. But the final decision was held by the archprelate and would be made at this gathering of the members.

In addition to being the governmental sovereign, the queen held the office of archprelate, the highest ranking member of the Prelature. The office of the archprelate was signified by a white sash across her vestment, not that it was really necessary since Queen Bryana was rather unmistakable. Next in order of seniority were the master prelates, having gold sashes, prelates with red sashes, and acolytes who had only the blue robe to identify them outwardly as members.

A semi-religious institution, the wizard Prelature defined a system of beliefs and practices related to the nature and application of magic as well as of the philosophical or moral code to which the community in general should adhere.

The Prelature controlled the use and study of magic through its teachings and by declaring as immoral and illegal all doctrines contrary to its themes.

It had been Torrin's lifelong dream to be ordained a prelate, a true member of this esteemed order devoted to the peaceful and defensive use of their combined power. Torrin rejected as insidious lies the dark rumors spread from time to time that the senior members studied and plotted the means for conquest and enslavement of all people. Such stories were absurd, products of ignorance and jealousy no doubt. It seemed that power, even that which is well used, inevitably inspires suspicion and scorn in the hearts of others. But they were only foolish rumors and easily dismissed.

By the time Torrin found his seat within the hall of the Prelature, his hands were sweating and his stomach churning with worried anticipation.

In Torrin's eyes, to be here among these talented wizards and in the presence of the queen and, World Spirit willing, to pass the First Rite of Ascension was a tremendous honor. It still galled him that Aragon, after having been given the honor and privilege of being ordained a prelate, had quit this revered order, thereby insulting the Prelature and everything Torrin respected. What is more, this meant that Aragon was forbidden to practice magic, as was anyone born with the ability but living outside the Prelature. However, though he did not like to admit it even to himself, Torrin knew that Aragon still practiced magic and studied theories and methods of application that were heresy and illegal.

Publicly it was said that those who were born with magical ability had been blessed by the World Spirit. But Torrin, as did every other member of the Prelature, knew the true history of the origin of their magic. As he waited on the arrival of the other members and the ceremony's beginning, Torrin mentally retraced that history.

Long ago, ages before the birth of Queen Bryana, there were no human wizards and the world was uncivilized. Human society was loosely organized into clans that were continually at war with one another. They fought for land, power, wealth, weapons, livestock, and often for nothing more than the sheer joy of killing. Each clan aspired for dominance and nurtured hatred among their people directed toward the other clans to further fuel their appetite for conquest. And although they were incapable of uniting their forces against them, all human clans shared a common hatred and envy of the elves.

The elves were a cultured race organized into several kingdoms united under a central rule. All elves possessed innate magical ability, although not of wizard caliber. Wizards were unique among the elves and their creation required conscious effort and arcane skill. Elfin wizards were created by elfin holy men exercising particular magical rites and incantations over a male and female elf as the pair conceived a child. These rites were well guarded secrets even among the elfin race and were completely unknown to humans.

The practice of creating wizards was confined to elfin monarchs, barons, and dukes. These elfin wizards had enhanced inherent talent and keen intellects with which to develop their skill. However, the elfin wizards were born sterile and could not reproduce second generation wizards. An elfin wizard was typically the second or third child born to a royal couple and would serve as the court wizard and trusted advisor to its elder sibling; the reigning monarch, baron, or duke.

The humans coveted the wealth and power of the elfin people. They frequently made raids upon the elves attempting to capture riches and, more importantly, weapons as well as other objects bestowed with magic. Magic in the form of weapons, particularly wizards themselves, were desired by the human clans to aid them in their feuding conquests. But the elves were effective in their defense, and no wizard was ever taken prisoner. Other elves, however, were less fortunate. Those that did not escape or kill themselves, either by their own hand or by refusing to cooperate with their captors, were forced to serve the purposes of the humans as guides or aids. But these were few.

One clan, under the rule of Farrel Durendal, had been particularly successful in acquiring elfin prisoners and coercing them to his will. Farrel had captured an elfin holy man named Sogin and, from the information Farrel elicited from him, devised a plan for conquering the other human clans.

Farrel amassed a sizable army from his own clan and others he had defeated. This mighty army was used by Farrel to attack an elfin barony. The elfin soldiers were defeated and killed. The remaining elfin citizens, including the Baron, Baroness, and the barony's holy men, were captured alive. Farrel tortured and killed many of his captives while the others were forced to witness these acts. From living victims, body parts were methodically removed, backs were flogged, and skin flayed from muscle and bone all before the horrified observance of the other elfin men, women, and children. After Farrel had thus obtained the attention of his elfin audience through his display of pain and power, he at last issued his demand.

Farrel informed his captives that the elfin holy men would perform the magic rite for the creation of a wizard as he, Farrel, conceived a child with the Baroness. This struck the elves with a horror nearly as profound as they had felt at witnessing the previous torture. Farrel stated that if they did not meet his demand, the torture and killing would continue, beginning next with the Baron and his children. Furthermore, if Sogin informed Farrel that the rite was not being performed correctly, the acts of torture would not only continue but would be administered with enhanced brutality.

The elves complied and thus, Kalob, the first human wizard, was conceived. Following this, most of the elves were killed, but quickly and with mercy. The holy men and the Baroness and her children were spared. Farrel claimed the Baroness as his wife, intent on producing more human wizards to serve him.

Anxious to implement his plan to become the sole ruler of the known land, Farrel forced the elfin holy men to employ their magic to speed the growth and maturation of the first human wizard. However, this unnatural process and family life stressed Kalob mentally and emotionally. Therefore, although he was powerful, Kalob was also unpredictable. In spite of Kalob's shortcomings, Farrel did expand his realm of influence by conquering many other clans in the years that followed. But he was ineffective in achieving complete dominance.

After conceiving many more wizard children, Farrel became increasingly paranoid of his captive elfin holy men and eventually had them killed. He no longer trusted his control over the elves and concluded that they had ceased to be an acceptable risk. In his opinion, Farrel had sired enough magic to serve him.

Not wishing to repeat the mistakes made with Kalob, Farrel's other wizard offspring were allowed to develop more naturally. However, jealous plottings developed among the siblings and several were captured by other clans for their own combative applications. Sometime later it was discovered that the human wizards were fertile and capable of reproducing wizards without the burden of the elfin magic rites. But, not every child born to a wizard inherited the power of magic. A single wizard parent, regardless of if the other parent was a wizard or mundane, could produce both mundane and wizard offspring. In time, it also became evident that two mundane parents could produce a gifted child, provided the power of magic was a trait somewhere present in their ancestry, such as in Torrin's case. Not to imply that wizards were anything but a scarce minority. The birth of a wizard was still a relatively rare occurrence.

Years passed and the human wizards increased in number among the various clans. Because of their innate intelligence and power, the human wizards naturally became the leaders of their clans. The war of the clans continued. The human wizards grew in strength, focusing their knowledge in the art of warfare. During this brutal age of war, the elves decreased in number in the face of a more powerful and savage enemy. Eventually, the remaining elves were driven from the known land.

During the clan wars it was discovered that if one human wizard killed another, a measure of the dead wizard's power would pass with a sudden violent fury into the wizard who had killed. Absorbing another's power in this way was both tortuous and exhilarating, a fearful test of a wizard's strength but one which most were eager to take.

Although clan leaders were generally wizards, other clan members who retained physical characteristics that suggested their partial elfin heritage did not have elevated status in human society. Rather, these half-breeds were persecuted because they were different and linked to a former enemy. But more importantly, they were oppressed out of fear that they may be capable of magic. Other mundanes did not trust them. The wizard clan leaders allowed and even encouraged this persecution and bigotry because they too feared that the half-breeds may be concealing their magical ability and might prove to be a potential rival.

To survive the misery of their oppression and drawing on the fragmented relic beliefs of the vanquished elves, an underground half-breed religion developed. The hope that preserved and united the oppressed half-breeds was a religious prophesy.

"It is said that from his chosen brethren, the Redeemer's power and knowledge shall grow, so that he may reshape the land in the image of the Great One, creating a new order by which the Oversoul's flock shall be guided. Through his reign, the Redeemer shall attain the greatest good for all the land. The world shall be purged of its corruption and the chosen shall inherit this new age and all it contains."

The harsh reality of the continuing clan wars and worsening persecution dominated everyone's lives, so much so that virtually no cultural development of any kind occurred for many years. Then, a force of change rose out of this bleak landscape of hatred and death. A powerful clan lord by the name of Gannon Murgleys sought to unite the clans and finally establish order in a world too long embedded in chaos.

The attempt was made initially through the use of reason and negotiation. But given his contemporaries' fondness for violence, such efforts typically failed and force was required to gain cooperation. Fortunately, Gannon's sword was as sharp as his intellect. When his enemies would not bow to his wisdom, they were forced to succumb under the brutal beating of well planned military attacks. And these clan lords who had been foolish enough not to yield to Gannon's reason were defeated and then killed by Gannon himself so he could, in that primitive yet mystical way, absorb their power and advance his efforts in attaining unification and peace.

But before Gannon could fulfill his noble vision, he was mortally wounded in battle. His daughter, Bryana, had fought with her father since the time she came of age and was as skilled a warrior as he. So naturally she was with her father on this occasion. Fearing that he could not recover from his injury, Gannon begged his daughter to kill him before he died of his other wounds so that she may absorb his power and complete his ambition.

Bryana did as her father ordered and there upon the field of battle immediately assumed the role of clan lord. She won the day and the hearts of her people. Her victories in battle along with her social reforms enhanced both her power and popularity. Bryana became the Redeemer the half-breed religion had prophesied. The lives of wizards who pledged themselves to her were spared. She united the clans and established a unified government and religion for the populace, human and half-breed alike. She created the Prelature so that wizards could gather together peacefully, to share knowledge and study without fear of their fellow wizards. She became the most powerful human in all the known land, but without abuse. Under her direction, a system of law and government was created which immortalized her as the symbol of excellence and justice. To Torrin and nearly everyone else, Queen Bryana was an epiphany, the manifestation of a divine being, and the foretold savior of their people. She was no longer just a woman, or even just a queen; she had become something like a benevolent god, loved as much as feared.

What about the elves? Torrin wondered. *If they had not been driven from the known land before the coming of Queen Bryana, could her reforms have embraced the elfin race as well? Are there any elves left in existence? It was rumored that they lived deep within the wastelands, the home of the exiled. But who knows what merit these rumors have. In fact, who even knows what a true elf looks like, since none have been seen in generations?*

The myriad of murmured conversations among the members of the Prelature began to silence, indicating that the ceremony was about to commence. Ushers closed and sealed the doors after the guards left the hall. Only wizards were allowed to remain.

The room was large enough to hold two hundred people without crowding one another. The assembly hall had been constructed in an oval shape with a domed ceiling supported by marble pillars magnificently carved to resemble dragons, griffons, minotaurs, and other beasts both real and imagined as well as in human likenesses. Gifted artists had painted the ceiling in an intricate and complex pattern representing the seemingly unfathomable design and purpose of the World Spirit. Stained glass windows and brightly woven tapestries adorned the walls of the enclosure, depicting for eternity the glory of the World Spirit, the Prelature, and Queen Bryana's reign.

The acolytes sat in the center of the hall facing the opposite direction of the massive, iron-bound mahogany doors from which they had been admitted. The prelates were positioned to the right of the acolytes and the master prelate sat to the left. All faced the throne of the archprelate, raised upon a dais high above the heads of the assembly. Stairs led up to the tiered platform and currently vacant throne, a chair of gold, richly jeweled with rubies and sapphires and padded with white velvet.

An unbroken silence descended upon the quiescent hall as the archprelate entered through a small passage to the left of the throne. A retinue of robed attendants followed her. All eyes focused on the archprelate. The sight of the archprelate cloaked in her noble garments imbued Torrin with intense veneration and awe.

The strong and beautiful aspect of the archprelate was an apotheosis, a glorification of her power and wisdom. She was old but the physical evidence of her longevity communicated no hint of senility, bore no indication whatsoever of weakened strength or diminished ability. Her appearance reflected aptitude rather than infirmity. Her face was firmly set though lined with age and battle scars. The archprelate's eyes were bright and piercing. Her sinewy frame stood tall, lean, and erect, sheathed in firm, tanned skin. Long, sleek silvery hair that remained soft and full despite her years crowned the archprelate's head and draped about her rigid back.

Archprelate Bryana stood before her throne with arms spread wide in symbolic embrace of the Prelature. "Ignorance is a form of blindness that holds us in the darkest prison," intoned the archprelate. Although she did not shout, her voice carried clearly throughout the great hall. She followed her words with an arcane incantation that instantly extinguished all light within the assembly hall. There came no outcry of alarm at the abrupt stygian eclipse. It was anticipated. This formally initiated the proceedings of the First Rite of Ascension and served as a symbolic test of the acolytes' ability to use their magic cooperatively.

"Through learning and knowledge we shall light our way to freedom," droned the acolytes in unison and in the same manner recited the incantation to illuminate the hall in a magical, pale blue fluorescent glow.

"The power of the Prelature is the blessing of the World Spirit," pronounced the archprelate with imperial formality.

The acolytes again answered in a single voice: "We are open to the direction of the Oversoul, so that we may better serve its will and mirror its image." In a unified chant the acolytes spoke an incantation that made the ceiling of the assembly hall invisible, although physically it remained. Thus, the Prelature was placed under the full view of the firmament and subjected to the uninhibited scrutiny of the World Spirit.

The archprelate continued the ceremony by calling each acolyte before her for an individual evaluation of knowledge and skill. As a final measure of their aptitude, each would be asked a question and instructed to perform a specified feat of magic. No acolyte knew what these tests would be until it was their turn to kneel before the archprelate.

Torrin realized he should be listening to the examinations of the acolytes proceeding him. But he was nervous and so spent the time mentally reviewing basic tenants of the Prelature and fundamentals of magic in an attempt to anticipate his test.

After what seemed like both an eternity and the briefest instant, an attendant to the archprelate summoned Torrin to the throne. His heart stopped for a beat or two, then rushed forward with too much haste. Following beside the attendant, he progressed down the aisle and up the stairs with escalating trepidation, praying he would not stumble, sneeze, or do some other foolish thing he characteristically might to embarrass himself at such an occasion. But without mishap and before he knew it, Torrin stood before the archprelate. Her seasoned beauty and the staggering impact of her commanding presence enhanced with closer proximity. Grandmother or not, she was a daunting presence.

"Kneel," directed the archprelate in a stern command.

Torrin complied. His stomach clenched and burned with acid. Inside his mouth, his tongue felt swollen and thick. But he managed to bow and bend his knees to the floor with a fair degree of grace.

"First, your magic shall be evaluated," Bryana explained. "Give me your hand."

Torrin offered his left hand to the archprelate, which she gripped with hers, thumb over his palm and fingers along the back. The archprelate pushed Torrin's hand down and back, tightening his wrist and forcing it upward. Maintaining her hold on Torrin, Bryana used her right hand to accept a dagger from a waiting attendant. Attached to a white handle of carved bone, the steel blade possessed a wickedly serrated edge that gleamed in the magical fluorescence. At this sight, Torrin's pulse drummed at his temples in a fearful cadence, as his mind struggled with his body to remain still and calm. *Trust in the archprelate if not yourself,* thought Torrin.

The archprelate held the knife, its sharp edge coldly intimidating, against Torrin's forearm. Before he could swallow the fear choking at his throat, the archprelate plunged the dagger deep within Torrin's exposed flesh. She dragged it slowly across, pushing it deeper into the meat of his arm, severing muscle and tendons, and scraping bone.

Torrin held his body so completely rigid and his jaw so tightly clamped, he worried his teeth might crack, crumble, and grind to powder beneath the strain. But compelled by respect for the queen and his aspiration to prelate, a goal which had become the fundamental basis of his sense of self, Torrin did not move nor scream in response to the agonizing pain erupting in his arm.

Once the knife completed its cruel passage, the archprelate commanded in a harsh, inflexible voice. "Use your magic to heal yourself."

Torrin's mind felt confused and weak. He struggled to concentrate on his magic rather than on the sight of his blood pooling upon the floor.

I can't do it. I can't do it! I'm failing. I'm dying! His panicked thoughts screamed inside his skull.

Torrin pulled his consciousness back from the fearful pit into which it had begun to fall and suppressed his awareness of the pain clamoring for his attention. He concentrated, focused his magic, and spoke the words to initiate the healing process.

Blood slowed. Veins reconnected. Muscle fibers wove themselves back in place. And skin fused to close the gap.

Relief washed over him. Exhaustion imposed both by exertion and loss of blood gripped Torrin, demanding a great effort of him to remain cognizant of his circumstance. He wanted to slump to the floor, to let his eyes close, and sleep. But he knew he could not surrender to the ease of such comforting weakness.

"Very good," said the archprelate. "However, you left a scar. Keep it as a memento of this occasion. You have proven your skill and now you shall demonstrate your wisdom."

My wisdom? I'm having trouble remembering my name at the moment, thought Torrin, enervated by the ordeal.

She afforded no time at all for recuperation.

"A female dragon will fight with savage ferocity, sacrificing her own life if necessary, to defend her brood, her young. What moral lesson can be drawn from this to teach us how humans should behave?" she queried with profound solemnity.

What? What kind of a question is that? Why not ask which came first, the dragon or the egg? How am I supposed to answer such a question? wondered Torrin, his head beginning to throb again. Certainly ethical questions were a part of his studies but not like this. *How does the archprelate want me to respond? That violence is acceptable in defense, that we should place the welfare of our family above our own or above all else, that an attack on someone is a crime which extends beyond the injury done to that individual and includes the consequences to those adversely affected by the harm done to the original victim, or is there some other moral to this cryptic story? What does she want?*

"Can you answer?" asked the archprelate, an edge of impatience now added to her formal tone.

"Nothing! It teaches us nothing," exclaimed Torrin, committed to his position but unsure that it was the correct response. "Humans must determine standards of morality based on their reason, not on acts of nature which are merely evolved traits that assist the survival of a particular animal species. There is no moral example in this act of the dragon any more than there is in the widow spider's habit of killing the male once their mating is complete. Human reason is the law giver, the sole guide to moral behavior and the will of the World Spirit."

A long, silent pause followed that was nearly as painful to Torrin as the dagger had been. Bryana's eyes flashed with an unnatural brilliance. Her brow tightened. Everything around him seemed frozen in time. Torrin braced himself as the archprelate inhaled visibly, preparing to speak.

"Arise, Prelate Torrin, and accept your sash and the duty of the Prelature." The archprelate placed the red accolade over Torrin's head so that the sash rested on his shoulder and lay across his chest.

Torrin left the dais shaken but elated at his new status.

Chapter 2
Nadir

During the convocation of the Prelature, Devin amused himself amid the festive atmosphere of a nearby alehouse. He had slept much of the day, reviving his bold and bawdy spirit, and was ready again to indulge his penchant for social drinking and stimulating recreation.

People crowded the tavern, men and women having fun, relaxing from a day's work, taking their minds off tomorrow's troubles, speaking loudly and laughing with pleasure. A thin haze of pipe smoke drifted languorously upon the subtle currents stirred by the animated customers. The temperature was comfortably warm, the lighting appropriately low, a soft radiant glow that was easy on the eyes.

Devin enjoyed the company of the tavern's denizens, and at the moment one individual in particular captivated his attention. At his table, she sat very near to him sipping wine from a small pewter goblet while Devin gulped greedily at his brandy, posturing before the young lady. And she was indeed young, surely no more than fifteen; a slender, lineless, pretty girl with an alluring innocence.

"So, do you have a name or do they simply call you 'Beauty,'" inquired Devin.

She bowed her head in a blush of shyness. Long blonde hair fell forward across her cheek. Through her bangs, she peered up at him modestly and answered, "My name is Aileen, but you can call me what you like. Do you truly think I'm beautiful, or are you just teasing?"

SCOTT C. RISTAU

Gently, Devin placed his hand beneath her chin, tilting up her head. He smoothed back her mane of wheaten hair to reveal a sweet face with bright, trusting eyes. So fresh and untutored. So much to learn but the promise of such pleasing potential. Devin ever so lightly traced the pads of his fingers above the thin amber line of her eyebrow; down the narrow bridge of her pert, upturned nose; along the fullness of her lips; across a pale cheek; down the delicacy of her neck to the hollow of her throat, exploring the exquisite textures of her flawless skin.

"Oh, you're attractive all right, but I think your youth prohibits my full appreciation," sighed Devin to the enticing stripling. "You should meet my son; he's closer to your age. And I think you could be good for him."

Caressing the powerfully sculpted muscle of Devin's upper arm and gazing at him wantonly, Aileen murmured, "Is he strong and handsome like you?"

"Well he's off to a good start but he's got quite a ways to go before he'll be like me," boasted Devin. He took another long swallow of brandy. "Torrin is a decent boy, probably a little too decent, if you know what I mean. He needs to toughen up, roughen some of his smooth edges, get a little reckless once in a while. A man needs to indulge in base pleasures sometimes or he's not much of a man if you ask me. Smoke, drink, womanize, get in a fight once in a while— it's all part of being a man. And it's fun too. But my son has an unnatural aversion to life's pleasant vices. The self-righteous brat certainly fancies himself as too good for me. Nor does he want anything from me." Devin frowned and shook his head. "I've always tried to be there for my sons. But no matter what I do, it's never enough. I tried to teach Torrin to fight when he was younger but he wouldn't have me, thinks Tyrus is a better arms instructor than his own father. Well that's crap and he knows it. I was using advanced weapons before I was old enough to talk. I was the best in my class too. And if that dog's puke Tyrus is so damn good, why is my son still in the novice class?" Devin's fist balled with anger. "It's embarrassing."

"I'm sure it is, but I'm also sure your son still loves you," said Aileen in an effort to appease Devin's bitter resentment. "Maybe he just felt Tyrus would be a more objective tutor, even though he knows your skill is far superior."

Devin smiled. *Why couldn't his wife be as understanding as this pretty young thing?* he wondered. "No," Devin answered. "Torrin doesn't regard me in very high esteem. Part of the problem is we don't have much in common anymore. I sure don't know anything about what the Prelature does, nor do I care. About the only thing I still had left to help Torrin with was his horsemanship. I thought this at least was something I could give my son,

36

something we could share, something he might admire me for. A man wants his son's respect. But no, he had to go and show me that he didn't need nor want me for even that. He thinks he's better than me, that I'm just a drunken old fool with nothing to offer. The little bastard rubbed my nose in this fact by beating me in a race. The ungrateful bastard beat me, can you believe it? He might as well have just spit in my face. After all I've done for him, after all I've given up for him. Then there's Aragon, that's my other son, he doesn't like me much either and sometimes I think I understand him even less. But, I can at least see more of me in Aragon. He's a rebel, like his old man. He makes his own way and lives by his own standards. He sure told those old crones in the Prelature where to stuff their rules. And he sure never listens to a word I have to say. But don't get me wrong, they're not bad boys, my sons. I just wish I knew how to talk to them."

Devin paused in his reflection to finish the dregs of his brandy and order another. During this respite, Devin allowed his eyes to feast once again upon Aileen. She coyly rubbed herself against him, playful, tempting. His hunger grew.

The brandy arrived. Devin took his drink, dismissed the serving wench, and continued his desultory account of his domestic woes. It was a comfort to have someone to listen to his problems, someone so lovely, so undemanding.

"Even more so than my sons," continued Devin, "my mother regards me as a tremendous failure. I wasn't born with magic and, according to her, I didn't marry right and don't father well. But I've learned to live with her disappointment, even if she hasn't. And let's not forget my wife, dear sweet Marketa." Devin paused, looked down into his brandy, swirling the golden liquid around the sides of his glass. "She and I had been so much in love before. I wish I could go back to that time, I really do. It was so much better than it is today, and so long ago that it hardly seems like it was ever my life at all. I never thought she'd desert me. But in a way she did; she turned against me. It all started out so good but went quickly downhill as so many things began to go wrong in our marriage. The worst of which was that she made me doubt myself. Her appetite in our marriage bed was unnatural, more than I could satisfy, more than any man could. Her insatiable need made me seek out other women to reassure myself that I was competent. It sounds insane, but it's true."

"Oh, I have no doubt of your competence, my lord. I'm sure you could exceptionally please any woman. Your wife must be mad and does not deserve you," purred Aileen in unctuous coquetry. She wanted to distract Devin from thoughts of his family so he would concentrate instead on her.

"And she cheats on me in her own way, spending so much time with her books and those eccentric friends of hers, believing they can offer something I can't. She tells all our intimate affairs to that idiot counselor of hers. Damn it all; is nothing sacred? Family matters should be kept private." He sighed heavily, shaking his head in a kind of defeat. "I don't know what to do about my family. They hate me and yet because of my obligation, I am bound to them. If it were otherwise, I might leave the castle and seek adventure in the wild lands."

Devin drank deeply from his brandy, feeling its effect and playing out the idle dream in his mind.

"No," he continued. "I'm a family man and such adventure is behind me. But, it might be good if we moved to another kingdom, got a fresh start. Maybe I have treated my family poorly in years past, though I think they did the same to me. But I swear by all that I've done wrong, somehow I'll make it right. Tomorrow, when my head is clear and my heart is pure," finished Devin with a rich and vivid smile to his eager companion. Aileen's hand had brushed his knee beneath the cover of the table and lingered to massage between his parted legs.

"I think your family has neglected you and ignores the blessing you are to them. You need someone who understands what a good man you are and knows how to please you," argued Aileen in a dulcet voice as she continued to fawn at Devin. His resistance was waning as he began to enjoy more and more the way this lithe beauty stroked his ego as well as his anatomy. "Why don't we continue our conversation somewhere more private?" breathed Aileen warmly into Devin's ear.

By now Devin was full of lust and liquor, ready to meet the challenge this girl offered. He rose and let Aileen lead him out of the alehouse. Outside, the heavy door closed at his back, sealing away the background noise of the tavern.

"Come with me," she invited. Then Aileen walked a few yards ahead of him, casting a glance over her shoulder now and again to be certain Devin was following her.

For a moment, Devin lost sight of her. She seemed to vanish. Then he turned a corner and saw her standing in a secluded passage, waiting for him. When Devin reached her, she seemed to become suddenly overwhelmed by a lustful appetite, urging Devin to meet her need. His passion swelled, aching for release. He roughly kissed her face and neck. Aggressively, he fondled the firm tissue of her youthful bosom, teasing her nipple with his thumb, crudely caressing her ripening breast. Aileen responded by murmuring approval, moaning for more. She alternately gnawed at his ear and encircled it with the raw length of her tongue. She whispered to him, "If you want me, take me." Spurred by her encouragement, Devin tore open Aileen's thin blouse and attacked the exposed flesh with ardent lips.

To this and Devin's surprise, Aileen shrieked. "Rape! Help. Rape! Help me someone."

Devin jerked away in confusion and shock as Aileen continued her shouting.

"Shut up! Have you lost your mind? What in the name of the World Spirit are you screaming about," demanded Devin with alarm and angry dismay.

Then suddenly in answer to Aileen's urgent plea, there were two armed men in the passage with them. "Get away from that child, you bastard," barked one of the men as he raised his sword threateningly at Devin.

Regaining his composure and forcing a friendly tone, Devin explained. "Hold, friend. There's no rape here, just a girl with a confused attraction and an active imagination. She wanted it just as much as me. I haven't got a clue why she started screaming just now. Maybe it's some sick game she's playing or maybe the intensity of her own desire frightened her into making stupid accusations. I don't know. But, gentlemen, I assure you I was not forcing myself upon her. Tell them, Aileen. Tell them you went with me willingly."

"Like hell she did," cursed the man with the drawn sword who had spoken before. "That's my daughter. That's my baby girl you tried to rape. You'll pay for this, you son-of-a-bitch."

Something was wrong here. Very wrong. Something in the way the man used the word "pay" and in his companion's predatory grin aroused suspicion in Devin. The man's words were wooden, expressed as if he were reciting a prepared speech. How likely was it that Aileen's father would happen to be in this part of the castle at this particular inopportune moment? It was awful damned coincidental. It could be the man was an over-protective father, always following his daughter wherever she went, secretly guarding her safety.

Bullshit, thought Devin. He glanced at Aileen, who was calmly readjusting her blouse into a less revealing position, and his suspicion was confirmed. *The girl is too damned relaxed for someone who believes she's narrowly escaped rape. These swine have set me up. They no doubt orchestrated this rape and rescue scene to extort money from me in return for keeping silent about my crime. Apparently the other man was supposed to be the impartial witness who could confirm my act of rape if I refuse to pay them off. How dare they try to ensnare me with such an inane plan?* Uncontrollable rage at their attempted ambush boiled within Devin.

"I don't believe you three conspirators have considered all the possible directions your half-witted blackmail scheme might take, " growled Devin in an acid tongue.

Without further warning, Devin's ire exploded at the other two men in a wave of violence. His sword flashed from its scabbard as Devin moved to attack his ambushers. Gamboling from one to the other in adroit swordsmanship, Devin inflicted painful wounds upon his adversaries while parrying their less competent thrusts.

Devin opened a long, crescent shaped gash across the father's face.

In a whirl of steel, Devin spun, slashing the other man's chest, ripping through his leather jerkin and opening the underlying flesh.

Back to the father. Like the flashing sting of a scorpion's tail, Devin's sword bit deeply into the man's abdomen.

Blood flowed in abundance, but it was not enough. Their pain was evident, but that too was not enough. Devin's excited fury would not abate. It grew and grew. They had threatened him, dared to challenge him, and for their crime they would suffer the ultimate price.

They were no match for him. But the girl's father managed to sneak past Devin's defenses and land a clumsy blow to the muscle of Devin's upper calf. Warm blood streamed from the cut, soaking into his pants and running down his leg. But the wound was not so serious as to distract Devin from his enemies.

He would have preferred to prolong the death of these two men, to savor their execution, but knew there was not time, that the castle guards may be attracted by the commotion and that it might raise awkward questions. Yielding to this limitation, Devin's deft swordplay quickly dispatched the other two men, leaving him standing with imperfect satisfaction over their lifeless bodies.

Aileen gasped behind him, diverting Devin's attention and rekindling his rage. He leapt the distance separating them and struck her with vengeful fury across the tender face he had kissed not long before. He sheathed his sword, then gripped her violently.

"You bitch! You prick-teasing, back-stabbing bitch! Nobody tries to sham me and gets away with it," rasped Devin.

His face loomed in front of hers, mere inches separating them. His dark eyes glittered with impassioned savagery. His breath felt hot against her skin; she flinched from it as if it were a scalding vapor. She could barely hear him over her own thundering heart.

"You're going to get what you asked for and then some, you filthy little whore. And if you cry out again, I'll penetrate your body with my sword instead."

He pulled a torch from its cresset mounted to the wall and clamped his other arm around her slender waist, dragging her down the passage and into a remote room. The room was deserted except for packing crates, stacked barrels, and a table.

Devin forced Aileen into the damp and chill of the abandoned chamber. He slammed the torch into an empty bracket bolted on the wall. The flame writhed fitfully, covering Aileen with Devin's dark and wild shadow, an augury of what his body would soon do. He cupped her face between his broad, callused hands and ate at her clay cold lips, lips that earlier had been so hot with invitation. Devin struck her again, smashed his fist against the side of her head in a crushing backhand. The impact left her dazed. Resistance seemed hopeless. It would only bring more pain.

Savagely he ripped the clothes from Aileen's unwilling body. He then stepped back a pace to leer at her with eyes like broken glass, sharp and dangerous. While he removed his pants, he admired her in the way a predator views its prey. His vicious passion would consume her utterly, her body a sacrifice in atonement for her part in the conspiracy against him.

It was as if his life's previous emotional experience—lust, anger, betrayal, hatred, love—had been a drought and this was the storm. Now it rained, eroding Devin's restraint, freeing the maddened captives of his heart, transforming uncontrollable emotion into an act of horror. In feral brutality he violated her body with his masculine penetration, no act forbidden, no part of her anatomy left untouched.

Devin had never raped before. He discovered now that he hated it but also that he could not stop. Strangely, his own disgust seemed to propel him to greater perversity. He wanted to spend himself and be done but could not, which infuriated and prolonged his desire, forcing Devin to drive himself into her loveless form again and again. Her body was cold against the burning rivers of fire that boiled through his veins. The criminal debauchery, the cruel sexual battery continued for what to both seemed an eternity until during his frustration and ultimate shuddering climax, an odious paroxysm, Devin strangled the once lovely Aileen to death. As he came, her life departed.

After the ceremony, Torrin lingered only briefly to congratulate a handful of fellow newly ordained prelates and to speak with a few senior members of the Prelature.

"Torrin, my boy." A familiar voice called him from behind, accompanied by a heavy hand upon his shoulder. It was Master Barrage, one of Torrin's instructors and favored by many of his students for his avuncular style and amusing charm. Barrage was a short man, almost fifty years of age, with thick, bushy eyebrows and a thinning head of gray hair cut within an inch of his mottled scalp.

"That was an interesting answer you gave us tonight," Barrage continued. "Quite unexpected, really. I dare say even the archprelate appeared a bit taken aback by it. But it has given me something to think about. Would you care to discuss your ideas further? I'd be interested in getting your perspective on a few thoughts of my own."

Torrin was distracted from answering. From over Barrage's shoulder, Torrin saw Kyle waving feverishly at him and wearing a grin that nearly consumed his entire face. Kyle was a friend of Torrin's, a slender, plain-looking boy with thick, curly brown hair who was unfortunately burdened with eyes nearly always afflicted with a nervous twitch. But he was nice and possessed a quick mind.

"We made it!" Kyle shouted, eyes twitching excitedly and hands pointing to his red sash. "Come see me tomorrow and we'll go fishing, relax and have some fun now that it's all over, now that we graduated."

"I'll do that!" Torrin shouted back. "See you tomorrow."

Torrin returned his attention to Barrage, suddenly embarrassed that he had been yelling over the head of a Master. "I'm sorry, sir. I'd be glad to discuss my ideas with you sometime, but I'm afraid I can't right now. My parents are expecting me," Torrin lied. He just was not in the mood for serious discourse at the moment. He wanted to be alone for a while or at least find something more exciting to do than discuss philosophy with his teacher.

"Quite all right," Barrage answered. "There'll be plenty of time for us to talk latter. Perhaps we might even raise the subject during one of our classes."

Stepping from the hall into the cool night air, Torrin began his parade around the castle, subtly bragging of his achievement by continuing to wear his vestment and sash. It was too late to call on Lenore and too early to go home.

So he continued his stroll about the castle with a slight bravura to his stride, a swagger indicative of a budding self-confidence.

The ascension to prelate made it conceivable that Torrin could finally begin to construct something significant out of his life. A plan began to emerge for his life's direction that was both desirable and possible. He would select an area in which to concentrate his studies within the Prelature, perhaps in the field of food production, healing, sanitation, or some other beneficial service. Now that he was a prelate he may also be able to obtain his own living quarters. *Wouldn't that be wonderful*? he thought. And if that could be arranged, then perhaps Lenore would consent to be his wife. Providing that he could summon the courage to ask her. They would travel some, see a measure of the world's beauty and mystery, then come back to the castle and settle down. Torrin would apply what he learned in this adventurous sabbatical to his work within the Prelature. Then, after they became comfortable in their ways and with one another, he and Lenore would have children, a boy and a girl. His children would be proud of their parents and safe in a loving home. Yes indeed, a golden future seemed to be awaiting him.

In plotting his idealized destiny, Torrin had not been paying particularly close attention to where he was going in the here and now, nor of what lay immediately in front of him. He tripped and began an uncontrolled plummet to the floor, desperately grasping in vain for support and mentally bracing for the eminent collision. But the surface he impacted proved to be softer than the stone floor. Torrin opened his eyes to find himself sprawled across the prone figure of a man.

As heavy as any waterfall, a cataract of embarrassment pounded through Torrin, believing he had blindly collided with this man causing them both to fall. Any second Torrin expected the man to launch into an angry tirade, cursing him for being such a blundering fool.

But the man spoke no words, angry or otherwise. In fact, he did not move at all

Oh shit, thought Torrin. *Had the man hit his head on the floor and been knocked unconscious? Now I've done it; I may have really hurt this poor fellow. Why am I such a stupid idiot? Maybe I should get away from here, quick as I can, before he regains consciousness and wants to exact revenge for my cursed clumsiness. But I can't just leave him like this, suppose he needs help.*

Then as Torrin began to lift himself up, the realization came that not only was he not moving but also the man was not breathing. *Holy World Spirit, I've killed him, I've accidentally killed him*, thought Torrin, the red flush of embarrassment turning pale in a rush of cold fear and abhorrence.

Frantically looking about for help, Torrin discovered another man lying nearby, covered in blood and badly damaged by a sword. *No, not damaged, killed!* Torrin's attention snapped back to the man he still laid across. This man too was wet with blood, which by now had seeped into the fabric of Torrin's robe. Leaping back from the corpse and scrambling to his feet in revulsion, Torrin struggled to think above the loud, deep-toned beating of his vociferous heart.

Wait, calm down, Torrin cautioned himself. *Obviously these two men killed each other in a duel of some sort. The thing to do is simply call the guard and have their bodies removed.*

Regaining his self-control, Torrin looked about in an attempt to get his bearings and ascertain from what direction to most effectively obtain assistance. Then something puzzling caught his eye. A small and fragmented trail of blood extended beyond the likely battlefield of these two men. Either one of them had come here bleeding or someone else departed this scene leaving that trail in his wake. The latter suggested itself as the more probable alternative. Torrin glanced back at the two corpses, their ashen faces frozen in death and their bodies pooled in gore and laced with grisly open wounds. It was absurd to follow the assailant's trail, but curiosity is all to often enough to bolster courage and induce addle-minded behavior. Torrin decided he could delay in summoning the guards until he investigated this mystery at least a little further. After all, he was a prelate now. He could handle this situation.

The bloodied tracks did not provide a quick and unerring path to the murderer. The trail frequently disappeared, forcing Torrin to guess at which direction to continue his search, all the while fearing that at any moment he would stumble unprepared upon the cut-throat he pursued. When a suspected path proved false by failing to yield any new or continued evidence, Torrin would go back to where the trail had left off and select a new direction. Often Torrin would be on the verge of abandoning the investigation because the trail seemed to terminate entirely, when he would find it again.

Torrin halted, not because the trail had ended but because he knew his search was about to achieve its denouement. The mystery was about to unravel and explain the story into which he had stumbled. Torrin stood in a narrow corridor staring down a short flight of stairs to the dimly lit entryway below. A premonition whispered to him that disaster waited at the bottom of those stairs, filling Torrin with dread and attempting to discourage him from the continuation of his search.

Wiping the sweat building on his forehead with hands likewise slick with perspiration, Torrin called on his reason to overcome his fear, to mollify his craven emotional sense of despair. For some irrational reason, he felt that the room possessed more than a threat to his personal safety. Instinct advised him to flee. At some visceral level beyond rational thought, Torrin knew that if he went down those stairs, everything he valued would be put at risk, placed upon an irrevocable path destined for destruction.

Yet Torrin could not turn back. He crept forward slowly, attempting to reason away his fear with each careful step, using logic to erect a thin veneer of courage to cover the fear twisting in his gut. At the entryway, braced against the wall, Torrin forced himself to look within the room.

The air was thick with death and sin. The naked corpse of a young girl lay upon a low table, her stale body ornamented with crimson welts, bright against the white pallor of her skin. Her once smooth face was lacerated with red runnels scratched across pale cheeks. Beside her dead and damaged form, and with his back to Torrin, stood a man pulling on his shirt.

Damn my foolishness, thought Torrin. *What am I doing here alone and unarmed?*

His muscles began to cramp painfully from attempting to remain motionless against the stone wall. To relieve the discomfort, Torrin slowly shifted his weight but in doing so his robe brushed the wall, disturbing the silence with a whispery rustle of cloth. The man inside the room grabbed his sword and whirled around in the direction of the stealthy sound.

Father and son faced one another in mutual shock and alarm. They stared, unmoving, measuring the significance of their situation and conceptualizing the other's reaction to this startling encounter. In the space of a heartbeat, Torrin was forced to select between impossible choices, each with immeasurable consequences, and worry that such consequences should have no bearing on his decision. Torrin's heart spoke to him of loyalty and love for his father, taking painful note of Devin's beseeching expression which seemed to call out for Torrin's understanding and compassion. The voice of reason identified Devin as a rapist and murderer who must be punished in the name of justice. An unbearable dilemma demanding immediate resolution was forced upon Torrin.

Devin took a tentative step toward his son, thus commanding Torrin's full attention and provoking a decision. So Torrin acted, he believed more out of a sense of justice than of fear, although both were compelling.

"Guard!" bellowed Torrin in anguish as he scrambled up the stairs and into the corridor. "Help. Guard! Someone get the Guard, there is a murderer here," he continued shouting as he hurried down the corridor, expecting his father to overtake him at any moment, until he saw several castle guards running toward him, armor and weapons clanking loudly as they came.

Half a dozen guards quickly surrounded Torrin. "Back there," exclaimed Torrin. He was breathing deeply and having difficulty catching his breath. "To the right, a small chamber at the bottom of the stairs, there's a girl who's been killed. The killer has probably gotten away by now." He paused. "But it's all right, I saw who it was." He stopped.

Torrin strengthened his resolve and confessed. "The killer is Devin Murgleys. I saw him. Search the castle. Don't let him get away."

One of the guards began issuing orders to the others. "You two check out that room. And you two," he continued, pointing at a different pair, "go to Devin Murgleys' chambers and see if he is there. If so, bring him to me here. If not, tell the other guards to start looking for him or anything else suspicious. But let's keep this as quiet as possible for now. Go!"

The guards quickly left to fulfill their orders leaving Torrin alone with the two remaining guards. The guard in charge looked at Torrin for a moment without speaking, studying him as if Torrin were an equation to be solved. "Are you hurt?" he asked.

"No," answered Torrin. Then remembering the blood on his robe, he recounted how he had discovered the dead men and ultimately the girl. Through the story the guard just stared without reacting in any noticeable way, as if the incident Torrin described were as dull as the sound of falling rain.

"I'm Captain Barret," he finally said, then paused and continued his scrutiny as if waiting for something to be revealed before he spoke again. "We also found the bodies of those men. Do you know who they were?"

"No," said Torrin.

"How about the girl?" asked Barret.

"No," Torrin replied. "I mean, I don't think so. It was hard to tell." He shuddered at the recollection of the girl's ruined beauty.

Captain Barret rubbed his face, a face that disclosed nothing to Torrin in terms of what he might be thinking or what kind of person he might be. Barret's features were a neutral mix of contradiction. His nose looked as if it had been broken and improperly set, which together with his build and the scar above his left eye suggested Barret to be a brawler. But his calm demeanor and penetrating gaze were more characteristic of a scholar than an undisciplined, uncontrolled belligerent.

46

The two guards dispatched to the room containing the dead girl returned. They reported back to their captain in haste, their expressions grave. A chill breeze seemed suddenly to wash through the passage, raising gooseflesh on the back of Torrin's neck.

"Well?" asked Barret.

The older of the two guards spoke, his companion looked as if he were struggling to contain his dinner within the confines of his stomach. What they saw had been unsettling. "There's a girl, obviously raped, badly beaten, and unquestionably dead. We found no one else or anything to suggest who might have done it."

"Is that right? Well, let's go have a look ourselves now, shall we," said Barret completely without emotion. No scowl, smile, grimace, or any expression of feeling intruded upon his face. Torrin thought Barret was speaking only to the other guard but he gripped Torrin's arm like a vise and forcibly escorted him back to where he did not want to be, back to the unfortunate girl's resting place. Barret inspected both the girl and the room, careful in what he touched or disturbed, in that same detached manner, still seemingly unaffected by events even in the girl's disturbing presence. He intently scrutinized things which Torrin could not in any way perceive as clues or possible evidence. But his thorough investigation was interrupted by the return of the two guards sent to find Devin. They reported that they had been unable to do so.

Barret towered, cold and impassive, before Torrin. "You said before that you didn't think you recognized this girl. Do you now?"

"No, I've never seen her before. I don't know who she is," answered Torrin, shaking his head in a gesture conveying both sorrow and denial.

"You mean you don't know who she *was*," Barret corrected. "Well tell me, how extensive is your ignorance? Do you know *your* name?"

"What?" responded Torrin, confused by the odd question and the taunting nature of it.

"Your name, do you know it?" repeated Barret, again sarcastic in content but not in tone.

"Yes," said Torrin beginning to suspect the direction of Barret's line of questioning. "I am Torrin Murgleys, Devin's son, which makes me well qualified to recognize him. And it was him I saw."

"Other than your claim about what you saw, do you have any evidence that would identify Devin as the man who did this?" asked Barret, sweeping his arm back to encompass the room and reference the girl.

Torrin looked about him with growing anger and concern, then re-focused his attention on Barret, whose eyes had never left Torrin. "No," he admitted, "but you can't possibly think I'm lying, that I did this. I have no weapon and why would I have called the guard?"

"I didn't say that you did anything," replied Barret, irritatingly calm. "But, since you brought it up, let's explore the possibility. You are covered with blood, which might suggest you as the murderer. We did not find any clothes but those of the girl in this room. It strikes me as strange that a rapist discovered over the body of his victim would be so meticulous as to collect all his belongings before fleeing the scene. But if you were the one who did it, you could have hidden your sword before you called the guard. As for why you called, perhaps you thought that it would draw any possible suspicion away from you. And, perhaps you have some grudge against your father, so you chose to blame him for your crime."

"Are you insane?" snapped Torrin. He was nearly drunk with emotion now. Barret's accusation shook Torrin with fear and hostility, emotions he likewise felt concerning his father, mixed with disgust and invasive pity. "There is no way I could have done this. If you incompetent fools would find my father, you'd know that I'm telling the truth."

Barret's whole body seemed to clench momentarily at being called incompetent but his reticent calm quickly returned. "We'll find your father, don't worry. Until then, let's go visit the queen, shall we?" Barret invited casually. His words and manner were passive but there was no denying his commanding presence.

Barret, with Torrin in tow, were given immediate admittance to the queen's chambers without question, although the sentries were unmistakably curious. Queen Bryana sat at a table facing the doorway from which Torrin and Barret had entered. Arlen, the queen's legal advisor, stood at her side and at the other was seated Devin Murgleys. His clothes were different than that which Torrin had seen him in. He seemed composed but as if it had only recently been achieved. Both Torrin and Barret were taken aback by the sight of Devin and stared in dismay. But Barret quickly concealed his surprised reaction.

"Your Majesty," began Barret, his face unreadable, "a grievous crime has been committed. A crime in which, I regret to report, the Murgleys family name has been implicated." Barret paused and waited, again assuming the aspect of a man involved in mathematical computation.

Bryana, revealing only slightly her impatience, demanded, "What crime and who?"

Torrin was about to speak, when Barret's iron grip tightened painfully on his arm, bruising it to the bone and silencing him. "This boy alerted my guard to the apparent murder of three individuals. He claims to have witnessed the person who committed these crimes and that it was your son, Lord Devin."

Devin responded with an angry scowl. Bryana appeared surprised and somewhat wounded by Barret's report. But when she spoke, it was with a calm nearly equal to that of Barret's. "That is impossible. My son has been here with me since the Prelature concluded its business this evening. During the convocation of the Prelature, Devin was here as well, to which Lord Arlen can attest, for they awaited me together."

Torrin was stunned, struck with apoplexy. He could not move nor think in response to the queen's statement. *Surely I heard her incorrectly*, Torrin thought, his mind racing wildly. *It couldn't be. But, no, she had vouched for Devin's innocence. Maybe I am wrong, maybe it wasn't my father I saw. No, I know what I saw and it was Devin. She is covering for him, knowingly giving him a false alibi.* He couldn't breath; Torrin felt as if something was constricting around his throat, pinching off his airway. Thousands of tiny black spots peppered his vision, spinning and darting through the air in an agitated dance, like a swarm of unnaturally large gnats. Torrin's hands began to twitch spasmodically, as tremors ran throughout his body. He felt the castle crumble about him, saw the room spin violently, winced at the explosions in his temples, and gagged at the bile rising in the back of his throat. Truth, justice, law, and order became mere illusions, illusions shattered by the queen's lie. He had nothing to hold on to, no anchor that he could cling to during this emotional storm. The invisible minions of chaos seemed to rush forward from the shadows, gnashing their teeth and slashing their claws, preparing to rend his helpless soul.

In panic and rage, Torrin wailed in a tremulous voice. "You're lying! He did it. I saw him. What's the matter with you? What kind of person are you? How can you lie for him?"

Barret wheeled about to face Torrin, tightening his grip so painfully Torrin thought his arms might snap under the pressure. The look on Barret's face, the first hint of emotion he had shown, told Torrin more clearly than words that if he did not keep quiet Barret would beat him into unconsciousness. No further outbursts would be tolerated. Having achieved Torrin's silence and resuming his blank expression, Barret turned back to the queen.

"Your Majesty," said Barret, "your statement not only confirms Devin's innocence but establishes that Torrin has lied about what he saw. In view of this and in consideration of other evidence, it appears obvious that Torrin is the rapist and murderer."

Barret had laid out a small piece of bait but the queen did not bite. She did not carelessly admit prior knowledge concerning the full nature of the crime. But whether it was out of ignorance or cunning, Barret remained unsure.

"Rape? You did not mention a rape before," said Bryana.

"One of the murder victims was an innocent young girl who had clearly been raped," replied Barret.

Devin's scowl deepened at the word "innocent."

"I see," said the queen. She looked deeply troubled, as if a great weight rested on her heart. "However, I believe your pronouncement of Torrin's guilt may be premature. Perhaps when Torrin claimed to have seen his father by the body of this girl, he was mistaken rather than deliberately lying."

Damnation, thought Barret, gritting his teeth. *There it is; the old girl tripped herself up.* He had not told the queen where Torrin said he saw his father. It could have been an assumption but he suspected it was an unconscious slip, an unintentional revelation of prior knowledge. No one else noticed nor did Bryana notice Barret's nearly imperceptible reaction to her suspicious statement.

The queen continued, "I know that Torrin was at the convocation of the Prelature. But, there may have been time for him to commit this crime after the Prelature concluded its business." She looked directly at Torrin now, addressing him purposefully, though he was barely listening. He was still lost in shock, shattered by the lies, the seemingly all pervasive corruption. "Did anyone see you after the First Rite of Ascension who could testify to your whereabouts?"

Torrin just stared blankly forward. He had lost the energy to sustain interest in his circumstance, no matter how dire it appeared. What was the point of defending your innocence or fighting for justice in a world where law amounted to nothing more than the capricious whim of an unethical queen?

Barret again pivoted between Torrin and Bryana, demanding his attention. "Answer the queen," barked Barret. Then, in a whisper of virtually unmoving lips which spoke only for Torrin to hear, "Your life depends on it."

Torrin feebly returned to the reality of his situation and he gave the names of the prelates and master prelate he had spoken to at the end of the ceremony. But he worried that it would not be enough to clear him.

"I will bring them here at once, your Majesty," stated Barret. He turned Torrin over to the custody of another guard and left the room.

Standing there before the accusing stare of the queen and his father, Torrin thought Barret would never return. No one spoke. Time seemed to stop for what was akin to an emotional eternity.

Finally the iron bound doors opened and Barret passed swiftly through them, with a quick and courteous bow to the queen. Given the late hour, the people he had been sent to find were easily located. Virtually all had been asleep at home in their beds. One by one, Barret presented Torrin's witnesses to the queen to give their testimony. After which, it still seemed conceivable that Torrin could have committed the murders.

Pausing briefly but before the queen could speak, Barret called forth another witness, a soldier who said he saw Torrin walking about the halls not long before Barret's men reported to have found him. The soldier said that when he saw Torrin, his robe was clean, not soiled with blood. Clearly there would not have been time for Torrin to have committed these crimes.

Everyone in the room seemed to breathe a uniform sigh of relief. Torrin did not remember seeing this soldier in his walk about the castle, though admittedly he was not paying very close attention during his aimless stroll. Still, he could not help but wonder if the soldier was telling the truth, even though there was no reason for him to lie.

"Obviously Torrin is innocent," announced the queen. "Equally obvious is that the true perpetrator of these crimes is someone who resembles Devin, enough to fool his own son. Barret, continue your search for this man, though I fear he has most likely left the castle by now. Also, increase the number of guards on duty and the extent of their patrols to help reassure the populace that they are safe from the reoccurrence of such crime. That is all. I wish to be left alone now."

At her command, the room emptied. Torrin slumped to the floor outside the queen's door, alone with her sentries stationed there. He sat with his legs pulled up to his chest, his arms folded over his knees and cradling his head. He held this dispirited position for less than five minutes before one of the sentries was tapping Torrin's shoulder.

"Hey, you can't stay here. You'll have to move along," said the sentry somewhat sympathetically. Torrin pulled himself to his feet and complied with the order.

He had not gone far beyond the sentries' sight when Devin sprang at him from behind a corner and forced Torrin against the wall. Inches from his face, Devin glared at him with black baleful eyes seething with acrimonious contempt.

"You little bastard!" Devin spat at him. "How could you do that to me? How could you, you traitorous son-of-a-bitch? You self-righteous bastard. You think you're so damned superior, so perfect and pure. You think you're real hot shit, don't you? And you know what, that's exactly what you are—shit! Something nobody wants and their happy to get rid of. You look like shit. You smell like shit. And if I could get away with it, I'd drop you down a crap-hole along with all the other shit I've created in my miserable life. Are you listening to me? I want you to understand what I'm telling you. You're no son of mine, you back-stabbing brat. You hear me, you're no son of mine! I never want to see your ugly, disloyal face again for as long as I live."

Torrin thought his father might kill him and almost did not care. But without further criticism or abuse, Devin cast himself away from Torrin, leaving him alone. No one saw. No one would believe.

He could not go home, Torrin knew that much. So he fled to the abandoned depths of the castle in hopes of making sense out of what had happened and figuring out what he could do about it. Once there, enveloped in the damp and musty darkness, enwrapped in his blood encrusted robe, Torrin laid down upon the floor, curled on his side in an inch or two of rank water, his mood as dismal as his surroundings. He tried to stop shivering and organize his thoughts, give order to all that had transpired, but weariness overcame him. He had been awake for nearly twenty-four hours, a day more physically and emotionally draining than any he had previously experienced. The refuge of sleep came mercifully quick.

Torrin awoke in the early evening of the following day, when the horrors of his nightmares overwhelmed the desire for sleep. A scream that was his own echoed out of the dark. At first he was so disoriented that he could remember nothing of the previous day's events. He wondered if he was still dreaming and if not, why he wasn't lying in the comfort of his own bed. He created light from his magic, saw the blood on his chest, and it all came back to him in a torrent of tormenting remembrances. Combined with the vile stench of the air surrounding him, the memories sickened his already queasy stomach, causing him to vomit unprepared, spilling the putrid contents of his stomach. Chunks of partially digested food mixed with thick yellow mucus clung to the sleeve of his robe. He stood up, coughing and gagging at the gorge rising again in his throat. He brushed off his robe as best he could and wiped the scum from the corners of his mouth, beyond being disgusted by such things.

His father had committed rape and murder, crimes to which the queen had made herself an accomplice by lying to protect her son. And Torrin would be as guilty as they unless he did something about it, something to balance the scales of justice. But what could he do? The queen was the highest court in the land, so to whom could Torrin appeal? The legal system had been a victim last night as well. How could Torrin obtain justice without further damaging the law?

Why had his father done this, why? "World Spirit, what am I to do?" Torrin cried aloud, lonely and despairing, his fists held out at his sides and balled up with frustration.

Answers, divine or otherwise, eluded his grasp. In confused, frustrated anger, Torrin began smashing his fists repeatedly against the stone wall until his knuckles bled freely. Strangely, the violence and the pain had a calming effect, a perversely comforting quality. He struck the wall again and again.

Then suddenly, in a flash of insight, he understood what he must do. It all became quite clear to him. Relief rose within Torrin, then quickly gave way to a flood of grief. Tortured by his decision, Torrin cried for over an hour. Once it was over, he resolved never to be so weak as to give way to tears again. Such emotion was corrupt and destructive. With newfound determination, Torrin began the climb out of the nadir of his despair, preparing himself for what he knew was morally imperative. He accepted his duty much as a condemned man faces death, with a resignation that afforded a measure of renewed strength but an imperfect seal against the panic twisting in his heart. By accepting the inevitability of his fate, he forfeited his future. Having nothing left to hope for and nothing left to lose, Torrin carried with him the power of the damned.

In a mood pitch black and as foul as an open grave, Torrin left the catacombs of the castle's lower regions wearing the look of a madman. His robe, hands, and face were soiled with old blood and filthy grime. Dark blue circles ringed the eyes of an intense, turbulent, and fatigued lined face. His hair was greasy and wild.

Staying to the shadows, Torrin crept through the castle with the stealth and silence of a cat, so different from his strutting of yesterday. So much had changed in such a short time. He managed to avoid detection and arrived unmolested at Lenore's home. She was the only person left of whom he still had a hope of trusting.

"Oh Torrin, you look awful," announced Lenore in concern and confusion. "What happened, where have you been? Are you all right? Are you hurt?"

She seemed to struggle with conflicting impulses. A part of her displayed a desire to embrace Torrin, take him in her arms to comfort him and soothe his troubled soul. Torrin was clearly upset, with the aspect of a man who had lost all that he valued. But his appearance was also repellent to her and not merely because he was covered with filth and reeked of a horribly offensive odor. Beneath his armor of grime and stench, perhaps accentuated by it, he appeared out of control, almost crazed. It was this that most scared Lenore. Order in life and control over one's behavior were tremendously important to Lenore, fundamental to the way she dealt with and judged the world. She did not know how to react to wild emotion or unstructured conduct other than to condemn it.

"I'm fine, everything is under control," insisted Torrin with a forced calm, sensitive to Lenore's reaction and attempting to offer reassurance.

"I heard what happened, that you saw the murderer, the rapist," whispered Lenore. "It's just awful. They still haven't caught him. No one knew what happened to you. Is he after you? It that what's wrong?"

"No," said Torrin, "they haven't caught him, nor will they. It was *my* father. You must believe me. I'm not lying. I saw him. I know it was him."

"But the queen, She said that…" Lenore began, but Torrin cut her off.

"A lie. A cover-up to protect her son," rasped Torrin, fighting tears that swelled to breach the dam imposed by his will. "I need your help, Lenore," pleaded Torrin. "I need you to go to my home. If my father answers, just leave. But if my mother or brother answers, tell them that you think you know where I am and that I may be injured. Ask them to go with you to find me, but don't let Devin go with. Tell them I'm terrified of him or something. Tell them anything, but get them out of their chambers."

"What are you talking about, Torrin?" appealed Lenore, her anxiety growing. She was chilled by the desperate tone of Torrin's voice and frightened by what he asked. "I don't understand what's going on."

"I just need you to get my mother and Aragon out of their chambers for a while. Take them down to the stables or to the archives of the Prelature or something," urged Torrin frantically.

"No," insisted Lenore adamantly. "Not until you tell me what is going on. What are you planning to do?"

Torrin groaned in frustration, his body shook with it. He rubbed his face deeply as if kneading bread, then raked his fingers through his hair. Torrin fought to suppress his emotions, contain the outburst of feeling about to explode from within him. Still trembling with the effort, his face clenched in a knot of anguish, he focused on Lenore, fixed his gaze intently upon her.

"Lenore," rasped Torrin, no longer trying to keep the desperation from his voice. "I've never asked anything of you. Never asked for more than you were willing to give. And I swear, if you do this, I will never ask you for another favor as long as I live. But please, I beg you. Please do this for me."

"Torrin, I can't, not unless you tell me what you are going to do," sobbed Lenore. She hated herself for causing him more pain by denying him. "I love you but I can't."

"Please. I swear, when this is all over, if I can, I will explain everything," begged Torrin, reaching out to Lenore with open hands and pleading heart. "If you love me at all, do this for me. Please!"

Lenore's instinct for common sense and her need for disclosure warred with her love for Torrin. She worried that Torrin was out of control, but in the end love won both her trust and cooperation. "All right," she conceded. "I trust you. I'll do what you ask. But promise me that you won't do anything stupid or dangerous. I don't want you to get hurt."

"I promise." He desperately wanted to hold her and kiss her but felt that he should not. If he did, it would likely be their last kiss and he didn't want that memory to include such foul conditions as these. "I love you."

Torrin hid himself from view, watching as Lenore led Marketa and Aragon away from their home. He had been terrified for Lenore, worried that Devin might hurt her and he held himself poised to intervene if Devin tried anything aggressive. But she was safe and the three of them were now well out of sight.

Torrin cradled the battle axe Lenore had given him for his birthday, drawing comfort from its weight, solidity, and connection to the one he loved. He had retrieved it earlier and held it hidden within his robe during his conversation with Lenore. He looked up and down the hallway one final time, then moved quickly to the door of his home. Back braced against the wall, Torrin paused for a moment, breathing deeply and working up the courage for what he was about to do. Slowly, silently, he lifted the latch, eased open the door, and slipped inside.

Devin was there. He stood with his back to the door, leaning against the hearth's mantle, staring at the fire blazing within the large fireplace. The room was silent save for the flames crackling in delight, consuming the wood upon which they gleefully danced.

"What do want, Torrin?" Devin asked in a deep dispassionate monotone as he turned slowly, almost casually about to face his son. He wore a haunted expression.

Torrin took in the contents and arrangement of the familiar room. He nodded imperceptibly with approval, noticing the sword resting near the fireplace. Light glinted dully from the broad, double-edged blade and the gold runes inlaid along its length seemed to glow. Separated by a wooden grip cut with spiral grooves and covered in black leather, the graceful down-sloping crossguard and disk-shaped pommel were constructed of brass, an unintended symbol of Devin's impudence. Next to the sword and propped against the wall was a shield garishly painted in the image of a black stallion rearing up on its hind legs and silhouetted against a bright yellow background.

"What I want is the fair execution of punishment equal to the crimes committed," Torrin stated with grave formality in reply to his father's query. He had practiced this scene in his mind, working out the dialogue, readying himself to play the grim role he now assumed. Torrin held himself rigid in the cold, hard profile of a judge.

Devin sighed heavily with anger and disappointment. His brow furrowed and his dour features compressed wearily into a scowl. "I deserve no punishment," complained Devin. "It is you who disregard the law by continuing to accuse me. You heard the queen's verdict; I am no criminal."

"It was you and no amount of lies, regardless of their source, can disguise or turn away your guilt," rasped Torrin.

"Try to understand," said Devin. "You don't know what happened. It wasn't my fault. Those men and that girl, they weren't innocent. And the situation just got out of control. If you had been in my place, you might have done the same thing."

"Never!" Torrin snapped with hostility instead of sympathy, appalled at his father's suggestion.

"Don't be so sure, Torrin. You'd be amazed at how little we really know of our own capabilities." He sounded tired, defeated. "We're all human, Torrin, even you. And maybe I can forgive you after all, if you can agree to put this behind us and let be."

"You violated the law and the principles upon which our society are based, just as surely as you did that girl. If High Queen Bryana will not fulfill the duties of her office, I am honor bound to exact justice myself," recited Torrin with conviction, just as he had rehearsed, his voice faltering only slightly at the end, frightened by the conclusion to which his words had carried him. He finished his threat by raising his axe meaningfully.

Keeping his eyes on Torrin, Devin slowly bent down to slip the shield over his arm and grasp his sword. "Don't be a fool, Torrin. There is no way you can beat me," Devin appealed sternly.

"Justice will prevail!" Torrin roared in anguish and determination, rushing at his father with the axe raised in attack.

Instantly both men abandoned their reservations and committed themselves fully to the duel. Devin effectively repelled Torrin's initial frenzied attack. He employed his shield both defensively to parry blows or to knock Torrin's axe aside and as a weapon, thrusting it in Torrin's face or wielding it edgewise to strike at him. Devin's prowess was clearly equal to the advertised agility and daring emblazoned upon his shield in the heraldic symbol of a wild horse. Torrin hammered at that shield in a cannonade of blows, as if the shield were his target rather than the man behind it. Torrin's axe repeatedly bit into the shield's center and edge, trying viciously to chop down Devin's defense.

Devin managed again to beat back Torrin's attack and recapture the offensive. His shield arm was numb from absorbing the shock of Torrin's axe. Devin threw off the shield and went at Torrin with the broad cutting edge of his sword, carrying behind it the power to shatter bone. Torrin twisted and dodged, avoiding Devin's attack and returning it in kind.

Unbalanced by his rage, Torrin overextended his swing. Devin moved in to take advantage of his son's failing, turned his opponent's axe aside and kicked at Torrin's legs, knocking him from his feet.

Torrin lay sprawled on the floor, stunned by the impact of the fall, gasping and sucking air that seared his throat and lungs. But he regained his senses in time to see the silver arc of Devin's sword racing in descent toward him. Torrin rolled aside and scrambled to his feet, hearing the hard crash of Devin's sword against the floor from where Torrin had narrowly escaped.

Torrin struggled to lock away his emotions and fight with more intellect and precision. Fear, pity, and rage were distractions he had to ignore. He swung at Devin and Devin parried. He swung again. Devin shifted out of the way and Torrin's axe missed its target, cleaving the drop-leaf from a gate-leg table of finely polished cherry wood. Torrin tried to recover but his mistake gave Devin sufficient time to wield his sword. It ripped through the blue fabric in a spray of blood, biting out a large chunk of meat from Torrin's shoulder. But the pain, although excruciating, helped Torrin focus on his task, on his moral duty.

They battled wordlessly, expressing themselves with their weapons, exchanging blow for blow with terrifying ferocity. The room was a din of clanging metal, grunts, and breaking furnishings. Thrusts were parried or avoided. Those that were not succeeded in inflicting wounds, painful but not fatal. Slashing, slicing, and pounding at one another with their cruel weapons, they fought without mercy.

Devin came at his son again. With the speed and dexterity of a stag, Torrin leapt from the arcing path of Devin's sword, leaving it to rip through a large padded-leather chair, another inanimate victim of the battle's depredation. Devin gradually became impressed with Torrin's ability, almost to the point of feeling proud of his son. But this sentiment did not compel Devin to disengage from the conflict. The relentless press and retreat of their duel continued. Both men were bathed in rivers of sweat, breathing with open mouths and burning lungs. Their muscles ached from the repetitive effort of attacking and defending.

Still it continued, until the death blow was struck at last. Torrin saw an opening and effectively seized the opportunity it presented. Propelled with the speed of an arrow released, he drove the spiked-tipped axe forward.

The blow impaled Devin's chest. The spike punched through his sternum and pierced his beating heart.

Devin reached up with his free hand, as if in disbelief. His fingers curled around the protruding steel as if to substantiate what had happened before Torrin withdrew the spike. At the new wave of pain which accompanied the spike's retreat, Devin lost his grip on his sword and it clattered to the floor. Devin followed it there, slumping to his knees, both hands now clutching at his heart, trying to dam the vital blood gushing from the wound. He looked up at Torrin. The dark glimmer faded from Devin's cool black eyes. The color drained from his face, leaving a ghostly countenance.

The two stared at each other with shared expressions of betrayal. Devin began to speak but blood issued from his lips in place of words. Again he tried, this time with success.

Gurgling and choking, Devin managed, "You never loved me."

At that Torrin pivoted, bringing his axe up and finally down with crushing force against the base of Devin's neck, separating his father's head and body.

He stood there a moment, looking down at the gore, surprised that he did not feel nauseous or overcome with horror, feeling instead only a curious tingling in his hands and arms instilled by the impact of the killing blow. This was the only person he had ever killed. It was his father. Torrin thought he should be more strongly affected by the experience. He had cried after deciding to execute his father. But now that the decision had been implemented, there was very little emotion at all, just an odd sense of serenity. He felt wearily resigned to face the remainder of his verdict. He had accepted responsibility for the execution of his father. Now he must accept the consequences of carrying out that decision.

"Guard!" Torrin shouted in a stentorian voice. It was a strong cry, unshaken by fear or grief.

Torrin was unsure how long he went on shouting before his efforts yielded results but after a while the hard soles of booted feet could be heard clumping heavily toward him. The door burst open and crashed against the wall, leaving two of Gairloch's soldiers framed in the entryway.

Torrin stood pointing with his axe at Devin's decapitated corpse lying on the floor surrounded by a large spreading halo of scarlet blood. The soldiers quickly moved to seize Torrin's weapon and immobilize him. Without resistance, Torrin passively allowed them to do so and stated the obvious, that he had killed his father. He then demanded to be taken before the queen.

The soldiers did not respond nor did they comply with Torrin's demand. Instead, they wordlessly escorted him to a prison cell.

Alone in his cell, the full impact of all that had happened began to reassert itself, pressing like a weight on Torrin's heart. He turned the scene of his crime over and over again in his mind. The gruesome sight of his murdered father and his dying words were burned indelibly into his memory. The greasy sweat covering Torrin's body felt like a sheen of ice upon his skin. Chilled to the pit of his quavering stomach, he shook uncontrollably.

After an hour, or perhaps two, a guard accompanied by a pair of attendants entered Torrin's cell. They stripped him and with stiff brushes and buckets of soapy water scrubbed him thoroughly from head to toe. The guard gave orders to the attendants but no one spoke to Torrin despite his inquiries. He was given fresh clothes and stale food, both of which he eagerly accepted. Then he was left alone again.

He could hear movements and murmurs from the occupants of neighboring cells, but drew no comfort from their shared misery nor identified himself with them, as a true criminal. He was alone and felt that way. Lying on a thin lumpy mattress thrown carelessly upon the floor, Torrin stared into the darkness outside the barred window, listening to the wind blow softly against the exterior castle walls, a lonely, menacing sound. It whispered to him, not his name but his fate. The dismal wait continued until gradually Torrin fell asleep.

His dreams were troubled, filled with horrors offered up by his subconscious. He dreamed of a bright, golden apple set upon a bed made up with smooth, red linen. In the dream, Torrin reached out to touch the apple. Its surface gave way beneath his fingertip, leaving a rapidly darkening bruise upon the fruit, turning from brown to black before his very eyes. Slowly, he drew back his hand, watching in fascination as movement stirred beneath the apple's thin shell, its skin swelled and contracted in a shifting mass of chaotic distortion. Suddenly, the apple's integrity ruptured, a broken seam emerged along the curvature of its side. From the opening, thousands upon thousands of white writhing maggots spilled out over the vermilion sheets, their tiny bodies slick and glistening with the stench of corruption.

Chapter 3
Justice

The sun satisfied its daily duty by once again ascending in the eastern sky, gradually bleaching away dawn's deep purple haze, slowly lightening the hue, changing it from dark violet to a vermilion streaked indigo and finally to a glaring aquamarine. Life within the castle began to stir and fall into familiar routines. Dogs barked. Chickens clucked. Gates and doors opened and closed. Morning birds chirruped. The irregular pounding of someone's hammering competed with the metronomic pulse created by someone else beating the dust from a rug. People called greetings to family and friends. Merchants opened their shops for business. Muted by distance, the everyday patter of man and nature reached Torrin through the window of his cell. The world went on unaffected, if not unaware, of Torrin's plight.

Now that he was rested and awake, the waiting began to annoy Torrin. Even though it was certain to be unpleasant, he was anxious for his fate to be decided. He paced back and forth with restless energy. And the longer he did, the more impatient he became. Impatience gradually developed into a smoldering anger.

Why is she keeping me waiting so long? wondered Torrin. *Is she trying to insult me by ignoring me? I'm not just some petty thief. They can't just lock me up and forget about me. I have a right to be heard, a right to be judged.*

It was nearly mid-day before the guards finally came for him. He could see them through the bars which composed the forward wall of Torrin's cell, bars pitted with years of rust except where the desperate wringing hands of past prisoners had kept the metal smoothly polished. One of the guards sorted through a large ring of brass keys, found the one he was looking for, and inserted it into the lock. It released with a hollow click and the iron gate of Torrin's cell swung open.

"So what happens now?" Torrin inquired angrily. "Has the queen finally decided to haul her lazy ass out of bed and see me? Or are you two here for a game of dice?"

"Watch your tongue," the guard commanded, "or I'll rip it from your head and watch it for you. Your days are numbered as it is, and right now you haven't got a single friend in all of Gairloch. The queen sure as hell isn't going to protect you. So you'd be wise not to aggravate your jailers. Otherwise, your stay here could become a whole lot more unpleasant. Now, turn around, do exactly as you're told, and keep your fat mouth shut."

The guard grabbed Torrin's arms, forced them behind his back, and bound his forearms together with a long, narrow strap of supple leather. He shoved Torrin through the open gate and out into the hall, where they proceeded to lead him toward the queen's tribunal chamber. Those people they encountered on their way backed off, giving Torrin and his guards a wide berth. Torrin heard their condemning whispers, felt their accusing stares. Many of them were people Torrin knew, but thankfully Lenore was not among them. He thought he saw Dora, but she turned away before he could be certain. Torrin wondered what she was thinking.

It doesn't matter, Torrin told himself. *No matter what anyone thinks, I know I did the right thing. They are in no position to judge me.*

But despite his inner protests to the contrary, Torrin was wounded by the malicious rumoring that was certain to be running rampant throughout the castle. Once again, he felt betrayed.

The queen's tribunal chamber was capable of holding many but on this occasion only a select few were in attendance, suggesting that Torrin's trial was to be a private affair. Balconies and benches provided for spectators or an occasional jury stood empty. Also vacant were the tables and chairs used by contending legal ministers during disputes in which full contested case procedures were employed. The chamber itself was a masterpiece of artistry and architecture. Sunlight burst through the translucent planes of immense stained-glass windows, rising over two stories to reach the vaulted ceiling, illuminating the room with a mosaic of rainbow tinted light. Between decorative moldings, murals had been elegantly painted on the walls, murals that with grace and purity depicted images of historical significance or judicial inspiration. From the ceiling hung a large central chandelier. Its nucleus appeared as a sun whose radiating beams extended to a metal ring that encircled the golden solar disk. Above the ring perched a galaxy of burning candles and above the sun stood the sculpted icon of justice, a gilded human figure intended to represent the fair administration of law. Beneath the impressive chandelier, the flooring had been made from slats of hardwood stained in various shades and laid in a magnificent pattern of triumphant expression. The ceiling was held above the floor by glossy pillars of smooth, circular marble with dynamic figured scenes carved into the capitals.

Torrin's mother and brother were there. Marketa appeared tired and hurt, her face swollen and strained with tension, her body languid, struggling with the effort of keeping on her feet. Her shoulders hung slack and her fingers twisted nervously together in a quiet despairing pose. Aragon stood beside her, rigid and inimical to everything, glaring malevolently at Torrin with eyes that were flat and hard. Torrin found it too uncomfortable to return their gaze and so focused instead on the High Queen and on his purpose.

Bryana sat before him, outfitted in full battle dress as if she had prepared for war rather than justice, for attack rather than adjudication. Her face was a solemn mask, imperfectly concealing the emotion bubbling beneath the surface facade and fighting for release. With white knuckled, talon-like fingers curled tightly around the arms of her chair; she held her body in a stiff and dangerous pose.

Arlen, the High Queen's legal advisor, was also present. Previously, Torrin had held tremendous respect for this man, believing Arlen's adherence to the law to be as stout as the man's rotund figure. But that belief had been shattered by Arlen's collaboration in the queen's deceit, her violation of the law for personal gain. Arlen had supported the queen's lie, abetted her malfeasance. In Torrin's estimation, that act had demonstrated Arlen's lack of integrity and proven him to be nothing but a shameful lackey. He was the queen's running dog and nothing more, although admittedly Arlen's appearance was more porcine than canine, more pig than puppy. He was nothing but a fat, culpable, dishonest man with a pudgy face and tiny eyes yellowed with the stain of immoral complicity. Sweat ringed his underarms and dripped from his temples. He reeked even from a distance, stinking of cowardice and lies.

When Bryana broke the silence, her voice was as taut as a bow string. She dismissed the guards, then turned on Torrin. "Do you have anything at all to say in your defense?"

Torrin found the situation strange and, in a way, contradictory. He had never before felt so utterly alone yet at the same time so completely surrounded and observed.

"Yes, and no," Torrin answered with stoic self-possession, then continued on without further prevarication.

"I murdered Devin Murgleys, this I admit. And with your permission, I would like to briefly explain why I killed my father. But I do not present this information as an argument of my innocence nor as a petition for mercy. My father violated the law but the law set him free. He committed rape and murder, crimes against basic human rights, the right of people to be secure in their persons, safe from assault or unwarranted abuse. Justice demanded that he be executed in punishment of his crimes so that society could be protected from criminals like him. But justice was denied by the law, something which moral people cannot abide. If evil is tolerated and left unchecked, it will grow until it poisons the whole society. If I did nothing about my father's crime, my inaction would be an evil nearly as great as that of my father's. Society would suffer and we would both be accountable for the resulting injury. Therefore, I saw it as my duty to execute my father, a duty defined and derived from these moral principles and thereby possessing an inner moral worth. I acted out of reverence of moral law even though I transgressed the written law of our people. It is because of my sense of duty and my respect for the law that I stand ready to receive my punishment. I submit to the death sentence that the law demands I receive."

Escalating with the utterance of each word, Torrin's statement seemed to excite the queen's wrath and indignation. She seethed with outrage.

"How dare you presume to take the law into your own hands?" Bryana shouted. "You have no right to pass judgment on Devin or yourself. This childish and pompous speech of yours cannot justify your sin nor ease your guilt. How dare you bring this disgrace upon the Murgleys family name? You have sullied our reputation and pilloried our honor." Bryana was livid, her faced flushed, as she continued to reprimand Torrin, her scolding words as sharp as a lash. She shook with rage. "Does filial piety mean nothing to you? Don't you feel any love or sense of obligation to your parents, to your father? You knew the pain and disorder that your accusations against Devin and your murder of him would cause, that it would hurt not only your family, but Gairloch itself. You knew this yet you would not desist, thereby increasing your malice and the magnitude of your crime."

"Of course I was aware of the harm that would result from killing my father.

I love my family. I didn't want to hurt anyone and I grieve for the loss we have all suffered," admitted Torrin. "But the interests of justice are paramount, above even kinship, more important than family. The law must apply to all people, without contradiction or exception. Judgments of conscience must be based on moral reason, not on emotion or self interest. Reason is the arbiter between self interest and the interest of the public good. Duty demands that we fulfill the dictates of reason, of justice, even when it may be emotionally and physically burdensome. A man must do what is right regardless of the cost. I acted out of duty. My action was unlawful, but it *was* moral. For what is good or evil about an act is what the person intends rather than the consequences that the act produces."

"You don't see any contradiction in what you've done?" demanded Bryana furiously, her face contorted with grief and anger. "You claim to respect the sanctity of human life and yet you stole that from my son, a man whose existence had in itself an absolute worth. Devin's life constituted an end in itself. He had value. He did not live to serve merely as a means, a thing for you to use in an attempt to prove some philosophical point, to demonstrate a mercenary principle of your diseased ethics."

"No!" Torrin cried in obstreperous riposte. He was becoming increasingly irritated by the queen's continued recrimination of him. Torrin acknowledged that he had broken the law and saw no reason for her to belabor the point. "When my father committed rape and murder, he destroyed his value as a rational being, as a person. He did in truth become a thing, having only conditional worth, a relative value. I did the same thing you did. I killed my father to promote a higher social purpose, to support a greater good."

At that, Bryana became enraged. She threw something at Torrin but it missed its mark and hurled by too quickly for him to distinguish what it was before it crashed against the wall.

"How dare you compare yourself to me?" Bryana shouted in savage disapproval, vehemently protesting Torrin's declaration. "There is no similarity in our acts. My father begged me to take his life and even so it ravaged my heart. I loved my father and took his life at his request out of love and respect. You murdered your father and now try to justify it with hazy logic and a set of irrational ideas that you hope to pass off as a moral code. It was murder, pure and simple, empty of any noble purpose no matter what you claim."

Torrin remained intractable, unwilling to yield his position. But he realized that it was hopeless, that Bryana would never accept his argument or understand his reasons. "I agree that I am a murderer," answered Torrin bitterly. "I recognize that the interest of society and of the self must be balanced through the use of laws and sanctions to give binding force to moral rules so as to promote conditions consistent with the dictates of absolute moral principles. Yes, I have violated the law and I should be executed for my crime. I accept and am prepared to receive my death sentence."

"Well you're not going to get it," snapped Bryana savagely through tightly clenched teeth. "You executed my son in the name of your perverse beliefs. But I won't let you force me to carry out your own twisted self-sacrifice. You won't use me to provide the martyrdom you covet. I'm not going to let you use this to turn the people against me. I always knew the day would come when you would try to bring me down, but I'm stronger than you'll ever be. You'll not be remembered as anything more than a pitiless criminal, a cold-hearted killer. Perhaps I went too far in trying to protect my son," Bryana admitted, her thoughts drifting off in new directions, her speech distracted and issued in an offhanded manner.

"I cannot forgive what you have done but I will not have any more killing within our family. Your punishment will be exile. You will be cast out. My soldiers will escort you to the boundaries of my realm. And your mother and Aragon shall share your exile, for they too are a disgrace."

"No!" Torrin forcefully interjected. "You have no right to punish them. I take full responsibility for my action. I will not share the blame for my crime nor its punishment with anyone."

"Silence," roared Bryana. "Listen to yourself, you speak as if you are proud of what you've done, as if I'm offering a reward that you're unwilling to divide. You sicken me, Torrin. You are deranged and corrupt. And I can only assume that you acquired these traits from your mother and that you share them with Aragon. Marketa failed to control you, and your brother is as retched and undisciplined as you. The sight of any of you is more than I can stand. I knew from the beginning that you were wicked. I should have done something about you years ago. You dishonor our family; you always have. You challenge my authority. You made my son's life unbearable and ultimately caused his death. For this you shall be punished. In three days time, the three of you shall leave Gairloch forever. If after you have been exiled from my realm, any of you are found back within my kingdoms, you will be killed."

Bryana summoned the guards and ordered them to take Torrin back to his cell. Marketa and Aragon were allowed to remain free during the three days before their journey into exile. The trial was over; justice had been served.

Torrin was not asked nor allowed to attend his father's funeral. However, the small barred window of his cell permitted an awkward and distant view of the event.

Devin's body was ceremoniously transported outside the castle walls for burial. A festoon of bright flowers and painted ribbons hung about his casket in a repetitive series of suspended curves. The casket itself rested on a richly decorated carriage pulled by cream-colored horses adorned in ornate caparison of gold tassels, black cloth coverings, and yellow harness. The funeral procession included an honor guard riding on both sides of the carriage in solemn tribute. Devin's funeral procession was well attended, containing mourners from all levels of Gairloch's social structure.

Marketa and Aragon were of course at the forefront of the sorrowful parade. Bryana rode apart from them, keeping a purposeful and symbolic distance. Bag pipes and drums joined the procession in morose accompaniment, musically saluting Devin's memory with threnody. The grandeur and pageantry of this memorial service seemed unprecedented. All to honor Devin, a man who was killed for his immoral behavior. For his death, the sinner was celebrated and his son condemned.

The line of mourners progressed through the gates, outside of the castle, and into the royal cemetery. The pallbearers placed Devin's coffin upon the funeral bier surrounded by heads bowed in sorrow and respect as they listened to Bryana deliver her blessing. Following the prayer, Devin's body was buried, laid to rest in the ground's eternal embrace.

Torrin envied his father, not his popularity nor the respect he was being shown but his death. He had thought that after killing his father, he would be executed himself, not forced to continue his life enduring the pain of what he had done. Torrin had planned on receiving a death sentence, and by dying to atone for his act of murder, his life's blood to provide ablution for spilling that of his father's. Death meant atonement.

The prospect of living turned his thoughts to Lenore. Torrin settled back upon the floor again in a hopeless state of dejection. But he held true to his promise against the release of tears.

He had no idea how he could manage to go on living now that everything which had given his life meaning was lost. Home, family, Lenore, and even hope. All gone. The substance of his life, that which defined who he was, had been destroyed. His dreams of continued study and advancement in the

Prelature, his hope of making a significant contribution to society as a member of that venerable institution, were now impossible, along with his dreams of marrying Lenore and raising a loving family.

The queen's decision to spare his life and banish him to exile had reduced Torrin from prelate to pariah in a matter of minutes. As an outcast, Torrin felt pointlessly alive, like an animated corpse. True death, physical as well as social, would be easier to abide. The idea of suicide flirted with Torrin suggestively and he found it sensuously attractive. For a long, lonely time he wrestled with its soft and soothing appeal but in the end rejected its seductive proposition. Suicide was the avenue of a coward, a path for the weak to escape responsibility, to shirk the burden of life and its obligations. His mother and brother were being exiled because of him. Torrin knew it was not his fault but it was undeniably a result of his actions. Therefore, he felt grudgingly obligated to assist them, to ease the hardship they would undoubtedly confront in the land of exile. The wasteland it was called, but not because the land was barren. There would be trees, water, wildlife, and even crops. It was referred to as the wasteland because that was where society dumped its human garbage, social refuse considered undesirable or unsalvageable. Torrin, along with his mother and Aragon, now bore the mark of such a person—an outline of an eye branded on his right palm, the identifying mark of an exile.

No family or friend visited Torrin while he was held captive. His jailers were his only company and they were no great comfort. They refused to tell him if his isolation had been ordered or if it was simply that no one was interested in seeing him. In truth, there was only one person Torrin wanted to see anyway—Lenore. The thought that she stayed away by her own choice hurt beyond imagination.

I wish I could tell her how sorry I am, thought Torrin miserably. *I never meant to hurt her; I hope she can forgive me. If only I could see her one last time, tell her I'm sorry and that I love her. But then, truth be told, I doubt my heart could stand saying goodbye in person. Perhaps it's better this way.*

The guards refused even to give him paper and pen with which to write a message to Lenore. So in desperation, Torrin attempted to communicate with her telepathically, mentally reaching out to her, sending thoughts of love and regret. But he doubted its effectiveness, more good intentions yielding poor results. Such was the pattern of his life.

Despite Torrin's loneliness and imprisonment, for him the three days of solitary confinement passed surprisingly quick. The thought of exile made even his cell attractive and painful to lose. The cell was dry and warm and generally comfortable. But most importantly it was a part of Gairloch, his home, his heart. The castle was a jewel among a field of gold. It was beautiful not only in material and construct but in occupation as well. The people of Gairloch cared for their home, maintained its elegance and architecture, kept it clean, polished, and ordered. Torrin lovingly caressed the cool, rough surface of his prison wall and considered how terribly he would miss Castle Gairloch, a castle held together as much by magic and memories as by mortar and masonry.

On the third day, Torrin was released and instructed to return to his former living quarters for the purpose of collecting what few belongings he chose to carry with him into exile. The guards never left him, and Torrin found it peculiar trying to assemble a lifetime of keepsakes and memories into a parcel you could carry on your back while under the constant supervision of armed guards.

He counseled himself to be practical, take only what might be useful: books, paper, ink, quills, clothes, and tools. But it was difficult. Most of what he was leaving behind seemed the most meaningful. There were stories and sentiment bound up in nearly everything. Torrin took a couple of his blue robes. Foolish really, there would be no Prelature where he was headed and hence no need for a wizard's robes. Perhaps as nostalgic but outwardly less frivolous, he also took the axe Lenore had given him, or rather his guards took it, assuring Torrin that he would receive it upon reaching their destination.

Thinking he was done, Torrin prepared to leave when one final item caught his eye. It was a large, gaudy medallion his father had given him a long time ago. Torrin had not worn it in years. To be honest, he had always considered it a very ugly piece of jewelry. The medallion bore the image of a pair of silver eagle wings encircling an oval shaped, blue-green larimar stone. Tarnish, grown out of neglect and spreading like a malignant disease, now obscured the fine detail of the feathered wings.

Shaking his head, Torrin stared thoughtfully at the medallion for a moment then slipped the chain around his neck, tucked it inside his shirt, and let the guards lead him through the castle and into the courtyard where the others were assembling for their journey.

Their escort consisted of eight mounted soldiers led by Captain Barret. Marketa was there loading supplies and her personal belongings into a small wagon she had been allowed to take provided she tend the horses' reins herself. The guards flatly refused to drive the wagon for her. She was clearly overloading the wagon and increasing with each additional item the odds that it would fail to reach their destination. Marketa had never considered herself unduly attached to material luxury. But she was scared by the notion of a future in exile, frightened by the prospect of being dropped in the middle of nowhere without any of the comforts she took for granted as part of her previous life. She had no idea how she would support herself in the new land. Her education and eclectic knowledge now seemed trivial in comparison to her lack of more basic and practical skills.

Aragon finished assisting Marketa with her packing and was preparing to mount his horse. He remained angry over the murder of his father but not at his forced exile. Aragon long ago became disenchanted with Gairloch, the Prelature, and the formal institutions of higher learning. He considered life his school and the world its classrooms. Exile was merely another course in which he was enrolling and from which he envisioned great opportunity for gathering interesting information. The only facet bothering him was the mandated nature of his enrollment. For Aragon, personal independence was a fundamental value, a precious right. Only the knowledge that someone had ordered him into exile angered him, not the exile itself. However, the anger Aragon experienced also provided him with a curious pleasure, granting him a justification for his habitual animosity and a peculiar sense of superiority in the knowledge that their punishment did not burden nor injure him.

Torrin loaded his saddlebags on a horse saddled and selected for him. He rubbed the sorrel's neck, its sleek hide pilosed with velvety, reddish-brown hair, letting the horse get accustomed to his presence before climbing on its back. Despite his precautions, the spirited horse threw its head, stomped, and shifted in unruly protest. But the recalcitrant animal actually helped improve Torrin's mood. It felt surprisingly good to impose his will upon that of the horse, to force it to yield to his control, when so much else in life seemed beyond it.

Torrin looked about, taking in the grandeur of Castle Gairloch one last time, hoping to capture and preserve its image in his mind. Pleasant laughter and other friendly sounds of life could be heard. Soldiers patrolled the lofty battlements and marched behind protective parapets. Raised high above the peaks of gilded spires perched atop stone towers, bright colored banners of red, white, and yellow snapped briskly in the wind. Brilliant shadings reflected from stained glass windows in radiant splendor. Torrin could not believe that he was looking upon this treasured sight for the last time. What beauty. What loss.

From his rapt appreciation of Gairloch's ubiquitous beauty and strength, Torrin was disturbed by the approach of an unexpected rider.

"Lenore, what are you doing here?" Torrin asked with quick surprise.

"Coming with you," Lenore answered blithely as she positioned her horse next to Torrin's.

"What? You can't. Don't be absurd, it's not safe where we're going." Torrin spoke with genuine concern. "Whatever fate we're riding into, it's sure to be full of danger and misery."

"Give me some credit, Torrin. I know it's dangerous and I don't care. I'm coming with," insisted Lenore casually. "Unless you did all this just to get away from me?"

"No. I'd give anything to be with you, believe me, but I can't let you do this. I won't let you throw away your future because of me. I love you too much to let you ruin your life this way. I can't ask you to come with me. You've no chance of being happy unless you stay here," explained Torrin.

Lenore remained adamant. "Well if you'd give anything, give your mouth a rest. This is my decision, not yours. You didn't ask me to do anything, although there is something you should ask. I do what I want and right now I want to be with you. So, keep quiet and consider yourself lucky."

Torrin was about to continue his protest but with diminished enthusiasm, when Barret interrupted them. "What's going on here?" he barked.

Lenore faced him, squaring her shoulders in preparation for a nasty confrontation. "I'm coming with," she said plainly but firmly.

Barret studied her for a long moment before responding, then shrugged his indifferent approval. "You will have to keep our pace or fall behind. We won't wait for you and we won't bring you back if you change your mind."

With that, the issue was decided. Barret wheeled his horse about and galloped back to the forefront of their party, issuing the order for their departure, shouting to be heard above the clattering of the horse's hooves upon the paving stones. Flanked by soldiers, they rode beneath the raised portcullis of the castle's main gate and into the open countryside, thus beginning their journey into exile. From high atop Gairloch's walls and towers, their withdrawal was supervised by stone gargoyles sculpted in forms ranging from the fearsomely grotesque to those humorous in design. Yet they watched without concern. Their fixed, silent gaze held neither sorrow nor malicious joy over the exile's plight.

Torrin estimated it would require several days to reach the wasteland and that the road they followed would fail long before they arrived. But the road would make their travel easier while it lasted.

The conditions of the day seemed inappropriate to the situation. One might expect a cold drizzle beneath a gray overcast sky, a day oppressive and miserable. But it was not. The day was warm and sunny; the sky a resplendent azure dotted with scattered milky-white clouds, like islands in a vast blue sea. It was late spring and life was abundant. The forested hills were full and green and the plains contained an explosion of colorful wildflowers. The air was sweet and filled with the chorus of singing birds. It lightened the heart and made the journey less like banishment and more like a pleasure outing. This was also in part attributable to the mind's natural tendency to reject unpleasant realities, to deny the existence of pain in defense against it. These factors together with Lenore's comforting presence helped improve Torrin's spirits, but apprehension and despair would not entirely forsake him.

In spite of all the beauty which the land possessed, Torrin found his gaze constantly returning to Lenore. She wore a teal blouse decorated with floral embroidery about the delicately scalloped neckline and front lacing. Her lower anatomy, however, was clad with greater practicality, pants made from sturdy brown fabric and soft leather boots that hugged her calves. Beautiful, yet sensible. That was Lenore in thought and form, and the inspiration of Torrin's affection.

Lenore rode her horse with dignified difficulty. It would have been cute if not for the knowledge that her discomfort would increase to unbearable proportions if her skill did not quickly improve. For the time being she would be all right, while the road held out and the terrain remained relatively even. Her hair was knotted in a single braid that hung at her back and glistened in the sun. Her face was smooth and pale like polished ivory, her lips full and moist. He would have to make sure that her skin did not burn or her lips crack and blister from continued exposure to the sun and wind during their journey through the hinterland. She looked so soft, so lovely. Riding her horse, she bounced in a most delightfully intriguing manner. Delightful to Torrin anyway. Lenore did not find it pleasant in the least and cursed the existence of even her modest bosom.

Changing the subject of his thoughts, Torrin asked, "What did you mean back at the castle when you said there was something I should ask you?"

"Forget it," said Lenore.

"Come on, don't keep secrets; tell me."

"No, I shouldn't have to. If you can't think of it on your own, I'm certainly not going to tell you."

Torrin smiled at the game she appeared to be playing with him despite the fact he seemed to be losing, then sobered at a different thought. "What did your parents say when you told them you were leaving?"

Lenore did not answer. She stared ahead and Torrin could see that she was softly crying. A slow current of tears began to stream from her eyes. He hesitated to speak again, not wanting to further provoke her misery but his heart ached to find some form of comfort he could offer. Feebly he asked, "Lenore, are you all right?"

"Yes," she answered, her voice fragile. But she continued with strengthening resolve, "It's just that I'm going to miss them all so much. They understood my decision, of course. And they supported me. Last night my mother and I talked for hours and then cried together for several more. I'll miss her most of all. We were so close. I could tell my mother anything. I'd say we were like best friends but that would be trivializing our relationship. She was much more than a friend; she was my mother. Listen to me, I'm already talking of her in the past tense." She paused and wiped her eyes. "I feel like I'm running out on my sisters. I won't get to see my nephews grow up. I'll never...." Her voice trailed off. Lenore stopped talking and sobbed quietly to herself.

"I'm sorry," Torrin offered pointlessly. He wanted to tell her that everything would be all right. He wanted to promise that he would protect Lenore, that he would never let anything hurt her. But he knew it was already too late for such promises. He could think of no way to comfort her, so he left her alone to find it within herself.

When at last they halted for the day, Torrin knew it would still be several hours before he could lie down and rest. There was work to be done. He removed the bridle and saddle from Lenore's horse as well as from his own and unhitched the harness from the horses that pulled his mother's wagon. After setting the gear out in the sun so that the sweat would dry, he currycombed the horses and saw that they were watered and secured in an area in which to graze. Torrin also fetched water for Lenore and his mother to drink and to wash their hands and faces free of the equine smell and the film of dirt acquired over the course of the long day.

After finishing these menial chores, Torrin looked around and saw Lenore sitting on a blanket in the shade cast by the lush overhanging canopy of a tall oak tree. He walked over and knelt beside her on the grass.

"I imagine being on that horse all day has left you with a fair share of discomfort," he remarked. "Would you like me to see if I can help make you feel better?"

"Oh yes," groaned Lenore, grimacing as she struggled to pull off her boots.

"Anything you can do would be greatly appreciated. I hurt all over. I wish I never had to look at another horse again for as long as I live, much less ride one. I don't see how I'll ever be able to get back on that cursed beast again tomorrow."

With her consent, Torrin began to use his magic to ease the aches and pains her body had suffered during the day's arduous ride.

"You know," said Torrin, "in addition to voicing the applicable incantations, the magic requires a laying on of hands for the healing to be truly effective."

"Is that so?" asked Lenore, well aware that he was lying. "I suppose that would be all right, but be careful about where you choose to lay them. Understand?"

"Of course," Torrin assured with exaggerated piety. "My intentions are entirely honorable. I wish only to ease your suffering, nothing more. Now lay down on your stomach and let me get to work."

He began by kneading her shoulders, working his fingers deep into her flesh, then moved down to massage the strain from her back. His rubbing caress soothed the saddle sores from her pert derriere and well formed legs. Lenore released a sigh of relief followed by soft moans of pleasure. With sly carelessness, Torrin brushed nearer and nearer to forbidden zones as his hands continued to glide over the graceful curves of Lenore's pliant body.

She enjoyed the luxury of his attentive message but only permitted it to go so far, shifting her body when necessary to block Torrin's lascivious advances. After all, they were hardly alone.

Once Lenore's physical hurts had been lessened and she was resting comfortably, Torrin left to find his mother and offer the use his magic to do the same for her, minus the more personal attention he had given Lenore. But she declined. Torrin was not sure if Marketa did this out of spite or because she considered her pain minor or perhaps because she thought such pain should be endured so as to strengthen the body and spirit. Whatever her reason, Torrin felt offended. As for his brother, Aragon continued to be less than approachable and besides he could probably heal himself.

Leaving his mother, Torrin saw Barret dispatch a few of the soldiers into the woods to hunt the party's evening meal. It was likely Torrin would have been assigned this duty too had they felt he could be trusted with a weapon or against escape. His status as a prisoner remained clearly evident despite the absence of a cell or physical restraints.

Barret's presence as leader of this expedition was curious and Torrin had been somewhat bothered by it all day. But an appropriate occasion to speak with him never seemed to present itself, until now.

"It's quite a coincidence that you were chosen to escort me into exile," Torrin commented, "you being the one that found me that night."

"No," answered Barret, continuing his inspection of a map drawn on heavy yellow parchment while he also idly sharpened his sword, dragging a whetstone over the blade's keen edge in long easy strokes that repeated again and again. "It was no coincidence at all. I volunteered for this detail."

"Why?" Torrin asked, puzzled.

Barret looked up, his face expressionless. "Because I understand what happened. I know that Devin was guilty. But so are you. I implement the queen's will and abide by her command. You are a criminal and the queen rightly ordered your punishment. I mean to see that punishment carried out, because that's my job. Devin was all charm and ruthlessness, but a popular man nevertheless, well liked by a lot of people. There are others," Barret said gesturing at the camp, "who don't understand what happened that night and feel your punishment is too lenient. I thought you at least deserved to reach exile alive. And besides, that was the order of my queen."

Torrin still failed to fully comprehend this man but was beginning to see ramifications of what Barret said and of what Barret had done. "The night we found that girl, the one my father killed, you told that soldier to vouch for my whereabouts? You did that to protect me, to give me an alibi, didn't you?"

"Maybe I did." Barret shrugged his disinterest, holding up his sword and inspecting the sharpened edge of its blade. "But don't expect me to do anything else for you except fulfill my orders," Barret stated with characteristic nonchalance. "The hunters will be back soon, go build a fire. And when they do return, I want you to clean and cook whatever food they've found. Get to it."

The culinary arts had never been considered one of Torrin's strong suits but he found the meal of small game surprisingly satisfying. Lenore, however, disagreed. A finicky eater, she considered anything more exotic than chicken or beef unfit for human consumption. But despite her discriminating tastes, Lenore managed to eat something from her plate, although not without considerable complaint.

After dinner, when the camp finally settled down for sleep, Torrin was bone weary and slipped eagerly into slumber. Lenore did not share the luxury of Torrin's sleepiness nor his capacity to accommodate the desire. She had never slept outdoors before nor understood the appeal of recreational camping. This experience confirmed her anticipated distaste for the activity. The romantic notions others had tried to impress upon her of how life in the wild and in harmony with nature liberated the human spirit, delighted the senses, and expanded consciousness were now unequivocally disproved. Such ideas were sheer nonsense. She felt entirely too close to nature at the moment and would have appreciated a far less intimate relationship. She longed for the comfort of a warm bed complete with down pillows and clean linens appropriately enclosed by walls, floor, and ceiling. *Anything else is uncivilized, might as well walk around on all fours and howl at the moon*, thought Lenore.

"Torrin," she whispered, reaching over to shake him and thereby assure he received her words. "I can't sleep."

"Huh?" Torrin mumbled as he slowly came back awake. "Why? What's wrong?"

"The ground's too hard. There's huge rocks everywhere and every time I move a sharp branch or thorn stabs me in the side. It's like we've bedded down in the middle of a rose garden. They're all over and I can't get comfortable."

"Ok. Get up," said Torrin with a slightly exasperated sigh, agitated but not truly disgusted by her complaint. From the area in which Lenore attempted sleep, Torrin removed the small rocks and sticks that Lenore had enlarged beyond reality by her exaggerated description. He then spread out his own blanket for Lenore to use as a mattress. "There you go. That should be more comfortable. Now, try to get some sleep, tomorrow promises to be another long day."

Her face inches from the uncovered ground, strong earthy odors assaulted Lenore's nose and olfactory nerves, offending her fastidious sensitivities. *Dirt was not something one slept on*, thought Lenore. *It was the reason you washed sheets and swept floors*. Feeling unclean, she began to itch. And with each new itch she became more and more convinced that an army of ants joined by spiders, centipedes, and other contingents of insects had infested her blankets, clothes, and person. After a few more minutes, the feeling became quite maddening.

"Arg! Torrin, I feel like I'm crawling with bugs!" she groaned, scratching furiously.

"Don't worry, it's just your imagination. The frogs around here probably ate all the bugs," joked Torrin. "Just be careful you don't roll over and squash a nice, fat, friendly amphibian."

"That's disgusting. I'm not sleeping with any damn frog," grumped Lenore.

"I'm glad to hear it, my love, since your not *sleeping* with me either. But don't worry about them, I'm confident the snakes in turn keep the frog population under control. In fact, I saw a nest of them earlier in those tall weeds over there"

"Snakes!" she shrieked, leaping to her feet and throwing off her blanket.

"Shh," Torrin hushed, struggling to hold back his laughter. "I'm just joking. Lay back down. You won't be swallowed up by any snake. I promise."

"Don't laugh," she said heatedly, kicking dust at him. "You jackass! It's not funny; I hate snakes. How do you know there aren't any around here? How can you be sure they won't crawl in bed with me in the middle of the night. I've heard they do that, because they like the body heat or something."

"If they do, I'll crawl right in after them. I like body heat too."

In answer, she kicked more dust at his face, folded her arms over her chest, and turned her back to him.

"I'm sorry, please don't be mad," Torrin pleaded. "I didn't mean to laugh at you. I was just having a little fun, trying to lighten the mood that's been hanging over us most of the day. I apologize. But seriously, you don't have to worry about snakes or nasty little creepy crawlers."

"Why not?" she demanded.

"My magic; it repels them. It holds them at bay," explained Torrin.

"Really?" Lenore asked, still distrustful as she slowly turned and laid back down.

"Yes. Of course, the repellent emanates from me so the effect is strongest closest to my person."

"Well then get over here, damn it."

Torrin smiled mischievously as he snuggled up next to Lenore, his body pressed against her back. He put his arm around her waist, his hand over her stomach. "There, feel safe now?" Torrin whispered into her ear. "You know, your language has become decidedly less ladylike recently."

"Bullshit," Lenore cursed jovially. "And don't go getting any ideas," she scolded, stopping the lustful exploratory progress of Torrin's hand. "Behave yourself."

"You're no fun," Torrin pouted.

She closed her eyes and tried to shut out visions of snakes, insects, and the many other elements of nature she perceived as unpleasant. Far off in the distance, a wolf howled. Toads croaked, an owl hooted, and crickets sang. Despite their calls, Lenore's qualms about midnight attacks gradually subsided and eventually she succeeded in attaining sleep.

The days followed in much the same manner as the first, except that the growing acceptance of their situation began to slowly alleviate some of the tension between Torrin and his family. They talked little but at least they talked and did so with a civil tongue. However, Torrin's relationship with his guards progressed in the opposing direction. The soldiers became increasingly restless and disgruntled with their journey. Some even made it clear that they would have preferred to kill their captives, claiming that it had been done in response to an escape attempt, and return to Gairloch. Fortunately, they were not all so cold blooded as this and Barret was certainly not the type of man to allow those that were to carry out such a villainous plan. But the soldier's irritation and boredom enhanced their hostility toward their prisoners. And Torrin became the focus and outlet of their malice.

One of the soldiers, Kayne, assumed the role as informal leader of the campaign against Torrin. Kayne was a husky brutish man of a crude and combative nature. He was foul both in body and spirit, cloaked in a malodorous stench that became more pungent with each new day. Nevertheless, he won the hearts of his fellows by instigating and encouraging abusive entertainment at Torrin's expense.

It began simply enough. Kayne would ride alongside Torrin spitting and hurling insults at him. Although Torrin burned with rage, he thought if he ignored the harassment, Kayne would lose interest. Kayne did not. Each day Kayne became more cruel in his persecution of Torrin, spurred by Torrin's weakening tolerance and his cohorts' delighted appreciation of the sport. Every barb and act of torment was applauded by grating, sardonic laughter.

One morning, Kayne added a new tactic to his repertoire of abuse. Riding where Torrin was sure to see him, Kayne openly studied Lenore with a disquieting intensity.

"It's been too long since I've been with a woman," Kayne complained to the other soldiers. "If I don't dip my wick pretty soon, I'm afraid it might fall off. Maybe this young slut here could remind me how it feels. She's not *too* ugly and I bet she's had enough experience that she knows how to please a man."

Kayne saw the effect he was having on Torrin and continued mercilessly in his assessment of Lenore's womanly attributes, providing a detailed vulgar description of how he intended to enjoy her flesh.

"Yes sir, she's a ripe little bitch," Kayne grunted. "I'll wager she's shared a bed with half the men of Gairloch. Probably not as tight now as she was a few years back, but tight enough to suit a man of my considerable size. Course, I'd be running the risk of ruining her for all the men who'll follow me. But what do I care? I'll risk it."

"Ignore him, Torrin!" Lenore commanded as she attempted to follow her own advice. She knew Kayne was just trying to rattle Torrin and that Barret would probably protect them from any real harm, but she was beginning to scare anyway.

But Torrin could not ignore it. Hatred filled his soul and screamed for release. Heedless of his unarmed status, he was not going to let anyone talk about Lenore that way. He could not allow Lenore to be subjected to such abuse and intimidation. Kayne's talk alone was more than Torrin could stomach. He would do whatever necessary to make certain it went no further.

"…Yeah, I've been long enough away from Gairloch that she's beginning to look mighty appetizing. Not much of a chest on her though. Why, I could cover all of one breast with a single hand, maybe even get the whole thing in my mouth. What a sweet morsel that would be." He laughed and so did the other soldiers listening. "Look at her nipples harden up, she's getting excited just thinking about it. I've seen the way she looks at me, the way she wiggles that little ass of hers whenever I'm around. Yeah, she wants it and she wants it bad. Hey girl. Hey bitch! You ready to get off that horse and ride something else for a while? Come on over here and unbuckle my pants. Give me a kiss where it counts the most. A nice, long wet kiss."

"Shut up!" Torrin roared. Tiny droplets of spittle sprayed from his mouth carried by the explosive force of his shouted, rage-filled words. A cruel and murderous desire burned through the marrow of his bones, blazing with white-hot intensity and fueled by an acerbic temper. "Shut up, you filthy pile of shit. Shut up or I'll tear out your vile tongue and shove it down your throat. You lay one hand on her and I swear you'll pull back a stub! I mean it, damn it. I'll kill you if you don't shut up and leave her alone."

Kayne grinned wolfishly. "Oooh, Torrin the terrible, how you frighten me. Look, I'm shaking like a leaf," he chortled behind his grizzled beard, his hand engaged in a mocking, exaggerated tremble. "You should learn to have more respect for your elders, boy, and your betters."

Kayne kicked his horse and drove the animal hard against Torrin's sorrel causing it to buck and rear wildly, catching Torrin unprepared and dumping him to the ground. It hit him solidly, knocking the wind out of Torrin.

"Torrin the tormented had a great fall. Hear how pitifully the baby bawls," jeered Kayne in rhyming mockery.

His ego as badly bruised as his posterior, Torrin climbed to his feet amid a chorus of laughter and ridicule. Dusting himself off, flushed with anger and embarrassment, struggling to regain some semblance of dignity, Torrin suppressed his homicidal impulse but vowed silently that he would see Kayne dead before this journey ended. Somehow, some way, he would see it happen.

Tension escalated as the day wore on and the group continued its trek through green forests and fields. Kayne's taunts went no further. Torrin and Lenore passed the hours in silence until the sun slowly dipped behind the hills lining the western horizon, leaving a darkening sapphire sky in its fiery wake.

That night, when their party made camp, Lenore confronted Barret. She had no intention of suffering through another day of mistreatment by Kayne and his brutish cohorts.

"Why don't you keep your men under control?" she demanded defiantly.

"Excuse me?" asked Barret, rising to his feet and towering above her.

"Your soldiers, they're animals in need of a tighter leash. You're their captain, control them! They've got no right to treat us this way. We don't deserve their abuse. And if you're a man with any honor what so ever, you won't continue to allow it. So tell that damn Kayne of yours to leave Torrin alone and to stay the hell away from me."

"Don't worry," Barret said calmly, unaffected by her tirade. He casually dismissed her concerns as if they were of no consequence at all, his manner so serene he seemed to have lost interest in all earthly matters. She felt like slapping his face just to shatter that annoying calm and force some stronger reaction from him.

"Kayne's no real danger," Barret continued. "He's just a little ornery. But if you don't believe me, if your unconvinced by my faith in Kayne's character, be assured that I won't let him hurt you. He'd have to get through me to get his hands on you, and that's not something Kayne could manage, even if he were twins. As for Torrin, tell him not to be so sensitive. He shouldn't let Kayne get under his skin."

"No! That's not good enough," snapped Lenore, determined to get results from this man. "He's a prisoner. He can't protect himself against your soldiers. It's your job to do it for him, damn it. So do it!"

"Now look here, little girl," Barret grumbled. His eyes narrowed and his brow drew close, implications of anger beneath a surface calm. "You don't tell me how to do my job. I don't answer to you and I don't have to put up with your uninvited criticism. My assignment is to see that these prisoners are exiled,

That means I'll do what it takes to keep them alive in order to fulfill that obligation. But that's it, you hear me, that's all I'm paid to do. I'm a captain in service of the queen, not Torrin's damn nursemaid. And not yours either."

"Please, isn't there something you can do?" Lenore pleaded. She saw her prospects darkening like the night and feared that she had now alienated her best hope of protection.

Barret massaged the perpetually placid features of his face. His disposition softened at the frightened look in Lenore's eyes and the gentleness left in her voice now that the angry demands were gone.

"All right, I'll talk to Kayne. And like I said, I won't let him hurt you, so don't fret about that. I'll tell him to ease up on Torrin if that's what you want. But you should realize that where you're going there will be a lot worse than Kayne. He'll seem like a prince of etiquette compared to the men who occupy the wasteland. Torrin's going to have to learn to take care of himself all on his own. He has to learn to be a man, because neither you nor I are going to be able to fight his battles forever."

Disturbed by his warning but content with what Barret had promised, Lenore went to find Torrin. She did not tell Torrin of her discussion with Barret and hoped Barret would not speak of it either. She suspected that if Torrin knew of her appeal on his behalf, it would injure his pride and quite possibly their relationship.

In the days that followed, Kayne's abuse of Torrin lessened somewhat but did not cease entirely. It became more covert, always done just outside Barret's protective view or just inside Barret's tolerance. Kayne continued to taunt and belittle Torrin in front of the others but not so boldly as before. It was more private now, a contest between Torrin and Kayne alone, no longer a spectator sport. Often, when no one else was looking, Torrin would suffer the furtive and unexpected impact of Kayne's knotted fist or waken to the concussion of Kayne's booted foot against his face or ribs. Torrin remained a toy for Kayne's sadistic entertainment. And an unspoken threat promised worse things to come.

Although it was plausible that Barret did not actually witness Kayne's actions, he could hardly be ignorant of their occurrence. The evidence clearly displayed itself in the cuts and bruises adorning Torrin's person. But then Torrin was unaware of Barret's previous intervention and therefore had no reason to expect it now. For the time being, he was content that Kayne at least left Lenore alone. So he suffered his torment but all the while continued to nurse his hatred and a festering desire for vengeance.

Time passed in a manner similar to the prisoner's progress through the land, each marching forward into an unknown future without hope of return. The terrain became increasingly formidable as they moved further westward and the road eventually abandoned them entirely. Their route meandered below the foothills of a immense mountain range, its slopes strewn with large rock masses which bore the appearance of a fallen city, like a ruined castle razed to its foundation by the ravages of time, war, or some equally powerful conquering force. Talus accumulations collected at the bottom of the foothills, the broken and eroded remnants of earlier rock slides. The grassy plains of the valley through which they rode gave way to oaks and pines and then to scrub with increasing elevation, their greenery a sharp contrast to the jutting gray and auburn stone.

The landscape was striking in its rugged splendor but challenging to the party's movement. It would not be necessary to actually cross over the mountains but even at their base the ground rose and fell in fatiguing undulation, possessed of ravines, rubble, and other natural obstacles which combined to form a unified barrier that was particularly hindersome to Marketa's wagon.

Marketa urged the horses forward with as much force as she could muster. Each time she snapped the whip against the animals, Marketa flinched at the cruel sound and in pity of the pain she imagined it inflicted. Her face was lined with worry for herself and sympathy for the horses laboring under the strain of meeting her command, pulling the heavy wagon up the land's increasing incline. Time and again, she looked to Barret, not in the hope of receiving aid but in concern that he would at any moment demand she dump some of the wagon's contents so that the speed of their pace might be preserved.

"How soon until we reach the wastelands?" Marketa asked with a strange blend of hope and apprehension.

"Few more days yet," stated Barret, reining in his horse and calling the rest of the party to a halt. He turned his attention back to Marketa and continued, as if in answer to her unspoken thoughts, "You're slowing us down and overworking your horses, neither of which I'll tolerate. It's time to cast off some of that crap in your wagon. I never should have let you take it in the first place. We'll take a brief rest while you toss out half that stuff. But be quick about it."

"No. Please don't make me do that," Marketa pleaded. The thought of her last worldly possessions littering the landscape like jetsam from a sinking ship wrung her heart. Even something as simple as a chair can become infinitely precious when you have not the skill to make one nor the means to acquire another. "Is it really so important that we get there so quickly?" she continued. "What difference will a few days make? No one will care. But if we take the extra time and keep what we have, our lives will be much easier in this harsh and forbidding land. Can't you understand? Can't you help me with the wagon? Use the strength of your men and their horses to keep it moving until we come upon smoother ground."

Torrin, Lenore, and Aragon rode forward to investigate the reason for the delay and the nature of the discussion between Barret and Marketa.

"I have deadlines to meet," Barret asserted with cold indifference. "And I won't have my men pushing this damn wagon over every hill and rock we encounter between here and the wastelands. I'm not interested in your problems and whining won't change my mind. Now, get rid of what you don't absolutely need or I'll do it myself."

Defeated, Marketa began looking through her belongings to determine what items possessed the greatest inverse relationship between weight and value, what was heaviest but the least important. Torrin stopped her.

"Wait," Torrin called to his mother. "Get out of the wagon and step away. Our kind Captain Barret may not be able to help but I believe that I can."

Initially Marketa thought Torrin intended to take the items from the wagon himself and she moved to protest. Then she realized that this was not the type of assistance being offered and complied with his command.

Torrin dismounted and walked over to stand before the wagon. With arms held out before him, he brought forth his magic. The air grew palpably heavier with the weight of the magic's strange emerging power. Blue fire sparked at the fingertips of Torrin's hands. The spell wove its enchantment through the fabric of the wagon and its cargo, causing both to mysteriously diminish in weight but to remain otherwise unchanged.

After composing himself, Torrin returned to his horse and swung back into the saddle. "The wagon will now appear lighter, but the effect is only temporary. It can be reapplied though. That should solve the problem for a while."

"Dwarves!" someone shouted from behind them, stealing the import of Torrin's accomplishment. "Dwarves!" The angry call went up again.

The soldiers quickly rode up to join Barret and the others. After being reined in, the horses stamped and shifted with nervous energy. Bridle rings jingled in answer to their restless movements.

"Sir, there's a pack of dwarves on that hillside," one of the soldiers said pointing. "Most likely spies or scouts for their army. Give the word and we'll take care of them. We'll cut them to ribbons, the beady-eyed, little worm-eating moles."

"There's no reason for violence. They're not warriors," interjected Aragon. "They're only children and a few adults."

"What? How can you tell at this distance?" Barret asked.

"I can see them. My sight is enhanced by magic," Aragon explained with growing irritation. "Most of them are just children, best if we ignore them and move on."

The soldiers grew impatient, waiting for Barret to deliver their orders. This chance encounter with the dwarves presented relief from the boredom of the march and an outlet for their bloodlust. Their racial hatred provided a convenient motive for brutality, a justification to engage in an age-old barbarous sport.

Kayne took the initiative. "Children, my ass. Demon spawn is what they are. If they're stupid enough to stick their heads out of their grubby holes, then they deserve to have them heads lopped off. Child or not, the only good dwarf is the one spited on my sword. Stop stalling, you cowards. Come on!" Kayne shouted, wheeling his horse about and charging in the direction of the dwarves, taking six of the other soldiers with him.

"Damn that bastard," Barret mumbled under his breath, then yelled, "Get back here you idiots!"

Torrin took quick notice of the fact that at the moment they were guarded only by Barret and one other soldier. This would be their best opportunity for escape, to make a run for it, provided there was somewhere to run more appealing than the wastelands. Still, at least they would be away from Kayne and his despicable friends.

But Lenore distracted his thoughts before Torrin could decide if an escape attempt was worth the risk. "Torrin, is it true, are they really only children?" she asked, wide-eyed with fear, horrified at the thought of murdered innocents.

"Hm? Oh yes, Aragon's right about that. They're mostly children. I too can see that clearly enough," Torrin answered, half is mind still measuring the chances for flight.

"Then for the love of all that's holy, you've got to do something," Lenore begged with great concern. "Don't let them kill *children*!"

"But ..." Torrin began to argue but discovered he could not in the face of Lenore's beseeching expression, her green eyes filled with mounting horror and injured gentleness. He could deny her nothing.

Barret had not been listening to their dialogue and so was taken by surprise when Torrin bolted from the group, galloping at a breakneck gait in the direction of the soldiers.

"Son-of-a-bitch!" Barret cursed, choking on his anger. Exercising great restraint, Barret bridled the urge to chase after Torrin. He would be remiss in his duty if he left the remaining prisoners guarded by only one soldier. So he stayed and hoped his other men would subdue Torrin and have the good sense to return to their duty.

The soldiers had spread out, leaving Kayne nearest Torrin. But this was not his only reason for aiming at Kayne. Torrin had much more personal motives for making that enemy his first target.

Torrin spurred his sorrel to a furious pace, using communicative magic to instill in the horse's mind Torrin's need for speed. He also employed his magic to draw strength from the horse, stealing some of its physical vitality, not so much as to slow its gallop but enough to fortify Torrin's own energy. Thundering forward in a fusillade of pounding hoof beats, the ground flew past beneath them. Man and horse became a blur upon the landscape.

Almost there, thought Torrin, putting his heels to the sorrel's flanks, kicking the beast harder and harder. The horse's stride lengthened. The muscles of its powerful legs rippled upon impact and rebound from the land. Breathing hard, neck stretched, black mane flying, ears bent back, the sorrel labored to achieve the speed Torrin demanded. Faster. He gained on Kayne. Faster.

Torrin moved swiftly up behind Kayne, pulling along side him, matching the other horse's rhythm. Torrin pulled his left leg up and cocked his foot against the saddle horn. Then, before Kayne had a chance to recognize him, Torrin made a deft and mighty leap from his mount, launching himself from his saddle and sailing into the air.

Torrin collided with Kayne, wrapped his arms around him, and carried them both to the ground. They impacted hard and bounced apart, staggered by the crash. Torrin bit his tongue deeply; his mouth filled with the coppery flavor of his own blood. Kayne was quick to recover from the fall, eager to confront his attacker. Then, seeing it was Torrin, Kayne's eyes gleamed with inflamed fury, an atavistic need to shed blood, a primal urge to kill.

The two fought violently against one another, each savagely wrestling to overpower the other. Kayne pinned Torrin beneath him and slammed his fisted knuckles into Torrin's throat. Pain blurred his vision and he struggled to catch his next breath. But Torrin could not free himself or gain the upper hand no

SCOTT C. RISTAU

matter how he tried. In a flash of steel, Kayne drew his dagger and moved to strike with the force and ferocity worthy of a wild boar. Torrin rolled to the side avoiding the attack. The dagger bit into the earth. Frantically he struggled to get out from under Kayne's imprisoning weight, knowing that if he did not the dagger would not miss its mark a second time. Torrin clawed at the dirt, trying to gain a purchase he could use to pull himself free. Digging into the earth, two fingernails snapped painfully from his hand. But it was no use. Death was surely no more than a few heartbeats away. Torrin let go of the ground, began to turn toward Kayne, and saw one last chance. In what might have been the last remaining beat of his heart, Torrin called on all his power to fulfill his final hope.

In fervid desperation, Torrin grabbed a stout tree branch lying next to him and rolled back bringing the branch with him, striking against Kayne's skull. Kayne was surprised not only by the attack but also by the strength with which Torrin delivered it. The branch broke on impact, leaving Kayne dazed and sprawled helpless on his back. Torrin knelt beside him, grasping the branch with both hands. In a wild euphoric furor, he drove its broken, jagged end deep within Kayne's chest. His heart erupted, spattering Torrin with a grotesque spray of blood. The warm geyser spotted Torrin's face and arms before subsiding under the loss of pressure.

Torrin returned Kayne's horrified stare, watching his hands clench and his robust body twitch in the throes of death. In reply, Torrin's own heart erupted, but in an arterial gush of *exhilaration*! This was nothing like when he killed his father. Nothing like it at all. He had felt empty then, emotionally numb. That was a rational execution for which he suppressed his feelings and performed with imposed indifference. But this, this was a killing he not only reasoned to be justified but one in which he delighted in emotionally, finding it delightful at all levels. All the tenants of heart, soul, and mind danced in jubilation. Torrin's whole being became engorged with untainted ecstasy, suffused with the pure joy of power released. The feeling came upon him like a whirlwind, emerging out of substance as intangible as the air before his mind could focus on the event, and it expanded rapidly to greater height and proportion.

"YES!" Torrin shouted in cathartic release, freeing the wild emotions seething within him. He leapt to his feet, knotting his fist in blissful triumph, a posture that seemed to communicate a threat to the whole world.

But there was more to do. Torrin took up Kayne's sword, thrilled by the added empowerment offered by its possession, comfortable with the weight of its deadly purpose. He summoned his horse using voice and magic. The animal responded to his call without hesitation.

Mounted once again, Torrin targeted a second soldier and charged at him with eager anticipation. The soldier was bearing down on a young boy that had wandered farthest from the dwarves' central group, prepared to murder a child simply because of its race and the history of war between their cultures. But Torrin intervened in the execution of that heinous act. Before the soldier was aware of his presence, Torrin struck him in the back with a thunderbolt of steel, nearly cleaving the man in half with the powerful force unleashed and concentrated along the cutting edge of the sweeping broadsword.

The sorrel's momentum carried Torrin past the fallen soldier and beyond the dwarven child. His shoulder ached and his arm tingled from the aftershock of the powerful sword stroke. He curbed his horse sharply, bringing it to a halt amid a plume of dust. Pulling mercilessly at the reins, Torrin turned the beast around, sheathed the sword through his belt, and again put his heels to the horse, racing back toward the child. Without breaking stride, leaning low against the horse's flank, Torrin plucked the child from the ground and lifted the boy into the saddle before him. He held onto the boy with one hand and fisted the reins in the other. Fortunately, because dwarves are incredibly strong even at this young age, the child did not greatly resist his rescue.

As his horse galloped toward the other threatened dwarves, Torrin used his magic to probe the child's mind, exploring the boy's thoughts and experiences, and studying the dwarven dialect. From this brief examination, he discovered the language to be composed of harsh, guttural sounds, the words articulated in something like grunts or hard barking noises but enunciated in a sharp, well defined and forceful manner. In this way, Torrin gained an imperfect yet rudimentary understanding of the language and a brief insight into the dwarven way of life.

Amazingly, Torrin managed to reach the dwarves before Gairloch's soldiers. "Tomrok! I am Tomrok!" Torrin shouted as he approached their group, conveying a sense of self-assured authority in his tone as he used the dwarven word to identify himself as a comrade, an allied friend in battle.

There were only two adult dwarves. They reacted with surprise to Torrin's knowledge of their language and his offer of help. Torrin quickly jumped from his horse and turned the child over to their custody. They accepted the offering but stood poised to attack at the slightest provocation, remaining yet distrustful of this human who professed to be their friend.

The five remaining soldiers were nearly upon them. Torrin addressed the male adult dwarf, issuing an appeal he hoped would be acceptable. "Run. I will fight the humans and give you time to escape into the cover of the mountains. Go quickly!"

"Dwarves do not hide from battle. Such disgrace may come easily to humans, but ours is a noble race. We will fight, as we always have, with honor. We were born to fight and we are prepared to die," insisted the dwarf.

The glimpse of dwarven culture garnered by Torrin during his magical communion with the child's mind readied him for this. He had expected to confront such an attitude and so formed his final argument.

"Your death in this battle would be without purpose or honor. Save it for the coming war. The time is drawing near when every dwarven warrior will be needed to defend his homeland and crush the invaders. Don't cower from that responsibility, don't be so quick to accept an easy escape from the brutal challenge of that imminent and ultimate battle. Now go, while you still can. And ready these children for war." Torrin issued his demand with heartfelt conviction, despite the fact he knew of no war being prepared against the dwarves.

He hoped the dwarves would be convinced by his argument for flight but did not linger to find out. Instead, he turned his back to them and faced the approaching soldiers with his arms spread open. He spoke a select sequence of mysterious words, invoking the magic, calling forth and releasing a wall of fire at his back. The flames flared to life, bounded at the left and right by large rock masses and imposing a blazing barrier between the dwarves and the human soldiers. Again he experienced the thrill of power released, excited by his own abilities. The fountain of adrenaline erupted anew. When the first soldier arrived, Torrin met his challenge with intense passion. His fierce blue eyes glittered with expectation.

Swinging his arm in a high-handed arc, the soldier discharged the awesome striking force of his flail. Torrin thwarted the assault, holding the sword blade in one hand and its hilt in the other, letting the spiked ball and steel chain of his opponent's flail wrap around the sword under its own momentum. Once the flail was fully encumbered about the blade, Torrin pulled violently, wrenching the soldier from his horse.

Torrin slipped his weapon from its entanglement but was prevented from using it to finish the downed soldier by the arrival of another. He blocked this soldier's sword then stepped in close, grabbing the man's hauberk and dragging him from the saddle. Wasting no time with this adversary, Torrin rammed the point of his sword, followed by half its length, into the man's rib cage.

But the onset of panic quickly displaced the thrilling satisfaction of another kill. Torrin's sword lodged in the soldier's body, wedged between bone, and resisted his efforts to secure its release. He tugged at it frantically but to no avail.

Torrin placed his boot against the corpse to gain leverage, pulling and struggling with the single minded purpose of extricating the sword, fearing another attack yet forgetting his other defenses, oblivious even to his victim's sword left abandoned on the ground. Just when these factors were beginning to invade his awareness, Torrin was struck with a blinding flash of pain. It lasted only a few seconds but shot through him with unbearable intensity. A brief and deafening crack exploded in Torrin's ear, the sound of his skull fracturing under the crushing force of the other soldier's flail.

Instantly, the ground rose up to receive Torrin's limp body. Mercifully, unconsciousness was quick to descend and cloak the extreme trauma. He slid into a dark, comforting place behind his eyelids, an inner refuge where he could not be reached by the crackling fires of agony ignited by the wound, a quiet place to wait the arrival of everlasting peace. As he lost consciousness, the seam of orange-yellow fire died, leaving only a swath of blackened grass in evidence of its passing.

"NO!" Lenore shrieked, her eyes wide with fright, her stomach clenched in anguish, cramped and burning with the acid of despair. The sight of Torrin's injury brought terror to her heart and tears to her eyes. She moved to run to his rescue but was restrained. Barret gripped her horse's bridle. The mare whinnied and jerked to a stop.

"Damn it, let me go!" Lenore screamed, her voice a high pitched wail that sounded like the wounded cry of a wild animal. "Let me go! He's hurt, I've got to help him."

"All right. But we go together," said Barret flatly in that insufferable neutral tone of his, his expression fixed and uncaring. He led them toward Torrin at a swift but controlled canter, insanely refusing to rush into anything, even though a life might be at stake.

When they reached him, the soldier who had struck Torrin returned from an unsuccessful search for the dwarves. They had escaped. But Lenore's concern for the dwarves' welfare was overcome by her fear for Torrin's.

She slumped beside Torrin's unmoving body and touched his bloodied temple, her hands quivering and her heart swollen with grief. An area on Torrin's head the size and shape of a fist had been caved in, forming a hideous depression along the right side of his skull. He remained alive but mortally wounded, unconscious and so incapable of healing himself.

"Somebody help him. Oh please help him. Don't let him die!" Lenore wailed in desperate behest, glaring fiercely at those crowded about her. She was angry and scared, more so than she had ever been in her life.

The soldiers stared back, mute and unsympathetic. They were disinclined to feel compassion for a man they now considered a personal enemy. He had attacked them and killed their comrades. They were incapable of viewing Torrin's death as a tragedy.

"There is nothing we can do for him. The injury is fatal. I'm sorry." Barret spoke with a tiredness that bordered on regret, weary of death and of this assignment, the senselessness of both.

"No," Lenore sobbed, shaking with the palsy of fear, shuddering uncontrollably at the thought of losing Torrin forever.

"Aragon, can you save him?" Marketa asked her son in stern appeal.

Grim and forbidding, Aragon stood unresponsive in quiet dilatory thought. He was not without feeling but rather troubled by a perception of wickedness he saw growing in Torrin, a hint of spiritual disease that seemed to be swelling like a malignant tumor. More and more, Aragon had recently come to fear Torrin's capacity for evil. If he used his magic to cheat death, what would he be saving and what would be the cost?

"He's your brother. If you have the power, use it," demanded Marketa. "You can't turn your back on your family."

Aragon scowled. "Certainly not. Torrin has already demonstrated just how dangerous that can be."

Aragon's sarcastic interpretation of Marketa's premise was wasted on Lenore. She was oblivious to such subtle word play, seeing only hope where before there was none and eagerly running toward it. With her heart in her throat and renewed supplicatory vigor, she added her voice to Marketa's entreaty, pleading on Torrin's behalf, begging for his life.

For a moment more Aragon remained unmoved, refusing to be swayed by outside influence. Then he acted. Swift and aggressive, he pushed the others aside as he moved to kneel beside his dying brother. Calling out his magic, Aragon placed his strong gaunt hands over Torrin's wound, correcting the damage, reforming his cracked and splintered skull, knitting together torn flesh and broken bone.

What he could do to restore Torrin's health he had done and knew that the treatment would be effective. Filled now with a need for solitude, Aragon left his patient and the onlookers. It galled him that he had been forced to display his powers before people like that. Pensive and aggravated, Aragon shrugged off Marketa's gratitude and departed what distance Barret would tolerate.

With the exception of Lenore, the rest of the group also lost interest in Torrin's recovery. Despite the early hour and the potential for retaliation by the dwarves, Barret gave the order to make camp.

It took a while for Torrin to revive. When he did awaken, Torrin was confused by the incompatibility of remembered pain and his present wellness. His head still hurt, throbbing with a punishing ache, but not at the magnitude it should have. The first thing he focused on was Lenore. Framed by a brilliant sky, her face hung above him streaked with tears and expressive with loving concern. Her moist green eyes sparkled. If not for the thin veil formed by a filigree of tan highlights, the beautiful iridescence of her emerald irises might have been blinding. Her eyes were welcoming, as they so often were, offering an unspoken invitation to share a long visual embrace. More than ever before, Torrin wanted to be held by the captivating grip of Lenore's gentle gaze, and he wished never to be released.

"Are you all right?"

"Yes," Torrin answered, his voice a weak, raspy whisper.

"Does it hurt much?"

"Yes. What happened?"

"Lie still and don't talk until you feel better. I should never have told you to go after them. You might have died. When you went down, I was so scared."

As he rested in her cradling arms, Lenore gave Torrin something to eat and filled the gaps in his memory, explaining how his life had been saved by Aragon. But the couple's quiet moment alone was short lived and interrupted by Barret's return.

"Has he recovered?" Barret asked without compassion.

"I'm fine," answered Torrin.

"So glad to hear it. Thought we lost you. Unfortunately, not everyone had your luck today. Those men you killed, they were under my command," Barret stated, his words embedded in a growl. "You understand what that means? It means they were my responsibility. I'm accountable for their deaths. I'll have to answer for what you've done and I'm not at all happy about that. And if you ever attack my men again, nothing and no one will save you—save you from me. They were good men, damn it. Kayne may have been a little unruly but he wasn't evil. Egon had a wife and kids and now I've got to tell them their father is never coming home. Damn it! And Ryley, shit, he was just a kid, not much older than you. Just a callow, damn kid. You both had a lot more growing up to do. But you took his chance away."

"They were animals, preying upon children," said Torrin, glowering at his accuser, his face twisted in revulsion.

Barret reached down, grabbed Torrin by his shirt, and hauled him to his feet, holding him close as Barret spat. "They hadn't actually done anything yet. You drew first blood this time."

"Leave him alone!" Lenore demanded, standing as if poised undecided on the verge of flight or aggression.

Barret released him. "Start digging. You've got three graves to finish by early tomorrow morning."

"He can't do that," said Lenore. "He's not well enough yet. Have your soldiers do it. Torrin needs his rest."

"No," Barret commanded, jabbing a finger against Torrin's sternum. "You killed them, you bury them."

"With what?" Torrin asked.

"With a stick, with your hands, I don't care. Just do it. Do it now!" Assured that his point was made, Barret left Torrin to his task.

Fortunately, Torrin found that Marketa had actually chosen to pack something useful. He discovered a small shovel tucked away in her wagon. Nonetheless, it was still hot, tiring, and grisly work. By the time the first shallow grave was dug, a stiffness had invaded Torrin's shoulders and he found himself covered in a sheen of muddied sweat. But sticking to the task, he dragged and dropped Egon's body into the first hole.

Damn, thought Torrin, shaking his head in regret. *I dug the hole wider than need be. Wasted effort. Oh well, live and learn. Hm, maybe that phrase is a little inappropriate for the occasion, perhaps even a bit insensitive. Sorry Egon, no offense intended.* Torrin smiled at his own grim humor.

Truth was, Torrin felt somewhat guilty about Egon's death. Egon was the last soldier Torrin had killed, the one in which his sword had become encumbered. He had not even known Egon's name before Barret mentioned it, much less that he was a family man. Actually, Torrin could not recall ever even noticing the man before. He had been one of those people who just blend into a crowd, even one as small as this. The only recollection he had of Egon's face was the expression it held upon his death. But, despite these misgivings, Torrin remained confident that he had acted correctly and that Egon had really brought this unfortunate fate upon himself. *Don't commit violence against others if you're not prepared to have it returned upon you,* thought Torrin.

After Torrin finished shoveling the soil back into the hole, he began collecting large stones and placing them upon Egon's grave. Barret told him to do this to mark the site and prevent wild beasts from digging up the body. This possibility seemed unlikely to Torrin and he wondered if it might not be more sensible to leave the bodies above ground and let the animals eat them. Certainly it would be more efficient. Torrin would not have to waste energy digging useless graves. The animals would expend less energy hunting other prey, and by eating the corpses possibly spare the life of someone else who might otherwise have been killed by the hungry animals. But Torrin doubted that Barret would be reasonable enough to accept this logic, so he kept working.

The day burned into late afternoon. Torrin completed Egon's stone cairn and the hole for the second grave, but narrower this time, no more wasted effort. Lenore came to him bringing water for his refreshment and a pair of leather gloves. He should have thought of that himself and earlier. Blisters were already visible on his palms and on the insides of his thumbs.

She left quickly, not caring for the sight of bodies or of Torrin's own foul appearance, his clothes mottled with dirt and his face awash in rivulets of perspiration. *Just as well*, he thought. Supervised work generally seemed to take longer anyway and he had always found it particularly uncomfortable when the supervisor was an attractive member of the opposite sex. It is difficult to concentrate on any job when your mind is preoccupied with how you looked while doing it.

He placed Ryley in the second grave but without the hint of sympathy he had felt for Egon. Torrin remembered Ryley, remembered him as Kayne's insufferable ally. Ryley clearly admired Kayne. With laughter and imitation, Ryley faithfully encouraged Kayne's abuse and abasement of Torrin. Although his hands and back hurt with the effort, Torrin had to admit a certain perverse pleasure in covering Ryley with dirt and rock.

But it paled in comparison to the satisfaction experienced at seeing Kayne lying lifeless in the third grave, face down in the dirt, food for worms and insects. Torrin had gotten the last laugh after all and he felt very good about it. A despicable human being, Kayne deserved to die and Torrin was pleased to have been the one to make it happen. Unfortunately, however, the purity of this feeling was not as strong as it had been while delivering the killing blow. That ecstasy was already fading to memory. And a part of his mind now took the time to question the morality of finding pleasure in another's death, even someone as vile as Kayne. Yet strangely that nagging intrusive question rekindled Torrin's disgust of Kayne. He hated him, still hated him. Death was too easy; Kayne deserved worse, much worse. Torrin wished for the chance to degrade and humiliate Kayne as he had done to him. *Piss on his grave, cut out his tongue and shove it ....* Grim ideas flashed through Torrin's mind, contemptuous and disturbing, but too hazardous to act upon.

What has happened to the brother I used to know? Aragon wondered with mounting concern and deep disapproval while observing Torrin, the subject of his critical thoughts. Aragon sat far removed from Torrin and secretive in his watchfulness.

How did you become so judgmental, so casual about killing? Even now as you bear the burden of burying your victims, you do so with an icy practicality in place of penitence. There is no remorse, no reverence for their former lives. The act of burial is more a physical exercise than a commemorative ceremony. You dig and fill a grave employing certain muscles then stack stones for the cairn, exercising different muscles and allowing the former an opportunity to rest. Practical. Dangerous. I fear you've acquired an appetite for destruction, one ravenous and growing. The remnant of the brother I once loved is all but gone. Perhaps I am somewhat at fault. For the past several years I have been hesitant to reveal too much of myself to you because it seemed that as soon as you became aware of a belief or characteristic held by me, you denounced it and worked to develop its opposite for yourself. So I thought if I distanced myself from you during this formative period, you would develop your character unbiased by resentment of me. And that later, we would discover we were not that different after all and unite again as true brothers. But it hasn't turned out that way and I wonder now if there exists any commonality at all between us. Maybe if I had labored with greater care in maintaining a close relationship between us these problems could have been avoided or at least minimized. What relations do you have, Torrin? Is there anyone, friend or family, that you care about? Lenore, of course. Danger lies there too. You have made her far too important. I can see that; it's evident. You depend too deeply upon her. Very dangerous, indeed. Has she blinded you to the rest of us? If you love her with all your heart, does that leave you with none for the world? You took my father, Torrin. Have you taken my brother, too?

Finished, thought Torrin as he positioned the final stone. Most of the others had already retired to their bedrolls for the night's slumber. Barret had been with Torrin since dusk, guarding against escape or other misconduct. He nodded his approval, accepting that Torrin had completed the appointed chore. Torrin's demand to bathe in a nearby stream also received consent. But not even its frigid water could enliven his bone-weary body. Sleep, after cleanliness, became his greatest desire. And when that need was finally fulfilled, it was with his right hand shackled to a rear wheel of Marketa's wagon. So he slept, safe and sound, happy to be alive despite his disturbing circumstance.

This restricted level of freedom carried into the following day. Torrin rode with his hands bound together at the saddle horn and his horse tethered behind a soldier's mount. The journey proceeded without incident and considerable distance had been covered by the time Barret gave the order to halt and make camp.

Torrin was allowed freedom from his restraints, almost to his regret. All day he had been putting off talking to Aragon, but Lenore would let him delay no longer, gently nagging him to do the right thing, to acknowledge gratitude for his brother's help.

Aragon relaxed against the gnarled trunk of a large willow tree. From his vantage and wearing an all too familiar smugness, he watched Torrin's advance.

This is going to be unpleasant, Torrin thought as he approached slowly, mentally fortifying himself.

For years now, attempting pleasant conversation with his brother made him feel like a sacrificial lamb, bleating friendly discourse as Aragon cut him open him with sharp looks and words. Torrin felt acutely vulnerable at this particular moment. The perception both distracted and disturbed Torrin. Inside, it seemed as if he were preparing for battle. But this internal preparation that fueled courage and readied defenses had to be masked by an external cloak of good-natured gratitude.

"Aragon, I want to thank you for saving my life yesterday," said Torrin, finding his words lacking and continuing apologetically. "That almost sounds ridiculous put that way, doesn't it? Those words of gratitude are pitifully weak considering what you've done. I may not know how to adequately communicate my appreciation but please realize that you indeed have it. I just wanted you to know that. It was very kind of you to help me after all that's happened. But I must admit, I find it rather uncomfortable to be so indebted to someone. So if there is anything I can do for you in return, please don't hesitate to let me know."

Aragon scowled mildly in disappointment and irritation. "How warped your values must be. You don't help people in order to gain their servitude. Don't you understand the concept of compassion at all? Or do you believe self-interest to be the only motive in life?"

Here it starts, thought Torrin, still hoping to keep this conversation friendly or at least civil. "I didn't mean it that way. I simply meant I'm very grateful and that I would welcome the opportunity to demonstrate the depth and breadth of my gratitude by doing you some service."

"Damn it, Torrin. Why can't you talk to me like a brother instead of some kind of legal minister?" complained Aragon. "Tell me what you really feel. Tell me what's in your heart." He made a stabbing gesture at Torrin's chest. "Is there any heart, any brother left in you at all?"

The friendly mask began its fall as anger rose to the surface. Controlled, Torrin answered, "I'm sorry if you find my manner disconcerting, but you've never made it particularly easy for me to talk with you. I feel bad that you and Mother were exiled because of me. Despite that, you saved my life. For that I thank you and I apologize for creating the circumstances which made it necessary for you to do so."

"What does that mean, that you're sorry you let that soldier hit you or that you're sorry you attacked and killed those men or that you're sorry you killed our father?" queried Aragon.

"No. In that I acted correctly. Our father committed a sin that could not be forgiven, one that demanded retribution, required swift punishment."

"You don't punish a crime by committing another," argued Aragon, his scowl intensified and more deeply lined with bitter resentment. "He did something wrong, granted. But he was not without value, and virtue too. But by killing him you destroyed the opportunity for its enhancement, denied him the chance to repent, and denied the world the chance to experience the positive contribution he might have made. He had good qualities too. And with time and help, I'm sure his negative attributes could have been eliminated or controlled. Whatever crimes he might have done, I believe he would've one day suffered genuine remorse and accepted a path of rehabilitation. No one is a lost cause. Where there is life, there is hope. He was our father and still worthy of our love, regardless of his faults. Compassion, remember. He made a mistake, Torrin. We don't know everything that happened. We know he committed a crime but he might still have been redeemed. People aren't perfect, you know. It doesn't make them evil, it makes them human."

"No, in this case it made him inhuman," Torrin stated, captious and cold. "For some crimes there can be no repentance and for some criminals there can be no reform. No amount of remorse or community service or prison sentence could undo the damage done to that girl nor offer up adequate protection from and assurance against the repetition of such horrible crimes. The only rational solution was his elimination. What I did had to be done."

"And that's your decision to make," snapped Aragon, infuriated at Torrin's casual dismissal of his father's life, reducing the whole of the man to one criminal act. He thought he understood the potential of Torrin's convictions and was frightened by it. "You placed yourself above the queen's authority. Do you also place yourself over the World Spirit's authority? You think you're qualified to make the choice of who lives and who dies?"

"Maybe not, but I was forced to. It was really the queen's responsibility. However, she tossed aside the sacred duty of her office to protect a savage man. She chose to discard the dictates of reason in exchange for those of the heart."

Aragon replied in weary rebuke, a tired but severe reprimand, "But heartlessness, that wasn't a problem for you. And your reason is also not without its flaws. Find your heart, Torrin, lest the world finds it has no place for you. Try offering love and understanding to your fellow man in place of death. You may find it better received."

"Love? Compassion?" Torrin spat out the words, words turned obscene by Aragon's use of them. Aragon's self-righteous condemnation of him caused Torrin's anger to flare and erupt in vitriolic retort. "I find your lofty altruism to be both ludicrous and abhorrent. The level of mercy you would extend to criminals is disastrous in its unrealistic demands. I wish we did live in a world in which there existed no crime nor need for its punishment. But we do not. Until you accept the reality of the world we live in and act in accordance to it, you will enable victimization. We need to protect the lawful by severely punishing the lawless. My actions against our father and against those soldiers were motivated by benevolence, a rational intent to protect and serve the interests of others, of innocents. You, on the other hand, have always been one of the most selfish people I have ever known. What have you ever done for anyone but yourself?"

Damn, thought Torrin immediately. *I should not have made that last statement. It was stupid and has laid me open to attack.* He had been rattled by his rage, angered at having to again defend himself and at the reminder of his dead father. The memory hurt, a fact he could not let be revealed.

Aragon saw the mistake as well and mentally played with ways to use it against his brother. He was quite angry himself. He wanted to hit Torrin, to physically punch through his narrow-minded self-assurance, wanted it very badly. His younger brother had become much too arrogant, in urgent need of being humbled. But Aragon restrained, growing very tired of the whole discussion. He suspected that Torrin was more interested in delivering punishment, as he called it, in beating up on the lawbreakers than he was in helping real or potential victims. His self-professed desire to help the innocent might merely be a justification for acting out his own propensity for violence.

When it came, Aragon's reply lacked the sting it might have bore. "What have I ever done for anyone? Why, for one, I saved your life, my dear brother."

"Well from now on, leave my life to me!" Torrin shot back bitterly, his face flushed. Then he turned and left.

Torrin walked with clenched fists. His fingernails burrowed into his palms and he found a kind of relief afforded through the pain. Loathing, it wrapped its twisted coils around his soul, hating Aragon and the fact that he now owed him his life. *No, you owe him nothing*, Torrin's hatred hissed in sibilant protest.

Marketa stopped Torrin on his way back to the central encampment. She took hold of his arm and pleaded, "Torrin, please don't fight with your brother. We need each other now more than ever. Can't you see that? We have to be able to depend on one another if we're going to be able to have any chance at all."

"It's not my fault!" Torrin yelled, reading more into her statement than perhaps was intended, thinking it an accusation about the cause of their present plight, another condemnation for killing his father. "Just leave me alone." He pulled away and put distance between them.

By the time he finished his daily chores and evening meal, Torrin's anger had subsided. He sat resting against the wagon wheel, his arm shackled to it, and Lenore nestled beside him. More than work or time, Lenore helped dispose of his anger. With caring objectivity, she listened to Torrin's account of his confrontation with Aragon and offered what advice she could. She also offered confirmation of Torrin's assessment of his brother. Aragon could be very difficult. However, she had criticism for Torrin as well, suggesting that he might have handled the situation better. But that was all right. They did not argue with each other, she and Torrin never really did. They may at times disagree and discuss their opposing views but never in a manner that could be considered a real fight. After any debate between them, which is the correct term, for they never yelled at each other, they always came back closer than before, even if the issue remained unresolved. They were even able to joke about their own positions or the ridiculousness of the issue over which they disagreed. Their love for one another held them together and life's vicissitudes were incapable of weakening that bond.

It was dark. The fire settled, its flames less active and bright, the red embers glowing warmly. The trees and hills around them were only distinguishable as darker shadows amid the pitch of night. The moon hid behind a scattering of clouds and distant stars shown like faint sparks between the overcast. A cool, gentle wind heavily laced with the scent of pine breathed over and around them in an airy caress. Responding to its touch, the land rustled and soughed. Torrin found it soothing and relaxed into it. Contented, he cradled Lenore closer, exchanging warmth.

Lenore worried. The inspiration of her distress had many sources. The night Torrin found so soothing harbored for Lenore unseen horrors certain to be both wild and vicious. She was afraid of the soldiers too, but more afraid of how they would survive when the soldiers inevitably left. Torrin said they were going to a settlement but how would they live, where would they live? Most significantly, however, she worried about her judgment. She loved Torrin, loved him more than she had ever loved anyone, but to go into exile for him? It just seemed too unlike her, not at all practical. Being here was recklessly romantic, in no way the smart thing to do. Unlike so many girls her age, she prided herself on being sensible, even in matters of the heart. So her decision to be here troubled her prudent, realistic nature.

Closing her eyes, she was haunted by remembrance of what they had lost and by fear of what they could yet lose, of what else might yet go wrong. *You can still go back*, a part of her suggested.

No, Lenore decided. She would abide by her decision even if it had been swayed more by the heart than the head. But from here on out she would be practical all the way. No regrets. Make the best of it come what may. That decided, sleep followed resolve.

Two days later they arrived. The party came to a halt at the bank of the Purl River, the declared boundary of Queen Bryana's realm. A town, of sorts, lay sprawled upon the other side, haphazard in its design and composed of several squat buildings constructed of age-gray boards. The squalor of the community seemed capable of offending all of one's senses equally. The rotting, ramshackle structures were shrouded in dirt and grime, accentuating their level of disrepair. Reeking odors carried upon the shifting breeze made Lenore wince and her eyes start to water. Littered with excrement and other decomposing refuse, the muddied streets appeared to be shared equally by people and animals. In fact it was almost hard to tell some of them apart. Angry shouts and shuddering laughter met their ears in disturbing greeting.

It was not until that moment that the full magnitude of his predicament was revealed to Torrin. They were doomed. It would be impossible for him to survive here, especially with Lenore. A single night without shelter in this cesspool would unquestionably find them all dead before morning witnessed the first rays of light of the ascending sun. Even if their lives were spared, they would surely be robbed of what little else they still possessed. It was hopeless.

Before them was a wooden bridge, narrow and decayed. Its ability to support its own weight appeared suspect, let alone the weight of anyone desperate enough to set foot upon its rotting planks. Suspended above the bridge was a board and upon its surface the word "ABANDON" had been painted in large white letters.

"What does it mean?" Lenore asked, pointing at the sign.

"That is the name of this settlement," said Barret. "It was given that name because when you cross this bridge you are thought to have abandoned everything of value—peace, law, love, respect. Hope."

Torrin understood its meaning immediately and felt it drain his soul. He needed no explanation.

"Lenore, go back," Torrin pleaded urgently. "This is no place for you. You should never have come. Go back. Please, I beg you. Forget about me and return to Gairloch."

She stared across the river, for a moment unresponsive. "No Torrin, I'm not going back," she said quietly determined, brave and firm in her resolve. "I'm sure it's not as bad as it looks. We'll be all right."

"That's the spirit," encouraged Marketa. "We must be fearless, trusting in the power and grace of the Oversoul. We shall persevere undaunted by adversity. Fearless."

Torrin glared at his mother as if she had gone suddenly and completely mad, violently irritated by her insane affirmation. But the matter was decided.

The soldiers departed once the four of them were across the bridge. They entered Abandon slowly, each assessing in his own way the merits of their new home.

Torrin felt trapped, as if he were being swallowed by this loathsome place. An icy prickling nagged at the base of his neck and descended down his back, as if a trickle of frigid water had been poured down the yellow core of his spine.

The people they passed all bore a grim and dangerous aspect. He tried not to meet their eyes but kept doing so despite himself, like a mouse in a room full of hungry cats, expecting everyone he saw to pounce at him but unsure who would be the first.

The cruel, the crazed, and the wretched shared this place together with a heartless quality common to all. Each seemed to have lost the ability to care about the welfare of another human being. Wasted men and women, comfortable in the squalid condition of their environment, as if they had chosen filth and degradation as a preferred lifestyle. Human wreckage. Derelicts clothed in filthy, stinking rags lay slumped in the street at virtually every corner. Ahead, a pathetic child quarreled with a mongrel dog over some scrap of food. A thick gray-green stream of sewage flowed sluggishly through the rutted dirt street. A suffocating odor rose from the foul, putrid discharge, forcing Torrin to cup his hand over his mouth and nose. The shrill cry of a baby pierced the air again and again, a miserable and indefatigable call that went ignored by its mother. Rats, bold even in daylight, scurried here and there. Vicious looking men also prowled the streets, lawless thugs that were no better than animals, worse in fact as they refused to be bound even by the laws of nature.

They stopped at what could only loosely be referred to as a boarding house and negotiated a room. They quickly unloaded their belongings and each laid a claim to one corner of the small room. Despair folded over Lenore's spirits like a burial shroud.

"I think I'll go for a walk around town, get the feel of the place, see what it's made of," Aragon announced, turning away from the open window.

"Do you really think that's wise?" asked Lenore. "I mean, it can't be safe for us to be roaming around out there all alone. You saw what it's like."

"You shouldn't judge places or people by appearances alone," answered Aragon. "We haven't gotten to know Abandon yet. Besides, I've always been able to take care of myself and I'm quite confident in my own defenses."

"Who cares?" groused Torrin. "Let the arrogant fool find out for himself that these people are as corrupt on the inside as they appear on the outside."

Aragon mocked him with a crooked smile. "Maybe you should set up a ministry and offer salvation to these poor lost souls. I'm sure once they see how wicked they are in your eyes, they'll flock to you seeking redemption, drawn by the sheer magnetism of your moral purity. Ah, but then I nearly forgot. You believe that redemption must come in the form of execution. That might be rather difficult for your congregation to accept."

"Go to hell," Torrin cursed, his words sharp edged and bitter.

"Hell's only as bad as you're willing to make it. Well, I'll be back later, try not to worry about me." With a quiet chuckle, Aragon walked to the door, opened it and pulled it closed behind him.

"I'm going out for a while too," said Marketa.

"Do you want us to go with you?" Torrin asked, genuinely concerned for his mother's safety.

"No, no. I need some time alone and so do you. I'll be fine."

Marketa left, went directly to the local tavern, and proceeded to get drunk.

Torrin and Lenore stayed in the room, the door bolted and the window barred.

"Torrin, I'm scared," Lenore groaned.

The usual inner strength upon which her hopes and resilience relied had begun to crumble. The evidence showed in her face. Waxy and pale, her skin sagged like a melting tallow candle. Her eyes lost their clarity and luster. Fear did that. Fear and depression were breaking her spirit, and seeing it was breaking Torrin's heart. He sensed that Lenore now believed in a future promising nothing but physical and emotional pain.

To himself, Torrin swore that he would protect her, that he would assume responsibility for her health and happiness, encourage her self-reliance while providing an ever-present shield for her safety. He had to make her believe in a better future and then transform that belief into reality. He would. Somehow, he would do it. Inwardly, he swore to offer Lenore shelter and comfort in whatever measure she required. A sacred oath he would never break, no matter what.

"I'm really afraid," she repeated.

"I know." He put his arms around her and she leaned into him. "But it'll be all right. You'll see, we'll all be all right. Things can only get better. They have to."

He tried to convince her that they should leave Abandon, that it would be safer if they went into the forest and lived there. But she refused. Lenore was afraid of the wilderness, believing it overcrowded with wolves, snakes, trolls, and other untold terrors. "Abandon may not be much," she said, "but at least it offers some semblance of civilization." Torrin believed the opposite, seeing people as representing a far greater danger and much more worthy of their fear. Nevertheless, he yielded to Lenore.

For half an hour they sat without talking, sitting together with Lenore cradled in his arms, until she again broke the silence. It was enough just to be close.

"I know you don't want to talk about it," Lenore began, "about your father I mean. But I want you to know that I think what you did was right. I also know that it hurt you deeply. The brave mask you're always wearing around this issue doesn't fool me. If you want to talk about how you're feeling, I'm here for you anytime. I'll always love you, Torrin. And I respect you and the decisions you've made. Like you said, we'll get through this. We'll face the consequences together. Whenever you need me, I'll be there."

The next morning they discovered one of their horses had been stolen in the night. They quickly sold the remainder for what they could get, which was considerably less than what the animals were worth. But at least it was one less thing to worry about. Realizing they could not stay in the boarding house forever, they agreed to share the single room, conserving their resources while they built a house.

Two days later, Torrin and Lenore were married. It was a private ceremony, attended by just the two of them. Torrin used some of their personal funds to rent a private room for the day. He decorated it with magic, creating the temporary illusion of luxury and glamour. Lenore provided the genuine beauty. They exchanged vows composed themselves, pledging hearts and lives to one another.

After the wedding, Torrin's magic transformed the dilapidated chamber into an opulent suite bathed in a warm, radiant splendor and designed for the consummation of marriage. The rich appearance of the room enhanced Lenore's womanly provocation. She had never before looked more beautiful, dazzling to the eye and thrilling to the touch.

Uneasy about entering this new dimension of their relationship, their kisses were tentative at first, nervous and shy. But as they touched, their timidity quickly yielded to a stronger, more physical yearning. Their kisses gradually took on more force, became hotter and more demanding. Torrin's tongue flickered against Lenore's ripe succulent lips, darted between parted teeth, and thrust deeply into her mouth. Lenore placed her hand flat against Torrin's chest, sliding it slowly down the firm musculature of his abdomen, sinking lower to stroke the stiffening muscle of his manhood. Torrin shuddered with pleasure. His kisses again became gentler, moving from her lips, over the delicate features of her sweet face, and down her throat. His breath was warm, almost hot on her neck, heated by the conflagration of his burning passion.

Lenore tossed her head to the side, then unwrapped from their embrace and took two steps back from Torrin. Her eyes told him nothing was wrong.

She looked down as her hands came up and found the buttons of her shirt. Beginning at the top, she began to undo the buttons, revealing more of herself inch by sensuous inch. Her shirt laid open, she slipped her pants over her hips, stepping out of them as they fell to the floor. Torrin followed her lead, removing his own clothes as he watched Lenore.

When their eyes met again, they were bright with growing excitement. Torrin moved forward and gently pushed the folds of Lenore's shirt back over her shoulders. His right hand glided down her waist, savoring the velvety soft contours of her body and kneading her flesh when his fingers reached her naked buttock. With his left hand, he cupped and squeezed the creamy skin of her small up-turned breast, skin soft and silky smooth, like the pedal of a new white rose. Lowering his head, he put his mouth to her bosom; kissing, suckling, and nibbling her turgid nipple, delighting in every subtle aspect of her taste, scent, and texture. Her sex moistened and throbbed with anticipation. Lenore's breathing became ragged, as if she were panting with eagerness. She murmured her approval, an anxious invitation for more, a breathless urging for Torrin to provide her with other, greater sensations.

Outside, thunder cracked and rolled. The storm blew rhythmic gusts of wind, hurling rain and rattling against the exterior walls. The clamor of the storm was not frightful but welcome for it served to camouflage the passionate sounds emanating from within the room and left its occupants uninhibited. While the night sky was rent by lightning and shook with thunder, the air inside their room was electrified with erotic energy. Chaste no more, their lustful desires at last achieved release as Torrin and Lenore relinquished all restraint and fully gave themselves unto one another.

The pair celebrated their union in a manner previously unknown to them, as husband and wife, knowing the full pleasure of the flesh in consort with a loving spirit. With uxorious care, Torrin massaged Lenore's responsive body, like an artist working clay and bringing it to life, drawing out the beauty of her pleasure, finding no greater satisfaction than witnessing it in his wife. Their lovemaking was comfortable, yet exciting. Both were amenable to the other's touch, zealous and trusting. Rife with irrepressible desire, they explored the outlets of passion and the depth of their love.

Chapter 4
Abandon

A year passed. And in the early months of that difficult year, the new residence of the Murgleys family had been assembled with great haste. It was a simple domicile consisting of one common room, which the four of them shared, and a small private bedchamber reserved for Torrin and Lenore. The special privilege of having their own room caused Torrin no guilt whatsoever. In fact, he was frequently of the mind to believe he held an exclusive right over both rooms. He felt as if he had built the entire house almost completely unassisted, that Marketa and Aragon had participated in its construction only in a token amount, just enough so they could claim a right to its occupation. In Torrin's estimation it was his house and Aragon and Marketa were merely his guests. But they did not see it that way or treat his house with the proper consideration expected of humble guests

In addition to their physical shelter, Torrin also provided for the family's financial support. He became a jack-of-all-trades, all which were available anyway. As the opportunities arose and only for payment, he offered his services in healing the ill, cleaning stables, butchering livestock, building barns, and nearly anything else that paid a wage. It did not make him rich, but it let them survive.

With mounting intensity, Torrin grew to despise everything in Abandon, everything, that is, except Lenore, who remained the singular focus of his love. He adored and respected her. She was all that sustained him, became the only thing that now gave his life meaning. Love and hatred became the paired halves of Torrin's cleft soul. Together they shaped his character and defined his essence in unique ways.

Love gave Lenore courage, provided her with the strength to cope with the myriad of hardships that had been forced upon them. But love had a different effect on Torrin. It filled him with fear. Because of his love for Lenore, to see her hurt devastated him in unimaginable ways. The thought that new hurts lay around the corner tormented his already tortured soul. He worried constantly that Lenore would come to harm or that she was unhappy or that she regretted her decision to stay with him. These and a million other anxieties gnawed at him every day and every night.

It was true that there was very little about Abandon Lenore did like nor did she ever feel particularly safe. But she tolerated it. She accepted it in order to be with Torrin. However, his overprotective concern often created dissonance between them. Torrin's incessant apologies for their predicament and unnecessary fretting over her welfare became unbearably annoying. At times it intruded upon their relationship, their oasis of happiness within the dismal landscape in which they were compelled to reside. Furthermore, Torrin's over protectiveness offended Lenore's confidence in her own self-reliant abilities.

Torrin's fear also fed his anger, nourished his hatred. Umbrageous, he viewed everyone in Abandon with suspicion, seeing each citizen in varying degrees as vile, corrupt, wicked, depraved, and repulsive. But his growing animosity was not limited to the citizenry of his present community. Torrin's hatred spanned the hinterland, directed itself back even to Gairloch, to High Queen Bryana, the villain who mandated his family's misery. He hated too that Aragon and Marketa were forced to live here because of him. Not to imply that Torrin retained any great affection for his mother and brother, because he most assuredly did not. Quite the opposite, his loathing of them grew daily. He simply hated the guilt he felt at having caused their exile. It interfered with the anger he directed at his mother and brother, weakened the justification of his ill will. Torrin hated them because of the irreverent way they treated him, he hated his guilt at hating them, and he hated them because their presence stimulated his guilt. If not for Lenore, hatred would have been Torrin's only friend.

Two or three days a week Marketa held classes in the Murgleys' household, teaching many of Abandon's children and a few curious adults to read and write. It may have been a noble service but it was one that contributed nothing to the family's finances and it stole more of Torrin's meager privacy, a rare commodity he greatly prized. At night Marketa drank, never alone but always as a social fellowship with her neighbors. That is what she called it anyway. Her drinking was for friendship and relaxation, she said. Frequently, she went out to drink and only returned inebriated, sometimes alone and at other times accompanied by guests. These "guests" came in a multitude of varieties and objectionable combinations, shameless in their deviant and shameful recreation. No consideration was afforded Aragon, who shared the same room with these degenerates, let alone for Torrin and Lenore who attempted sleep in the adjoining room.

Abandon's lowlife, its most wretched dregs, seemed drawn to Marketa. They fed on her, taking more and more until the day came when she would have nothing more to give. Then they would surely discard her like the trash Torrin believed she was becoming. But she was blind to the truth and ignored Torrin's warnings. She welcomed these predators and parasites with open arms. She wanted to help them all. Marketa took it upon herself to save Abandon's most worthless citizens. She said the mercy and love we give to others should be as great as that which we receive from the Oversoul.

Torrin did not understand nor could he tolerate it. His mother brought thieves, vagrants, drunks, and prostitutes into *his* house, fed them *his* food. Torrin considered Marketa's friends to be unbearable, filthy, diseased vermin. Torrin was convinced that not a one of them had any hope of redemption and that Marketa was only deluding herself. Torrin was certain that she could not save these people and that in fact they did not even really want salvation. By trying to help them, by caring about them and calling them friends, Marketa was doing nothing but becoming one of the degenerates herself.

Almost immediately, Torrin put Marketa's strays back out on the street. But Marketa always found more or brought the same ones back, as if thinking Torrin would fail to notice or that he would somehow be inspired to change his tolerances. It was insufferable. Marketa foolishly believed she could help them, solve their problems, give them comfort and salvation while searching for her own at the bottom of a wine bottle.

As a drunk, Marketa was sickeningly demonstrative, gushing with inappropriate and excessive fondness for anyone in her company. The wine allowed her the freedom to express herself with sweet words, kisses, hugs, and fond caresses. Her companions' worthiness of affection was irrelevant. In her overwhelming need to help the downtrodden, or perhaps to find love, Marketa allowed the unscrupulous to avail themselves of the Murgleys' property as well as of the less tangible yet equally important elements of their existence. She gave away the peace and comfort that a home was supposed to provide. Seeing only the good in people, Marketa appeared untroubled that by her hospitality she and the rest of the household were taken advantage of, if not abused.

At least thirty pounds had been added to Marketa's frame during the past year but the increased weight failed to lend solidity to her appearance. Instead, she continued to deteriorate, looking more unstable, unhealthy, unreliable, and unkempt as time progressed. There existed no synergism to any of her relationships. She gave but received nothing healthy in return. Her "friends" fed upon her like parasites and she seemed unwilling if not incapable of freeing herself of their destructive influence. The thought appalled Torrin that he might be allowing his mother and Aragon to feed upon him in much the same fashion.

Aragon was hardly better to live with. His presence in the house fluctuated without notice. He refused to discuss where he went or what he did. Always hostile and secretive, his inimical and enigmatic nature became increasingly more pronounced. When there, Aragon took freely from their supplies while adding nothing in return. Nor did he feel obliged to assist in the home's maintenance. There was always work to be done but Aragon would have none of it. And yet a word of thanks never crossed his lips for what he took, as if everything and more were owed to him.

Hate grew inside Torrin's heart. It maddened Torrin that such people violated his home, his last remaining refuge, his only sanctum. At least once each day he entertained the notion of evicting his mother and brother, throwing them out, ridding himself of their burden without a care to what became of them. But there lay the flaw to this attractive scenario—a small corner of his heart did care. And from that corner, words were spoken of loyalty, of responsibility. He could not deny that their being here directly resulted from his actions. Nor could Torrin expel from his conscience the few good memories he had of them and which haunted him with guilt. As yet, Torrin had not found a way to get rid of them and still feel righteous in his actions.

So he could not lock them out. He fought with them frequently, sometimes even getting them to promise improvement. But it never materialized. Torrin was disconnected from his family and the world around him. Hate and Lenore were all he had left.

Late in the evening, Torrin trudged through the streets of Abandon, headed for home and returning from an exhausting day of labor. He had obtained fairly steady employment with a relatively prosperous farmer just outside of the village. It was steady in the sense that he had remained working for the man for over two weeks.

It was a long walk back to town, always seeming longer coming back because his legs were tired. The farmer, an old man named Flynn, had offered to let him stay at the farm while the work lasted. But Torrin could not ask Lenore to sleep in a barn any more than he could stand to be separated from her for so long. So, he walked, tired though he was.

For the first few days Flynn hired Torrin to repair and build fence, then to assist in the construction of an earthen berm designed to divert rainwater runoff away from Flynn's hog confinement. The hogs were fenced in a large area on the slope of a hill, which was not an ideal location because the animals denuded the ground of vegetation, leaving bare soil susceptible to severe erosion. But the location left the flatter terrain available for crops and pastureland on which Flynn could graze his cattle. At the bottom of the hill, Flynn built a shallow pit that collected the mud and manure that flowed downhill after it rained. As a side benefit, this helped protect the quality of the stream that ran at the base of the hill, but the intended purpose was to capture the manure, a valuable resource that would otherwise be lost. Making use of that resource had been Torrin's task for today and it had been the most unpleasant thus far.

Torrin spent the day shoveling the contents of the manure storage pit into a wagon. He then hitched the wagon to a horse and went through the fields applying the manure to fertilize Flynn's crops. The smell still clung to Torrin despite having taken a bath and nearly scrubbing his body hair off. Soap and water simply were inadequate to the challenge.

Although he expected diligent work from his laborers, Flynn was a generally decent and likable old man. He did, however, have one most bothersome quality. He whistled. Constantly, all day long, Flynn whistled and never once hit a note on key. The man could not carry a tune to save his life, which almost became necessary. After the second day, Flynn's quavering, inharmonious melodies began to chafe Torrin's nerves to the point he considered slitting Flynn's throat just to end the infernal sound, the shrill wheeze that made Torrin's skin crawl and teeth ache in irritation.

But Torrin restrained himself. The thought of murder did not manifest itself in action and Torrin managed to control his annoyance. His capacity for killing had not yet reached such a level carefree ruthlessness.

During their year in Abandon, Torrin had killed only four times. As far as he knew, Lenore was unaware of this fact and he intended to preserve her ignorance. Torrin kept this secret not because he was ashamed but because he was certain that such knowledge would needlessly upset Lenore. She did not like fighting, thought it much smarter to walk away from a fight if you could or run if you had to. Perhaps this stemmed from their experience en route to Abandon, all the trouble they had with Kayne and the other soldiers. Torrin tried to accommodate Lenore's desire for nonviolence. He was not particularly fond of fighting either, but found it often forced upon him. He had killed these individuals in self-defense, with one exception. Torrin had taken one life without sufficient provocation. But it was not a human life. It was a dog.

In addition to human strays, Marketa adopted dogs as well, having at least six around the small house at any given time. When home, Torrin chased them out, but their aftertaste was unmistakable. The smell of their urine permeated the floor and walls, fur coated the furnishings nearly as much as the animals themselves, and they ate far too much. *Six dogs, it was insane*, thought Torrin.

Apparently Marketa's dogs eased her depression in a way her human companions and alcohol could not. But the unconditional love she received from each new pet became a destructive addiction in its own fashion. Melancholy in Marketa was often followed by a collie of a different sort or a terrier or some other mutt for which they had no room. But for Marketa the twenty minutes of blithe love afforded by a new stupid, slavering puppy was worth the cost and inconvenience. Then, when the depression passed or took a new direction, Marketa neglected her canine "sedatives" just as Torrin believed she did most other responsibilities.

One of her dogs (Torrin refused to learn any of their names, referring to them all simply as "damn dog") made itself particularly annoying. It was a husky with a pure white coat, an attractive dog physically but not so in its demeanor. The cur was overt in its dislike of Torrin, growling at him, chewing up his things, getting in his way. But worse than any of this, the dog barked. It did so incessantly, with a special fondness for choosing the hours Torrin slept in which to issue its canine vocalizations. More than the rest of the pack, Torrin hated that dog.

One day, when Torrin returned home from an odd job, he was relieved to find his house for the moment unoccupied, by people anyway. He desperately needed a brief moment of solitary peace, some time to himself without anyone bothering or pressuring or worrying him. It had been a trying day and he wanted to avoid all confrontation. But the dogs were whining to be fed, a task that Marketa had once again failed to accomplish, much to Torrin's irritation.

Such a damned irresponsible woman. Well, they're not my dogs so let them starve, Torrin thought as he herded the pets out the door.

The husky started barking, of course, and objected to being ushered out.

Then in response to his prodding, the dog bit Torrin's leg, not a deep or painful bite, just a nip that barely broke the skin. But it was an attack Torrin could not forgive. It cracked the floodgates of his rage, releasing a stored reservoir of hatred, an irrational fury that quickly focused on the dog.

Torrin kicked the dog in its right flank, eliciting a yelp of pain from the animal. It felt so good that Torrin kicked it a second time. The dog barked in protest and its lips curled back into a snarl. So again Torrin kicked it. Seething with excessive brutality, Torrin went on kicking and beating the dog until it became unmistakably evident that the animal would never bark again. It laid dead on the floor, its white fur mottled with blood, its body limp and broken.

With the brutal act complete, Torrin felt suddenly sick and conscience stricken. It was just a dog, but his actions felt like murder and unquestionably took its form. This was the nearest Torrin had come to weeping since he took his oath against that particular form of weakness back in Gairloch. It scared him that he could be so savage, that he could lose control and kill for no just reason and draw such pleasure from that killing. In shame, he sought to cover his crime and did so by burying the animal's body far away from the house. As an alibi, Torrin planned to tell his mother that the husky must have run away. But she never asked, she never even noticed its absence. Her apathy toward a life she had chosen to be responsible for nearly sickened Torrin as much as his own murder of the animal.

But that was behind him now together with the path to his house. Coming home was never easy. He never knew what to expect upon returning, a condition he found very unsettling. Torrin had a powerful need for stability, for order in conformance to his own designs and tastes. The unpredictability of his capricious home environment and the instability of his mother filled Torrin not only with anxiety but also with disgust. Home was supposed to be a safe haven, somewhere you could shut out the world's cruel demands. Silently he prayed that his home would be peaceful tonight. He just wanted to relax in his own house. If possible, he planned on finding sleep without stopping even for the luxury of a meal.

But even before he opened the door, Torrin suspected that this was too great a goal for which to hope. His mother was entertaining again, hosting a party for her friends. Once again his home had been violated by drunken freaks and degenerates. The scene was a hackneyed one, far too common in its occurrence. And the sight stole away his last reserve of strength, leaving him completely without the energy necessary to deal with the situation. There were people everywhere, laughing and yelling, drinking and smoking, pushing and groping one another. The place was a mess, littered with food and broken clutter. The house he worked so hard to build, the house he wanted to preserve, was being thoughtlessly damaged and fouled. But he was too tired. Torrin felt he just could not deal with it tonight, not tonight.

Trying mightily to ignore the revelers and their acts of impropriety, Torrin hurried toward the entry of his "private" bedchamber and discovered it bolted. "Lenore, let me in. It's me, Torrin," he said knocking loudly to be heard over the roar of foolish talk at his back.

"Torrin, is that you?" came Lenore's voice through the door.

"Yes. Now open up."

She did, then quickly bolted it again after Torrin entered. She was clearly upset, scared by the people that cavorted on the other side of the perilously thin wall.

"Where have you been?" Lenore snapped, her face red.

"Working. I told you I would be late, that Flynn had a lot of work for me to do. For a while I thought he might keep me there all night."

"I've been waiting for you to get home for hours. I can't stand this anymore, Torrin. It's too much! I can't live like this. We can't live like this!" Extremely agitated, she was on the verge of crying, screaming, or some other form of catharsis. Her eyes were puffy and she was shaking visibly.

"Calm down. Are you hurt? Has something happened, did someone try to get in here? Are you all right?" Torrin asked gently, trying to hold her.

"No!" she groaned, pulling away from his embrace. "They've been out there all day, drinking and doing who knows what. I hear things. It frightens me; I don't like it. I've been too afraid to leave this room, too afraid to sleep, too afraid to do anything. I kept waiting for you to come home but you never did. Why didn't you come home?"

"I'm sorry," Torrin apologized, "but I'm here now. And I'll put them out, right now. You stay there and try to relax."

"No Torrin, don't," Lenore protested. "There's too many of them and they're too drunk. Just get me something to eat and drink, or let's get out of here ourselves. Why does it have to be like this? Why? I just can't take this any more!"

As she said the last, Lenore flung her arms wide, emphasizing her desperate conviction. But in her frantic gesture, she accidentally toppled a small ceramic doll from the nightstand on which it rested. It hit the floor and shattered, accompanied by Lenore.

Her mother had given Lenore the figurine many years ago, and it had been one of the few physical mementos she still possessed of their relationship. It was a reminder of old love and better times. Now a moment of emotional recklessness had made trash of the sentimental treasure, smashed it into a dozen worthless fragments. And having broken it herself, Lenore had no one else to blame or against whom to vent her anger. So she slumped to the floor and cried in abandon, oblivious now to all but the broken doll and her grief.

It was too much. The sight of Lenore's emotional pain pushed Torrin past the limit of his restraint. Torrin's heart pounded furiously at the interior walls of his chest, filled with hate howling for release. He could not find any soothing words within himself that might calm his wife's gasping sobs or dry her bitter tears. Outrage at those who had truly caused Lenore's misery overwhelmed Torrin's sympathy for her. Hate was all that held him together.

"Bolt the door after me," Torrin commanded before he slammed it behind him and left Lenore alone.

The air reeked of smoke and beer. The evil in the room was palpable. His body hardened by fury, Torrin cut his way through the mob of revelers. His shoulders back and jaw firmly set, Torrin felt invincible in his rage. His stomach knotted and relaxed over and over again, an unconscious mimic of his repeatedly clenching fists. His eyes were afire, his breathing heavy and through flared nostrils.

He scanned the room looking for his mother. He found her in a disheveled condition, lost in an alcohol-induced oblivion, clothed in nothing but a loose and partially open robe. Unconcerned by her reckless wardrobe, Marketa swayed in her chair while indulging in an absurd conversation with a glassy-eyed man who leered at her carelessly dressed body.

Torrin stood over them, feeling his rage gather within himself, a rage grown a hot as the core of hell's furnace.

"Get these vile scum out of *my* house!" Torrin bellowed at his mother. His fiery voice carried throughout the room, cutting through the clamor.

Marketa's head bobbed weakly as it turned to face Torrin and her watery eyes struggled to focus. "They're not scum. They're my friends," she slurred.

"I don't give a flying horse's hind end who they are! I want them out of here and I want them out now!" Torrin punctuated his demand by slapping the wine goblet out of Marketa's hand, sending it crashing against her lecherous companion.

Wiping at the fresh wine stain on his shirt, the man rose slowly to his feet. "What's your problem, lad? I don't like you talking to the lady that way," the man said threateningly.

Torrin turned and fixed his feral eyes on the man. The white-hot blaze of Torrin's anger flared explosively. "Shut up and get out of my house, you ignorant, sheep-humping son of a bitch!" Torrin ordered in a clenched growl.

The man swallowed his reply and backed off.

"Oh Torrin, lighten up. Why don't you have a drink and sit down here beside me and talk with your poor old mother like a good boy. Come on, have a drink. It won't kill you," she murmured, searching for the flagon of wine to replace her lost goblet.

But Torrin was no longer listening. Something else had caught and captured his attention, something even more offensive than the sight of his mother. He saw that a man stood urinating on the floor in the corner of the house. New unprecedented explosions of fury detonated within Torrin. He walked away from his mother and stepped quickly up behind the man. The second he reached him, Torrin delivered a powerful kidney punch, interrupting the man's relief. As the man doubled over in pain, Torrin grabbed him by the collar and the seat of his pants. Ferociously, Torrin pushed the man forward, slammed his head soundly against the wall, and hoped that his neck snapped in the process. But before Torrin could ascertain the truth of this dark desire, he was himself accosted.

Someone gripped Torrin's shoulder, spun him round and struck his face with a fist so solid it felt more like stone than mere flesh and bone. Before he could recover, someone else punched Torrin, then another, and another. There were too many, too fast. All he could do was tuck his arms up and hide behind them in defense.

But the defense failed. The blows rained down on him sadistically and Torrin was beaten to the floor. Curled in a fetal position, Torrin lay face down in the other man's urine. The attack continued but Torrin was unable to summon the strength necessary to move. He could not get up nor escape the tidal wave of abuse crashing over him. He was being repeatedly kicked and stomped and punched from above. The onslaught continued unrelenting, without mercy, until the individual attacks blended into a continuous sensation of pain. Torrin could feel unconsciousness approaching and seconds before it reached him, his mind's eye flashed on the image of that white dog buried several yards away.

Then all went black.

Torrin awoke slowly, remaining perfectly still in the pretense of death. That he was not dead initially surprised him. Every part of his body ached with an intense severity.

Unmoving, with the exception of his spinning head, Torrin listened. It was quiet. He heard no talking, no movement. It seemed that the party was over. But Torrin could not be entirely sure. Maybe he was alone. Maybe they were not still standing above him ready to resume their abuse as soon as he indicated his return to consciousness. Maybe.

In a painful act of courage, Torrin opened his eye. Only one, as the other was quite swollen and held closed by the inflammation. He lay facing the wall but could see that a soft, lambent light filled the room, the unmistakable illumination of early morning.

His raspy breathing was shallow but growing stronger. His swollen tongue was coated with a thick mixture of mucus and blood. He opened his mouth a fraction of an inch attempting to swallow the bitter, coppery taste it encased. That was a mistake. His jaw proved to be extremely tender and its movement yielded a stinging hurt accompanied by the release of a fresh stream of blood. It trickled out between his lips at the corner of his mouth. Torrin shifted his weight and moved slightly, trying to diagnose the extent of the damage that his body had suffered.

Every inch of his body felt raw. He was a mass of bruises, all agonizingly sensitive. Oddly enough, however, it did not seem that any bones had been broken, with the possible exception of a few cracked ribs. But, thankfully, it seemed his lungs had not been punchered by the fractures. He could still breathe. But the presence of other internal damage was more difficult to determine given his blurred level of consciousness and muddled cognitive powers. He hurt so badly he could hardly think. With his magic, Torrin reached within himself to tone down a fraction of the fierce pain, ease some of his physical distress. His breathing grew heavier now, winded from the effort of fighting the bodily hurt. Relatively assured that his persecutors had gone, Torrin risked discovery by lifting his hand to touch his face, finding the battered flesh crusted with dried blood.

Slowly, Torrin pulled himself to his feet. He leaned against the wall waiting for the dizziness to pass. The room was spinning all around him and for a moment his vision tunneled, blurred by the mind-splitting pain howling inside his head. A million tiny droplets of sweat erupted on his forehead, flowed together, and ran down his face in meandering, braided streams. Anger was all the strength Torrin had left and he used it as a crutch to keep himself up and moving. He drew upon its power to steady himself.

Looking around the cluttered room, Torrin spied his mother amid the wreckage left in the party's aftermath. Torrin's features twisted in revulsion as he focused on his mother who lay sprawled out upon the floor. Angry and standing above her, Torrin thought about killing her, seriously thought about it for a fleeting, violent instant.

"Get up," Torrin said dryly, nudging her with his foot.

"Hmmm. Oh, leave me alone. Let me sleep," Marketa moaned without opening her eyes.

"Get up!" Torrin shouted, slamming his fist upon the table like the blow of a blacksmith's hammer against an anvil. The blow carried such force that the wooden surface was immediately cleared of all its cups and half emptied tankards of stale beer. They crashed to the floor in exclamation of Torrin's command.

"What?! What is it?" she asked, fumbling to her feet in bleary eyed confusion and weak annoyance.

Actually, Torrin was not sure himself what exactly he wanted or what he was going to say. He was angry and simply wanted to communicate that fact in no uncertain terms. He needed a witness to his anguish and an outlet for his rage.

"What is wrong with you?" Torrin began. "What the hell gives you the right to do this to me? After all I've done, this is the thanks I get. I don't care if you've lost all your self-respect, but damn it all, you will at least respect me. I've had enough of your crap. How dare you bring those lowlife scum into *my* home and let them destroy it?"

Squinting and holding her forehead, Marketa groaned. "Torrin, don't yell at me. It's so early. I'm tired and I don't feel good. My head and stomach hurt."

"You don't feel good," Torrin scoffed in stunned disbelief. "You don't feel good?!" he shouted. Enraged by her self pity, he attacked her hangover. A sudden and intense urge to hit her washed through him. His fist clenched, his arm muscles bunched, flexing their potency. But he did not touch her.

"Look at me," Torrin commanded. "Look at me, you stupid bitch. Look at this place! Your whimpering won't get sympathy from me, damn it. I don't care about your damn hangover. I don't give a rat's ass about you at all. I'm glad it hurts. Hell yes I'm glad, the pain can only be a small part of what you truly deserve."

She focused on him then, her eyes like shield bosses, gaping with wide-eyed sympathy at Torrin's injuries and recalling fragments of the previous evening. Her heart turning suddenly tender and heavy with emotion, Marketa tentatively reached out to her son. Then she pulled back slowly, seeing something darker about Torrin than his bruise-blackened skin.

"Torrin, I'm sorry," confessed Marketa. Her words carried the remorseful weight of defeated love. "I'm so very sorry. I don't know what happened; but I suppose it doesn't matter because nothing I say will help you. Nothing I do seems to please you. And I can't make you love me, if you don't. I can't make your heart feel something it doesn't hold. I never wanted to hurt you. Can you understand that?"

Torrin said nothing. There seemed no hope of forgiveness in his cold blue stare, only an icy wrath.

"Why do you hate me so much?" Marketa continued. "It's been hard for me, and you haven't made it any easier. Sometimes you make everything so much harder than it has to be. You're always finding fault and fights were there aren't any. But I never stopped loving you and I never will. Try to understand that I'm just struggling in my own way to be free, not from you but to find my own kind of happiness in life. I would never intentionally hurt or betray you. And if you believe I have, I hope you can get beyond it. If you feel I've wronged you and you can't forget, maybe you can at least forgive."

He did not want to weaken. Torrin did not want to let her manipulate his emotions, to play his childish need for a mother's love against him. But something in her words or perhaps her look managed to touch Torrin deep inside, sundering his resolve with hairline fractures, allowing doubt and affection to penetrate the barrier he imposed around his heart. A part of him wanted to bury his face in his mother's shoulder and cry like a little boy. The desire was sickeningly attractive. But in retaliation, hatred rose to seal the breach in his resolve and keep his anger pure.

"Forgiveness? Love?" Torrin scoffed at his mother. "You don't know what you're talking about. And your words are empty of conviction," he snarled. "You say you're sorry but by tomorrow you'll repeat your abuse. You speak of love but hold no respect for my rights, my needs. You bully me with sentiment and mock me for allowing it. No more!"

"That's not true," Marketa argued. "You're the bully, Torrin, and I'm so very weary of hearing you criticize me. No matter what I do, you find fault with it. You seem to have forgotten just who is the parent here. Why don't you stop blaming me for everything? It's more likely that your own hot temper caused your injuries than anything I did. If you want to improve your situation, you had best first improve your manners."

"Parent, ha!" Torrin exclaimed. "You're a joke. I nearly died last night. I was nearly beaten to death in front of your very eyes and all you cared about was getting your next drink. Or deciding how many and who next to invite into your bed. You rank whore. You dog shit slattern!"

She moved to slap him but Torrin caught her wrist before she could land the blow. Holding her wrist in the tightening vise of his grip, Torrin's face clenched and his voice rumbled. "Too slow, too fat, too stupid. I won't be cowed by one, you bovine bitch. You have no right to criticize me or tell me what to do. You have not behaved as a mother should and so cannot lay claim to being one. We are nothing to each other. You are a fat drunken fool, deserving the foul fate you're headed for." Still gripping her wrist with one hand, Torrin raised his other in a fist.

"Easy, Torrin." A voice low and menacing suggested from behind him.

Torrin spun around to face the familiar voice. "Aragon! What are you doing here?" Torrin asked in surprise. Annoyed at the interruption, he released his hold on Marketa.

Staring at his brother, Torrin wondered, *Was Aragon here last night? Did he watch, doing nothing, as the others beat me? Did he participate?* "When did you get here?" Torrin asked aloud.

Slow in answering, Aragon stood relaxed as if by example he attempted to instill calm upon the emotionally turbulent room. A dark cloak with the hood thrown back over his shoulders clothed Aragon's tall, sinewy frame. Aragon's hair had grown long in back but his face remained bare although shrouded in a sullen shadow of disappointment. In his left hand, Aragon clutched a strange staff. Polished and black, the staff appeared to be made of wood although Torrin was unfamiliar with the species of tree from which it might have been cut. Spell laden runes were carved into the surface of the staff, strange symbols and script no doubt rich with mysterious power. As if possessed of life, the runes seemed to shimmer and shift in the morning light. A silver heal protected the base of the staff. And its apex was crowned with a silver, three-taloned claw embracing a green gemstone that pulsed faintly with an alien inner light.

Torrin's curiosity in the staff's origin and power distracted him from the current conflict. But he was forced to ignore it, knowing Aragon would reveal nothing of the staff's mystery no matter how Torrin might question him.

"By the look of things, I'd say I arrived when needed," stated Aragon in answer to Torrin's question. "This is no way for a family to treat one another, certainly no way for a boy to address his mother."

"I have no family in her or you or any other," insisted Torrin.

"Hard words," answered Aragon, "which I trust you do not mean. Don't forsake your family, Torrin. Don't deny our flesh and blood. We are family; Mother and I are undeniably a part of you."

"Like a wart or a gangrene limb that I would have removed," spat Torrin. "You and I are as different as night and day."

"Ah Torrin, you and I are of the same blood, born from the same love. Can our spirits truly be that different? I suspect not. Look within your soul, surely there must be more there than anger and contempt."

"What the hell are you babbling about?" Torrin snarled. "You don't know anything about me."

"I know your rage runs beyond your reason. You're not thinking clearly; you're too thrilled by the heat of your own temper," Aragon responded calmly. "Don't waste your life blinded by fear and hatred. Learn to accept the differences, the troubles of others with better grace. Shake off your ignorance and hate will follow. And once and for all, would you put aside your resentment of me? Just because our feud goes back to our childhood is no reason for you to continue behaving like a child. When I left the Prelature, I didn't leave you. Nor was it meant to insult you in any way. I simply didn't believe in everything the doctrines of the Prelature held as unquestionable truth. By the World Spirit, Torrin, you're still my brother. That's what's important. You are one of the only reasons I come back here at all. Despite your faults and my conflicting interests, I come back to keep an eye on you, to help you if I can. But you won't let me help you just as you refuse to help or tolerate anyone else."

"Help me?" Torrin responded in stunned disbelief. "You only come back here to rob me, to sleep in my house, to steal the food and other items purchased by my labor. You do not regard me as a brother anymore than that diseased tramp treats me as her son. No, in your eyes I'm just another dupe, someone you can deceive and cheat, just a gullible little fool for you to prey upon."

"You're wrong, Torrin." Aragon collared his anger, held it back with a heavy leash gripped by an iron will. "I see you as a brother but also as a self-pitying little boy, crying because you believe the whole world has let you down. Where will it end, your unforgiving nature, your demand for absolute respect, your insistence that all people live in accordance with your design? Tell me Torrin, where will it end? Where can it end but in destruction?"

"Damn it, Aragon!" Torrin cursed, fuming at Aragon's arrogant condemnation of him. "You have the audacity to judge me? You're overstepping the bounds, crossing the line into dangerous territory. From here on out I suggest you be very careful in what you say and do. You've both pushed me far enough. I warn you, don't provoke me further, for I could rend you limb from limb with magic or mundane arts. Here it ends, for now and forever. I will never again be made a victim, not by you or her or anyone else. That above all else I hold as an absolute truth, a paramount principle upon which my actions shall now be based."

Aragon raised the index finger of his right hand and point it at his brother like a threat. "First, Torrin, I am not your enemy. But if you insist on making me one, be advised that it is considered wise practice to understand your enemy as well as possible before attacking. And you are in fact quite ignorant of me and my capabilities. Secondly, what are you to become in your absolute fight against being made a victim? You have always talked of kindness for your fellow man in the conceptual but what about the flesh and blood dimension? People have failings; they need help or at least tolerance to overcome them. But you look upon the needs of others and view them merely with contempt."

"Only where they are contemptuous," Torrin snarled. "Failings caused by a weakness of mind, soul, or body that need not be. Such people are victims more of their own choosing than by the world's cruel misfortunes. True victims, those that suffer unjustly at the hand of others or by conditions outside their control, I sympathize with and would offer them my aid."

"Please don't," Aragon chided. "For what help would you provide? Butchery, training to become themselves a self-righteous persecutor such as you? No, you're too prejudiced and narrow-minded for social work. It doesn't suit you. Looking at the struggles of others, you are witness to only if and how it burdens you, how you may be inconvenienced. But you're blind to the true nature of the struggle. Mother has struggled and she has suffered. A measure of which relates to you in ways you've never bothered to notice. She protected you. You owe her life and more. Is respect and compassion too much to ask? Apparently so. Your kind of internecine reaction doesn't change anything, doesn't help anyone. You've got to believe in people before you can help them and, before all that, you have to care. What do you care about except yourself?"

"Enough!" Torrin thundered. "This discussion is pointless. It goes nowhere and I find now that I'm utterly bored by its futility. I've had more than I can stand of either of you. Not one second more can I stomach. I'm leaving, today. Lenore and I will pack our things and go. The two of you can stay here and wallow in your vice and madness together. You can suffer all the pains the world has to offer for all I care. I'm sick of caring about either of you. Its product has been nothing but my victimization. Caring about you is too expensive; I'll not pay the price for it any longer."

From the infighting, Torrin stormed to the door of his bedchamber. He rattled its handle until the door was hastily unbolted from the other side. Then he entered.

Lenore stared at him, her look full of concern.

"Are you all right?" she asked, meaning both his physical and emotional state.

"Fine," he said flatly. "You heard?"

"Yes. But why do we have to leave? We're the ones who built this place, why should we leave it to them?"

"Because *they* won't leave. Even if we throw them out, as long as they know we're here, they'll keep coming around, interfering in our lives and begging for handouts. We'll never have any peace in this house."

He was right but Lenore suspected that Torrin wasn't being entirely honest, not even with himself, that he had other reasons for not throwing Marketa and Aragon out. She was certain that he still felt guilty over their exile, still felt loyalty toward them, and even love. He would never admit it, but Lenore was confident that these were the unvoiced reasons that motivated Torrin to leave rather than force his mother and brother out of the only home they had left.

"But Torrin, we can't move out immediately," Lenore insisted. "Where would we go?"

He sat Lenore down and with as much self-possession as he could muster explained what had happened last night and why they had to leave. In the end she was swayed by Torrin's arguments and his bruises. She agreed with his decision. They packed in haste, by necessity taking less than they were entitled, and departed without another word to those left behind.

Marketa and Aragon stood in the doorway and watched the couple march down the street and out of sight. Disheartened by this loss, Marketa said gloomily, "Poor Torrin. I didn't mean to hurt him, or anyone for that matter. Yet I've hurt everyone who ever reached out to me. Tell me, Aragon, have I hurt you very badly?"

"Not at all," he answered, placing a lank hand upon her shoulder. "And I think it is Torrin who you describe rather than yourself."

"Do you still receive visions of the future?" Marketa inquired. "Do you know what will become of him?"

"The portents are unclear, although there is cause for worry. Everyone gets angry once in a while. But with Torrin it's becoming clear that he has such a deep and turbulent reservoir of hatred that he is very likely to find himself drowning in it one day. But don't lose hope. Although the omens are menacing, Torrin's destiny is not necessarily unalterable."

"I thought it was over," Marketa remarked. "I thought the prophesy of doom had been fulfilled last year."

"I don't know. Maybe, or maybe there is more yet to come. But leave the worrying to me," Aragon answered.

"Will you stay a while? Stay for a few days and keep your mother company. This house is going to seem very lonely now."

"No," Aragon replied. "There are things to which I must attend. I regret that I must leave by sunset."

"My mysterious son with his solitary ways." Marketa smiled weakly. "Don't worry, I won't press you to reveal where you go or what it is you do. I would like to think you're just going off to meet some pretty young girl somewhere, but I suspect it's more than that. Keep your secrets, if you must, and I'll keep to my wistful notions. It's a mother's prerogative. But promise me that in your exploration of either love or the wild lands you will be careful. Both can hold great peril for a man as much as great reward."

After Torrin and Lenore left, they went first to Flynn. The farmer had not yet reimbursed Torrin for his labor, so he intended to settle that debt before departing Abandon. When they arrived, Flynn was already hard at work and wondering why Torrin was late. Then seeing him, Flynn had other questions as well.

"My word boy, what happened to you?" Flynn asked. "You look like you got run over by a cattle stampede. And who is this cute little filly you got with you? Did your wife find out about her and cause that damage to your face? She must pack a hell of a punch."

The old man's concern and jovial friendliness helped dampen the anger still simmering inside Torrin. He smiled at Flynn's wry humor. "No, this is my wife, Lenore."

Flynn pulled the brown work glove from his right hand, wiped his palm on his trousers, and then extended it to Lenore. She shook his hand and said hello.

"I'm pleased to finally meet you, Lenore. I've been telling Torrin to bring you out. But I can see why he'd want to keep someone so pretty all to himself." Flynn winked at her.

For some reason, Lenore liked the old man immediately.

"Listen Flynn," Torrin continued, getting back to business. "I'm sorry, but I won't be able to work for you anymore. Lenore and I are leaving. We're moving away. So I'll have to ask for payment now for the work I've done."

"Well don't be too sorry. The work I had for you was nearly finished anyway. But tell me, you aren't running from a fight or something, are you boy? Because running isn't always the answer and maybe I can help you find a better one."

"No. It's nothing like that, we're just leaving," said Torrin.

"Uh huh," said Flynn with a shrug, suspiciously eyeing Torrin's bruises. "Well it's your business. Lenore, have you had breakfast this morning, darling? No? Well come on up to the house and we'll get you two something to eat while Torrin and I settle our accounts. Come on, don't be shy." Flynn led the way whistling. The shrill sound once again set Torrin's teeth on edge.

The house much resembled its owner, aged but solidly built and well maintained. It was also a compliment to Flynn's wife, Kara, as were the couple to each other.

Bright and robust, Kara was unlike so many women whose spirits sour from a long life. She greeted Torrin and Lenore with honest good humor, then set cheerily to preparing what would obviously be the second morning meal. But her kind, life-worn face reflected clearly that she felt no imposition and was in fact quite pleased in offering her unpretentious hospitality.

In no time, the house was redolent with the smell of freshly brewed coffee and reheated apple dumplings served with cinnamon and sugar. Kara also offered them biscuits with sausage gravy along with so much other food it seemed as if she were convinced that the young couple was nearly starved to death.

Flynn sat at the crowded table across from Torrin and Lenore. Kara playfully spanked Flynn's hand as he reached for a piece of spice cake, stating that the food was only for their guests. Flynn let out a short bark of laughter, leaned forward, and filled his mouth with words instead. "So where are you two bound for, if you don't mind my asking?"

"We haven't exactly decided that yet," Torrin explained while chewing his breakfast with a hardy appetite that surprised him.

"Uh huh," remarked Flynn. "Well if that's the case and you're still set on leaving, maybe you could use some advice. If not, just tell me to mind my own business and I will. I know how you young folk hate to take advice, especially from an old timer like me. No, all right then, my advice is go north. By the brand of exile on your hand, I can see that east is not an option and west is no better.

But north of here there is a settlement called New Hope. Now don't get overly excited by the name, it's not all that it promises. I've done some trading up that way. New Hope is still a pretty rough town but maybe a little better than Abandon, certainly no worse. If you choose to go that way, follow the Purl River north a few days, maybe more depending on your speed. The river will lead you there. But watch your step along the way. Between here and there is dangerous country, frequented by outlaws and raiders. So keep your eyes open and be quick to cover if you should see anyone. Anyone you meet along the way will most likely have it in his mind to rob you, or kill you, or worse. So make a cold camp. The light of a fire attracts more than moths. And stay out of Cravenwood, that foul forest is haunted by every form of death imaginable."

"Dear," Kara interrupted, a look of pure horror on her face. "You're scaring that poor girl half to death."

"Well there's reason enough to be scared," Flynn snorted. "It's dangerous terrain, but you'll get through all right as long as you're smart about it. You know, careful."

"Sir...?" began Lenore.

"Stop that *sir* business. I told you, call me Flynn."

"I'm sorry. Flynn," continued Lenore, "I don't suppose you could come with us to New Hope, as a guide?" The question stung Torrin's pride but even he had to admit the sense of it.

"I wish I could, honey, but I can't get away right now," Flynn explained with sympathy. "If you want to hold off for a month or so, maybe then I could."

"No," said Torrin. Having made up his mind, he was eager to act on the decision. "We have to leave today."

"Dear, do what you can for them," Kara lovingly insisted of her husband. "Make sure these kids have what they need to make the journey."

Smiling, Flynn answered. "I will, hon, just give me half a chance. Torrin, if you're done eating, come with me and we'll settle up my debt and get you outfitted for travel."

Torrin received more than he rightfully had coming. Flynn gave him a bay gelding, an old horse but still strong and sturdy. The horse was then loaded down with blankets, tools, a bow with a full quiver of arrows, and other necessary provisions. Meanwhile, Kara detailed her life history to Lenore and during her great flow of talk prepared and packed additional supplies—dried fruits and meats, black bread, cheese, soap, bolts of cloth, needles and thread, and other simple luxuries. Kara and Flynn argued over the necessity of traveling light and the importance of each other's contribution. But in the end, they elected to let Lenore and Torrin decide what to take. As much for fear of offending their benefactors as for their own personal desire, they kept everything. After repeated thanks, Lenore and Torrin began their trek, now well provided for in material and morale.

The sky was as clear as the conscience of a newborn. Birds wheeled across the cloudless sky above flocks of sheep and cattle. The air was sweet. To Torrin and Lenore, the sky never seemed so bright, and strangely neither had their spirits. Despite the danger they might well be walking blindly into, it felt good to be leaving a hurtful past and moving forward into the promise of a better life.

With the fall of evening's dark drape, Aragon privately slipped away unseen and headed south to Shantung Crypt. He discovered the place several months ago but had only recently gained access and claimed it as his home. Located in a wooded hollow encircled by the slopes of the Barisan Mountains, Shantung Crypt was a forgotten elfin burial ground. He uncovered its existence by chance during his exploration of the wilds, but unlocking its mystery had required far more than luck.

Stairs of moss-covered stone descended to a portal carved into the earth and recessed in a small grassy knoll. Its simple exterior belied the crypt's significance. Locked and impenetrable to forced entry, the door was flat and smooth, unadorned save for a few immemorial runes chiseled into its stone surface.

It was obvious that the runes were the key to opening the door, but possession of a thing does not automatically impart knowledge of its application. For a wizard to magically learn a foreign tongue, he must be in contact with a living person who commands the language he seeks to understand. Magic alone will not let a wizard decipher unknown inanimate text. Furthermore, the runes themselves were magic and merely pronouncing their words would not release their power. An understanding of their meaning was also required.

Aragon had camped outside the door, speaking every word or phrase for entry that came to mind and writing the words down so as not to repeat himself. He also studied the runes, trying to find links to his own language. Eventually he unraveled their riddle, not in a flash of insight but as the undramatic result of earnest investigation and careful calculation.

He felt a rush of excitement that first time he spoke the words and gave voice to their meaning. "Shantung, Children of Navar." He had surmised that Shantung was the name of some long-lost elfin kingdom and Navar the elfin name for World Spirit.

The rune inscribed door slid into the earth. To his keen vision the crypt was empty, devoid of anything but the ink-like blackness that faced him. In stepping forward, Aragon kicked gravel out before him. The pebbles bounced and plummeted, disappearing into the darkened void with a rattling echo that faded slowly into silence. There was no floor, only a pit that seemed to descend to the world's very core. After casting light into the chamber's darkness, Aragon searched along the walls until he found the trip lever that returned the floor above the fathomless pit. Once he stepped within, the door closed behind him and another barred further advance. He was confronted with more runes, more riddles, and more traps, all of which he set to solving with greater urgency as he had left his food rations outside. Hunger, and fear of starvation, worked to significantly enhance his motivation for discovery.

With care and skill, Aragon worked his way through the crypt's defenses and reached its inner chamber. The cool, dry room was large, and his breath echoed in a manner that seemed to surround him with the whisperings of unseen hosts. The sepulcher's walls were lined with sealed tombs of elves long since confined to their place of internment. To Aragon, the dead imparted an odd, contradictory sensation, one not only of isolation but also of companionship, as if perhaps their spirits lingered here to keep him company. The crypt also contained a rich trove—gold, silver, jewels, and other tokens to which the living assign value. But Aragon scarcely noticed these trinkets, having spied what was in his estimation a greater treasure.

Adjoining the main chamber was a somewhat smaller room that must have been used at one time by the elfin kingdom's holy men or perhaps even their wizards. Within the room were ornate chairs, a finely crafted desk, a table, and the wooden frame of a bed. Upon the desk and at shelves lining the walls sat leather bound books, bulky volumes possessing the arcane wisdom of the lost elves that had long ago met with ruin. He was at first hesitant to touch them, afraid the ancient books would crumble beneath his fingertips. Then he saw to his amazement how miraculously the books had been preserved. Actually, not so miraculous, as the crypt had obviously been designed for the preservation of artifacts, be it the shells of once living elves or the books they scribed. It was here Aragon had acquired his staff. It was here he now returned, intent on fully uncoding the elfin tongue and reading these bound treasures of paper, words, knowledge, and magic.

Chapter 5
New Hope

Three months had passed since their arrival in New Hope, the time and move doing much to improve Torrin's mood and revive Lenore's optimistic spirit. The village of New Hope was no less of a challenge than Abandon had been and one they were only beginning to confront. But they met it together and with greater peace of mind.

To others it may not have appeared that the couple's standard of living had in any way been improved by the move, but to Torrin and Lenore it had immeasurably. Although their house was only a small single room, it possessed a commodious illusion, seeming more spacious than its true dimensions because they shared it solely with each other. Alone, they were happier now than they had been in a long time.

On this evening, Torrin and Lenore prepared for a lighthearted ceremony that they had planned as a way to formally declare their new dwelling as their home. Torrin and Lenore had definite beliefs about what a home should be that extended beyond the simple trappings of size, design, and furnishings. A home was a place for people to feel love, security, and peace. The couple had high hopes that here these needs would finally be satisfied.

Leaving Lenore to prepare their supper, Torrin walked to a village tavern not far down the road. Torrin almost never drank, generally considering alcohol to be a weakness, but he thought a flagon of wine might be appropriate to celebrate this special occasion.

The tavern was typical, smoke filled and crowded with the despairing and the intemperate. Torrin felt their eyes upon him, each assessing him as prey or predator.

It was a rough crowd but Torrin had learned how to survive in such places. However, he had not yet learned to accept such people as his neighbors. Without realizing it himself, a sneer of revulsion crossed Torrin's lips with unconscious ease as he glanced from one side of the room to the other. A fat man with a full beard, seemingly grown to excess in compensation for his receding hairline, sat at a table by the door. He was smoking a pipe filled with a noxious blend of tobacco. A swirling cloud of stink rose above his balding head. At another table sat a gaggle of young girls, enticing prostitutes still pretty but becoming hardened by the life they led. Their eyes were filled with a vacant look, as if their minds had gone off somewhere while leaving their bodies here to be used in whatever manner the clientele may choose as well as afford. Yet within their vacant stares, a glimmer remained of their latent hunger. They craved something. Torrin did not know exactly what, perhaps nothing more sinister than money, men, and booze, but certainly nothing more noble. For a second, Torrin wished it were otherwise, wished that they would look at him with a desire for friendship. Although they were happy with each other, there were times when Torrin and Lenore were lonely for the company of friends. But he would not find them here. Torrin felt certain these people would never like him and they were not worthy of his friendship anyway.

Without any clear reason, Torrin felt himself getting angry at the prostitutes. He began to see them now as conceitful trash and imagined that they were laughing at him. And he found he wanted to hurt them for this presumed sin against him.

Moving forward, Torrin noticed someone else casting a bitter glance at the girls. An older woman sat poised upon a bar stool, legs exposed, her appearance carefully tooled to seem more youthful than what truth wanted to reveal. The camouflage failed and only seemed to hide the real beauty of her age. She was probably a competitor in the prostitution business who was loosing business to the newcomers in the trade.

Men were standing around, talking and drinking heavily. Someone bumped into Torrin, spilling warm beer down his back.

I was wrong, thought Torrin, *alcohol is not a wicked thing; it's these people. The manner in which they imbibe and their resulting actions constitute depravity.* Eager to leave, Torrin moved quickly to find the barkeeper and place his order.

Quinn McCall was one of those who watched Torrin. His narrowed eyes carefully followed Torrin, measuring him. Beside a round table of stout wood, Quinn sat balanced on the rear legs of his chair with his broad back braced against the wall. Resting his feet in their heavy boots on the chair before him, Quinn idly stroked his moustache, repeatedly running thumb and index finger from the center of his upper lip, around each corner of his mouth, and down his chin. Whenever he came to the tavern, he always sat at the same table because it was a place near the warmth of the fireplace and because he was able to see the entirety of the room from where he perched. He focused now on Torrin. He studied Torrin's bearing; saw the sense of superiority and aloofness it possessed, the kind owned by noblemen. Torrin also wore the blue robe of the Prelature, a fact Quinn found quite curious. When Torrin waved to attract the barkeep's attention, Quinn saw the brand upon Torrin's palm that marked him as an exile. Every fact and suggestion conveyed by Torrin's person was assimilated and analyzed in relationship to each rumor and ambition known to Quinn. The man in blue presented a curious blend of characteristics. But as yet, what he saw and what he suspected of Torrin held only a passing interest, a curiosity of little significance.

Waiting on the barkeep, Torrin's eyes settled on an unsavory scene. In a far corner, a pair of ruffians entertained themselves by tormenting an elderly man. Their victim appeared half blind and was missing one leg below the knee, hardly a challenge for the two who used him for sport. They were big, stupid, and malicious, an ugly combination. One drank from the old man's jug, laughing at his companion who played with the man's crutch. Clearly not enjoying their company, the old man was forced to suffer the pair's mockery. They spilled wine on his chest, spit in his cup, and forced him to dance a one legged jig. Humiliated, pathetic, and defeated, the old man now sagged in his chair waiting for them to lose interest.

Torrin's skin warmed, heated by annoyance and disgust. His anger was kindled not only at the ruffians and their crimes but also at the old man, at his infirmity that permitted the abuse and which made Torrin feel obligated to intervene.

The cripple should stay out of places like this, knowing what would happen if he didn't, Torrin thought. *How dare the old fool set himself up to be a victim and compel others to risk themselves on his behalf?*

And risk it would be. The two men looked to be mercenaries. One wore an iron-studded gambeson of thickly padded quilted cloth with a sword strapped to his back and a brace of daggers at his waist. Mantling the other was a short mail hauberk, the interwoven iron ringlets of the chain mail shirt shimmering in reflection of the firelight. Thick dark-brown leather vambraces heavily studded in brass encircled both his forearms and a sword hung scabbarded at his side. Both men were wide of chest and had arms with swollen muscles.

Torrin suspected that he had probably received better formal weapons training than these two. But by the look of them they had known battles and possessed considerably more actual combat experience, the kind that mattered, when life was on the line rather than simply reputation. Coming to the aid of this crippled old man might be the right thing to do, but it might also very well be a fatal thing to do. It was a frustrating situation that had been thrust upon him, a situation that attacked pride, conscience, and common sense. Should he help the old man or stay out of it? Infuriated by the whole affair, Torrin made his decision.

He had come here unarmed, not expecting trouble and believing that weapons were often as much an attraction for violence as they were a deterrent. So Torrin turned to the man standing at his right and asked. "Excuse me sir, could you lend me the use of your sword for a moment?"

"Go hang yourself, you beggar," came the reply.

Awash with new waves of irritation, Torrin tried again. He slapped a copper coin on the bar. "I'll pay you for its rental and not leave the building with it. Fair enough?"

The man snatched up the coin. With a quizzical arc to his eyebrow and a bemused smirk, the man handed over a broad-bladed, short sword. Torrin had actually wanted the man's other longer sword, but grudgingly accepted the offering, as he had not specified. Armed, he turned and approached the pair of ruffians.

"Leave the old man be," Torrin ordered, his voice flat and direct. "Find some other way to amuse yourselves."

Their attention shifted quickly to address Torrin. The man in the chain mail shirt positioned his bulk before Torrin, grinning wolfishly with broken, rotting teeth. He voiced his words in a snarl carried on breath fouled by decay. "Is that a threat, little man? Or are you volunteering to take his place?"

Torrin tightened his grip upon the borrowed sword, still keeping its tip pointed at the floor while he held his ground, refusing to be intimidated. He drew deep breaths, forcing himself to relax, to calm his heart and yield to the inevitable. There was no hope of walking away from this without a fight and still take away with him any dignity. His nerve grew suddenly stronger. By forsaking the hope of a peaceful resolution, he strengthened his commitment to violence and diminished any fear of it.

"Actually it was more an appeal to your sense of decency," said Torrin. "But I see now that it was wasted effort, that threats are all you can understand. I'll keep this simple so even you can follow it. Leave now and you may do so in possession of your life. Linger and I'll take it from you."

Overhearing, the others of the tavern gathered around Torrin and the pair he challenged, circling like buzzards hungry for the sight of blood, a brutal show that would cost them nothing. An opening broke in the crowd making room for Quinn, who pushed his way to the front of the spectator's ring. But no one moved to intercede or lend support on behalf of Torrin or the men he challenged.

The ruffian facing Torrin stepped back and to the right while his cohort charged forward, freeing his sword and swinging wildly at Torrin. He parried and dodged then blocked the attack of the other man who had now added his weapon to the fray.

One of them threw a tankard of ale in Torrin's face, leaving him confused for a dangerous moment. Holding his sword before him in blind defense, Torrin wiped the salty brew from his eyes and took a glancing blow across the thigh.

These swine did not fight in accordance with the codes of conduct under which Torrin had been trained. To survive he may not have to sink to their level, but he must certainly remain conscious of their disregard for the civilized rules of combat. A small mistake in a tournament may cost you a point; here it may cost you your life. Torrin recuperated quickly. Once again he felt anger's gelid fire rage through him and himself borne upon its euphoric flow.

Turning from one to block the other, Torrin sliced through the man's wrist, dropping the piece of meat to the floor with the fingers of the dismembered hand still curled impotently around the sword hilt. The man screamed in uninhibited agony and fell writhing on the floor. In the same instant, Torrin spun back to turn the other combatant's blade aside, stepped in, and smashed the pommel of his sword soundly between the ruffian's eyes. He staggered, dazed by the harsh blow. Torrin grabbed the man's collar and with his other hand held the tip of his short sword to his adversary's throat.

Recovering, the man dropped his weapon, his eyes bright with unaccustomed fear. "Mercy," he blurted. "Sir, I beg you. Have mercy."

"Mercy is a privilege reserved for persons of honor, not villainous scum such as you," Torrin answered in a tone as cold as death. His arm tightened in preparation of driving home the point. Torrin's lips pulled back in a death's head grin, a triumphant expression of lethal power. "Get over there by your friend and on your knees. Now!" Torrin shouted, kicking the man's fallen sword out of reach and pointing at his maimed companion.

On the floor lay the other man trying desperately to tie a tourniquet around his forearm. But the crude, one-handed approach scarcely slackened the bloody discharge issuing from the mutilated arm. Torrin knelt down beside him and placed his hand around the wound. The crowd watched in wonder as Torrin invoked his magic. Cracking and hissing sounds broke the hush that had fallen upon the tavern. Blue fire, like miniature bolts of sustained lightening, leapt from Torrin's hand and crawled over the man's injury. The man screamed. The sorcerous flame cauterized the wound and the smell of burning flesh crept through the tavern. The man's arm no longer bled and his cries died away.

Torrin stood up. "Old man," called Torrin, holding the defeated pair with his forbidding gaze and keeping his sword at ready. They stared back with a mixture of awe, fear, and muted temper. "These men," Torrin said in disgust, as if the word had been made bitter in using it to identify the ruffians, "have wronged you and will compensate for it by performing you some service. What do you require? Tell me and I will make them do it. Don't be afraid, speak up."

The old man moved forward, squinting and smiling at the humbled state of his persecutors but worried at the prospect of continued association with them. "Well, my roof could stand to be re-thatched. It's kind of hard for me to do it these days. It's not as easy for me to climb up there as it used to be."

"So be it," Torrin proclaimed. "You two will thatch his roof tomorrow. If it is not done or if he meets with any harm, I will kill you both. It's that simple, so even you two should be able to understand. And be advised that if I'm forced to kill you, I just may do it in a manner so slow and tortuous that it will leave you begging for death long before it comes." Torrin placed his sword tip to one of the men's Adam's apple. He pushed against it firmly enough to draw out a small trickle of blood. "Any questions? Any comments?"

Glaring malevolently but effectively intimidated, the two agreed to Torrin's mandate and left the tavern in shame. The old man giggled like a fool. He tried to thank Torrin but Torrin wanted nothing more to do with him.

Torrin wiped the blade then returned the borrowed sword to its owner. The man now wore a broad grin, apparently entertained at the part his sword had played in the little drama. A few well-wishers congratulated Torrin on his victory or endorsed his actions. Torrin ignored them, picked up his flagon of wine, and tipped the barkeep a little extra to cover the disturbance he had caused.

"Not to worry," snorted the barkeep as he pocketed the coin. "In this business such episodes happen, and when they do, it gets the clientele's adrenaline pumped which tends to make men thirsty. Come back again. I never turn away a man with money to spend."

Turning quickly to leave, Torrin nearly collided with a brick wall of a man. And once he saw past the man's presence to his form, he was startled yet again.

It was Quinn. Broad shouldered and thickly padded in muscle, Quinn stood a head taller than Torrin. And it was this that had taken him by surprise, not the height but the head. It was deformed, not grotesquely but noticeably, in a way that made it uncomfortable for Torrin to meet Quinn's eyes squarely. His skull appeared slightly warped, contorting his features so that they looked off center and twisted. His face showed further abuse by the beatings of weather and a hard life.

"Pardon me, sir," Torrin apologized, stepping aside to give the deformed giant his place at the bar, which is what Torrin assumed he wanted.

But Quinn grabbed Torrin. His big, thick knuckled fingers curled around Torrin's right bicep in a grip that was gentle yet firm.

"Can I speak with you?" Quinn asked.

Despite his anger at another interruption and annoyance at being touched, Torrin almost smiled at the unintended irony of Quinn's question. The man's speech was slow and ponderously stuttered, as if each word had to wrestle its way free of his mouth against an unwilling tongue. Immediately, he knew what Quinn would want, that he had seen Torrin's healing magic and wanted treatment for his own physical disorders. But Torrin was impatient now, feeling already imposed upon and eager to get back to Lenore.

"Stop by and see me tomorrow," said Torrin. "I live just down the road. I don't have time to help you right now. I'm busy at the moment. But see me tomorrow and maybe we can work something out."

"Wa-Wa- Wait. R-R-Reconsider. You sh-sh-should be more care-care-careful. You may want my escort," stuttered Quinn with tedious difficulty. As he talked, Quinn patted the pummel of the sword strapped at his side.

The lumbering question further nettled Torrin's impatience. And misinterpreting it, the question angered him initially. His first thought had been that Quinn was threatening him. But the time required for the question's utterance allowed Torrin to think past his paranoia and comprehend its actual intent. Quinn was referring to the men Torrin had defeated, that they and perhaps a few of their friends may be laying in wait to ambush Torrin and that Torrin may need protection.

Wise counsel, thought Torrin. *Perhaps safe passage home was worth the price of his inconvenience in having to deal now with Quinn.* His wariness persisted, but Quinn seemed the lesser risk.

"Very well. Follow me. We can talk at my house," answered Torrin. He spoke quickly, as if he were trying to compensate for the extra time Quinn's part of the conversation required. "My name is Torrin. What's yours?" he asked as they shook hands.

"Q-Q-Q-." He stopped. Frustration lined Quinn's face as he drew in a heavy breath. "Quinn McCall." With great effort, his name exploded from his lips in a well-concentrated burst of clear syllables.

"Pleased to meet you," returned Torrin. "Shall we go?"

They arrived at Torrin's home without incident. No one tried to ambush them and Quinn did nothing to suggest his motives might be sinister. Torrin opened the door and showed Quinn inside. Torrin's guest surprised Lenore but she quickly concealed her reaction.

"Lenore, this is Quinn McCall," Torrin explained. "Quinn, this is my wife, Lenore."

"It's a pleasure to meet you," Lenore offered. She was forcing herself to look straight into his disfigured face, trying to treat him as she would anyone else. The sight of Quinn unnerved her but she did not want to be rude. And it was not just his facial abnormality. It was fear as well as good manners that motivated her to be polite. Quinn was an imposing figure of a man. He looked like a man who could drop a bull with one punch. His shirt was tight against his broad shoulders. His sleeves were rolled up to the elbow, exposing the thick meat of his forearms. Quinn was all muscle. And his face was so ugly; she hoped the poor man never had to see himself in a mirror. But in stark contrast to his face, he had the most beautiful wavy blonde hair.

From the first moment he laid eyes on Lenore, Quinn's heart swelled with what he thought might be love. She was beautiful certainly, but it was more than that. Her luminous emerald eyes held a gentle quality that was spellbinding. At that moment, he wanted nothing more in the world than to be her friend, something he had not dared to want of anyone in a long, long time. If she were to cringe or to laugh at his ugliness, as most women did, he believed it would crush his soul to dust. No one had held such power over him in a long time. He found himself both drawn to her and terrified of her.

Afraid to speak, Quinn merely nodded in reply to Lenore's tentative greeting.

With the introductions out of the way, Torrin offered Quinn a chair at the table. Torrin took the seat opposite Quinn. Lenore went back to the kitchen area to fix their plates and clean up. Although she acted as if nothing concerned her, she watched the two men carefully, keeping an eye out for signs of trouble.

"You said you wanted to talk to me. Why is that? Do you want medical attention, healing like I gave that man in the tavern?" inquired Torrin, unsure how better to phrase the question without giving it offensive implications.

"N-N-No," Quinn said. Then he paused, thinking how best to explain his need and how to minimize the words necessary to convey it.

Tapping the table top with anxious fingertips, Torrin intruded upon the pause. "Well, if not that, what is it you do want?"

"You," Quinn hurriedly announced in succinct phrasing.

"What? What do you mean? Is that some kind of threat?" demanded Torrin.

Lenore was growing frightened. The man was strange and obviously Torrin did not know him or trust him. Like Torrin, she was beginning to suspect he meant them harm, that he might kill Torrin and rob them. And what would he do to her, she wondered and shuddered at the thought. Hoping he would continue concentrating on Torrin, Lenore took the axe from the wall and moved slowly to her husband's side.

Quinn threw up his hands, trying to hold back their fear. The large Adam's apple in his neck bobbled up and down nervously.

"No, n-n-no. I m-m-mean no h-h-harm. P-p-please, l-l-let m-m-me explain. I w-w-w-want you t-t-to b-b-be s-s-sen-sen-seneschal for N-N-New H-Hope," asked Quinn in a speech so broken and stammering that it was almost painful to listen to. But again, the patience of listening helped Torrin put his volatile temper to rest.

It was at times such as these that Quinn most despised his speech impediment, his infernal stuttering. He had something important to say but the way in which he was forced to say it would make a mockery of his words, belittle his proposal. His appearance and speech made him seem stupid, no matter how strong the intellect behind his deformity. He looked and talked like an overgrown simpleton. How then could he employ reason and dialogue in persuading Torrin to support his plan? He was like a muted singer or a sculptor without arms, his skills disbelieved because they lacked adequate means for expression.

Torrin caught a hint of this struggle revealed in the frustrated yet intelligent gleam in Quinn's eyes. Torrin was also surprised at the idea of himself as seneschal. Lord and ruler of New Hope? It was an intriguing proposition. He wanted to hear more and was annoyed by Quinn's slow explanation.

"Let me see if I can help you," said Torrin, moving over by Quinn.

Torrin placed his hands over Quinn's throat and lower jaw, delivering the invocation to release a slow, pulsating, blue glow around the area. Magic poured from his hands. If a physical ailment, Quinn's speech impediment would probably be cured by the magic. If the problem's cause was psychological, then perhaps Quinn's faith in Torrin's magic would allow his mind to abandon the stutter.

"There," said Torrin, "maybe now we can talk more freely. Say something so I can hear how good my work is."

Massaging his neck, Quinn stood up next to Torrin as if in reverence of the occasion. His skin tingled and felt strange. He looked at Lenore then back at Torrin. They both watched him expectantly. In the back of Quinn's mind, a voice whispered that this was all a joke, that they gave him false hope so that they could laugh at his failure and disappointment. Jokes like that had been played on him before. But no, he did not believe that they were playing with him, not truly. Torrin and Lenore did not seem like the kind of people who would do that sort of thing. He trusted them. But having lived so long minimizing his words, saying only what was absolutely essential, Quinn was at a loss to find and speak words with no other purpose than to test the sound of his voice.

"What should I say?" asked Quinn in a voice as smooth and unimpeded as a practiced orator. The sound shocked him and disbelieving he spoke again. "Is it true, is that me?"

Now certain of having heard his own clearly articulated words, Quinn's face broke into a smile that was pure and boundless like the innocent joy of a child whose heart's desire had been unexpectedly delivered. It was a smile infectious and beautiful, despite Quinn's misshapen features. Torrin and Lenore could not help but be touched by Quinn's joyous outburst of emotion and smile almost as brightly in return.

"My Lord Torrin, I knew I rightly recognized you as the one destined to be New Hope's seneschal, the leader it so desperately needs. Let me be the first and most proud of its citizenry to swear fealty to you," pronounced Quinn, full of solemn emotion. There were tears in his eyes. He fell on bended knee in obeisance before Torrin and stared up at him with intense sincerity.

Torrin and Lenore exchanged glances and nearly burst out laughing at the preposterous notion. Then looking back at Quinn, his face lined with scars from the past and hope for the future, Torrin sobered.

"Come, on your feet," urged Torrin. "I can't accept your oath of fealty, and as for the rest of what you propose, I do not understand it. What makes you think I could impose myself or make myself accepted as seneschal? Look around you, this is hardly a palace and I have no army to enforce my will. And I will never have the backing of the High Queen; I can guarantee you that." Torrin returned to his seat at the table and the other two followed his example.

"Perhaps seneschal is not the correct word. For you're right, there is no monarch for whom you would be managing New Hope's estate," explained Quinn. He still could not believe the sound of his voice. It was wondrous but distracting. "Gairloch doesn't care about us. So, I guess in truth you would be king of New Hope, such as it is, but more importantly of what you could make it."

"King?" snorted Torrin in amusement. "Hear that Lenore, you're my queen now. A queen with dishpan hands and a king with holes in his boots. What a noble sight we are! Listen Quinn, you seem like a good man but I think too much ale has crossed your lips tonight. No?" Torrin continued as Quinn shook his head. "Well then, just how do you envision this crowning to occur?"

"You've seen New Hope's problems," remarked Quinn. "They are many. Heal them, as a king should, as you've done for me; and like me, all its people will loyally support your rule. You have the power to do it. I've seen what I need to know. You have the knowledge, the skill, and the judgment that makes a king. And more than this, you've demonstrated your possession of the wisdom of justice. Not only could you rule New Hope, but you would rule it justly. I know it. Regardless of if your selection comes from the World Spirit or mortal men or both; kingship, here, is your duty and your right."

Quinn's conviction and enthusiasm were contagious. Lenore was growing excited by the idea without any further thought to how it might be implemented. She smiled at Quinn, who reaffirmed endorsement of his plan by nodding with such vigor that his shoulders shook as well.

Torrin leaned back, scratching the back of his head, thinking. "I suppose it's not an entirely ludicrous notion. You wouldn't know this Quinn, but I come from royal blood. So I've learned a thing or two about managing an estate."

"So, it is true," remarked Quinn. "I heard rumors that you were Torrin Murgleys, grandson to the High Queen. But Murgleys isn't the name you've been using around New Hope."

"Yes, it's true," Torrin confirmed. "And no, I haven't been using the name Murgleys, though it's my birthright to do so. But around here that name wouldn't win me any friends, would it? That name carries no favor here. And there are many who might consider it a twisted thrill to kill a Murgleys, particularly when they know the royal house will do nothing to punish that act, provided I'm the victim. But if I were to ask New Hope to accept me as their king, who knows, maybe the name might add credibility to my claim. Outlandish as it may sound, your plan might work, if done properly.

"For example, the community empties its waste into the same river from which it draws its drinking water. This has made typhoid, dysentery, and other diseases common. With magic, mechanics, and nature's help we could collect, treat, and utilize this waste. Furthermore, we could build cisterns or holding tanks above ground that we could pump water into from the river, purify, and supply to the people through a gravity-fed distribution system. And because these services would be centrally controlled, we could levy taxes for their construction, operation, and maintenance. Controlling something like that would certainly bring power with it."

"Yes, my lord," Quinn agreed. "But it would also require power to retain it. Taxes and fees for other services would also have be used to maintain a standing army or militia to defend against attack from those who might oppose you or seek to steal your newfound power. But this same army, as well as other necessary defenses, would serve to protect New Hope from raiders and outlaws."

"That's right," interjected Lenore. She clapped her hands in excitement. "The people would pay for such protection and outlaws who were captured could be forced to labor on the construction of a defensive wall or on other public buildings. In fact, the people's taxes could be paid in either material or labor as their resources allow."

The three continued to plan Torrin's rise to power as ruler of New Hope, identifying immediate and long-term objectives and the methods for their attainment. Their mood remained buoyant, full of ambition and promise, well into the early morning. And together with the design of a kingdom, a bond was being forged between the three, a bond of trust, friendship, and shared dreams. It was as high as Torrin and Lenore's spirits had been elevated since before their departure from Gairloch. It was still only a dream, but at least it was something they could envision and to which they could aspire.

"We've laid a solid foundation tonight, but even a king needs his sleep," said Quinn, still savoring the fresh, sweet clarity of his words. "I'll go now and let you rest, my lord. I'll begin preparing the stage for your entrance as king, setting what wheels in motion I can. Thank you again. Thank you for everything."

Torrin rose to shake Quinn's hand. "If I am to be king of this estate, small and humble as it may be, I can't do it without you. You must be my right hand in this and you must be true, not simply loyal to me and our laws, but also honest, always honest. I have to know that I can trust you with my very life. Trust doesn't come easy for me. But I consider you a friend who I can trust."

The two stared at each other, their hands locked and their lips silent. And in that wordless pause, both men felt an unspoken covenant pass between them.

"Before you go," began Torrin uneasily. "Would you like me to use my magic to try and heal your face?"

"Oh," said Quinn, not offended but aware that Torrin worried he might have been. He had not thought of asking Torrin for this service. Over the course of the evening he had forgotten about his looks. Quinn's appearance did not seem to matter to his newfound friends and so he stopped worrying about it. Putting fingers to his features, Quinn wondered how to respond. "It's not necessary," he said finally. "But I guess it would be all right."

The attempt failed.

"I'm sorry. I really am," Torrin said. "Have you been this way from birth?" Quinn nodded and Torrin continued his apology. "The bones apparently have had too long to set. Perhaps if I could have attended you when you were younger, I might have been able to help you. Please forgive me if I raised your hopes for nothing."

"It doesn't matter," sighed Quinn. Oddly, he felt almost relieved that his facial features were unalterable. "I've gotten rather used to the shape of my face, ugly though it may be. Besides, the hope you have given me will not be for nothing. Goodbye."

Before Quinn could leave, Lenore surprised him with an unexpected hug and kiss to his cheek. She had been put off by his looks when first she saw Quinn, but in the familiarity that developed during the evening, she came to see him as a gentle, handsome man and the closest thing to a friend they had known in a very long while.

"Thank you, Quinn," said Lenore smiling. She stepped back and rested her hand over her heart. "You can't know how much you've helped us, how much hope you've given us."

Quinn smiled too but he was too choked with emotion to respond. He kept smiling long after he left. The seeds of belonging had been sown. Belonging, it was Quinn's greatest dream, his heart's most fundamental desire. His parents had abandoned him when he was very young, perhaps because of his deformity, he never learned why for certain. He was not even sure who his parents were. They could be anyone. They might still live here. He may even know them without knowing it.

Quinn had been raised by his grandmother, at least that was what she told him to call her. However, Quinn was relatively certain that this title lacked any biological truth. She was kind, elderly, and loving. And she treated him well, which was more than his parents had done. But she died in Quinn's tenth year. After that he was forced to raise himself alone. And alone was exactly how he spent the next fifteen years in New Hope. His face and stuttering combined to make others uncomfortable and essentially ostracize him. He probably would have been taunted and abused for these differences if not for the deterrent of his size and strength. When provoked, his appearance could be frightfully intimidating. So he was mainly left alone. People had been civil and even respectful to him, but never close. Yet it was this closeness that Quinn coveted. He wanted people to care about and who would care about him. He needed to belong in the way of friends, family, and community. This was the object of desire for which he long hungered and for which he had this night finally sampled, finding it a morsel so magnificent that his appetite for it now grew more conspicuous.

It started slowly, but after a month their plan began to bear fruit, rich and golden in its promise of a larger harvest to come. Most people were skeptical of Torrin, distrustful of his motives and doubtful of his potential effectiveness. Gradually, however, he won over the incredulous by showing how they would benefit with him as king. Torrin wished for speedier progress. Things were moving too slowly to suit his needs. Although the temptation to strong-arm their support remained ever present, he managed to refrain from force, knowing that a pledge freely given was stronger in its loyalty. But it frustrated him knowing how much more he could do for the community if he was universally acknowledged as king.

Then a fortunate stroke of luck ended Torrin's frustration. At the time it did not seem lucky but rather like a prelude to failure. Rumor had come to New Hope that a large band of raiders was riding for the village bent on plunder and destruction. Without a sense of unified community, the residents responded by hiding and hoping their neighbor might be victim enough for the brigands. Unlike most of the village, Torrin responded to the threat by preparing for battle, despite his meager handful of followers and the fact that virtually everyone expected his quick demise. Torrin's army was small and ill equipped in weapons, horses, and training. His soldiers were primarily those who owned very little and so had little to lose by supporting Torrin. But they did have a fighting spirit along with a leader possessing the ability to heighten their enthusiasm for combat and unify it pervasively against the attack.

Torrin did not have time to prepare an elaborate surprise defense or drill his army in smart tactics. When the raid came Torrin's army met it head on, like desperate and doomed fools outnumbered at least five to one. Without even a horse of his own, marching in front of his band of foot soldiers, Torrin led the charge against their attackers. Quinn followed faithfully at his side carrying a long spear with a red flag flying from its tip as a symbol of Torrin's authority.

When the raiders came into view, Torrin could feel doubt ripple through his army. He could sense their fearful desire to run for cover. To salvage the courage of his men, Torrin raced forward to assail his enemy. Shouting "Attack!" in a voice amplified by magic and swinging his axe with berserk fury, Torrin rampaged against the raiders. He fought with a wild fervor that infected his army. He seemed impervious to fear and radiated an aura of power that cast him in an indestructible light.

The battle's beginning went poorly and defeat loomed imminent for New Hope. But from the center of the melee, Torrin pulled victory out from the hands of the raiders. Valiantly, refusing defeat, Torrin unhorsed a brigand and stole possession of his mount, a fleet horse with a glossy white coat unspotted except by the blood of men. Well trained for battle, the animal was strong, fast, and fiery. It reared. Hooves flailing and with a long pealing whinny, it protested its new ownership. Then it yielded to Torrin's control. From his seat, Torrin stood out as a paragon of power and command, a living rallying marker. His blazing eyes and scarlet-smeared axe radiated skill and supremacy. As quick and blinding as a lightening flash, his axe delivered the promise of death held by both Torrin's look and his blade. Not only Torrin's soldiers were moved by the sight. Many of the cowering citizens of New Hope, inspired by Torrin's leadership and the deadly hew of his axe, now ran to lend support with staves, clubs, picks, knives, and whatever else lay readily at hand.

The foray was stopped and those raiders who broke to flee were quickly hunted down and killed. The battle was brutal and not without cost, but still a decisive victory for Torrin. On the field of battle, he immediately began caring for the wounded. Under Quinn's careful supervision, the dead raiders were stripped of their armament, which together with the surviving horses would be added to Torrin's growing arsenal.

Finished with his last patient and free of the concentration his medical treatments required, Torrin noticed it was late. Daylight had faded into dusk.

He noticed too that fires had been kindled and people gathered. Their look, focused on him, was strange, almost reverent. They seemed expectant, wide-eyed and waiting for some yet unfulfilled act of Torrin's. Then one of them, a man who identified himself as Connor, came forward out of the crowd to kneel before Torrin. Torrin remembered this man from the battle, recalled seeing Connor wield a mattock with all the bravery and half the skill of a practiced warrior.

"My lord, we doubt you no more," pronounced Connor with ceremonial esteem. "You are king, proven beyond doubt by your dominance in battle and the courage in your veins. You are the savior of New Hope, sent to us by the World Spirit. All our hearts and lives are yours to rule."

Men, women, children, virtually all New Hope's populace assembled on the field, ringed around Torrin, nodding in affirmation of Connor's pronouncement. Quinn stood with them, energized. Then to seal the moment Quinn shouted, "King Torrin!" The crowd chorused the proclamation, repeating it in an uproarious chant.

It was done. New Hope lay now firmly under Torrin's control. The coronation may have lacked the profligate splendor of richer kingdoms, but it possessed a simple vitality and youthful glory that more intimately bound the ruled to their newly crowned king. A feast was hurriedly prepared. It was a vigorous celebration with music, drink and dance. Nearly everyone took part. It was a night of triumph and merriment, a night which Torrin and Lenore shared together, as they did everything.

The following months witnessed a rapid elevation in Torrin and Lenore's quality of life, coupled with the rise in New Hope's order and organization. Both ruled and ruler felt adequately compensated for their investment in the other. People came to Torrin to describe their problems, which at first they had in full supply. He listened patiently and did what he could to help them.

Torrin's old house became merely an anteroom to the structure built for the new king and queen. First an adjoining large chamber was built as a throne room where the modest monarch could conduct business in a style better befitting his status. A bedchamber and lesser rooms were attached later.

The public services Torrin promised were delivered and their implementation managed by Quinn. Quinn had the ability to make men work both fast and willingly at his direction. He also was not afraid to lend his own muscle to the labor and work alongside those he supervised if the job or time demanded it. Connor too joined the royal circle, charged by Torrin to oversee the development and maintenance of New Hope's defensive arsenal. Responsibilities were delegated to Lenore as well, which she accepted with great enthusiasm and fulfilled with unerring competence. As minister of finance, she supervised the budget and treasury, tracking the levy and payment of taxes, disbursement of resources, and inventory of accounts. At any given time, Lenore could say what was owed to the king, by whom, and if the payment was delinquent due to hardship or greed. She grumbled and complained about the job at times, but it was clearly evident that she enjoyed the work. This was fortunate as there was no one else Torrin would have entrusted such power; and without her flawless skill in this capacity, all their other endeavors would have soon failed.

Torrin ruled well, in accord with principles of justice and benevolence. But his constituents' well being was not his motive nor his primary interest. For Torrin, their connection with him was too abstract for intimacy. It was his relationship with Lenore that remained his main concern and the source from which he molded his identity as husband, friend, lover, man, and even king. He ruled as he did because he thought it right but also because it made Lenore happy and him through her.

Torrin felt good, happier than he and Lenore had been in a long time despite the pressures of leadership. One such pressure, and it of a recurring nature, was currently being applied by Connor. Torrin sat in the central room of his royal home listening to his friend's appeal.

"Torrin, you must devote greater resources to production at the arsenal," urged Connor. "We need more weapons and more soldiers to carry them. We never know when an attack may come and of what size. We must be prepared. And if we had a larger army we could expand our sphere of influence. Surely you can see the wisdom in that?"

"Connor, you're doing an excellent job managing our military," answered Torrin, attempting to placate him without insult. "But at times I think you're more paranoid than me, your need for conquest is certainly greater. Sometimes I think your nights are filled with dreams of world domination. Try to remember, ours is only a defensive army. Besides, my wife tells me we simply have no more funds at this time to divert your way."

"That's correct, Connor," argued Lenore in a tone of mock grievance. "There's more to life than sword and spear and it all carries a price."

Torrin looked her way and smiled. Rich and royal, a purple gown wrapped her lovely frame, unrevealing but unavoidably curved and padded in provocative proportion. A shaft of sunlight streamed through the window's embrasure and sparkled against her modest jewelry, but pale in comparison to the cool green pleasure of her eyes. He never tired of looking at Lenore. She did not necessarily talk or dress or do anything in a way commonly characterized as sexually enticing, but to Torrin, she just was and uncommonly so. Certainly he noticed the temptation of other women, but never more than that. His love and respect for Lenore prevented infidelity, knowing also that if he were unfaithful, their relationship would be irrevocably changed. And he was certain that the pleasure advertised in the physical appeal of other women would be an empty horror compared to the satisfaction delivered with love by Lenore. She was all he needed and despite the fact they spent so much time together, they remained fresh to one another.

"Lenore, are you happy my love?" Torrin inquired, his question casual, but voiced with genuine concern. "Is there anything you need?"

"Yes, I'm very happy," sighed Lenore. "And I have all I need. But, well you know, I do still miss my mother, my family. It's hard sometimes. I wish I could see them again, even just to let them know I'm fine and they needn't worry about me."

"Well, as much as I would hate our separation, you could go back, for a visit I mean. I'm the exile, not you. I could send an escort back with you. Connor and Quinn are both free men. One of them could lead you back. You trust them, don't you?"

"Certainly, they're our friends. But I don't think we should be apart right now. Maybe later," finished Lenore, slightly downcast.

"My lord, if you wish, I could deliver a message to Lenore's parents at Gairloch," suggested Connor.

"Yes!" Lenore exclaimed excitedly. Delight abruptly returned to her features. "What a great idea. I'll start writing a letter immediately. Oh Connor, this is so wonderful of you. Thank you."

Connor reached Gairloch swiftly, eager to present his message—his message, not Lenore's. He destroyed her letter during his travel, it having been merely a pretense used to mask his true purpose.

Claiming to have urgent news from the west, he immediately requested an audience with the High Queen and waited impatiently for it to be granted. After keeping him waiting for several hours, she finally received him at the time of lamp-lighting.

"My attendants tell me you have information which you will reveal only to me and that you have been insufferably tight lipped about its nature and your identity," Bryana said in controlled aggravation. Connor did not look to be a royal messenger and she was naturally suspicious of him. "Who are you and what is your news? I'll decide what it's worth after I have heard it."

"Your majesty, I thank you for your gracious reception," he said in a voice free of the sarcasm he felt. "My name is Connor and I come to you from west of the Purl River with knowledge of events of grave importance to you. There is a rebellion under preparation in the village of New Hope. It is a rebellion led by Torrin Murgleys, your grandson. His army is small but growing and with designs against you. A handful of your soldiers could stop this rebellion before it starts, preventing a greater confrontation at a later date. I have seen him. He is a dangerous man, only a worry to you at present but one which could become a real threat if left unchecked."

Surprised frustration mixed with anger twisted across Bryana's face. As if frozen in the hostile scowling pose, she held it long before responding. "Torrin," she grumbled to no one in particular while mastering her surprise. "He is a curse I cannot shake. I should have listened to the prescient warnings that said this boy would prove to be my bane. But I showed him mercy. Now here the jackal is again nipping at my heels like a mad dog, foaming at the mouth and hungry for my blood. Tell me, is Torrin's brother with him?"

"His brother?" Connor returned in genuine confusion. "No."

"That at least is some comfort," said Bryana with curious relief. "You have done well in coming to me with this report and you will be rewarded in gold for the information."

"What will you do, my queen?" Connor pried.

She scoffed and said curtly, "That is not your concern. You may go." Connor was ushered out and Bryana turned to her minister of defense. "When you can spare the soldiers, soon but no hurry, send a contingent to New Hope and check out this man's story. If there is a rebellion in the works, crush it. If not, leave be and return."

Connor went quickly to his waiting horse. Its breath puffing in a fine white mist on the chilly night air, the fretting horse stamped restlessly, tugging at the bridle the groom held out for Connor. He took the rein and swung into the saddle. Then Connor's mount leapt forward under the spur, withdrawing from Gairloch in haste. He thought about lingering to see what Bryana would do, but if she did send soldiers, Connor did not want them too close on his heels. So he left, bound for New Hope and emotionally charged.

He did not consider himself a traitor, believing his devious actions were performed in the best interest of both New Hope and Torrin. Connor believed that if properly motivated, Torrin could vastly expand his power. But he was not motivated. Torrin was content in New Hope with his meager kingship, a kingdom that remained easy prey for a multitude of greater forces. So Connor devised this plan, thinking that a small attack on New Hope could possibly be defended against and if not, they should be able to recover quickly because they were still only poorly established. Either way, Torrin would finally see the threats around him and devote greater attention to defense and, with any luck, perhaps even conquest. If Torrin would retaliate by strengthening the power and glory of his realm, then the reward would be worth Connor's sacrifice.

"Connor, it's good to see you home." Torrin welcomed his friend with warm-hearted joy. "You look tired. Did you come straight here? Yes, well sit and have something to refresh yourself, some cider perhaps. So did your mission at Gairloch go well?"

"No, my Lord Torrin, it did not," answered Connor.

"What?" Torrin inquired, noticing that Connor's face was lined with more than simple fatigue. "Drop the formalities and tell me what happened. Was there trouble?"

"No real trouble, but I failed to deliver Lenore's letter. I was denied admittance to the castle and the guards refused to bring Lenore's parents to the front gate," he lied coolly, his face free of any evidence of his treachery. "I tried to persuade them but they were unyielding. I considered sneaking into the castle, but this seemed hopeless, not knowing my way around inside Gairloch much less where I could find Lenore's parents. I am sorry, Torrin. I have failed you."

"Oh you did no such thing," asserted Torrin, "but this is peculiar news. I don't understand why you should have been locked out. Was there some special event in the works that required this additional security or was there fear of some kind of attack?"

"I don't know. Others were allowed entry. Perhaps they knew I was your messenger, I couldn't determine their reasoning and what rumors I heard were uninformative. The letter may have gotten through though. I asked someone to deliver it for me and for a price they agreed," Connor fabricated. "I waited to see if a reply would come back to me, but it did not. I don't know if this was because the guards prevented it, the messenger cheated me, or if Lenore's parents refused to send one. Again, I apologize."

"This is sad news, and strange too," said Torrin. "It's not your fault though and I appreciate your effort. I will explain what happened to Lenore. It might be wise if, from now on, we try to obtain better reports of what transpires at Gairloch and abroad. Anyway, you've come back in good time. The raiders are active again and in great number. A large band of marauders has been reported north of here attacking travelers and terrorizing settlers. The reports are frightening, stories of rape, pillage, plunder, and destruction. Farmers have been robbed of their goods and animals. Many are said to have been killed and their women carried off. I've heard accounts of farmsteads that were deliberately torched and the occupants, even children, cruelly left to burn. Tomorrow, Quinn and I are taking most of the army up that way to hunt the animals down, restore order, and provide what comfort we can to those who have suffered. In my absence, you will act as regent and keep things under control here while we are gone. It shouldn't take over a week."

Fright hit Connor suddenly, fear over how his plan might be affected by this unforeseen turn of events. New Hope would be more vulnerable with the majority of its army away, but if an attack did come this would mean fewer military casualties and therefore quicker restoration.

"I should go with you," Connor offered.

"No. You've just returned from a difficult journey and you deserve a rest. Besides, I need you here to keep the home front safe. I know it's hard for you to leave the fighting to others and it will certainly be slower work without the benefit of your mighty sword arm, but we'll manage. Stay, relax. You've earned it. Now, I need my rest as well. Good night, Connor," said Torrin in dismissal.

Sleep came fitfully to Torrin that night. He awoke several times, dampened with sweat. His pulse was rapid, his breathing hard, and he was afraid. He shook with it, but could not define the source of his fear. If he was having nightmares again, they were forgotten with each awakening. All that clung to him was a feeling, an impression of being pursued by some dreadful phantom he could not identify. Lenore slept still beside him. He thought the sight of her sweet peaceful slumber should calm him, but for some reason it exacerbated his fear, making it even more pronounced. For a long time he lay awake in his bed, staring at a dark ceiling he could not see and waiting for the disturbing sensation of unexplained anxiety to pass.

By morning, after the horses were saddled and preparations made for their departure, Torrin's anxieties had faded to a dim memory. He did not mention to Lenore the irrational and nondescript fears that had attacked him during the night. It would only needlessly enhance what worries she already owned. Perhaps in saying goodbye to Lenore, he held their embrace longer than was customary, but she did not see anything unusual in it. She kissed him, told him to be careful, and with her love sent him on his way. Riding the now trademark white horse, leading his army out of New Hope, Torrin felt mulled by his wife's love. Its effect warmed his heart, sweetened his disposition, and added delightful spice to his life.

On the third day since their hunt began, Torrin's troop of soldiers found and engaged the raiders. During those three days, his sense of foreboding had grown heavy, weighing down on him like a pile of stones or the burden of a six-foot layer of earth. But it could not, he told himself, be his own death he felt prophesied. The battle was going well and nearly won. It seemed that Torrin and his axe were developing such a reputation that the enemy felt defeated before the first blow was ever struck.

Valiantly, Quinn fought beside Torrin and with his sword just ended the career of another outlaw. "Torrin, why the long face? The day is ours!" he shouted above the battle's din, the clash of arms, the cries of victory and of pain.

"Something's wrong," said Torrin, feeling cold as if a cloud had passed between him and the sun and refused to move off. "I can't explain it, but I know something is very wrong. I feel we must get back to New Hope, and quickly."

Quinn saw the concern in his friend's eyes and without question adopted it immediately as his own. "Let's finish it then and go," yelled Quinn before escalating the savage vigor of his combat.

When the fighting was finally done, Torrin led his company home at an urgent pace that the others were hard pressed to keep. But when they saw smoke rising in the distance over New Hope, all put their heels harder to their horse's flanks. Finally reaching their home and charging into the town's center, they realized they had come too late. Smoke still curled from the smoldering remains of buildings, but the fires were old and nearly extinguished. More than half the buildings were leveled or gutted or charred to some degree by fire. Dead littered the streets and now that the fires were out, the survivors were collecting the bodies of their friends, families, and neighbors. But the enemy was gone. The damage had been done.

Torrin drew rein, bringing his horse to a sudden halt. The animal tossed its head. The beast was sweating hard and foam dripped from its bit. Torrin swung to the ground and stared around him in horrified bewilderment. In a walk that turned abruptly into a run, Torrin moved through the streets calling out his wife's name in a wild blend of hope and terror. Quinn followed him, concerned for both of them.

Torrin found her at their home. Someone had laid her out on the wooden porch, the spear that had been used to pierce her abdomen rested with Lenore by her side. Walking now, wanting desperately to slow things down and delay the truth, he methodically took each step. By the time Torrin reached the top stair, the tremors in his hands spread profoundly to his heart.

The sight of Lenore's lifeless, bloodied form hit Torrin like a hammer to the chest, horrifying him beyond words, beyond thought, beyond belief. Those green eyes that had once held such life and beauty had already begun to subside within her skull. Her skin had turn gray and sagged upon protruding cheekbones. To any man still in possession of himself, her death was undeniable. But for Torrin the loss was too great for acceptance.

The blood having drained quickly from his face, Torrin's complexion was now a near match to hers. He fell on his knees beside Lenore and with trembling fingers desperately searched her neck for a pulse. Finding none, he frantically tore open her scarlet stained shirt and placed his ear to her chest. Nothing, not so much as even a faint murmur of life could be heard within her. She was dead, a fact he realized and could not alter.

Quinn stood wordlessly by him, his hands keeping time with his heart as they repeated an unconscious knotting and unclenching in grief-stricken, nervous pity. He turned to Connor, who had joined them. "What in the name of the World Spirit happened here?" asked Quinn in a controlled, despairing undertone. "Who did this? Why?"

Connor was covered in bloody wounds, some of which appeared serious and in need of immediate attention. "They attacked us and destroyed everything. With you gone, we weren't enough to stop them."

Guilt now joined Quinn's grief. "What, more outlaws?" he asked. "Where did they come from? We had no idea there were so many or that they were planning something like *this*."

"No," Connor continued. "They were from Gairloch, the High Queen's soldiers. Look. They left their banner behind," finished Connor, pointing to the identifying cloth staked in the street's center.

Cradling Lenore's lifeless body to his chest, Torrin did not react outwardly to this revelation but only continued to stroke his wife's hair, an act that she had so dearly enjoyed when alive. When he used to do this for her, she would always say what a good father he would be someday because he was so gentle and soothing in running his fingers through her hair and across her brow. It had always comforted her, helped her lose her worries and drift peacefully into sleep. Doing it for her used to comfort Torrin's own heart too, but not now. His emotions were in turmoil as he sat there thinking how he would never see her again, never feel the warmth of her skin again, never again taste her lips or see her smile or hear her sweet voice. The bright part of his life had been torn away, leaving Torrin robbed of what had been his cornerstone, the rock on which he had built his identity, his self-worth, and his hope. What was life without Lenore? What was he?

His sense of self collapsing in ruins, Torrin wondered how he would live without Lenore. He was nothing without her, he realized as a soul-swallowing emptiness enveloped his person. The purpose, joy, and identity Lenore had given Torrin's life was dying. He felt his spirit slowly dissolve, felt his identity and strength drain from him, leaving his soul bereft.

A man can only stand to have so much taken out from under his control, to have his life manipulated by others, to have the objects and sources of his love destroyed. There was a limit, and Torrin knew that he had reached it.

Connor made to follow Torrin when he finally left Lenore and went inside their house. But Quinn grabbed Connor's arm, stopping him. "Leave him be, Connor. He needs time to himself. We'll take care of things in the interim. Let's see to the others that need help and tend your own wounds. Then you can fill me in on exactly what happened here."

Into the second week after the attack, some semblance of order returned to New Hope, despite the conspicuous absence of its king. Torrin had not left the confines of his home since his return, not even for Lenore's burial. The people were hurting and angry, desperate for leadership and hope. Quinn did what he could but they wanted their king, wanted to know what he was going to do. Connor was already rebuilding the armory, putting every available man into the production of arms. Initially, Quinn thought Torrin's hermitic despair was understandably normal, but now he was growing worried both over Torrin's mood and that of New Hope.

Quinn greeted the guards Torrin had placed outside his bedchamber. "Morning, Boyd, Ryun. You two enjoying this easy detail while the rest of us are breaking our backs rebuilding the town?" he joked. "Is the king in?"

"He never leaves," answered Ryun. "Nor is he accepting visitors."

"He'll see me."

"That's what Connor said," Boyd scoffed, shaking his head. "The first time Connor went in, Torrin just ignored him, never said a word. Second time, Torrin damn near tore him apart. Sent Connor running out of here like a scared puppy with his tail tucked between his legs. Connor was as mad as a wet cat but he ain't been back. That's for damn sure."

Quinn laughed but without any real humor. "Well, make up your mind. Was Connor a cat or a dog? I'll take my chances and the blame too, if there is any. Now step aside and let me in."

Inside the bedchamber, nausea wrestled with Quinn as he stood with his back to the door and allowed himself time to let his eyes adjust to the quick change in light. His jaw muscles knotted, suppressing a strong urge to gag. The window was shuttered, the room ill lit and reeking like an open grave. What light leaked in around the shutters or guttered from the untrimmed wicks of melting candles showed that the room was filthy. Like hope, most of the furnishings were broken and their pieces, together with clothes and other personal items, lay strewn about the place. Plates of rotting, uneaten food rested upon the table beneath a swarm of ants and roaches. The air was foul with it and the smell of rancid sweat.

Torrin sat on the edge of his bed, elbows on knees and chin against chest. He looked like a man lost in memories without hope of finding his way back. Prodded by the sound of Quinn's intrusion, Torrin slowly raised his head. His eyes were red with exhaustion, grief and hate. Though internally Torrin's attention addressed his makeup, outwardly he appeared to have lost all interest in himself, not having shaved or bathed or changed his clothes in the two weeks since the day he found Lenore dead. His face was grimed with old dirt and distorted with agonized mourning. He was struggling with the death of Lenore, the destruction of his ideals and identity, and the violent emergence of a new perspective. This struggle raging within him and the prospect of a life without pleasure or hope seemed to leave Torrin with little energy for anything else.

Torrin threw Quinn a smoldering look filled with malice and doom. Then he growled, "Get out." The command was hard and heavy with emotion.

Bewildered, Quinn was confused, if not a little frightened, by Torrin's state. He hardly recognized Torrin and certainly did not know how to deal with him in his present condition. The strange sight had shaken him so much, that Quinn nearly did as Torrin ordered without saying a word. But he could not leave, could not turn his back on his friend even though he had no idea what to do for Torrin.

"I'm not leaving," Quinn said with firm resolve.

"Damn those incompetent bastards. Can't those guards keep anyone out? Can't they do anything right? What do you want?" snapped Torrin, his tone savage.

"You asked me that the first night we met," answered Quinn, feigning nonchalance. "Do you remember? The answer is still the same. I want you. I want our king back. I understand your grief; I feel it too, but this—this isn't healthy; it isn't right."

"Right," Torrin shot back. A scowl hooded his burning, red gaze and the word carried a stinging venom. "There is no *right*. It was an illusion she took with her when she died, along with all else that seemed good and pure in this lawless, wretched world. Before, when I was young and then when Lenore was with me, I had dreams. Sweet illusions of love and perfect unity, of justice, of one law to bind all people; a law that was larger than ourselves and that we were duty bound to follow. Now look what they've done to my dream. They've killed it, together with Lenore and the man I used to be. And as I lie dying, they shove reality in my face. Reality is that the strong determine truth and define justice while feeding the rest of us lies to keep us weak."

Torrin's raving fueled the escalation of Quinn's worries. He worried that Torrin had, in fact, gone mad. But still he clung to the hope that Torrin could be brought back from madness, that he could once again be depended upon.

"Torrin, pull yourself together," admonished Quinn. "Get control of yourself. Lenore's gone, I'm sorry, but it's true. Try to understand. She doesn't need you anymore, but we do. She wouldn't want this; she'd want you to restore New Hope. She was kind and strong; and she loved you. What would she say if she saw you like this or if she saw this pigsty?"

Quinn thought Torrin might explode in anger. But he didn't. Instead, he nodded wistfully and a sad smile touched his mouth. "You're right. She'd have a fit if she saw this mess and probably knock me up side the head for it. She always understood the truth better than me. She was practical and strong, you're right, and she was oh so loving." Tears began to spill from Torrin's eyes and meander down his cheeks. Bringing the heels of his hands to his face, Torrin ground the salty fluid into his grime-covered skin and cursed. "Damn these tears! When will they end? Why can't I stop them? It is weakness, damn it, weakness."

Quinn thought he had begun to pull Torrin out from his abysmal madness but he seemed now to be slipping back. "It is not weakness, Torrin. I have wept for her myself, more than you can know. It's natural to weep, but don't let it destroy you. Weep and live again."

"You stupid fool," responded Torrin bitterly. His voice held a rough edge cut with jagged serrations of anger and grief. His red-rimmed eyes possessed a frightening cast and beneath those hot blood-veined eyes lay a dark shadow of ruin. "You don't understand. You don't understand anything! You're like I was, one of the stupid passive herd. Don't you see? It's my fault. I'm responsible for Lenore's death just as much as that piss-drinking bitch Bryana. I was a slave to my old morality, believing in rights and justice, that they were principles commanding reverence, and crying like an invalid when others violated these principles. My old faith in these infantile notions made me weak, made me a victim and allowed me to let Lenore be killed. I refused to see life as it actually is, a struggle for power in a world where the strong survive and set the rules, where the powerful determine truth and value. Blinded, I did not even compete but lay myself open for exploitation and let my wife be killed. I loved her, damn it. And now she's gone and it's my fault, all because of my weakness."

"Then stop crying and be strong, and with that strength make yourself the law you claim is lacking from the world," Quinn said in a burst of anger equal to Torrin's wrath. "Say yes to strength and all that preserves and justifies it."

"You sound like the Beast," stated Torrin, suddenly calm again. He coughed and licked his chapped, blood-crusted lips. During his lamenting over the past two weeks, Torrin had absently gnawed at his lips so that they now remained split and swollen.

"The beast?" Quinn asked, confused.

"That is what I call it, and no longer disparagingly, at least not entirely. It is what I found within myself now that all else is dying. It was stronger than the rest of the voices despite the shackles I had placed on it over the years." Torrin stood and paced in a lion's prowl as if the room where a cage. "The Beast is a hunger; a desire; a will to power, to dominate, to rule unfettered by the false morality that before held me bound as a slave and left me as weak and docile as a newborn cow. I denied the truth of man's naturalness. Now the Beast roars, pushing me to break free of the herd. It is the old self that weeps and less each day. It grieves for Lenore and because it knows it too is dying. Still it wrestles with the Beast, though it knows it cannot win. Listen to me. I speak as if I am merely a spectator to this inner battle, but that is not true. I am both sides. It is the divisions of my soul which are at war."

Quinn did not pretend to understand all of what Torrin was saying. But he was reluctantly encouraged by this talk of power and that Torrin's tone and manner suggested that he was recovering his self-command. If so, then perhaps he could regain command of his kingdom. He still believed in Torrin and saw hope emerge again.

"Torrin, I know you believe you've failed Lenore and that you think everyone and everything you ever cared about has left you or betrayed you. But if you don't quit on me, on us, then I won't quit on you. That's a promise I'll never break. You are my lord and king and more than this you are my friend. I swear you can trust my loyalty and with it all those who serve you. For yourself, for Lenore, for all of us, be king again." With that, Quinn turned and exited the room, leaving Torrin to find himself.

Torrin did not find but rather forged himself. Over the next twenty-four hours, Torrin hammered at the wreckage of his soul, shaping it anew and fundamentally altering his person. Old anger blended with the new, stirring within him a need for vengeance and power. In this time of turmoil, his attention naturally returned to his home, to Gairloch, but for the comfort he would find in taking it. He wanted to take from Bryana what she valued as she had done to him. His hate and anger fed the Beast, but the more it ate the stronger its hunger grew, an unquenchable hunger for power. For years the Beast had been penned by the morality of the herd. Now it was finally free, shedding the dying remnants of Torrin's former self, casting off his old values and identity. He saw that his old self was something to be surpassed and that he was now entering a higher stage of human development. He was becoming supremely human. For humility he substituted pride. Contempt replaced sympathy, and in place of love, he would now hold no more than tolerance.

Reason is not the law giver, he told himself. It is only a tool, a facilitator. His soul was now ready to receive the real truth, that power and a will to acquire and wield it is the essence of nature and of the individual. The weak deny this truth. The strong embrace it.

Exalted, the Beast was growing increasingly rampant for spoil and victory. With self-asserting impulses for power, Torrin forged a new unbroken strength. He was becoming a man again. But in his new eyes, he was a more complete and noble man, a man of power and one avid for more. He banished from his soul all sentimental weakness and accepted the fact that life is essentially a matter of appropriation through conquest of the weak. It was not physical strength alone that Torrin desired and proposed to wield in his quest for power. The weak could also be conquered through the use of intellect and emotional manipulation. What he could not take by brute force may be won with cunning and wit.

Power became the focus of his desire. *Power is its own reward but it carries with it pleasure,* thought Torrin. *Power, the spirit is intoxicated and exalted by it. A man of power, of strength, of virtue, must be autonomous, conquering, and imperious. Yes, I will be king again but greater than before. I'll be a king who insists on taking things, taking power profoundly and variously. I shall be a true and noble king and what I do for my subjects shall not be granted out of pity or benevolence but rather from impulses stemming from a superabundance of power.*

The next day Torrin's mind, soul, and body were made ready for war. The discipline he had imposed on himself in coping with Lenore's death and its ramifications were severe and steadfast. As part of this discipline he established goals of power and revenge. He turned now with ferocious enthusiasm to planning their attainment. The task before him was to prepare his people for war, to convince them to adopt his goals as their own and serve him so that those frightful goals might be achieved. Torrin felt confident that he could dominate the people and bend them to his will. But even through his burning need for revenge, Torrin realized that, alone, New Hope's force would prove grossly inadequate in fulfilling his ambition.

He washed, shaved, and changed, so that he now looked the part of the vengeful king. Dressed in a rich display, he wore the dark blue robe of the Prelature altered by the addition of brightly polished pauldrons of articulated steal that crested his shoulders. Matching demi-gauntlets with protruding knuckle spikes covered the backs of his hands and wrists, leaving Torrin's leather-gloved fingers exposed. Tucked in the crook of his left arm he held a shining spangenhelm, a steel helmet constructed of four convex plates riveted into a framework of steel bands with large, splayed, decorative bat-like wings attached to the sides above hinged cheek plates. A pointed nasal piece protruded from the helmet's front and a flaring neck guard was fixed at its rear. A circlet of silver crowned his forehead and the medallion Torrin's father had given him years ago hung from his neck. It hung there not out of sentimentality but because it served as a good compliment to the rest of his attire and because Torrin had grown to appreciate its gaudiness. The tarnish had been removed from the medallion's silver wings, so that its metal now caught the light in a brilliant sheen.

"Sound the alarm!" Torrin barked to his guards, his voice sharp and boldly commanding.

Axe in hand, his back straight as a spear, and bearing himself proudly, Torrin stood hardened like iron. He stood on his porch facing into the street while below him Ryun blew the horn in the code that would both alert the town to danger and call them to assemble. People came running from everywhere, quick with remembered fear. Soldiers carried weapons, mothers carried babes, and others brought only their fear and confusion in response to the summons. They gathered round their king and, as if willed by his presence alone, a hush fell over the crowd.

Torrin held the stiff and silent pose overlong, intentionally making his audience uncomfortable. It was done to demonstrate clearly that his appearance was not an act designed to allay his subject's fears or cater to their needs. They were not to make demands of him and they were to understand that the situation was his to control. And before the use of words, Torrin wanted to visually communicate his strength, power, and control; a peril to his enemies and a blessing to his friends. A turbulent, black storm seemed to brew behind his baleful eyes and his bearing promised that Torrin could direct that storm like a whip, expertly controlling the release of its violent fury.

When he finally spoke, it was with a strong voice and one that held a kind of cold, commanding energy that instilled confidence and enthusiasm in his listeners. "I am your king," he began. Then he paused, letting the weight of his words fall upon the crowd. "And as my subjects, it is your role to follow my rule. You are to carry out my bidding and do as I say. You are to be when needed my sword, my plow, my labor, and my sweat. And I, as your king, am to lead you, to determine what is needed and in what proportion. It is my part to decide what is best for my kingdom and how to obtain it, to decide in what manner the kingdom can best be improved and to see that it is done. I am your protector, your benefactor, and your judge."

Again he paused and let his gaze sweep over the crowd, meeting and holding the eyes of individuals for seconds that felt painfully long to those touched by it. Continuing, his voice took on a louder pitch and an angry temper. "I judge that we have lived too long under the heel of the High Queen. I judge that you, my people, have lived too long in fear, a fear that makes us less than whole. My people have suffered and we have lost what we held dear. I judge that this loss shall be avenged, that the High Queen shall pay for her crimes against us. We will take from her in greater measure what she so cruelly stole from us. She deserves our hatred. Your rage is righteous, but only if we have the courage to express it."

Punctuating the point, Torrin brought his axe abruptly to the porch in a violent single blow, its curved blade biting deep into the wood decking. He released the handle, clenched the freed hand, and wrenched the crowd's attention back squarely, firmly on him.

"If we do nothing," he shouted, "if we skulk away like beaten dogs, then we have truly lost. And when we die, it will be a coward's death, a shame to ourselves and to our loved ones who proceeded us and to those who will be forced to follow. But if you remain loyal to me and follow me in the course I chart, I promise you victory and reward. A reward of vengeance and of wealth shall be yours. I swear it! And those who die for its attainment will die a hero's death—proud, honorable, and purposeful. So I call on you. Do not cower, waiting for the High Queen to strike the next blow, but rather stand up and arm yourselves against it. Anyone with honor, with courage, who would follow a king and receive the blessings of his victories, follow me!"

A roar of public support went up in answer. They were moved by his appeal and inspired by his example. He took their anger and their bloodlust and exalted it. Torrin whetted within them a voracious appetite, an appetite for revenge. He made them crave a violent form of compensation for their misery. Then seeing their hunger, he promised them a banquet on which to feast.

Torrin raised a hand, silencing the clamor. "Now go and prepare yourselves for greatness. I will call on you when my plan is ready."

Having dismissed the crowd, Torrin took up his axe. He went back within the enclosure of the modest throne room and began to pace the floor restlessly. He was certain that Quinn and Connor would trail and join him. They did. Hot on his heels, they entered the room, their faces set with worry and relief. They were relieved at Torrin's renewed spirit but worried because they failed to fully understand the nature or sanity of his intent.

Torrin met their anxious looks with a broad yet wicked smile. He was enlivened with aggressive energy, like an animal released on a bright spring morning after a long winter of confinement.

"Come in, come in," beckoned Torrin, "and drop those troubled expressions. Put away your doubts my friends. Have faith and heart. We have work to do, a kingdom to conquer and a queen to crush." In saying the last, he raised a hand before his impassioned face and slowly curled fingers emphatically into an angry clenched fist.

"Not Gairloch, not the High Queen? Torrin, that would be mad folly." Quinn spoke freely as was their custom during counsels with their king. "No matter how appealing the thought of retaliation might be, it is hopeless. Our army is made up of farmers, tradesmen, and merchants not career trained, seasoned warriors such as Gairloch has. If we march against the High Queen we will be annihilated. We'll be slaughtered. With only a meager fraction of her force, she could destroy ours. As it is, she doesn't even recognize us as a self-governing kingdom. In fact, at this point she would laugh at even the suggestion of calling New Hope a kingdom. We cannot challenge her and live. Our best hope is to rebuild and defend."

"The best defense is to kill your enemy before he has the chance to raise his sword against you," said Torrin in cold defiance.

"There's truth in both your words," interjected Connor. "You're right, Torrin, conquest is the best defense. The High Queen is an enemy that must someday be brought down. To her we are no more than criminals. And if we have the audacity to better ourselves, to improve the prison in which she has condemned us, we receive her wrath and suffer further persecution. At present we are nothing to her, a petty annoyance or an evil plaything. But we can change that. We should begin a campaign of conquest, but one with realistic expectations. We should begin by adding other villages, like Abandon, to our demesne. Then as our power grows, we conquer some of the lesser kingdoms and ultimately, one day in the future, even Gairloch."

"No," answered Torrin flatly. "Cowards and children are satisfied with small bites. I want Gairloch. And I want it now. But you're right, we can't do it alone. We need allies. And with them at my command we shall be victorious."

"Allies?" Quinn asked. "What allies would stand with us against the greatest power in the known land?"

Before answering, Torrin smiled greedily at the prospect of absorbing that power. "Those we make and those we take," he stated mysteriously, pausing briefly before clarification. "The elves first."

"Elves!" Connor exclaimed in disbelief. "They're only a legend concocted from fear and idiocy, a story to frighten children who misbehave. You can't be serious; elves exist only in people's irrational superstitions. For crying out loud, Torrin, don't put your faith in fantasy. Base your ambition on reality, on the strength of real men and their weapons." His words were rash, spoken without thinking and with too much liberty, placing himself dangerously close to committing a grave offense.

Like a lash, Connor received an icy stare from Torrin. But when he spoke, his tone remained congenial yet strong. "Connor, my friend, your ignorance is showing. The elves were real. They existed once; there's evidence enough of that. And there is good reason to suspect that they do in reality yet live, as rumors say, in the forest of Cravenwood. Certainly there are stories aplenty of people who have braved that forest never to return or whose mutilated bodies are later found floating in the Purl River. But Quinn told me once of a man who claimed to have seen an elf and lived to tell about it. I believe the elves exist. Are you saying that you doubt me?"

Before Connor could respond, Quinn spoke. "Yes, the elves are more than mere legend. And that man I spoke of told the truth. He ventured into Cravenwood and had the misfortune to see an elf but was lucky enough to only have been blinded for it. For some reason the elf did not kill this man, as would be their normal practice. Instead the elf burned out the man's eyes with a heated dagger so he could not report what he saw, even if he did find his way back out of the forest. By thunder, Torrin, all we know about the elves tells us that they're cruel savages with a hatred for anything human. What makes you think they would want to help us or that we should want them?"

"Because their savage power may be of tremendous use to us," Torrin answered. "Their animosity and reluctance to interact with humans is understandable. Indeed, history tells us that the elves should have no reason to hold any great love for humans. Their fate was similar to our own; we have both suffered persecution. Perhaps we can use that commonality to bind them to us and serve our ends." Torrin paused, studying Connor and Quinn, daring them to challenge him.

"I have decided," Torrin announced. "We will continue to build our own army and we will seek out the aid of the elves. Connor, you will stay here and commit everything we have to the creation of a real fighting force. Do not fail me. Quinn and I will go into Cravenwood to find the elves and secure an alliance."

"You propose to do this alone?" asked Conner with skepticism. "Would it not be wiser to take a troop of soldiers with you for protection?"

"No," insisted Torrin. "We do not want the elves to feel threatened by us or perceive us immediately as an enemy." Then he addressed them jointly and demanded finally, "Are you with me in this, or against me?"

Each man worked his private thoughts prior to answering. Quinn was encouraged by Torrin's fortitude, the new courage with which he now seemed to be coping with the loss of Lenore and the adversity New Hope faced. But the focus and direction Torrin had chosen for his newfound courage could very likely prove tragic as well. The idea of defeating the High Queen and occupying

Gairloch was absurd. Even seeking out the elves looked to be a hopeless venture, one that would end in failure if not death. But Quinn knew the obvious truth of these realities would not matter in his decision. He would do whatever he could to protect Torrin, but he would not forsake him. Quinn would remain true to the heart and glory of who he thought to be a great man. A man who was Quinn's king and more. Torrin and Lenore had been the nearest thing to family Quinn had known since the death of his grandmother. Now Lenore was gone too, leaving him only Torrin and New Hope. He belonged to both, cared for them, served them. He felt a bond to Torrin and a loyalty because of it. The two had been brothers-in-arms, fighting alongside one another in shared battles, and they had been also like brothers in more peaceful times, times he wished for now. Quinn hoped that time, distance, and the work involved in this journey would temper Torrin's grief and hostility. But if Torrin was to be involved in any sort of fight, he would be with him, faithfully at his side.

Connor's thoughts were more pragmatic and without the measure of Quinn's sentimental loyalty. He too considered Torrin's plan doomed to failure but was glad still that at least it was a plan of conquest no matter how unrealistic or premature its goal. If Torrin worked a miracle and made a success of his plan, then Connor intended to willingly share the glory. And if Torrin should be killed in his efforts to gain elfin assistance, this too could serve Connor. If Torrin and Quinn were dead, then Connor as acting regent in Torrin's absence could permanently assume the role of king.

"You needn't doubt me," Quinn said. "You know that. You know that I will support whatever you decide. I am with you, my friend. Besides, I've always been curious about Cravenwood, if the perils it's said to hold are real or imagined." Quinn smiled good naturedly and Torrin answered it with a grin of his own.

"Aye, it should be quite an adventure," said Connor. "And you can be sure that I will be doing my part here. At last we shall have a real army."

"Good," shouted Torrin, cheered by their support and eager for action. "We will leave in two days. That will give us time to make the necessary preparations and be sure that things are running smoothly here. I will bring back warriors; you can be sure of that. And you had better see to it that the army we already have gets the training they need in the time allowed. You understand me, Connor? Make it so, or your incompetence may well kill us all."

The waiting was difficult for Torrin, particularly the nights. He still battled against the despair of Lenore's death. Never having had many close relationships, either with friends or family, Torrin had felt alone before but never a loneliness this deep. At night it was the worst. The memories of how full Lenore had made his life seemed to hang in the dark and painfully remind him how empty his life now was.

Many people would have turned to the comfort of others or even to alcohol to stupefy the senses and take the edge off the tormenting loneliness. But not Torrin; he did not want to show weakness to others and he despised the escape of inebriation. The opiate he used to quiet his pain was a mixture of hate and a new lust for power. His need for power and revenge grew hour by hour, day by day. With it and brutal discipline, he pushed reflections of Lenore from his mind. He used anger and hatred to drive aside his grief and a stubborn longing for lost love. He ate, slept, and dreamed vengeful thoughts of how he would hurt Bryana and take her strength away. He played out his plans over and over in his mind. Gradually the nightmares receded and were replaced by visions of power and vengeance, visions that would prove to be a growing hunger he could never slake.

Chapter 6
Cravenwood

The pair traveled on horse, but lightly and at a comfortable pace. They followed the meandering curve of the Kankeen River, a tributary of the Purl. The landscape they passed through on their trek west was pleasant enough. A vast blanket of tall, thick grasses spread out before them, accented by colorful fireweed and honeysuckle. The fragrant flowers bloomed in red, yellow and white. Lining the banks of the Kankeen were towering river birch whose branches, unlike the darker hue of their trunks, gleamed like mottled silver behind soft green foliage. The birches were kept company by other trees, such as willows, alder, and swamp oak. Between the trees, the travelers saw the river catch the sun and glimmer in brilliant reflection of that heavenly light. The plains' tall grasses reached above the horse's hooves to their fetlocks. From this lush carpet, the riders inadvertently scared up a rabbit from time to time or drove a pheasant into flight from its cover.

Apart from the need that drove Torrin, the westward sojourn was peaceful and subdued. Both were taciturn men and not given to idle chatter, Quinn because he had lived the bulk of his life with a heavy stutter and Torrin because he was by nature a private man. But the silence between them held no discomfort for either man.

They were good enough friends not to feel pressured to talk if it was not their mood. And when they did converse, it was done freely, because they wanted to and not because they felt they should. There was one topic, however, Quinn was now careful to avoid—Lenore. He had met with failure and even hostility when earlier he had tried to engage Torrin in conversation about her.

Quinn missed Lenore and for him it would have helped to keep her memory alive by remembering her with someone else who had known and loved her. Yes, Quinn had loved Lenore, as his queen, as a friend, and as the wife of his best friend. And if not for Torrin, Quinn would have loved her romantically, as a suitor. His romantic infatuation with Lenore, Quinn had never made known to her or to anyone. It was a secret he would carry to his grave. Nor did Lenore ever give Quinn the slightest reason to suspect that she thought of him as anything more than a dear friend or perhaps a brother. But even that love had been precious to him and a hardship to lose. He had never before known a woman so honest and so lovely, and he suspected that he would never meet another like her.

When they reached the edge of Cravenwood, it was clear that the horses would no longer serve them. From here Torrin and Quinn would have to proceed on foot. The forest was a dense woodland overgrown with bramble. With the horses, they would never be able to maneuver their way through the thick tangle of trees, fallen wood and prickly shrub. They had anticipated this and decided they would abandon the horses, sending them back to New Hope. It would not have been practical or safe to tether the horses at the forest's edge, keeping them for Torrin and Quinn's return. The horses would undoubtedly become easy prey to thieves or predators, and the men had no idea how long their search might last. So Torrin plied his magic on the beasts, ordering the horses to return straight to New Hope. Connor had been warned of this and so would not be alarmed at the arrival of the riderless mounts.

Despite his larger size, Quinn quickly demonstrated himself to be the better woodsman of the pair. He moved among the trees with a dexterity and silence that seemed at odds with his large muscular build. Torrin attempted to imitate his stealth but without success. With a clamor that he thought must surely have alerted the whole forest to their presence, Torrin forced his way through the heavy growth of underbrush. Fighting through areas of thorny, interlaced branches, Torrin's hands and face became crisscrossed with a series of small, red scratches within a few short hours. And try as he might to tread lightly, his boots continued to rustle and crunch as each step disturbed the dead leaves underfoot and littering the forest floor. Up from the bushes, Torrin's plodding was from time to time answered by the scolding of a jay. Finally, adding to the noise and insult, Torrin's frustrated cursing set Quinn into a fit of uncontrollable laughter. He leaned against a twisted lichen-covered tree trunk, shaking with

SCOTT C. RISTAU

mirth until Torrin could not help but share in his laughter.

Gradually Torrin did manage to improve his forest skill as they continued snaking their way through the wood's green maze, moving quickly but without any set direction. They pushed forward, keeping their bearings and knowing that the elves were the subject of their quest but nothing about where they might be found.

Hours passed. The dark comes quickly in the woods, and the pair noted its rapid approach. The day had been unproductive and they were growing weary, but continued on in the dimming light. Neither Quinn nor Torrin wanted to stop yet because they were in a low area filled with waterlogged depressions that would make for a poor camp. The bog was filled with stinking, stagnant water and rotting deadwood. The muddied ground of the swamp sucked at their boots, making each step laborious and tiring.

At a gesture from Quinn, Torrin stopped and held still. Quinn cocked his head up and from side to side, testing the air.

"Do you smell that?" he asked in a quiet undertone.

"Yes. Now I do," breathed Torrin in a hushed voice. "It's smoke from a chimney or a cooking fire. Can you tell where it's coming from?"

"Aye," answered Quinn. "Follow me and go quietly."

After a time, they came on the source of the smoke, a small squarish house with a thatched roof made of straw and rushes. Smoke curled lazily from a vent in the hovel's roof, carrying with it a homey smell and the faint odor of cooked meat. Neither Torrin nor Quinn guessed this to be an elfin residence, but they remained alert. Not wanting to surprise the occupant into rash action, Quinn called out to the house.

A poorly tanned, leather hide hanging over the doorway was pulled aside by a thickset woman. She was human but still something of an oddity. Her very presence here was unusual as well as the fact that she seemed to reside alone. Her large, nondescript frame was draped in dirty rags and her hair hung in a tangle around her shoulders. She stepped outside, squinting in the faint light, craning her neck to see.

"Who's out there?" she called. "What do you want?"

"Two travelers," shouted Quinn, taking a step forward. "We would be most grateful if you could spare us some hospitality, a warm meal and a dry place to sleep."

"Stop right there!" she yelled, halting their approach. "Are you men?"

Quinn arched an eyebrow at the odd question and turned to Torrin. The two exchanged amused expressions before Quinn resumed his dialogue. "Yes. We are men, but you needn't fear us, madam. We will not harm you, and we can pay for the food and lodging."

"Oh I'm sure you can," she said, and then launched into a long, gleeful trill of laughter that sounded strangely like a bird's high-pitched warble. "But you can't come in yet. No, not yet. I'm not prepared for visitors, wasn't expecting handsome men to be delivered at my door this fine evening. Wait right there! Wait right there and I'll get you food. I'll set it outside the door so you can eat and I'll tell you when you may come inside."

So they waited, holding back their humor at the woman's fey comic behavior, behavior that suggested she might be slightly crazed. She would have to be to live in Cravenwood, Quinn supposed. The food was surprisingly delectable and Quinn ate hardily. Ever distrustful, Torrin picked at his plate but made his meal mainly of the black bread and raisins from his own pack of rations.

When she finally let them inside, the woman had changed. Her hair had been combed and something done to camouflage the gray; perhaps she had smeared it with soot from the fireplace. She had put on a dress that, although well made and in good repair, was much too youthful for her. It was cut high at the knee and low at the bodice, exposing the pale plump skin of her full bosom. Somehow her hands remained soiled but her wrinkled face had been washed and applied with paint and powder. Quinn found it sadly amusing, thinking her a senile, lonely old woman that was trying to be pretty for her company. Torrin, on the other hand, was openly disgusted by her appearance.

She set out cups filled with mulled wine that she herself gulped greedily, occasionally allowing the sweet, red liquid to spill from the corners of her mouth and trickle down her chin. Responding to the spillage, she licked her lips and smiled. Quinn drank in moderation and Torrin ignored the wine completely.

She introduced herself as Colleen and insisted on hugging the two men once she learned their names. Her garrulous nature quickly became evident as she talked extensively but without making a great deal of sense. Her moods were unstable, however, for Colleen also proved to be a harridan with an evil temper that would flash suddenly and almost exclusively at Torrin. As the evening passed, the tension built between Torrin and Colleen. He had been fighting her evasive and maddening chatter for over an hour in a failing attempt to determine if she knew anything about the elves.

"Madam," said Torrin, his voice dry and icy. "For the third time, have you ever actually seen an elf and if so, where?"

"Well of course I've seen them. How could I not; I make my home in

Cravenwood, don't I? But enough talk of me; tell me about you. Quinn, my dear sweet man, does your cup need refilling?" she asked after draining hers.

"Damn it, woman!" Torrin roared at her in frustrated impatience, leaning across the rickety table and pointing an angry finger. "Answer my question."

She reached and enveloped Torrin's pointed hand in hers. Her grip was surprisingly strong and it began to hurt. "Don't use that tone with me, boy. I'm no gentle cow you can whip like you would your mother."

Torrin's face went scarlet with anger. "What?" he demanded, wrenching his hand free. He leaped to his feet and knocked the bench on which he had sat to the floor with a clatter.

"That's right, you little shit," she snapped. "You're transparent. I see right through you, and you're no match for me. What's mine is mine and you'll have none of it. You're not a man. You're nothing but a foul little boy."

In the face of her attack, Torrin regained his composure and said with threatening malice, "And you're nothing but a crazy old shrew with nothing any man would ever want. But if you know anything about the elves, tell me now!"

Colleen did not exactly back down, but rather her mood changed so quickly it was as if she had been suddenly possessed by another woman. She smiled genuinely up at Torrin without any evidence of fear or mockery. Her voice was suddenly calm, almost sweet with affection. "Elves? Oh no, there are no elves I'm afraid. There never were. I'm sorry. But there is wine; would you like some more wine?"

Taken aback by this change, Torrin threw up his hands in exasperation. He was still angry and felt as if he had been made the fool.

Quinn got to his feet sluggishly, his eyelids drooping heavily. He wanted to end the discussion before the fight began again between Colleen and Torrin. "Let's get some sleep, shall we," he suggested in a very tired sounding voice.

They agreed to follow his advice, each claiming a section of the sparse floor space. Quinn fell to sleep the moment his body met the floor. Colleen seemed to do the same. But Torrin lay awake. He stared at a burning log resting on the supporting metal andirons in Colleen's fireplace. *Colleen*, mused Torrin, *that crazy old bat is a living insult to that lovely name.* Torrin's thoughts were angry still. Although an abrasive and mad woman, she did not appear dangerous, but for some reason Torrin did not trust her. He had also come to hate Colleen and was in general growing very tired of holding back his hate and denying it expression.

About an hour later, Colleen stirred. She rose quietly and went outside. Probably to relieve herself, thought Torrin, as she had drunk heavily before retiring. Shortly after she was out the door, Torrin followed.

She walked a few yards from the house and, bending over, unlocked a door that opened on a series of stairs descending beneath the ground's surface. *It must be a root cellar*, thought Torrin, *and she's gone after more wine*. She took the stairs and pulled the door closed after her. Torrin waited a few minutes more and then resumed his pursuit. The wooden door was aged and gray but still solid. He felt oil on the hinges and he hoped it would be proof against the creaking of rusted metal. The door lifted a few inches, no sound, not locked. A yellow stream of light escaping the cracked door became a flood as Torrin lifted the gate fully open and found himself facing Colleen.

For Torrin it was one of those moments when a person is caught off guard, knowing he has committed a critical error, and everything seems to slow down so that the mind can catch up with its environment. It all seemed to be happening in slow motion, though it took no more time than a heartbeat. Colleen grinned with satisfaction and cast a handful of fine white powder in Torrin's face. An impulsive inhalation, in the reflex of surprise, carried the powder through Torrin's nose and mouth, deep into his lungs, and then quickly into his bloodstream where it continued its rapid distribution. He could almost feel the chemical working its way through his body, a tingling numbness that seemed to spread pervasively into his extremities and on up to his brain. He tried to lift his hand to wipe the powder from his face but could not feel his arm respond to the mental command. His vision blurred; Torrin blinked but it failed to clear. He sensed himself falling, and then nothing else.

When consciousness returned, it did so imperfectly. Torrin's eyes rolled in their sockets, split open, and struggled to focus. He was dimly aware of a deep ache in his wrists and ankles and a gentle throbbing at his temples. His mind confused, it required a few minutes for Torrin to realize the cause of these unpleasant sensations. His wrists and ankles were tied together with a leather cord. Ropes had been tied, one to his ankles and one to his wrists, and used to suspend Torrin upside down from the underground ceiling of Colleen's cellar. The length of the rope securing his hands measured longer, so that his head hung slightly lower than the rest of his body. Pulled by gravity, blood flowed to this low point, a fact that accounted for the heavy pulse of engorged veins throbbing in his neck and the pain across his brow.

There were shelves around the room set with labeled jars and chalky-white pottery. No, not pottery, Torrin realized. They were bones, some human, some not. Colleen used this cellar for more than merely storing food and wine. She was here too, behind a tall wooden table and wearing a brown leather apron.

She had something in her hand, a cleaver. She brought it down against the table again and again, butchering the carcass of some animal. There was surprisingly little blood and much of the flesh had already been stripped away from the bones. From time to time she paused in her dissection to put pieces of the carcass into a pot, presumably to boil off the remaining meat. Sluggishly, Torrin realized there was a foot on the table, resting on its side, one that could not have belonged to an animal. It was a human foot.

Not Quinn, Torrin hoped but without the intensity of horror his drowsy mind told him he ought to feel. With vision that kept shifting in and out of focus, he observed all this with a strange kind of detachment, an effect of the drug that had knocked him out. His emotions were numb. He knew that there was cause for fear, disgust, and anger, but these feelings simply refused to manifest themselves in any great proportion. The drug had left him emotionally paralyzed and his mind operating with profound lethargy, slow and uncaring. He was aware of danger yet felt safe and sleepy.

Colleen looked up from her work and saw that Torrin's eyes were open.

"You're awake," said Colleen, pushing the remaining body parts into a pot and toweling off her hands. "Not so arrogant any more, are you? You probably don't find me so offensive anymore either. I wish it didn't have to be this way. I don't like to use the drugs. I want people to like me for who I am. And the blood isn't as good when you use the drugs; it takes away from the purity. It's just not as pleasurable then. Fear adds ambience and flavor to the sustenance."

She picked up a bleached white skull and moved across to a corner of the room in which a small pen was located. Inside the pen, tethered against any movement, was a young deer, alive but weak. Its eyes, big and brown, were glazed with a look of hopeless despair. A tube had been inserted within one of the deer's major arteries. Colleen loosened the clamp on the tube and allowed the blood to pump into the hollow human skull. She used it as a cup, gulping down the scarlet liquid with a passionate indulgence.

"This is my favorite drinking vessel," explained Colleen holding up the skull. "It was my husband and my first. He wasn't able to adjust to life here as well as me. But sometimes I wonder if maybe he wasn't right, that I should leave these woods for a castle or village somewhere. I get so little company here and I often have to go extended periods without human dinner guests." She smiled, picked up a knife, and moved beside Torrin.

The knife's edge had been honed razor sharp, so that even a gentle touch was enough to break the skin. Watching Colleen, he felt the cool metal against his neck. But it did not penetrate. She smiled and moved the knife elsewhere, scraping over a small spot on his ribs. Her action left something on the flat of the blade, something slick and wet. Not his flesh, it was a leach, large and black. Colleen dropped the parasite into her mouth and chewed, one vampire feeding on another. Turning away, Torrin realized now that he was naked and covered in leaches, their dark slimy bodies dotting his arms, legs, and torso. His recognition of this fact lacked a complete and appreciative understanding. The sight sickened a part of his mind but the powdery white drug had anesthetized his full capacity for revulsion, as well as action.

Colleen was speaking again and Torrin dragged his muddled attention back to face her.

"...So you see, you and I are much alike," said Colleen. Torrin had missed hearing why she thought so. "And your friend Quinn shares my appetites, though he doesn't know it. The wine he drank was fortified with blood and laced with something to make him sleep. Plus, I'll wager that the meal he ate was not a meat he'd had before. What I take from others gives me strength. We're all victims of time, but I've fought it much longer and more successfully than most. My potions and elixirs are powerful but it's the blood that's the key. The key to youth, energy, and mastery. All that I have and all that..."

Victim, strength, power, mastery. These words broke through Torrin's drug-induced stupor to spark something inside his soul. *Strength, power, mastery.* It was as if someone were calling him awake by calling his name. *Strength, power, mastery.* That was his essence, who he was and what he desired. *Strength, power, mastery.* Like a catalyst, it set his magic in motion, but the confusion left by the drug robbed Torrin of his normal control. Unstructured and unprecedented sorcerous energy flowed within him, building with intense pressure to a cataclysmic breaking point. *Strength, power, mastery.* His impaired thinking told Torrin anything was possible. And that thought, blurred and agitated though it was, proved all the trigger necessary for the release of magic. Wild and reckless, his magic unleashed itself in a willful fury.

It hit Colleen first as an uncontrollable urge to move her bowels, to which her body obediently and immediately responded only to be quickly assaulted again by more magic. She was struck next at the feet, where the magic turned her flesh to stone with the effect spreading rapidly up her legs to the rest of her body but still slowly enough for Colleen to appreciate the horror and pain of this extraordinary spell. Her screams died shortly before the transformation reached her heart.

Blue wizard's fire crackled as it danced and crawled over Torrin's skin, wrapping itself about him like lightening and glowing like ignited natural gas. It encircled him with brighter and brighter coils, building strength and burning the leeches from his body. The leather cords snapped, dropping Torrin to the ground and detonating the explosive discharge of concentrated, undisciplined wizardry. Thunderbolts of magic energy ricocheted around the room with the force of a lightening blast gone mad, destroying the cellar's contents and shattering the stone statue that had been Colleen.

The surge of power died and calm settled back upon the ruined cellar. Torrin felt invigorated rather than drained by the experience, refreshed by the expression of power and eager to pursue his passions. He had been cleansed of the drug; its mind-numbing effects were gone.

Torrin denied the possibility that the drug had caused this wondrous release of magic, magic cast in spells he had never used before. Drugs are a weakness, a weakness that is passed on to the user. It must have been the challenge he faced that caused him to use his magic in these new and potent ways. *Yes,* thought Torrin. *The greater the challenge, the stronger I force myself to become. I grow mightier through what I overcome, more powerful by what I defeat.*

He rose, collected his clothes, and dressed. Pausing briefly before ascending the stairs, he looked around the room with satisfaction. Colleen, his intended victim, was dead, her altered form shattered. The rubble of her fragmented stone body littered the floor together with the broken bits of furnishings, boxes, and jars. The deer was dead as well. Torrin did not recall intending its death, but the animal had been caught in the blast and victim to the shower of debris. *Such is the fate of the weak,* thought Torrin.

Back at the house and to his great relief, Torrin discovered Quinn still there, sleeping soundly and undisturbed. From what he could ascertain, Quinn had suffered no lasting ill effect from Colleen's meat and drink. For reasons not entirely clear, Torrin decided against telling Quinn of the night's happenings or of what had become of Colleen. He did not think such information would sit well with Quinn's stomach. So Torrin made an excuse for her absence and later that morning the pair resumed their search for the elves.

Days passed one into the next with no hint of an elfin presence. Much to their frustration, Quinn's tracking powers and Torrin's wizard skill yielded nothing. Torrin used his magic through the forest creatures from hawks to deer to even mice, probing their weak minds for some clue about the elves and searching for them through the animal's eyes and other senses. But it was all to no avail. Another man would have seen the folly of this hunt—Quinn certainly did—and given up. But not Torrin, he remained driven by his hateful ambitions.

They were deep within the heart of Cravenwood's wilderness now and the woodland seemed to assume an eerie, indescribable change. Ahead of them, a flock of large black carrion crows started up from the carcass of a dead animal. *Not unusual in the forest, or anywhere for that matter*, thought Torrin. *The weak die and the strong survive. And scavengers take what spoil they can steal from the greater predator's kill.* But still a discomfort clung to them that had nothing to do with biting insects, soiled clothes and muddy boots, or heat and dirty sweat. There was an ill feeling in the air, like that preceding thunderstorms or tornados. But the sky shown bright and peaceful, its blue expanse a denial of any approaching danger.

Both the travelers shared this uneasiness in subtly different ways but kept it unspoken because neither could identify a cause to which the sensation could logically be attributed. Quinn halted their progress with increased frequency, listening and scenting the air. Each time he would shrug and move on, finding nothing tangibly out of the ordinary that he could point to or name. But the disturbing feeling persisted, a perception of being studied by unseen watchers and of an impending mortal threat that would come from somewhere just out of sight, like an arrow in the dark. It was the kind of feeling that prickles the hair on the back of one's neck and keeps one constantly looking over his shoulder. Out of the corner of his eye, Torrin swore to himself that he would catch unexplained movement, shadows that seemed to slip between the trees. But when he turned to focus, there was nothing.

"Damn," Torrin cursed under his breath.

"What's wrong?" asked Quinn, equally hushed.

"I don't know. But something is."

"You feel it too then," Quinn whispered. "It's said these woods are haunted and I'm beginning to believe it. I can almost feel their icy fingers on my skin. Though it sounds ridiculous, it must be ghosts. I know we're being watched, but I can't see or smell or hear who's doing it. And it's everywhere, like we're surrounded. Unless I'm going mad, I'd say we're in real danger. This, though little else, my senses do tell me."

When the arrow finally came, Torrin saw it. His awareness heightened against an uncertain menace, he heard the hum of the released bowstring and in a flash recognized the shaft shooting toward Quinn. Without thought or even doubt, he twisted his body into the arrow's path and miraculously plucked it from the air. Quinn saw it then and dived for cover, dragging Torrin with him still clutching the barbed and feathered length of ash.

Quinn brought out his dagger, but held it without much hope. He knew, as Torrin did, that the arrow must have come from elves, who no doubt now had them pinned down. Torrin reviewed his own arsenal of weapons, considering what magic would best serve him in this crisis. Although threatened, he still wanted to offer some show of friendship as well as force. He still hoped to gain an alliance with the elves. At the moment, it seemed a fool's hope, but not as foolish seeming as the act which followed.

Torrin stood up. With his arms spread wide and his chest exposed, he called on his magic to invoke nothing more substantial than a god-like corona about himself. He followed it with spells of warding and those designed for persuasion and to instill fear. It was uncertain what effect this had other than to hold off his immediate death and to keep Quinn from pulling him back to the ground beside him.

The elves came forward and at last into view. Torrin studied their appearance with quick wonder. Their height was less than that of the average human, their skin darker. Only males were present in this hunting party. They were dressed in simple greens and browns that blended with the forest, but Torrin suspected magic more than wardrobe was the source of their expert camouflage. There were ten in the group, positioned uniformly around Torrin and Quinn and advancing with slow caution, tightening their circle. At ready, they held smoothly contoured yew longbows fitted with arrows tipped by barbed or leaf-shaped heads. At the elves' backs, the colorfully dyed feathered flights of more arrows stood above cylindrical quivers of fine leather. Several of the elves were armed also with scimitars.

Quinn rose to his feet next to Torrin and eyed the long sweeping curve of the sword blades with a warrior's appreciation. He visualized how they might be used for slashing by bringing the entire blade across a target to produce heavy cuts or for making draw cuts that would be made even deeper by the barbed tooth forged at the tip of some of the blades.

With them, and as soft footed as the elves, were a pair of large hunting cats whose backs reached just above Torrin's knee. Unlike the elves, the cats seemed to have taken an immediate fondness for Torrin. Bright eyes blinking with curiosity and tails swishing, they rubbed their furred sides against his legs, ostensibly with affection. At least he hoped it was affection and they were not simply getting acquainted with what they saw as dinner.

By now Torrin had dropped the magical corona and Quinn his dagger. Face to face with Torrin stood an elf who gave Torrin the impression that he was the leader of this party and perhaps even a man of greater importance among the elves. He and his fellows all had raven black hair cut short so that it revealed their high pointed ears. Their eyes were slanted and of a dark color. Overall, Torrin considered the elves to be a handsome race. The leader directed an order at one of his men in a fascinating yet baffling language which Torrin ached to learn but for which he could not risk making physical contact at this point.

Carrying out the order to bind Quinn's arms, the man's action explained the other's words. To his regret Quinn resisted, falling victim to a blinding flurry of kicks and punches delivered with graceful yet devastating fighting skill. The elves' slight build belied their strength, which together with their speed and agility quickly brought the much larger Quinn to his knees. Torrin grabbed the leader, preparing to invoke his magic to learn his language but stopped in quick response to the dagger pressing at his throat.

"Wait. I'm not attacking. I'm a wizard. Let me use my magic to communicate," Torrin pleaded holding his hands up, palms open.

The leader looked Torrin up and down with great disdain, visibly regarding him with aloof contempt. "We understand you, human," he said, making the word "human" sound like a curse. "Now hold your tongue or be gagged. You will let us bind your arms and blindfold you or else you'll give us the pleasure of killing you here and now."

Torrin and Quinn did as they were instructed and soon found themselves being roughly escorted through the forest. The sun passed its zenith and moved on into early evening before they halted. With the removal of the blindfolds, Quinn's eyes beheld a spectacular sight never to be forgotten. They stood at the edge of a clearing populated by dozens of beautiful four-cornered tents with high central peaks and dyed in a myriad of bright colors. Elves moved about the tents, engaged in the daily rituals of living. It was staggering that such a rich and vivid colony could exist undetected. No doubt the elves chose to use men and magic to guard their home rather than give up the luxuries they owned in order to remain less conspicuous.

They walked slowly through the colony. Finally, their captors brought Torrin and Quinn before a large tent designed with overlapping colored streaks of black, spruce green, and gray. Outside the tent, red banners embroidered in gold fluttered in the light breeze. Within the colony, as well as outside this tent, sentries were absent and likely unnecessary. It seemed obvious that no enemy would get this far past the elves' woodland defenses.

They were ushered within the tent and its interior proved even more sumptuous. Soft furs and rugs carpeted the floor and above these lay a rainbow of large and lavish overstuffed pillows. Torrin and Quinn were made to sit in the tent's center beside a low metal brazier that burned with some form of coal in a fire that was virtually without smoke.

Despite their luxurious surroundings, Quinn remained tense, waiting for the hammer to fall. He caught Torrin's eye and mouthed the words, "We are dead men."

They were left guarded but otherwise alone for an uncomfortably long time, during which they had been forbidden to speak. Night had fallen and wrapped the colony in its dark embrace. Bored with waiting on death, Quinn's head hung forward as if he might be dozing. Torrin, however, remained alert, still intent on turning this situation to his advantage and purpose.

Both men were interrupted from their diversions by the arrival of others. Several elfin men and women entered and filled the tent. With all that was at stake and everything happening around him, Torrin was amazed at himself for what first caught and held his thoughts. The women, they were beautiful beyond belief. Their dark skin lovely against their fine silk coverings, they walked with a delicate grace and a pleasant sway to their narrow hips. Some wore their long black hair plaited with bright ribbons and flowers. All were slender and seemed to carry themselves with a shy diffidence that was strangely enticing. But Torrin forced his attention away from such thoughts and back to more critical issues.

A man positioned himself directly across from Torrin, sitting on the floor against the large pillows. He was older than Torrin, but their racial differences made it difficult to guess by how much. Following him, the other elves found their seats as well, all in unnerving silence.

When the elf opposite Torrin spoke, he commanded the room's full attention. His words were voiced in the human tongue, precise and calm but with an unmistakable strength behind them. There was nothing impulsive or over quick in his manner. He was not the kind of man who flared in violent, expressive outbursts of uncontrolled emotion. Not to imply that he was incapable of violence, but only that it would be carried out with a cool head and a calculating mind. He was a man who acknowledged the virtue of emotion and pleasure, but not its rash expression.

"This is Kweiyang and I am its Overlord. My name is Yoshindo. Your life was mercifully spared for this meeting and is now in my hands. Resign yourself to that fact and we can talk in peace like civilized men. I am curious about you. You are not like the other humans we've encountered in our woods and I'm told you claim to be a wizard, even showed some of your power." He paused, staring at Torrin. "Or was it all of your power?"

"It was not," Torrin answered stonily. "And it could be argued that I spared the lives of your men rather than the reverse. But I do not mean to offend or threaten you. That is not my purpose for being here."

"Which brings us to an interesting point. What exactly is your purpose here?" asked Yoshindo. "Who are you to trespass on our land, and what made you think we would allow it?"

"My name is Torrin Murgleys and my companion's name is Quinn. Please forgive our trespass. I came here to find you, because I need your help and because you will soon need mine. I am not your enemy but you do have one, an enemy we share and one who prepares to someday march against us both."

Torrin went on to explain in an extravagant blend of truth and lies how High Queen Bryana had attacked his village, that she was ravenous in her cruel conquest and abused her own people with impunity. Torrin said that Bryana would not be content with conquering the human lands, that she would one day extirpate the elves, root them out and utterly destroy them. But his vague threats were not enough.

"You can't believe that we would help you," said Yoshindo. "Humans have been a plague to my people for as far back as your history dates. If the humans had come to our ancestors, as you have come to us, they might have gained in friendship what they took in war. But after what the humans did to our fathers, how can we now, or ever, be expected to trust a human? Our ancestors were a proud and noble people reduced and broken by the human's treacherous and predatory greed. Still, we have reason to glory in the achievements of our ancestors and behold with a heavy heart the decline of our great race. Our hearts are heavy with sadness and with anger. We lament the fate of our ancestors and still today burn with an angry desire to avenge the wrongs visited upon them by the humans. You are human and carry with you a legacy of destruction. Everywhere the earth was touched by human hands, a mark of injury was left. I can't believe that your race has changed or improved. You separate yourselves from nature and wall yourselves up in towers and castles, where a man's heart must surely grow hard like the stone he inhabits. Through our nearness to nature we remain in touch with its sacred, unseen powers and with the wisdom of Navar. We acknowledge the intrinsic value of all creatures, using only deadwood for our fires and using without waste all that we kill. But the humans never shared this respect, not for beast, not for elves, not even for their own kind. How could we join with you in anything, let alone something so great as a commitment to war and all the damage it would cause?"

Torrin pulled a solemn mask across his face to hide the pleasure he felt inside. He believed that what he had learned about the elves would be enough to twist them to his purpose. Letting his voice take on the rhythm of a bard or prophet, he began to lay a snare for them.

"My heart is like a stone, hardened with determination and heavy with knowledge and power. And it is my heart through which the World Spirit, or Navar as you call him, has revealed his purpose. I will redeem your people together with my own and we shall create in our combined image a new world order. And it is not only in the elves' best interest to serve me in the achievement of this goal but it is for us all a moral imperative. Your principles and beliefs regarding nature are close to that of the World Spirit, but they possess a fundamental flaw which prevents you from realizing the truth. The truth is that nothing, not beast, not tree, not river, not human, nor even an elf has intrinsic value. None of these things have independent and inherent value.

"To demonstrate, I ask that you try to imagine a single elf isolated somewhere in a black, empty void, cut off from all other life. What value can this elf be said to have? What significant difference does his existence make? In what meaningful way is he able to define himself? Qualities such as fatherly, friendly, respectful, brave, and honest cannot be applied to him because his isolation prevents him from exhibiting these worthy traits or any other. This elf would need more than food and water to keep him alive. He needs a sense of self. And that can only come through interaction with other sentient beings, people and other living creatures.

"Our value is determined by how we interact with others, in a very real way, we are our relationships. A tree has value because of the oxygen, food, and beauty it provides the elves and likewise in return the tree values the elves. People, particularly we leaders, are the focus and creators of value. It is our right, indeed our fundamental nature, to maximize the utility, value, or pleasure of a thing regardless of if it is a community of plants or of elves. The best qualified individuals, aesthetic experts if you will, must determine and implement the plans which will provide for the greatest good or highest value for ourselves and our people. Yoshindo, you and I are those experts. And we cannot claim to value nature or other people or even to be moral unless we do just that, unless we implement such plans. That means we must stand up and fight together against those who would oppress us. Otherwise we are nothing but doomed.

"It is clear to me that the elves are a noble people, who should not be penned up and denied their liberty. Even a prison as lovely as this forest is still a prison. And so imprisoned, contentment cannot be expected from the elves. Nor can they be expected to grow and prosper. My rule will recognize you as equals and I offer you the chance to live with my people as such. Help me to take back what is rightfully ours."

Quinn didn't understand all that was being said, but still he thought he saw a flaw in Torrin's example about the isolated elf. The World Spirit, not the elf, is the focus and creator of value. And even isolated from all other life, the elf could still grow in value through his relationship with the World Spirit. But Quinn didn't think Torrin would appreciate having this question raised at this particular moment and the elves did not look as if they wanted to be troubled with such questions either. Something was happening to them. The elves seemed entranced, as if they had become intoxicated as they drank in Torrin's words. And as Torrin went on to describe the threat posed by the High Queen, Quinn wondered how Torrin could know of the plots he claimed she was making against the elves. He suspected Torrin was weaving lies into his arguments. Quinn knew Torrin's motives were good, but worried that a strategy of lies would prove disastrous, corrupting their goals and endangering their friendships.

Torrin's words acted like a drug. The expressions of the elves had gone from suspicion and hostility into curiosity and finally awe. They began to wonder if this human might not actually be an oracle of Navar and perhaps even the prophesied Redeemer. Like a fledged arrow to its mark, his words went straight to the elves' collective heart. These words, received almost like a revelation, promised the attainment of an age-old ambition in a way that could actually be believed. There were shades of apprehension which yet lingered in the air, but many could be seen nodding with inspired emphasis.

"We are thankful that you have come here to talk to us in a way we can understand," said Yoshindo. "It is the first time a human has ever done that. I also believe that it was the will of Navar that we should meet together this day. We were both able to speak our minds freely and we have listened to what you had to say. For the first time elves and humans spoke in peace as equals and I find this gives me great joy. There was a time, as we all know, when my ancestors were persecuted by yours, driven from the land they loved to find solace in another. You say that some things have changed. You say that not all humans are evil but that the human leader is, that she has driven you from your home and torments even her own people. We continue to listen. You say that you will help us retake what was ours if we help you do the same, and that we will all share the reward thereafter. You say that it is right to do this. We see the pain in your eyes and hear the conviction in your tone. You say that the evil High Queen is moving to war, that she is preparing to invade yet again the new home we have found and that your wife was among the first casualties of this invasion. The ambition and avarice of the humans destroyed our ancient way of life and now that they see our new lands and suspect us, they assemble for the final conquest. We have listened to what you had to say, but what you propose is a heavy matter. You must give us time to consider it thoroughly. We will give you our decision tomorrow."

"What is there to consider? He is a human and cannot be trusted," said an angry voice, trenchantly. It was the leader of the hunting party that had discovered Torrin and Quinn in the woods.

"Chiang, curb your insolence," Yoshindo commanded coldly and with a look of lightening. "I trust this human and we will consider the merit of his proposal." His anger having died, Yoshindo turned his attention back to Torrin. "Please forgive Chiang. He is at times beset with delusions that Kweiyang would be better served with him as Overlord. But rest assured that you and your man Quinn are welcome here. I, and therefore all the elves, regard you as friends. You will be treated as honored guests, given food and whatever other comforts you may require. Speaking of which, I have noticed the interest you seem to have taken in my wife," said Yoshindo, gesturing to the young woman at his right.

Torrin's heart stopped and his face went for a moment quite bloodless. It was true, he had found his gaze drawn to her again and again throughout the evening. Suspecting, but not knowing she was Yoshindo's wife, Torrin had repeatedly caressed this exquisite woman with his eyes. Though an Overlord's wife, her raiment was merely a simple white dress. However, she made the plain garment gorgeous. In striking contrast, dark black hair that looked as soft as silk lay loose and long about her shoulders. A slit skirt exposed a pair of extremely well formed legs and small delicate feet. Her body was petite and her face magnificent. Even now her composure seemed unruffled. She looked up at Torrin from behind the overhang of her lovely hair with long slanted eyes, bright and interested, and a demure dimple touched her cheeks all in a very attractive combination. The sight of her brought back Torrin's color and the beating of his heart. He had no interest in or illusions of love. It was desire he felt and pleasure he wanted, a pleasure which at this moment she seemed uniquely capable of providing.

"Don't be concerned," said Yoshindo. "I am pleased that you find her attractive. My wife's name is Midori."

She acknowledged the introduction with a slight nod and a faint smile that held a hint of playful mischief.

"We have been married only a short while," continued Yoshindo, "but I value her tremendously; she is very dear to me. If Midori is willing, the two of you have my blessing to share each other's pleasures this evening." He paused, taking Midori's hand and smiling at Torrin's shocked expression. "I see that you are surprised; don't be. Our ways are different from your own, different even from our ancestors. As a people, we had to make certain adjustments in our way of life in order to survive, adjustments which now seem natural to us, and desirable. I trust you, I suspect that Midori is intrigued by you, and I have no jealousy that would oppose what passions you might share. Of course no children can be allowed to come of this union and magic will be used to prevent that from happening. We can't allow our race to be polluted."

"You realize that I am a form of that pollution, a human with impure elfin blood, a descendant of some ancient intercourse between human and elf." Torrin responded, still somewhat amazed by this discussion of sharing another man's wife and the fact that the topic was discussed before a crowd of people.

"Yes," said Yoshindo. "I understand your heritage and there was no offense intended in my comment. I simply want you to understand that I wish to maintain the integrity of my race. I do not, however, consider you inferior because your magic stems from the elves. In fact, I am very curious about your being a wizard. You see, the elves have lost that ability. We no longer possess the art of making wizards. And our common magic has also changed significantly over the generations. We have lost many skills we once had and gained others we did not before possess, such as the ability of our women to regulate their fertility. There is much we have to learn from one another, but we cannot do it all in one evening. For tonight, I know enough to welcome you as friends and offer you our hospitality."

Not letting the opportunity pass him by again, Torrin seized it. "I am touched by the welcome you have extended us and I hope that we can join together in the campaign against the High Queen of Gairloch. Before retiring, I would like to clean up and have something to eat, if this can be accommodated." Torrin turned again to look at Yoshindo's wife, a woman who was a uniquely perfect blend of innocence and sensuality. "And Midori, I would be very honored if you would agree to share that meal with me."

"It would be my pleasure," came her reply, soft and willing. That simple phrase stirred Torrin's passions more than the most finely orchestrated song or any poet's verse could hope to do.

"Quinn, would you like a companion for the evening?" asked Yoshindo, addressing him for the first time. "I'm certain that there are many who would welcome the opportunity."

"No," Quinn insisted. He was relieved to be alive yet thought they should remain cautious and not let their guard down too much. But more than this, he felt a deep sadness creeping through him. He thought of better times and of his lost friendship with Lenore. "Food and a place to sleep are all that I require."

As they exited the tent, Quinn managed to catch Torrin's ear for a moment of private speech. "Torrin, we should not separate. We don't know if we can really trust them. We could be in great danger and should stay together. You shouldn't take your meal with that woman."

"I'll grant you that there is yet much we don't know about these people. But I think we're safe enough. Besides, if they meant us harm, I doubt that our being together will really matter that much to our ability to defend against it. You might as well relax and enjoy yourself. Of course, it might not hurt to sleep tonight with one eye open." Torrin smiled and walked away with Midori on his arm.

There was more bothering Quinn than simply their safety. He knew that his feelings were not rational nor perhaps even fair. But still he felt betrayed, perhaps on Lenore's behalf. *It's not so unusual that a man should look for comfort in the company of another woman,* Quinn told himself. And a respectable amount of time had passed since Lenore's death. It also seemed natural that a man should be driven by a need to avenge his wife's murder. But something about this whole affair troubled Quinn, something he could not quite explain. Torrin seemed changed. He had always been intense but his extremes now worried Quinn. So did Torrin's talk about how people were defined by their relationships. It had a ring of truth to it and matched things Quinn had often felt about his own need to belong. But if that were true and if Torrin believed it, what did that make Torrin? Lenore was gone, leaving Torrin without any strong positive relationships in his life, no family and no friends. Connor and Torrin called each other friends but in reality they were less than that. The people who mattered to Torrin now were those he wanted as allies and those he wanted as defeated enemies. Ambition and hate seemed now the only thing that moved Torrin and the only thing he sought. Quinn was deeply worried about Torrin's decisions and directions. But he was the only true friend Torrin had left. How could he forsake Torrin, what would he become then? Their friendship was Torrin's only hope. And if Quinn betrayed that friendship, what would that make him?

None of this should be this hard, thought Quinn, *this complicated.* He was becoming too much like Torrin, thinking too much about everything and what it all means. *Listen to your heart*, Quinn told himself. *It will tell you what is right. Be true to your friends—Torrin, Lenore, and New Hope.*

Torrin lounged in the warm soothing waters of an oversized tub. Standing, the water reached just below his waist and a bench ringed the tub that allowed one to sit, bringing the waterline shoulder high. The tub was placed inside a spacious tent with thick sculpted carpets covering the floor, decorating it with rich color and design. Candles and oil lamps burned around the room, filling it with a mellow, wavering light. The sweet scent of burning incense curled above their holders, mixing with and perfuming the air. From somewhere outside music played upon a dulcimer, the gentle sound of small hammers striking the taut strings stretched over the instrument's board.

From behind gauze curtains of pale rose, Midori moved with soft-footed grace into the wax light. With a touch, her white gown slipped from her supple shoulders and fell in a ring about her dainty feet. Poised and comfortable with her exquisite sensual beauty, she stood there a moment, allowing Torrin's eyes to feast upon the bewitching sight. Then, moving in a gentle sway as fluid as the wind upon the grass, Midori lightly stepped forward and flowed up the stairs to the tub's crest. A ring of small ripples spread out before her as she slipped beneath the water's surface.

Her provocative mystery and lithe figure inflamed Torrin's desire. But in an exercise of control and a demonstration of power, he let Midori come to him, letting her stand before him like an object for his inspection and appreciation. He touched the silken skin of her marvelously molded legs, sliding his hands leisurely up to her slim thighs and around her slender waist. Rising slowly to his feet, Torrin's eyes came to rest on hers. His fingers caressed her cheek, then slipped easily through the long, soft black hair that Torrin had longed to touch. With his hand gently cupped around her neck, he brought her closer to him. Only a breath away from his, Midori's lips were the color of claret, a dark and deep red. He crossed that distance, putting his mouth on Midori's, finding her lips remarkably moist and sweet, tasting like ripe strawberries. Torrin's eyes closed and, as visions of Lenore came back to haunt him, opened again, banishing the painful memory.

With Lenore, Torrin had shared both spiritual and sexual love. But the former was no longer a part of his emotional composition. He refused himself the continued experience of the sensation, even the remembrance of a love that he had once cherished. With mind and soul ruled by the Beast, he now regarded love as a character flaw, an affliction that weakens the will and power of a man. Eroticism, on the other hand, could be free of the adverse impacts inherent in sentimental weakness. It could be self-serving and indulgent without damaging a man's autonomous power. Torrin regarded Midori as he would a work of art, an object for his enjoyment. His interest in her was for his own pleasure. But if she received it in return or if it pleased him to satisfy her, so much the better. After all, drawing out the ecstasy of a woman was also a demonstration of power.

Despite Torrin's selfish perspective and his fascination with power, if Midori told him to stop, he would stop. Rape was still something Torrin despised but no longer entirely for the reasons that had moved him to commit parricide and kill his father. Torrin believed that rape would destroy the value of the sexual act, diminish its pleasure and thereby defeat its purpose. As a person who wanted to maximize his pleasure and the value of his possessions, Torrin approved only of consensual sex because he recognized it as infinitely more gratifying. So if Midori did not consent, Torrin would not force the issue by committing rape. However, although it was fine should she want to stop, if she stopped and wanted something of Torrin such as compassion or a kind ear on which to unload her problems or feelings, Torrin would have none of it unless it could in some way serve his own interests. In the past, he would have been eager to cater to Lenore both physically and emotionally, but no more. He no longer truly cared about the other person. What curiosity he might have about a woman's character was only for the mental seasoning the information added to the sexual union. As he did in his quest for power and revenge, Torrin conditioned his mind rigidly against a love that had once been and focused instead on simple passion. Mirroring this resolve, Torrin's muscles hardened as if his body were made entirely of erectile tissue.

He pulled Midori's svelte form closer to him, feeling the soft and erotic intrigue of her flesh. Leaving the water, they found a place on the tent's furs and rugs where their writhing bodies twined naked for hours and she taught him new lessons in carnal pleasure.

"Torrin, wake up. Wake up," urged Quinn, crouched at Torrin's side and shaking his shoulder.

Torrin's eyes opened, triggering the animation of his mind. It surprised Torrin that he had allowed himself to sleep so deeply. That could be a dangerous habit and one he would have to avoid in the future. "What's going on? Is something wrong?" he asked, rising to find and don his clothes.

"I'm not sure what's happening exactly," explained Quinn. "Yoshindo wants to talk to you. He and the rest are outside. They sent me, or rather let me come get you. What are you going to do, Torrin?"

"I don't know. Did he say what was on his mind, what he wants? No. Well then, let's go outside and find out shall we."

He pushed aside the tent flap. Squinting, he stepped into the bright morning air, finding it saturated with earthy forest smells mixed with the scent of pine and ripening fruit. The elves had turned out in sizable number. But their aspect appeared friendly. Yoshindo stood at the forefront with Midori braced demurely at his side. Torrin and Yoshindo exchanged a slight bow of welcome and acknowledged respect.

Yoshindo took the initiative. "Good morning, Torrin. It is good that you enjoyed yourself last night. Such pleasures give life half its meaning and serves to revive the body and soul. But labor is life's practical other half, pleasure's counterpart and an equally necessary component of existence. And we have business to discuss, you and I. A leader cannot afford to be rash nor should he be indecisive. Both can be destructive. A leader must make informed and timely decisions, and his ability to properly balance these often-conflicting needs will determine his success as a leader. I have made my decision. I support the concept of your proposal, that we should combine our forces to defeat the human High Queen. Now, to determine if we can support the implementation of your plan, I must hear the details of your recommendation."

"My plan is simple but effective. Quinn will return to New Hope to mobilize my army and inform them that the alliance with the elves has been secured. The elves and I shall march into the Tissima Mountains to the dwarven Kingdom of Prakrit. We do not absolutely need the dwarves to be victorious, but it will be an easier task with them for allies. They are ferocious warriors and I believe I can persuade them to help us. After that, it is on to Gairloch and victory."

Torrin went on to explain the numbers and capabilities of his army, padding it only slightly. He also described Gairloch's defenses and the challenges they would face. He flavored his words, however, with hypnotic spells to mesmerize his listeners and persuade them to his cause. He plied his magic to enhance the perception of Gairloch's vulnerability and his own credibility as a powerful adversary.

"Earlier you correctly described the qualities of a good leader," said Torrin. "A leader must be willing to listen to the counsel of others but ultimately there can be only one who in the end makes the final decision. In the thick of battle there is no time for bickering among warlords. I will treat the elves fairly and the dwarves too when they join us. But to win this war, I must know that you will adhere to my rule. If you follow me, we shall be triumphant and your loyalty will be compensated with rich reward. You have my word."

Their eyes firmly locked, Yoshindo measured Torrin one last time, assessing his conviction and his competence. When the stare was finally broken, it was Yoshindo who looked away.

"I believe you," Yoshindo announced. "And I believe that it is in the best interest of my people to do as you propose. We have lived in this forest a very long time and there is a sadness in leaving it. But we deserve more than it can offer and we would like to go home to our native land, a land made sacred by the dust and blood of our ancestors. We have a strong attachment to our homeland; it is a cord that was never broken. This forest has been kind to us but its soil is not equal to that of our native land. And even staying here appears to be a risk. It seems our choice is to remain and defend alone our surrogate home against foreseeable attack or to join with you in the hope of regaining what we most prize. I choose the latter. I choose the prospect of riches over ruin."

Yoshindo insisted Quinn have an escort to take him safely to the forest's edge and, despite Quinn's protests at the separation, Torrin sent him on his way. He told Quinn to let Connor know what had happened with the elves and to make sure the army was ready. Afterwards, he and Connor were to join Torrin at Prakrit to determine their next course of action based on what Torrin could accomplish there. Doubtful but resigned, Quinn agreed and left to fulfill his part of the mission.

Over the next several days, Torrin labored with Yoshindo in preparing all the elves for their exodus out of Cravenwood. Together they made arrangements for weapons and what other provisions they would take with them. The population was organized into units for improved defense, mobility, and other more basic logistic issues. The elves began quickly to accept Torrin as a leader. In fact, his status had been so elevated that many seemed to regard him as a demigod or savior. They thought he had come to lead them to the paradise of their ancestral home. Torrin began again wearing the silver diadem across his brow to crown his position here as he had in New Hope. And as they made their preparations, Torrin worked to raise and enliven the elves' passion for war, their aspiration for conquest and bounty.

At night, they attended to other passions. Torrin enthusiastically participated in their nighttime diversions, attending profligate feasts and lively celebrations held in anticipation of victory. The meals were exquisite and made of exotic foods. Spirited games and erotic entertainment were also part of the festivities. And the elves satisfied their lustful appetites as couples or in groups, dependant on the inclination of the participants.

A zealous partaker of these debaucheries, Torrin delighted in it all, the women and seeing his plans for war begin moving toward fruition. Finding the customs of the pleasure-loving elves wildly exciting, Torrin fervently indulged himself in these gratifying associations. But he never lost sight of his ultimate goal. Power, revenge, and conquest, that was what he wanted and he would settle for nothing less.

Chapter 7
Prakrit

"You were a fool to come here," Balinar rumbled. From his throne, raised upon a dais, the dwarven king glowered down at Torrin, regarding him with grim disdain. The throne was fashioned from dark green and richly veined marble, ornamented with carved designs and precious gems. Strong and unyielding, the throne served as a reflection of the obdurate man who occupied it. The sun-browned and weathered skin of Balinar's face held the appearance more of chiseled stone than of flesh. It was a stern face with heavy brows furrowed in an uncompromising cast and testimony to the ferocious fighting spirit of the dwarves. Balinar's manner and words were harsh and often ridiculing, despite what had already passed between he and Torrin.

Balinar stroked his graying rust-red beard with a small thickly calloused hand, a hand that suggested strength enough to crack diamonds in its grip. He, and the other dwarves around them, were armored in thick, hardened leather and heavy metal plate. Deeply dished metal pauldrons protected his stocky shoulders and were joined by sliding rivets to three lower lames on each arm. Fluted extensions with scalloped edges spread out like fans from the shoulder armor along his back. Over his body armor, Balinar wore a brick-red surcoat bearing his heraldic device, the black silhouette of a war hammer.

Balinar had not inherited his kingdom's throne; he had earned it. He acquired and secured his right to rule through unbending tenacity, fighting harder and ultimately better than any other in gaining his position as king. It had been a battle won not only for himself but also for his family. In some long distant military engagement, Balinar's great grandfather committed an act of cowardice, a high crime in dwarven society. And the stigma of this disgrace was passed on to subsequent generations. Balinar, through his victories and his demonstration of exceptional bravery, took the crown and redeemed his family's honor.

The dwarves held a reverent respect for all that was severe and hard. Theirs was a strong, stoic, aggressive, war-ordered society developed from years of struggle defending themselves against humans, ogres, and other unfriendly inhabitants of the mountains and surrounding lands. Even the natural character of the mountain environment demanded that those dwelling here be rugged and stalwart, strong and fearless.

The dwarves met Torrin's army of elves in the morning, a day uncommonly hot for the mountain altitude. Torrin had made camp, forcing the dwarves to come to him in an area that at least afforded Torrin a slight topographical advantage. A flag of truce flew above the elves but with no guarantee that the dwarves would acknowledge it. Weapons were held at ready by both forces even while Torrin exchanged words with the dwarven commander. The elevated tensions were palpable, feeling as if they might at any moment break into violence. The sun shown bright and uncomfortably warm. Sweat ran beneath the soldiers' armor, the dissolved salts burning skin that had chafed during the march. Ill at ease, the soldiers waited, alert for any signal that would trigger fighting. Equally expectant, buzzards winged above the armies in wide, lazy circles, hoping for the clash of arms and the feast it would supply.

But the vultures were disappointed; no battle erupted. After a few hours, Torrin and Yoshindo were taken, at their request, within Prakrit and before Balinar, the dwarven king. The elfin army was instructed to remain outside at the field encampment.

The dwarven stronghold Prakrit consisted of a complex network of tunnels and rooms excavated from the interior of a mountain in the Tissima range. It was not dank, moldy, dark, and dirty as one might expect. Although austere, the subterranean fortress was well constructed and maintained. Prakrit was austere in that it was marked by the absence of indulgent comfort and luxury, not in that it was simple and without decoration.

At working stone, the dwarves were masters of their craft, having no equal in the world. Their architectural and sculptural excellence was immediately evident and undeniably impressive in its grandeur. The portal through which they entered was a huge pointed arch with carved decoration around the doorway in an elaborate and zestful pattern of repeated scrolls. Guided by the dwarves, Torrin and Yoshindo walked over floors of smooth marbled pavements; down aisles divided by columns alternately incised with chevron ornaments and diamond patterns; and past banqueting rooms, living quarters, and other chambers exuberantly adorned in a profusion of geometrical decoration and heroic sculpture rich in symbolism and conceit. Given the occupants lesser stature, the rooms were more than spacious and the ceilings unusually high, always reaching at least twice Torrin's height.

In addition to the sculptural violence and bold muscularity of Prakrit's interior surface detail, the combative nature of the dwarves was evidenced in clashing stylistic change. Changing fashions and divergent opinions on how to express their architectural passions were reflected in the varied designs and diffuse patterning. Compromises, such as enclosing pointed arches beneath a larger round arch, were made in an effort to re-impose an impression of deliberate order. But regardless of its eccentricities, Prakrit was a triumphant expression of power and decorative glory.

Torrin now stood in the great chamber of the dwarven throne room. As side entrances to the enormous hall, its walls began as mighty columns wrapped with powerful spiral moldings that snaked around the circular piers. Above the flowers and leaves carved into the capitals of the stone columns, the walls rose several arcaded stories to the ceiling's ribbed vaults towering overhead. The chamber was overpowering in its magnificent structure, its glossy marbles, and the richness of its surface texture. What gloom there might have been was chased away by oil lamps bolted to the walls and massive iron chandeliers of magnificent metalwork and resplendent crystal suspended from large heavy chains and sparkling with light. The temperature of the hall was cool, pleasantly cool after the afternoon heat of the outside air.

Balinar and Torrin faced one another, embroiled in an emphatic debate of opposing wills. Torrin's show of strength on the field and in the hall had gained Balinar's respect but not his cooperation.

"If I was a fool to come here, as you say," argued Torrin, "it was not because my plan is foolish but rather the result of misinformation I received concerning your race. What I knew led me to believe that the dwarves were a stouthearted people, their warriors fearless and strong. There were those, such as those at Gairloch, who said the dwarves' reputation of strength and courage was overrated. Some even likened the dwarves to mice, cowering in their little holes and fearful of the human hawk, Bryana. But I could not believe this to be the truth. I remember the legends told to me that testified to the indomitable fighting spirit of the dwarves. Our histories hold records of battles in which a handful of dwarves decimated an army of humans three or four times their number. Am I to believe that this was simply an exaggeration, a story that grew more extraordinary with each telling so that it now bears no resemblance to reality? I thought that bravery flowed like molten lava through the veins of every dwarf, burning with a warrior's passion. Now what am I to think?

"I present you with a realistic opportunity to avenge the decades of injustice the dwarves have endured and the defeats you suffered that kept you from achieving the glory you deserve. And instead of grabbing up your sword and charging into battle, you refuse the prospect of victory out of fear for its cost. Gairloch is an oppressor to us all. I have told you of my human army that marches from the community of New Hope. You have seen the elfin army also at my command and surely you know of the elves' legendary magic. These forces under my leadership and together with my power as a wizard can defeat Gairloch. With the dwarves' help, we would have been assured of victory."

Balinar's scowl deepened; his look hardened. "Elves and wizards," he snarled with open contempt. "I know nothing of magic. And what I don't know, I don't trust. I put my faith in the strength of my weapons and the mettle of my warriors."

"Then your faith is ill placed," Torrin crassly interrupted. "For that mettle looks weak. Your response to the challenge Gairloch represents is not determination to do your best in conquering it but rather a determination to avoid that challenge. Where is the famed warrior spirit, the courage, and the fortitude I had thought to find in the dwarves? Timidity, faint-heartedness—these were not traits associated with the honorable and illustrious reputation of the dwarves. I am gravely disappointed. And you, you should be ashamed!"

In a quick froth of rage, Balinar sprang to his feet clutching the handle of his trademark war hammer and looking quite prepared to use the weapon in answer to Torrin's brazen insolence. To be accused of being a coward was a serious offense that no dwarf would easily tolerate. To Balinar, the accusation was particularly infuriating.

As king, he was the chief representative of Prakrit's honor. And the cowardice of his great grandfather remained a thorn in Balinar's side. It had been an enormous burden to overcome, and he still had to fight the stain left by it on the integrity of his bloodline. Complicating matters even more, Balinar was, in fact, a cautious leader, which in the eyes of many dwarves was a trait too close to fear. Balinar was not rash in committing his army into battles. He chose them wisely and to his advantage, being a calculating and prudent warrior. Prakrit had been effectively defended under his leadership and its population increased through years of avoiding hasty military engagements that would have needlessly resulted in excessive casualties. When he fought, he won and with an unmatched fighting spirit. But despite his success, there were those of a more brutish nature who criticized him as not being adequately aggressive. It was bad enough to be forced to defend himself against his own people; to do so against the taunts of a human was insufferable.

In answer to Torrin's insult, Balinar glared with intense malevolence, his eyes ablaze with anger and reflected light. The knuckles of his hand, knotted around the hammer, whitened from the tightness of his grip. The brawny muscles of his short, stout frame clenched in preparation of a violent explosion.

A deathly stillness enveloped the hall, so quiet it made the dwarves' mental shouts for blood seem audible. The attention of all gathered there fixed firmly on Torrin and Balinar. Most, if not all, would have welcomed the chance to attack Torrin in defense of their honor. But they waited, deferring to their king as it was his right to meet this challenge.

Then suddenly the spark in Balinar's eye changed. His brows relaxed and his snarl transformed into a wry smile. Arms akimbo, he threw his head back and a bellowing laugh issued from his lips, echoing about the cavernous hall.

"I like you, human," Balinar chortled. "You argue like a dwarf. You say what's on your mind with no holding back. Most of you humans are imbeciles or sycophants, using servile flattery to get what you want. And most would be begging for their lives by now. You got guts; I'll give you that much. Course, it brought you that close to having your head cracked open like a walnut," he said holding thumb and index finger near together. "But as you know, we dwarves appreciate daring in our rivals."

Torrin smiled in reply, feeling triumphant and admittedly relieved at Balinar's conciliatory humor. "Excellent! Then you will join us in our campaign against Gairloch?"

Balinar laughed again. "No human, my mind has not changed. You will not have the aid of the dwarves in carrying out your plan. I will not be goaded by insults into a war that does not benefit me or my people."

Torrin moved to interject with protest but was stilled by Balinar's upraised hand and the hard look that returned now to his face. "As I said," Balinar continued, "my mind is made up. I see no advantage in removing Bryana only to replace her with another human as king of Gairloch, despite what you've said about treating the dwarves equally. Humans and dwarves have never been friends. In years past we were often bitter enemies. Although our relations have improved somewhat, I have no great fondness for Bryana. But she has basically left us alone in recent years. She has launched no major campaigns against us. You say her aspiration for conquest is growing, but there is little evidence to support such a claim. All in all, I know more about her than I do about you. So if I were to support anyone in this war, it might well be Bryana. But this is not our fight and so we shall abstain from any involvement at this point. As I said, I appreciate the courage you demonstrated in facing me here today. It hasn't made me support your cause but it did inspire me to let you live. You and your elfin compatriot may stay here tonight. Your army will remain at their field encampment. My guards will show you to your rooms."

Torrin prowled his room in angry, anxious strides. He was infuriated as much by his own failure as by Balinar's refusal to cooperate. The only aspect of his conversation with Balinar Torrin remembered was the dwarven king's "no." To be denied like this was an insult to his power, told no and put to bed as if he were nothing more than a troublesome child. It enraged Torrin. It provoked the Beast within him, maddening it with a vicious, inflamed desire to dominate, to kill, to rule.

Although there were no guards posted outside his door, Torrin knew he could not get far without being discovered and apprehended. Confinement and unvented hostility animated Torrin with restless energy. Charged, his emotions screamed for an outlet. His breathing became heavier as the passion of his anger grew. The Beast howled for action, preparing to do anything to free itself, heedless of the cost.

The door of Torrin's room creaked open. Responding to the intrusion and using it as a focal point on which to direct his outrage, Torrin spun around to face the door. He felt primed for combat, hot with temper, fists clenched in defiance, and his heart pounding like the frenzied beating of a war drum. It was only with tremendous restraint that Torrin managed to hold himself back from instantly attacking the intruder in a wild fury.

It was a woman, a dwarf, looking rather prepared for battle herself. A thick brown leather jerkin clothed her short, sturdy, and well-proportioned frame. She wore steel vambraces on each forearm and matching pauldrons crowned her shoulders. A wide, metal belt encircled the muscular girth of her waist and accentuated her full bosom. Beneath the belt and over tight blue pants, a series of studded leather straps skirted the dwarven woman's hips. Heavy boots, also of brown leather, rose to meet her knees. Her hair, wavy and shoulder length, was a dark reddish brown.

From the compliment of weapons at her belt, she drew a broad, double-edged dagger. She held it ready for Torrin to attack or perhaps daring him to do so. A sadistic smile touched the rough-hewn features of her attractive face. Her smile shifted to a leer as if she were regarding Torrin's own ferocious look with ardent attraction.

In quick, fluid strides Torrin crossed the distance separating them and clamped his hand about her wrist in an effort to immobilize the dagger. When she resisted, Torrin struck her soundly across the cheek, not with an open palm but with the hard knuckles of his fist. She fought back and the two wrestled against each other like savage, untamed animals. Torrin could have called upon his magic but refrained, finding pleasure in the physical conflict.

Apparently so did she. After a few moments she broke from the fray, laughing and drawing the back of her hand across her mouth and chin to wipe away the fresh blood draining from her split lip. Torrin held back, regarding her with curiosity.

"So your blood does run hot, human," she said in a gruff, throaty voice. "Good! I'm sick of leaders with no backbone or stomach for war. And I'm not alone in my thinking."

Collecting his wits and denying any pain he had suffered from the brief exchange, Torrin inquired, "Are you saying there are forces who oppose Balinar?"

"Yes," she answered while restoring order to her disheveled clothes. "And those which may support your plan. My name is Darya. I can assist you in adding the dwarves to your army, but in return you must reward my help. Is it a deal?"

"How do you intend to accomplish this coup?" Torrin asked flatly and without commitment.

"It's quite simple, actually. Tomorrow, when you confront Balinar again, ask that you be permitted to present your proposal before the High Council. It's made up of high ranking military officials. A majority vote by the Council can override a ruling of the king. There are many factions among the dwarves of Prakrit who would like to replace Balinar. Along with those loyal to the king, the leaders of these factions sit on the High Council, but usually they're too busy fighting among themselves to be very effective against Balinar. From what I can gather, I think you could get a majority vote in your favor. They're hungry for war and each sees this as a good opportunity to enhance their own position."

"Then Balinar would be a fool to allow it. He won't let me anywhere near the High Council," stated Torrin.

"Probably not. I don't think he'll want to, but you may be able to force him. A citizen of Prakrit can demand to go before the High Council and the king cannot prevent it. But you are not a citizen and the issue must be raised by the one making the challenge. So, I can't do it for you. Before a dwarf reaches a certain age, he must pass the Labyrinth. It's a test, like a rite of passage. Each must do it and many fail. If a dwarf succeeds, he is granted citizenship. If you can get Balinar to let you enter the Labyrinth and you manage to navigate it successfully, he will have to let the High Council hear your case."

"Again, why would Balinar grant even this request?" Torrin asked, seating himself uncomfortably in a stiff-back, wooden chair. Arms folded across his chest, he leaned back, watching Darya.

"Because he won't believe you can do it. It's very difficult and very dangerous. It is a great source of pride for a dwarf to beat the Labyrinth."

"And if I fail?"

"Then you'll be dead and your problem solved," Darya said with a feral grin. Her cold blue-gray eyes gleamed like polished steel.

Still holding the vulgar expression, Darya approached Torrin. She grabbed him forcefully and pulled his mouth to hers, eating at his lips with voracious desire. Torrin met it like a challenge, kissing her back with the same brutish enthusiasm. Further aroused, she moved in closer, biting at his neck while working the fingers of one hand roughly through his hair and exploring vigorously with the other between Torrin's parted legs.

Growling in his ear like a wild creature, she insisted. "Prove to me that you are a man worth following."

Responding to the lusty, barbarous invitation, Torrin tore open Darya's leather jerkin, exposing her buxom chest and burying his head amid the luscious fruits of her full bosom. As if embroiled in a contest in which each advance was to be exchanged blow for blow, Darya ripped apart the back of Torrin's shirt, the fabric shredding like paper in her strong hands. Torrin felt his skin break and small trickles of blood leak forth as Darya, consumed in an erotic frenzy, raked her nails deeply across his bare back.

Her robust sexual appetite required nearly all night and virtually all of Torrin's energy and stamina to satisfy. It was like the mating of two savage animals in rut—stormy, loud, and physically demanding. Torrin felt certain that Darya's strong physique and aggressive style would leave him black and blue and suffering in the morning as a result of the fervent coupling, being about as frenzied and violent as their earlier brawl.

But pleasure though it was, it was for more than libido alone that Torrin chose to bed Darya, probing her mind as well as her body, eliciting information as well as passion. The strenuous nature of the activity in which they engaged, however, made it difficult for Torrin to concentrate on much else. But he did manage to use his magic to gather additional details about the dwarves, information he might well put to use in gaining their allegiance.

Torrin intruded upon Darya's mind, spying on her memories and stealing information. During his telepathic violation of her psyche, he cheated by acquiring bits and pieces about the Labyrinth from the recollection of her own experience. The Labyrinth would be a formidable challenge, he realized. Exploring further the stored data locked in Darya's subconscious, Torrin derived new knowledge concerning the dwarves that was relevant to his own ambitions.

For the dwarves, virtue and prosperity required essentially unremitting self-discipline. Strength of will was ascribed paramount importance, and pursuit of this uncompromising goal naturally contributed to their strength of body. They viewed fear to be the greatest evil, the most disastrous misfortune and failure that an individual could suffer. Nothing else, not pain, hunger, illness, nor even death, is by its own nature terrible. Only if feared do these situations become calamitous. It was the dwarven way to suffer in silence and, as much as possible, to regard adversity as an opportunity for personal growth. In the face of pain, a dwarf must not groan or complain, particularly he must not moan in spirit. The will must remain strong. A dwarf makes the best of what is in his power and endures the rest while ridding himself of lamentation. For a dwarf, it is not an assault or a tormenting situation that hurts the individual but the view he chooses to take of it. Pain is neither good nor evil but simply a neutral stimulus to which the individual responds. It is that response and the individual's interpretation of pain that may be regarded as good or evil, evil if it is one of fear or self-pity.

Their lives centered upon strict discipline involving an inflexible military structure and demanding labor. With this in mind, it was understandable that when the dwarves inherent but generally shackled passions were afforded an outlet, such as battle (or bed as Darya was currently demonstrating), it exploded in a staggering frenzy bringing skill, strength, and emotion into a nearly unbeatable combination. Their concept of individual will bore many similarities to Torrin's own, his will to acquire and wield power. Torrin realized that it would be difficult to restrain the will of the dwarves or to force them into yielding to his will. The only way to conquer their will would be by its own perversion.

"You want to speak to the High Council!" Balinar repeated Torrin's demand as if it were unthinkable. "Impossible! Only a dwarf may stand before the High Council. And you, regardless of what else you may be, are not a dwarf. I will warn you, human, you're beginning to tax my patience to the limit. You've made your request. I've given my answer. Now be on your way while that option still remains available!" With furrowed brows and a forbidding frown, Balinar's features hardened in an obstinate cast.

"Technically," Torrin began with smug impudence, "your law states that only a citizen of Prakrit may address the High Council. It does not stipulate that the citizen must be a member of the dwarven race. If I were to pass your little test of citizenship, the Labyrinth I believe it's called, then there should be no objection to my presenting my proposal to the High Council. Doesn't that seem logical to you?"

"Little test!" Balinar laughed at Torrin's gross understatement. "I don't know who's been giving you your facts, but it was poor advice I assure you. The Labyrinth is more than a little test. It's the most strenuous, exacting, and demanding challenge an individual can face. It is the supreme test of an individual's spirit and body."

"I am confident in both. And I am intrigued by, rather than fearful of, your infamous Labyrinth," Torrin flouted, his answer rife with undisguised arrogance.

Balinar grinned as if he were speaking to a daft or over ambitious child, his tone and manner patronizing. "Human, you would be dead by the time you took your eleventh step. If you want to kill yourself, do it somewhere else. Our sacred rituals are not the place for it."

"Concern for my safety and even the fact that the Labyrinth has traditionally been experienced only by dwarves sound like poor excuses to my ears," Torrin replied. "More than the appearance of a legitimate rationale, these excuses have the look of a smoke screen to mask your real motive. I suggest that it is your fear, not mine, that keeps me from the Labyrinth. You're afraid that I, a human, will complete with ease what the dwarves consider so difficult and hold in such esteem. You feel superior for having accomplished a feat that no member of any other race has yet achieved. But to preserve that feeling and the myth of dwarven supremacy, you deny any outsider the opportunity to enter the Labyrinth. You said it before and now I must agree with you, I was a fool to come here. I came looking for warriors. What I found are weak, lazy, complacent cowards who would rather arm themselves with cups of ale and brag about past exploits than risk the threat of new challenges. And worse even than this, you discourage others from testing their mettle for fear it will reveal the softness of your own."

In response to his effrontery, sparks flew, as Torrin knew they would. A shadow passed behind Balinar's eyes like a thunderhead about to break. His countenance extremely grim, his words came harsh and hard as a hammer. In true dwarven fashion, Balinar burned to requite Torrin's insult with injury.

"You long-legged, skinny piece of shit!" Balinar roared, precipitously discharging his acid temper. "I ought to break your filthy, scrawny little neck, you disrespectful pile of goat puke. I accredited you with daring, but I see now that it is only from ignorance that you speak and it is your ignorance which gives you the illusion of a brave tongue. What but your own feeblemindedness could explain the stupidity you have displayed in calling dwarven courage into question? You go too far! Even the actions of an idiot can be tolerated for only so long. You have exceeded the time for tolerance and no one would gainsay me for beating you to death for your clownish and insufferable behavior. But I wish to acquit myself of all responsibility in regard to you. You have provided me with the punitive answer to your outrageous offense. Let you kill yourself I say and let the Labyrinth be the means for your destruction. It will teach you respect, though it will cost your life to learn this lesson. And when you die, damn you to the darkest of the Seven Hells!"

It was cold, a cold that could not be attributed completely to the temperature of his environment or to the fact he was clothed only in a loincloth. The massive, stone door behind Torrin closed with a deep thud, followed by the scrapping of bolts and locks being secured from the other side. These echoing sounds faded slowly into the hollow caverns. A torch was all a challenger was permitted to take into the Labyrinth; all other provisions must be acquired as part of one's attempt to free himself from its confines.

Turning, Torrin held the lighted torch against the closed portal. The seal about the door was perfect and impenetrable. He noticed a few bones strewn at its base. Apparently, this door served exclusively in a one-way capacity. Failure meant death. There was no turning back. Torrin steadied his nerves, reminding himself that the more severe the challenge, the greater his power would be upon its achievement.

Natural, the product of earth power, the Labyrinth was carved by hands other than dwarves. Unlike the excavations of Prakrit's occupied cavities, the Labyrinth's floors, walls, and ceiling were rough cut and contoured with uneven surfaces. In carving out their home from the mountain's interior, the dwarves had stopped at the entrance of the Labyrinth not out of design but out of defeat. They simply had been unable to dominate its inherent internal defenses sufficiently to provide for sustained occupation. After years of attempts and attrition, it became evident that it was not worth the cost in lives and other resources. So with grudging acceptance, the dwarves resigned themselves to living only above the Labyrinth. Perhaps in an effort to save face, the dwarves incorporated the Labyrinth as an integral part of their society, establishing it as a mandatory rite of passage. With each dwarf that successfully fought his way free of the Labyrinth's dangerous catacombs, they reaffirmed the indomitable spirit of their race.

Torrin suddenly found the dwarves' professed distaste for magic ironically amusing, for magic resided here in abundance. He could feel it all around him. The Labyrinth was a wellspring of basic, natural, innate magic power. Manifest in unimaginable diversity, its energies prevalent and in various proportion, magic occupied these caverns. The hollowed out expanses of rock and the denizens that dwelled in it were a product of that magic. That dwarves should be the keeper of the key to such power was an entertaining irony.

Slumped against the slick, hard surface of a stalagmite, Torrin enjoyed a brief moment of rest. Gradually his metabolism relaxed. Just moments ago he had been fighting for his life, his pulse rapid, his breathing like a bellows, and his muscles strained. But emotionally he had already forgotten the conflict. You had to in order to take advantage of each short break before the next challenge presented itself.

He pulled his hand across his cheek, wiping away sweat and checking the time. Time, the concept had lost practically all meaning since entering this stone maze of death. Although a highly imprecise mechanism, the growth of his new beard was the only means by which Torrin could gage the passage of time. Cheeks that had been bare when he entered the Labyrinth were now covered in an ample mat of facial hair, perhaps a week's growth.

And what a week that had been. Torrin thought it would be easier than this, quicker than this. He had seen, defeated, and even eaten things he had never before imagined. Being redundant and unnecessary, the torch had been abandoned early on. The Labyrinth's magic provided illumination in many places and where it did not, Torrin relied on his own.

How did any of the dwarves beat the Labyrinth without personal magic? Torrin wondered. He had to give them credit. The Labyrinth was exceptionally difficult and he was beginning to wonder if he had not made a grave mistake by insisting that he be allowed this experience. Undoubtedly the dwarves' numbers would be greater if they stayed out of these catacombs. Torrin had stumbled upon several sets of bones and the decomposing bodies of a few hapless dwarves. But if it reduced their numbers, which it undeniably did, the Labyrinth produced a stronger people. It culled the weaker members from their society. The fittest survived. After his own experience, Torrin had a deeper respect for those survivors and hoped with deteriorating confidence that he would stand among them.

Earth demons resided here, massive, hulking stone monsters that seemed to detach themselves from the very walls. To fight them physically was like chipping away at the mountainside and if you were not quick enough, the strike of their incredibly powerful limbs left their victim shattered. In directing wizardry or muscle against these creatures, Torrin used their own properties to assist his survival through combat or evasion. In one case, he had evaded an earth demon by diving headlong into a lake. His assailant sank while Torrin quickly swam to safety.

But he soon realized that such rash actions, even committed in the interest of survival, could prove fatal and not only because of the monsters often present in these waters. Lakes of acid and fire also existed in the Labyrinth and as barriers to be crossed. Fingers slick with sweat, the temperature unbearable, Torrin had been forced to work his way along a narrow ledge above a vein of running magma. He had also nearly been consumed by another type of river. Upon first glance it appeared simply as a rapidly flowing, shallow stream. But closer inspection showed it to be composed of millions of small, ravenous snakes mindlessly charging forward and capable of devouring anything that interfered with its fluid course. Torrin, however, managed to instead draw a meal for himself from a minor fraction of the swarming current.

Dynamic, adaptive illusions also occupied the Labyrinth, assaulting the mind as well as endangering the body. Sanctuary was all but impossible to find and lingering too long in any one place was always a danger, one that gave the Labyrinth's active denizens an opportunity to scent your presence and close in for the kill. Among a horde of other dreadful beasts, Torrin confronted giant scorpions with pincers capable of cleaving a man in half and stingers that could impale a victim with devastating consequence. If they held poison too it seemed unnecessary. Sleep was all but impossible. Anything more than light dozing could quickly turn permanent. Regularly, Torrin's sleep was interrupted by banshees, their voices howling, shrieking in a maddening pitch and volume as they advanced upon him from all around. Narrow escapes became the norm.

Like a fixed position, movement was also a danger. An incautious step could trap a person in a patch of quickrock, where the floor bore the appearance of solid stone but the consistency of thick mud, bottomless and thirsty. The more you fought to get free, the more entrenched you became, the more avidly it drank, dragging you under to its airless depths. There were also regions in which a tunnel opened into a vast chamber whose floor appeared uniform but proved to be a patchwork of solid footing and illusion hiding severe drop-offs.

Things that looked harmless typically were not. A seemingly innocuous set of roots could reach out to entangle prey if one passed too closely. Danger, it was prevalent, diverse, and frequently subtle. There were small clusters of rock covered in deep, cushiony layers of lichen in which a person felt strangely safe, filed with a pervasive sense of serenity and incredibly tired. The traveler was inspired to rest upon the lichen, inclined to sleep beneath an illusion of contentment and security. But once yielded to, it became a fatal inclination. A stone slab would then descend upon the slumbering victim, crushing him and providing more readily utilized nutrients on which the lichen fed.

In making his way through the Labyrinth, Torrin would acquire weapons only to lose them again through various mishaps and encounters. At present, he owned nothing but the loincloth, tattered and dirty, he had worn on entering the Labyrinth. Bruises and cuts seemed to layer every inch of his person and fatigue threatened to overwhelm him. Using magic to heal the injuries had become nearly as draining as the injuries themselves. Unless life threatening, it was easier simply to endure them. Torrin did employ sorcery to help guide him through the stone maze, but the Labyrinth's powers at times confused his magic in addition to his other senses.

Although still intrigued by the Labyrinth, Torrin now desperately wanted to be free of it. He could not understand for what reason earth magic would produce such a hostile environment and such formidable creatures for its occupation. That the Labyrinth was the product of natural evolution seemed an unlikely possibility. Certainly there were characteristics of chaos and random developments caused by natural selection, but there was also the impression of something else. The work of a conscious mind seemed behind the activities of the Labyrinth, creating its complex structure and varied creatures for a purpose. The obvious answer was that they were generated for a defensive purpose, but in defense of what? Power. What else was worth defending? *But what was the character and capacity of that power?* wondered Torrin. *Could it be dominated and bridled?* Exciting questions, but ones for which Torrin presently lacked the luxury to investigate. He would keep them in mind, however, for later consideration.

When Torrin first discovered the door, it was recognized with disbelief, thinking it to be another illusion designed to torment. But it was solid, it was real, and it opened. It opened on freedom. It opened on victory. Once through the portal, Torrin collapsed to his knees, exhausted and overcome with relief. Following the initial rush of weary elation at having at last freed himself from the Labyrinth, Torrin rose, taking note of his new surroundings.

The dwarves named it the Victory Room for obvious reasons. The chamber was immense in size and roughly oval in dimension. Several tiers of balconies overlooked the central arena in which Torrin stood on a floor of multicolored tiles patterned in a fierce design. There were numerous entrances spaced evenly around the room, the doors constructed of plates of beveled, leaded glass joined by a framework of blonde ironwood. Recessed wall niches lined in black and white marble encircled figurative and abstract sculptures of bronze gilt intended to glorify the dwarves' strength and triumph. Circular staircases twined upward to the balconies that like the ceiling were lavishly adorned with emblems and inscriptions.

A large, circular, bronze gong hung suspended in a wooden frame. Torrin understood its purpose and used the mallet against it, calling the citizens of Prakrit to assemble and receive the announcement that a new member had joined their ranks. They came, filling the balconies and looking down on Torrin from behind the intricately carved railings. In reaction to Torrin's success, many of them held looks of surprise and disgust. Some may have looked neutral at seeing Torrin but none appeared pleased, except perhaps Balinar.

Balinar stood on the same level as Torrin and at the opposite end of the room, a faint smile upon his lips. *So the human did it, and in record time*, thought Balinar with an odd sense of satisfaction.

Balinar had no children. It had long been a dream of his to one day sire an heir and to see his offspring emerge from the Labyrinth. It was also a dream he knew would most likely never manifest as a reality because Balinar's wife was quite probably barren. They tried for years to conceive but without success. Balinar loved his wife and would never leave her in search of a more fertile mate, as others had encouraged their king to do.

It might have felt something like this, Balinar mused. He respected Torrin despite the harsh words they had exchanged; even children will fight viciously against their parents at times. He had worried that Torrin would die in the Labyrinth and felt somehow responsible for Torrin in this whole affair. It was with relief and a strange kind of pride that Balinar received Torrin.

"Victory!" Balinar shouted and the assembled dwarves repeated the exclamation as a single voice. "It is my responsibility, indeed my honor, to welcome you, Torrin, and recognize you as an esteemed citizen of Prakrit." Balinar spoke with sincerity, his voice formal but warm. "Congratulations, Torrin. You have accomplished what no other human has ever done. You walked the Labyrinth, and lived. You now possess the rights belonging to each of Prakrit's citizenry and I will not unjustly restrict those rights. But I will ask that you remember the responsibilities that inherently accompany them. When ready, you may have your meeting with the High Council."

"That is no longer what I want," answered Torrin. He stood rigid, arms clenched at his sides, muscling his courage and his strength. Focused, he faced Balinar with an intense and unwavering expression. "Instead, I challenge you to the Crown Match as is my right as a new citizen of Prakrit!"

The room erupted in shock and outrage. The Crown Match Torrin had learned about during his intimate association with Darya in which he magically examined the information filed in her mind. It was a duel to the death and Torrin's real motive for entering the Labyrinth. Each new citizen had the right to challenge the king to this duel. If the contender wins, or if the king rejected the invitation, the challenger becomes crowned as the new monarch. But the challenge must be made immediately upon exiting the Labyrinth and only with those weapons acquired there by the contender. The king likewise could use only what he brought with him to the Victory Room, but which was generally a great deal more significant than any weapons found in the Labyrinth. This custom evolved in order to ensure that an infirmed monarch could be replaced by someone stronger and better equipped to rule. This tradition was another way by which the dwarves sought to safeguard the strength and integrity of their kingdom. But the challenge was seldom made since most departing the Labyrinth were young, inexperienced, and exhausted by the recently completed ordeal and the demands required in simply becoming a citizen.

Anger and betrayal crossed Balinar's face, leaving it hard and fiery. His previous affection for Torrin made his newly kindled hatred all the more vehement.

"Quiet!" Balinar bellowed, silencing the room with his commanding voice, a voice like thunder and with a bitter edge. "Be quiet!" he barked. "A challenge has been issued."

Balinar, clad in battle-ready garb and with his war hammer hanging at his belt, further approached Torrin, who stood armored only in tired muscles and a tattered, linen loincloth.

"Are you sure you don't want to rescind that challenge?" asked Balinar in a manner that was more warning than inquiry. He unholstered the hammer, holding it threateningly before Torrin, glaring at him indignantly.

"The challenge stands, as shall I over your defeated corpse," snarled Torrin, posturing for the crowd in an attempt to convey an image of fearlessness and power.

Truth be told, he was somewhat apprehensive. Unlike his opponents in the Labyrinth, Torrin could not run from or apply his wizardry against Balinar, at least not overt magic. Beyond seeing Balinar as a formidable adversary, an obstacle to be overcome in pursuit of a goal, Torrin scarcely recognized the dwarven king as a person. Torrin gave no thought to Balinar the man. In Torrin's estimation, Balinar was simply a means to an end.

Balinar roared in a wrathful battle cry, swinging his hammer in an arc aimed at Torrin. Torrin dodged and using the fighting techniques learned from the elves, he kicked, planting the ball of his foot against the bridge of Balinar's noise. The pair fought cruelly. Torrin was soon reminded of the brutal damage a blunt weapon was capable of inflicting. An evasive move too slow in its reaction caused Torrin to incur the crushing impact of Balinar's hammer to his left side, breaking ribs and puncturing a lung. But he kept fighting and hitting Balinar with kicks and punches. Gradually the hostile crowd grew impressed with Torrin's agility and tenacity. A few even cheered Torrin when he accomplished a particularly dramatic counter or attack.

Beyond everyone's expectation, the struggle went on for quite some time, a thrilling contest of fecund violence in which the combatants battled mercilessly against one another. It stirred the dwarves' essential character, their savage natures, their primitive bloodlust. The impassioned excitement of the crowd and the adrenaline-charged combat seemed to feed on one another, each fueling the other's frenzy.

Torrin grappled with Balinar, for the moment clear of his hammer but not the abusive power of his arms, punishing Torrin's broken ribs and threatening to snap his spine. From Balinar's belt, Torrin managed to free a dagger and slice deeply across the dwarven king's face before he could break free. In quick darting moves, Torrin lunged at Balinar, trying to stab him with the newly won blade. Not quick enough, Torrin soon found himself again unarmed. Turning aside the dagger, the head of Balinar's hammer met Torrin's forearm with crushing force. The splintered edges of the fractured bone poked grotesquely through his skin and bright crimson blood erupted from the wound. Shock waves of tremendous pain sped from the useless, mangled limb to Torrin's mind. Nearly overwhelmed by the agony, he just barely stayed on his feet and managed to avoid another blow from Balinar's weapon.

In spite of his hurts, Torrin kept fighting. Defeat meant death as well as failure. Instead of holding back and in true dwarven style, Torrin mastered his pain and attacked with renewed vigor, striking Balinar with a flurry of kicks and left handed punches. His nose broken, one eye swollen, Balinar's face was battered and bloody. But none of his injuries were life threatening. Torrin was losing.

Then his luck changed, although Torrin would never admit the victory had been won by anything but his own skill and excellence. Torrin struck Balinar with a powerful kick to the chest. Recoiling from the blow, Balinar fell backwards upon a spear held by the bronze figure of a statue. His eyes widened in horrified astonishment at the fatal change in fortune. The ornamental spear pierced his heart, its blood-covered tip penetrated Balinar's sternum. In a death-rattle, his hands trembled and his body shook. Then the limp, lifeless form slumped forward. Balinar died quickly, perhaps never knowing exactly who or what had killed him.

But the crowd knew. They saw what happened and applauded Torrin's ingenuity. Despite his dissimilar race, Torrin's courage and victory impressed the dwarves.

Forgetting his injuries, Torrin flushed with exhilaration, exalted by the power of his triumph. He went to the fallen king, took Balinar's hammer, and with his left fist clenched around the weapon's handle, raised it above his head in a symbolic gesture and an emotional rush.

"Quiet!" Torrin roared, echoing Balinar's earlier command and deadening the clamor of the hall. He turned slowly in a circle, looking to the balconies, holding the dwarves with his intense, stormy gaze. "I am your king! I am king of New Hope, Kweiyang, and now Prakrit. Soon I shall add Gairloch to my expanding realm, and after that—all the world shall be mine to rule. To my followers, wealth and glory. To my enemies, ruin!"

He paused to glare at the crowd for a silent moment, mentally mastering the anguish of his wounds and conveying an image of untainted strength and unbending will. "Anyone who would dare question my kingship, my claim on Prakrit, do it now! And prepare your soul for death." Again he scrutinized the crowd, daring them into contest and with controlled body language promising certain defeat to any foolish enough to challenge him.

Lost somewhere in the throng of people, Darya exclaimed, "Hail, King Torrin! Long live the king!" Not privy to Torrin's plan, she had not expected this turn of events, but was excited by its prospects.

Dwarves love a winner, the stronger the better. Like it or not, Torrin had won his place through mortal combat. And if the gods chose a human to lead them in battle to power and glory, so be it. Their passions stirred, their hunger for war inflamed, the dwarves threw their support at Torrin's feet. They began chanting his name over and over, louder and louder, so that it rolled like thunder through the hollows of Prakrit.

"Torrin! Torrin! Torrin!"

Smiling wickedly, Torrin raised the hammer once more, then left the Victory Room in a flourish. Right now all he wanted was to find a place alone where he could tend his wounds. But Darya was waiting for him in the outside passage.

"My lord king, you have done it. You have the dwarven army you sought," stated Darya.

"Yes," answered Torrin distantly. "And as promised, I reward my friends. As my first official act, I hereby appoint you as the highest ranking general of my newfound dwarven army. You shall enforce my will among your people. Disappoint me and you will regret it to your death, which will be excruciating if not immediate."

"What is your will, my lord? Do you need a healer? How can I serve you?" asked Darya, eager to flex the muscle of her new office.

"Where is Yoshindo?"

"He is with the other elves at their encampment. They were joined two days ago by your human contingent from New Hope."

"Excellent," said Torrin. "Go to them. Bring back Yoshindo and two humans named Quinn and Connor. Then you can begin mobilizing the dwarves. They must be prepared to march in three days. Understood? But first, show me to the king's living quarters."

By the time they arrived, Torrin had mended his broken body and was resting comfortably in a stiff, wooden chair. There was a long table spread out before him set with delectable victuals—fruits, meats, cooked vegetables, and pitchers of ale. A feast had been prepared for the new king and his friends, but it was a banquet for a select set, a private celebration. The guard, a man Darya swore could be trusted implicitly, announced the guests. Torrin rose to receive them.

Not one for ceremony, Quinn rushed forward, embracing Torrin in a fond bear hug. "Thank the World Spirit you're alive," exclaimed Quinn, grinning from ear to ear and affectionately slapping Torrin on the shoulder, a shoulder still sensitive from his earlier conflict. "I knew it. I knew you couldn't be dead. We waited, on the hope you'd return."

"Good to see you too, Quinn," answered Torrin warmly. "It's good to see all of you and you did well to wait."

"You continue to amaze me, Lord Torrin," Yoshindo said with sincere respect. "You are indeed quite an astonishing individual. When I left here, I felt certain that you had perished. Now to my great pleasure, not only do I see that you yet live, but Darya informs us that you have been crowned as Prakrit's king.

"That's right and I shall be king of Gairloch just as easily," Torrin boasted. "Ah, you brought my pets."

Two large hunting cats padded forward to Torrin. He reached down to scratch beneath their chins and pet behind their ears. Torrin had adopted the felines, or they him, back at Kweiyang. Torrin straightened from the cats and they walked off, tails swishing and ears alert, to curl beneath his chair.

"Come, sit down and we'll fill each other in on what's been happening," invited Torrin.

Torrin, Quinn, Connor, Yoshindo, and Darya found their places at the table. They gave Torrin what news they had and he related the events that had brought them to this point. While they ate, Torrin provided a cursory outline of the next phase of his plan. He would wait to discuss the specific details of that plan until tomorrow, after he had time to recuperate more fully from the ordeal of the past several days.

The dinner complete and the social obligations satisfied, Darya prepared to depart. "With your consent, my lord, I shall take my leave. There are matters to which I should attend before retiring," Darya explained.

"Not plots to supplant me, I hope?" Torrin joked.

"Never, my lord," said Darya with a feral grin. "Such a plot would only bring me down with you. And I have no wish to fall so far or so hard."

Torrin nodded at her self-motivated loyalty. "Make sure you remember that. Good night."

In the spirit of celebration, Connor overindulged in his consumption of ale. Dwarven ale was stronger, more stout, than the beer to which Connor was accustomed. He did not, however, become overly drunk. Connor retained most of his control, but the alcohol did leave his speech slightly slurred and his attitude a bit more at ease than was customary.

Connor was excited, intoxicated as much by current events as by ale. Torrin had done everything he said he would do. Out of fantasy, he made the elves a reality and now even the dwarves called him king. And Connor intended to rise in power right along with him. Regardless of his ambitious nature, Connor knew his own limitations enough to realize that if it had been him instead of Torrin, he could not have come this far this quickly. But why strain yourself to do a job when someone else can do it for you? Let Torrin rule, there would be power enough to share. *And Torrin would reward those loyal to him*, Connor thought. In stark contrast to Quinn, Connor was exuberant, emotionally charged and talkative. He was free with his thoughts and opinions.

"This is a landmark day," pronounced Connor enthusiastically, raising his cup in salute of his proclamation. "We are writing history. A united army of humans, elves, and dwarves against a common foe; it's unprecedented. What we do will change the world and our exploits will be recorded for posterity. Soon all the world will know our names."

"Yes," Yoshindo affirmed. "This is most assuredly the eve of a new era. We have embarked on a momentous adventure. Regardless of the outcome, life as we knew it will be changed forever."

"Hey, I know what we need," Connor blurted, his eyes aglitter with inspiration. "We need a heraldic devise, a symbol to represent our unified army, a banner around which we can rally our combined forces."

"A good idea," Torrin acknowledged. "Anyone have a suggestion as to what this devise should be?"

"Well, the oak tree is a powerful image and one representative of…" began Yoshindo before Connor cut him off.

"Wait, I have a better idea," Connor interjected. "The griffon. It's perfect. You see, the lion hindquarters are symbolic of the ferocious physical might of the dwarves and the eagle front section represents the powerful wisdom and grace of the elves."

"Not bad," said Torrin. "But where is the human element to this devise?"

"The eye," answered Connor, as if revealing a great revelation or secret. "The eye is human because it is we who have the vision. We see our destiny and compel the rest toward its fulfillment."

Torrin stared at Connor. Then his gaze shifted to the eye branded upon the open palm of his right hand. "Yes. The griffon, it sounds right. That shall be our standard," Torrin proclaimed, and with remembered anger, slowly curled his right hand into a tight fist.

"It's a good choice," said Yoshindo. "I will have our women begin sewing banners and painting shields with its design immediately." With that and Torrin's leave, Yoshindo departed for the elfin encampment.

"Well, I suppose I should get back to camp too," said Quinn in a dispirited tone and rising wearily from his chair. Growing increasingly reticent, Quinn's earlier elation had melted away over the course of the evening so that he now appeared troubled and forlorn. "The soldiers have been on edge. They're willing to fight alongside the elves but living next to them still has them a little nervous. Besides, they'll be anxious to hear what the plan is. And there's always things that need tending in a camp of that size. The soldiers can fend for themselves well enough, but there's families out there too, and they're not conditioned to this kind of life."

"If anyone can pull them through this, Quinn, it's you. Thank you for all you've done. Soon it will all be made worthwhile," promised Torrin.

"I hope so," murmured Quinn, then louder. "You coming too, Connor?"

"No, I'll stay here tonight. See you in the morning."

"Good night then," said Quinn, closing the door on his way out and leaving Connor alone with Torrin.

Torrin moved from the table to lounge in a settee. The sofa was thinly padded and covered in lavender velvet. The cats followed him, one sitting at Torrin's side, the other across his lap. Torrin idly smoothed the animal's fur and scratched around its neck. The feline began to purr and its eyes closed in contentment. Connor poured himself another cup of ale and the two talked in a relaxed, friendly atmosphere.

"Cats are impressive animals, superior to most and they know it," Torrin thought out loud, idly stroking the animal's fur. "Virtually from birth they are self-reliant, whereas most newborns are dependant and helpless, even human young. A kitten has claws and will use them in its defense even before its eyes can see. As adults they are proud, vain, arrogant and predatory. They will do almost nothing just to please their master. Even if they hunt for me, it's done partly for the thrill of the kill. Their mood dictates when you may pet them. And they purr not for your enjoyment but to let you know that you are pleasing them and not to stop." As if in proof of Torrin's point, the cats jumped from the settee, bored with Torrin and ready to explore Prakrit.

"I had a dog once," offered Connor.

"Arg," groaned Torrin in disgust. "I hate dogs. Dogs are vile, stupid creatures. They are completely dependant on the attention of others. They crave it so desperately that they will urinate on themselves in excited expectation of it, begging with their round vacant eyes and lolling tongues. All a dog wants to do is love someone and be loved. They will do anything to win that love no matter how demeaning. And as a result, they allow themselves to be abused and neglected."

"But you can train a dog," argued Connor.

"That's true," Torrin admitted. "I'm not saying that they can't be made useful, just that they are in no way admirable."

Torrin left the settee to refill his glass with water and change the subject. "Well, Connor, the day is almost here, the day of reckoning. We are on the verge of greatness, the defeat of Gairloch. What an army we have. The very sight of it will strike terror into Bryana's heart. We've come so far in so short a time, accomplishing so very much. And we did it all on our own and from nothing. Gairloch must be brought down. We shall have our vengeance and we shall show no mercy to our enemy. We owe nothing to Bryana, except perhaps a bit of credit for being the push that set our conquest in motion," Torrin stated sarcastically.

"Perhaps not even that," Connor answered carelessly. The rash words were out before his ale-soaked mind realized what he'd said.

"What do you mean by that?" asked Torrin with solemn intensity. In response to Connor's peculiar statement, Torrin focused his full attention on him, contemplating his words and scrutinizing his manner. Unable to meet his gaze, Connor flushed and appeared shaken. His suspicious behavior suggested Connor was hiding something, something dangerous to him if not to Torrin.

Unsettled, certain he had revealed himself, the words began to roll off Connor's tongue in a nervous tumble. "It didn't turn out exactly like I planned. I never meant for Lenore to be hurt. I didn't think they would kill women and children," confessed Connor, rising from his chair and backing slowly across the room to the wall.

"I did it for you, you've got to believe that. When I went to Gairloch, I told

Bryana that you were in New Hope and that you were building an army. I thought that if she sent her soldiers to investigate you would see how vulnerable we still were and devote more attention and resources to our military force. I never thought for a moment that they might attack the village, and I certainly never believed Lenore might be killed in such an attack. I'm sorry, Torrin. You've got to believe me. If I could turn back time and bring Lenore back, I would. I am sorry. It just didn't work out the way I planned. But it did work. In a way, it did work. You have to admit that it was the catalyst that brought us to this point. You said it yourself, we are on the verge of greatness."

"Was Quinn involved in this plan?" questioned Torrin. Concealing his emotions, his face as transparent as the stone walls around them, Torrin revealed nothing of how he felt.

"No. He doesn't know anything about it."

Unsure how his revelation was being received, Connor worried. He stood ill at ease, shifting his weight from foot to foot. Sweat beaded thickly on his brow and Connor scratched nervously at his forearm.

"I understand your motives, Connor. It was a bold plan," Torrin said calmly as he approached Connor.

In a forgiving and companionable gesture, Torrin placed his hand on Connor's shoulder. He felt Connor relax slightly and returned his uneasy, sheepish smile. But only for a moment.

Torrin's smile shifted to a malevolent scowl as he tightened his grip on Connor's shoulder and invoked his magic. With wizardry he immobilized Connor, paralyzing his movements.

"No one betrays me and lives," snarled Torrin.

He placed his other hand firmly on Connor's chest, his nails biting into the skin. Torrin called upon his magic again to gain control over Connor's heart. He had done this before to save lives, to resuscitate victims of heart failure. Now he applied the power to attack the organ, to kill its host.

Outraged, Torrin wanted to repay Connor's treachery with pain and death. He derived a kind of ecstasy from the act of killing and wanted to maximize its pleasure. For this reason he even took time to consider in which direction to take Connor's heart. He chose to progressively increase its rate, believing this would be more painful and terrifying than the more gentle death that would result by gradually slowing down the pace of his heart. Excited pleasure swelled within Torrin as he watched Connor's face contort in horror and misery. It was with a hint of disappointment that Torrin felt Connor's heart burst, disappointment because the climax seemed to come too soon. Perhaps

Connor's heart was weaker than he thought or maybe Torrin rushed it. But the premature end left Torrin feeling inadequately satisfied.

He carried Connor's lifeless form back to the table and sat him slumped forward in a chair. Leaving the corpse at his dinner table, Torrin retired to his bed. In the morning he would tell the others that he had gone to sleep before Connor and that Conner must have had a heart attack during the night. Torrin did not want anyone to know of Connor's treachery much less that he had killed Connor. Both had the potential to weaken his subjects' faith in their king. It would be best if Connor's death was nothing more than the unfortunate product of natural causes.

Having murdered the man who was arguably the cause of Lenore's death, one might think that Torrin's hatred of Bryana would abate. But it did not. The Beast had taken full possession of Torrin's soul and could no longer be restrained. Torrin's anger was as cold and hard as ever. He still blamed Bryana for much of his misfortune. In his estimation, she had attacked and persecuted him relentlessly, attacks that must be redressed so that Bryana would rue the day she ever thought to threaten him. And her doom would be for his delight as much as it would be for his advancement. Bryana was as much to blame as Connor and she would meet the same fate. Unstoppable, Torrin's hatred continued to grow together with his lust for power. Earnestly he wanted to take Bryana's life and absorb her strength, personal and political.

"I can't believe he's dead," Quinn sorrowfully expressed, shaking his head over the loss. Connor's body had been removed, leaving Quinn and Torrin alone.

"Neither can I," agreed Torrin. "If only I had been awake when it happened, I might have been able to save him. Let us at least remember him as the first casualty in the defeat of Gairloch. He would appreciate that more than being remembered as dying of a heart attack before the battle ever began."

"The first casualty," Quinn echoed sadly. "I'm sick of death already and it hasn't even started yet. Damn it, Torrin! Why are you so determined to have this war? It's madness. You wouldn't listen to me before, and I kept hoping you would come to realize it on your own. Tell me, what is it that we are fighting for? If it's for Lenore, she's dead and nothing we do will change that. Is it justice? War with Gairloch will kill innocent people as well as those who attacked New Hope. How is that just? And how can this war be for New Hope if we are leaving it behind? Please, let's forget about war and go home where we might accomplish something positive, where we can honor Lenore's memory through things that have more to do with life and beauty. This course of destruction we're on, it isn't right. Let's stop while we still can. Like that night we met, when it all began, let's start over with a new beginning."

In response to this unexpected challenge, Torrin struggled to control his temper. "You've reminded me several times of that night we met, the night I asked you what you wanted and you said a king. But you have never asked me what I want. Well, I'll tell you. I want it all. I want it all, blood, power, revenge, wealth, strength, pleasure. Nothing shall keep me from it. I want it all and I shall have it, and you shall have your king."

"What about love?" asked Quinn, thinking again of Lenore.

"What about it?" Torrin snapped. "I can't want what I can't see. But should I find it serves me, I'll want that too."

"For crying out loud, Torrin, what do you mean you can't see it? You can see love in your memory of Lenore. And what about me? Haven't I proven that I care? I've been right beside you every step of the way. But you won't listen to my advice and you won't let me help you in the way I know I should."

"Yes," said Torrin, "you've proven your loyalty. But can I count on it? Are you turning on me now or do you hold true to the pledge you made? Are you a fair weather friend only? You speak of love, but if you love New Hope how can you not want to avenge the attack made upon it? And what about Lenore, how can you let her murderer go free? You swore to serve me, to be my friend and my loyal subject. I took it as a solemn oath. Was it a lie? Are you telling me now that your word, your commitment, means nothing? I counted on you more than any other; was I wrong? Did I judge you poorly? Are you now ready to betray me like the others, now when I need you more than ever?"

The words hit their mark, stinging with a cruel venom. Conflicting emotions threatened to tear Quinn asunder, the things he knew to be right pulling him in different directions. He had a strong loyalty to his friend despite the fact his friend was moving toward a destructive purpose. Although opposed to war, Quinn could not bring himself to try and physically stop Torrin, if that were even possible in view of Torrin's abilities. And abandoning him would change nothing except to damage the way Quinn felt about himself. To leave would violate the value Quinn placed on friendship. If he wasn't a friend, if he didn't belong, what was he?

"You are still my friend and I won't let you face danger alone," Quinn said finally and in a defeated tone. "My loyalty remains steadfast, you needn't lose faith in that. I am here for you, no matter what."

The continuation of their conversation was halted by the appearance of Yoshindo and Darya. "My Lord Torrin," said Yoshindo. "You asked that we join you here. Are you still prepared to discuss battle plans or in light of Connor's demise would you prefer to delay the strategy meeting?"

"No. This war cannot wait," insisted Torrin. "Come in and let us organize our attack. As I've said already, each of you shall serve as general of your respective forces, Yoshindo for the elves, Darya for the dwarves, and Quinn for the humans. And all of you shall answer to me. We will remain here two more days, drilling the armies so that they can fight together effectively and so that we can assemble the necessary war machines and weaponry. Then, we march on Gairloch. I want a fast pace. But given our size and mobility that should take us at least another five days. We'll have to push them hard, drive the soldiers under the whip," Torrin said it as a figure of speech, but he would literally do that and more if he had to. He would have Gairloch; nothing would stop him.

The planned conquest Torrin proposed was grossly understated in terms of its difficulty. Gairloch possessed strong defenses that would not be easily overcome. But Darya's dwarven sense of fighting superiority and Yoshindo's ignorance of the human lands kept them from raising such questions. Quinn had a better idea of what they might be up against, so it was he who asked for more clarification and assurances.

"Penetrating Gairloch's defenses won't be easy," suggested Quinn. "And I'm not sure we could survive a long siege. From what little I know of Gairloch, they have ample internal food and water supplies. So starving them out would be difficult. And they have the full might of the Prelature on their side as well as a large army of trained soldiers. I shudder to think what all those wizards might be able to throw at us. But even if we can defend against the Prelature, if our siege takes too long we may have a force to battle against other than that behind Gairloch's gates. Word of our attack will inevitably reach the other human kingdoms. They will come to Bryana's aid and we will be caught in the middle."

Darya nodded. "Quinn has a good point, several of them in fact. Perhaps it would be better if we started by attacking one of the other human kingdoms, such as Braemar or Parhelion."

"That might be prudent," agreed Yoshindo. "We could take one of these lesser strongholds, building our force so that we can attack Gairloch at a later date. Or by taking one of the other castles, it may force Bryana to come to us, giving us the more secure position of being on the defensive."

Torrin drew a deep, heavy breath, his chest rising slowly beneath folded arms. The sound focused the other's attention on Torrin as effectively as if he had sounded a trumpet. His eyes smoldered with a dangerous light.

"Fools. Cowards," Torrin growled. "You want to march our army right past Gairloch's front door and halfway across the known land to Parhelion, hoping Bryana won't descend upon us en route. Do you think she will give us free passage across her land out of gratitude for having postponed our attack on her? And I suppose Parhelion's king won't think to use all that time to firm up his defenses. After all, what tactical advantage could the element of surprise possibly give us? No, I want Gairloch and I will settle for nothing else. Once we crush Bryana, the other kingdoms will be easy pickings. They will fall into chaos fighting among themselves over who will take the lead in Bryana's absence. It's Gairloch and it's now. But I agree that there remains some serious problems we need to work out. Quinn's right, Gairloch must be taken swiftly. We need to figure a way in so that we can breach the gates and, if possible, immobilize the Prelature. All I need is a way to get inside and I can blast Gairloch wide open."

"Why don't you just fly in?" said Darya casually.

Torrin shot her an angry look in response to what he took as a sarcastic remark. "What is that supposed to mean? I warn you, I'll not tolerate any more insubordination."

"No, no. You misunderstand me," Darya quickly explained, trying to turn aside Torrin's wrath and regain the composure his angry stare had stolen. "I wasn't being flippant. I thought you knew; I thought that was why you took the griffon as your standard. There is a special bond between the dwarves and the griffons. We can't exactly tame or domesticate them, but at times we can compel them to tolerate us. Once under control, they can be ridden. You could fly right into Gairloch under cover of the night."

As she spoke, a smile gradually broadened across Torrin's face. When she finished, he released an amused chuckle while rubbing his chin with one hand and thumping the table enthusiastically with the other. "Well I'll be damned. Perhaps old Connor's choice for our standard was divinely inspired after all. How many griffons do you think we can get?" demanded Torrin excitedly.

Hopeful that this information would raise her standing with Torrin even further, Darya bristled with satisfaction as she elaborated in answer to Torrin's question. "There's a small griffon pride in the mountains north of here. Not all will yield to a handler, but I'd say out of a pride that size we should be able to bridle four, maybe five griffons."

"I would have wanted more," said Torrin. "But that will have to be enough. I'll take one, Darya you'll take one since we need you to control them, and the rest will be ridden by human soldiers who will be less conspicuous than elves or dwarves as saboteurs inside Gairloch."

Darya shook her head. "I can't do it. Only certain dwarves have the skill to be griffon handlers and I am not one of them. But I do know someone perfect for the job."

"Good," Torrin proclaimed. "You each shall lead your respective forces when we march on Gairloch in two days hence. In my absence, Quinn will be in charge. You are to follow his orders as if they were my own. I, and the other griffon riders, will meet you at Gairloch and put up a signal when the gates are ready to be stormed. It's only a matter of time now. Victory is ours!"

Chapter 8
Aragon

Darkness and silence permeated Shantung Crypt, unbroken by the elfin lords locked within their tombs and their eternal rest. A single sleeper stirred, the only one who lived inside the crypt as well as resided there. Resting upon a stuffed mattress and tangled in light blankets, Aragon twisted unconsciously in an attempt to free himself from the grip of a nightmare. The vision he saw in his dreaming state was a horror yet to be, a premonition of a world fouled and abused by a growing evil. This evil spread out across the land like a plague devouring life and destroying everything in its path. The massing black death progressively swallowed up each point of light and beauty touched by its spreading wave of annihilation. And at its dark, ravenous center, laughing with gluttonous and malevolent delight, was his brother—Torrin.

Thrashing at his covers and damp with sweat, Aragon came awake with a start in a hard, shuddering seizure of fear. Disoriented by the choking hand of terror, strangled for air, he felt as if incredible danger was closing in all around him.

Awake now and remembering where he was, Aragon forced his breathing to relax, slowly drawing in deep cleansing breaths through his nose and releasing them just as gradually through parted lips. Still his ragged breathing echoed through the quiet tomb. Under the control of his magic, Aragon's pulse returned to a more normal pace but the muscles in his neck and arms still ached from the nocturnal ordeal of his frightful dream.

Aragon swung his legs over the side of the bed and slumped forward as if weighed down by anxiety, resting his arms upon his knees. The dream had not vanished, its memory lingered and it scared him deeply. Augury was not new to Aragon and he believed this dream to be a tocsin, a warning, a signal of disaster.

He tried to convince himself otherwise but the feeling would not leave him. The dream of catastrophic destruction weighed his spirits down like a heavily sodden cloak. The haunting vision refused to be pushed completely from his mind. He kept seeing the blistered, tortured land melting beneath the terrible darkness, an expanding affliction bred by his brother's cruel designs.

The dark drew back with the lighting of a large candelabrum. Aragon could have used wizard light but at times took comfort in the soft, warm glow of natural candle flame. The morning routine unfolded unchanged. Aragon put himself through a familiar series of physical and mental exercises, bathed, and then went to his desk to continue his studies of the elfin records. The language was easy for him now and several volumes had already been committed to memory. The spells took time to learn and to perfect. But his abilities had by this time increased ten-fold, so that his skill was at least a match for, if not better than that of, any wizard alive. And he had learned applications of magic that no other possessed. All this scared Aragon too.

Aragon viewed power in a way vastly different from his brother. Aragon was by nature curious, thirsty for knowledge and wanting it largely as an end in and of itself. But with knowledge came power and, for Aragon, power was something to be feared. Where Torrin was hungry for power, Aragon was a reluctant recipient of it. Power led to abuse. It always, even if only unconsciously, was used to force others to conform to the powerful one's view of how the world should be structured. It stifled diversity, killed creativity, and enslaved individuality. The use of power changed things irrevocably. What is more, a person's power never seemed to grow proportionate with his intellect. At times it seemed to Aragon as if some natural law dictated that the two possess an inverse relationship. A wise man should be more cautious as his power grew, not less so.

For Aragon, these ideas were the source of a good deal of self-recrimination and self-doubt. As his own power grew, he began to distrust himself, fearing that it would pervert his values and make him far too dangerous. This belief that he was a potential threat served as one reason why Aragon chose to isolate himself from others. He could never again live among large numbers of people as in a castle or village. That kind of life was simply too great a risk. Aragon knew people thought of him as moody, intolerant, and aloof. Truth be told, perhaps he was. But the cause of this perspective, his forbidding public aspect, was more the product of the effort he was required to exert in preserving his control and maintaining his tolerance. It troubled Aragon that people regarded him with suspicion and contempt, particularly since he believed he tried so very hard to always look upon them with goodwill. It was safer here, but often lonely.

Still, although it frightened him, he could not stop his magic from growing stronger. The best protection from power came through understanding it, which in the course of a vicious and inevitable circle led to its acquisition. He had to know what he could do. So, although his power was vast, he practiced magic in small ways, in those that tested his control but in a manner least likely to affect others.

Preoccupied, Aragon had read the same page three times and still without knowing what it said. His mind was elsewhere. He could not dismiss the dread hanging heavy over him, the nagging vision of his dream, the foreboding of widespread ruin wrought by his brother's hand. He closed the book, rubbing his eyes and wondering where Torrin might be. The answer to that question refused to come but in the pit of his stomach, Aragon knew what Torrin's aim would be.

But what am I to do? wondered Aragon. *Do I take action to stop him, or kill him if I have to, under the assumption that the strength of my magic makes my judgments accurate, that might makes right? What would be the consequences of such action?*

You see, Aragon told himself. *That's the first thing I thought of, to force Torrin to act as I believe he should. Power breeds impatience and is too easily self-promoting. Why am I so certain that Torrin will not be more effectively swayed by reasoned arguments than by physical mandates? I should give him that chance. I must find him and make sure he understands what he is doing. It is a time for clear thinking. Only that can save us from ourselves.*

From the cool earthen enclosure of Shantung Crypt, Aragon stepped outside. It was late in the afternoon, the air warm and humid. Still, it felt good to be under an open sky. He spent too much time shut up in his study, he told himself reprovingly.

Nestled in the foothills of the Barisan Mountains, the natural beauty of the landscape around Shantung Crypt held an arresting impact. High upon the peaks of the surrounding mountains, rivers of snow and ice flowed down cracks and crevices and pooled in circular recesses of the jutting stone summits. Around the rock mountaintops and intermittently obscured by the mists of gauze like clouds, dark green pines marched part way up the slopes and reached for the sky as if in envy of the altitude attained by the mountains' zenith.

The green forest spread out upon the foothills and in a ring around the valley in which Aragon stood. To his right lay a serene wetland, its quiet surface a watery mirror of the clear sky. The wetland was jeweled with orange spotted touch-me-nots, water lilies, pickerelweed with its crowded spikes of purple flowers, the white blooms of water hemlock, and floating emerald duckweed. Beneath the gray bark of pumpkin-ash and the brown, scaly trunks of bald cypress, reed canary grass and dogwood shrub grew in thick clusters.

Hanging upside down or flying to and from their perch, hundreds of bats crowded the surrounding tree limbs. Black bodied with heads hooded in reddish-brown fur, they were called flying foxes, large bats, many possessing wingspans of up to three feet. In Aragon's estimation, they were remarkably beautiful and graceful creatures.

From the large flock, he recognized one who was a friend. In need of this friend's help, Aragon called to the bat with his magic, inviting it to approach. Also as part of this invitation, Aragon gripped the edges of his own dark cape, moving his arms slowly up and down, unfurling and retracting the material in imitation of the flying foxes' wings.

The bat left the tree, its black, leather-like wings flapping in an eloquent rhythm as it flew toward Aragon. It landed lightly on his chest, hugging his cloak with its claws and passively regarding Aragon with small round eyes, bright and brown.

"I need your help my friend, if you will give it," Aragon spoke to the animal's mind, not controlling it but merely communicating with it. For Aragon, possession, even of an animal's will, was an unjustifiable wickedness, an inexcusable evil. "I need you to fly to the northern lands to search for my brother. He will have an army with him. Find Torrin, then find me so that I may know where he is located."

After the bat communicated its consent, Aragon planted in its mind an image of Torrin together with further instructions. Wasting no time, the bat lifted into the air, flying away in great haste. Gradually it became a smaller and smaller black spot in the vast blue expanse of the overhead sky until it slipped from sight and was no longer visible at all.

This completed, Aragon found a large rock on which to rest and prepare himself for the next required task. It was an arduous task he faced and one with unlikely prospects for success. He needed to obtain the help of another but one who would not willingly give it. The individual he sought shunned people, being even more of a recluse than Aragon himself, and in certain ways he was as powerfully magical as Aragon. Aragon had caught glimpses of this elusive creature before and knew that he lived somewhere in these woods.

Entering a state of trance-like concentration, Aragon's eyes rolled back beneath closed twitching lids. He focused and directed his thoughts into the woods, reaching out in expanding concentric rings, searching, calling. It took a long time even to locate him, but once Aragon did, he locked on, resisting his subject's strong willed attempts to sever the communication of Aragon's projected thoughts. Magic to magic, they connected. Aragon did not use his power in an attempt to command or control him. Instead, Aragon relentlessly explained his need and repeatedly recited his petition to the other's mind, trying to acquire his service and cooperation. The other resisted defiantly, angry at Aragon's unwelcome intrusion and persistence. Aragon did not use his full power but its potential was visible, which although unintended may have been perceived as an unspoken threat.

Hours passed and Aragon still had not won the other's assistance. But he continued to struggle toward that goal, calmly and diligently describing his need. The day began to wane. In the wake of the setting sun, the sky was awash with color. Blue, lavender, red, and orange flowed together at the horizon and above the treetops. Over and over, crickets chirped the repeated chorus of their monotonous song. And with the deepening of dusk, clouds sailed serenely past the rising moon. Leaden with fatigue, Aragon's body began to feel heavy and his head ached from the prolonged labor of his concentration. But he was close, very close. He could feel it.

So, apparently, could the other woodland inhabitants. As if aware of the mental struggle and that it was about to reach its climax, a hush settled upon the forest's nocturnal stirrings. The silence amplified the creature's approach. It broke from the trees with a crash, charging into the clearing.

This was the first time Aragon had seen the pegasus in all its gallant glory, unobstructed and for more than a fleeting instant. The sight was intimidating even though expected. The dapple-gray winged horse faced Aragon, its eyes like cut garnet, gleaming with a deep red fire. The animal's movements together with the nighttime breeze animated the stallion's silvery mane, making it dance around the beast's muscular neck. Agitated, the pegasus continued to protest the wizard's intrusion, threatening Aragon if he did not stop and leave him in peace.

But the harassment continued as Aragon persisted with his appeal. In stormy annoyance, the pegasus threw its head back and from side to side as if trying to shake Aragon from its mind. Its nostrils flared and snorted. The ground pounded in answer to the pegasus' curvet, its tense and forceful prancing. On its hind legs, the pegasus reared, unfolding its extraordinary feathered wings and flailing hooves as beautiful and deadly as polished steel.

As the pegasus stamped and shifted, its milky white tail swished violently. The tufts of hair growing above its hooves were also white, making the fetlocks appear like wisps of cloud surrounding the stallion's legs. An exceptionally striking culmination of magic, strength, and agility, the pegasus' actions were intended to intimidate, an effect not wasted on Aragon.

Aragon had been slowly but steadily approaching the pegasus and now stood directly before it, within striking distance of its hooves. Aragon controlled his apprehensions, projecting an air of confidence despite the fact that he had communicated to the pegasus not only that he would not harm it but also that he would not defend himself even if attacked. Aragon wanted it made perfectly clear that he was in no way threatening the pegasus to submit to his will. Aragon wanted only cooperation freely given, nothing taken.

After several nervous minutes, his unrelenting approach succeeded. The pegasus agreed. Its name, as Aragon learned through their telepathic debate, was Helicon. Helicon, reluctantly swayed by Aragon's impassioned appeal, consented to carry the wizard to his destination. Taking hold of the pegasus' withers, the ridge between its shoulder blades, Aragon pulled himself onto Helicon's back, sitting astride the magical beast behind its neck and in front of its immense wings. For support, Aragon held tightly to the mane and used his legs to hug Helicon's flanks.

Then, without warning, Helicon charged forward and with a strong, vigorous bound leapt into the air. Helicon's wings beat powerfully, carrying them higher and higher above the ground. They traveled northward, gaining altitude. The features of the land, dimly lit by the moon, passed below them in miniature detail. Unlike Torrin and his father, Aragon had never been an skillful horseman. So, rather than by his equestrian skill, it was through Helicon's acceptance of him that Aragon kept his seat. Helicon endeavored to make the ride as smooth as possible, shifting when necessary to preserve Aragon's balance. The flight took them far and away.

Two days later Aragon found Torrin but forever lost his brother. The bat Aragon had dispatched led him here, to a hollow pass in the foothills of the Tissima Mountains. Concealed by the trees and the cloak of night, Aragon spied upon the horde of soldiers camped in the valley below. The sight stole away what hope he yet had of peacefully turning Torrin from his course of destruction. It was clear that Torrin was beyond reason now and for Aragon to approach him would be suicide.

Careless in their bravery or believing that Gairloch was yet too far away to notice them, the army did little to hide their presence. Fires, large and bright, illuminated the scene with a wild, ghoulish glow, glinting as if in warning off metal armor and idle weapons. Drums beat, exciting soldiers' passions and with such force that Aragon felt the frenzied rhythm in the marrow of his bones. There were scouts patrolling the surrounding terrain, a constant danger but one Aragon had successfully eluded thus far.

Aragon waited and waited until finally Torrin emerged. The crowd received him with a deafening roar, saluting their king with an emphatic cheer. They began chanting his name, to which the ground seemed to tremble in answer. Torrin was clothed in a blue robe adorned with steel armor and shrouded in a cloak of evil. His aspect sickened Aragon, filling him with grief, pity, and dread. At Torrin's signal, the crowd silenced to hear his speech, words which elevated the bloodthirsty greed of the murderous horde, words which drove a stake through Aragon's heart, killing hope of Torrin's redemption. Where once brotherly affection had lived inside Aragon, he now felt only a grieving, hollow ache.

"By all that's holy, Torrin, what have you done?" wondered Aragon aloud. "Damn it all. Your own hate wasn't enough for you; now you've got them hypnotized and hysterical. Dwarves, elves, and humans hungry for blood, screaming for war and justice, your brand of justice and by whatever cruel means serve your avaricious ends." Rising from his cover, Aragon threw himself upon Helicon's back and together they took flight into the dark sky, bound for Gairloch and at an urgent pace.

A rude shock awaited Bryana in her private chambers, rooms protected by posted sentries and thought to be unoccupied. Yet, someone was seated at her desk scribing notes upon a piece of parchment. "What in the…?" she began in surprised exclamation, a reaction which increased with improved recognition. "Aragon! What are you doing here? How did you get in?"

"Ah Bryana, I was beginning to wonder if you would ever show up," Aragon remarked calmly, folding his arms and leaning back in the chair for a better view of his bewildered host. "I know that my being here carries with it a death sentence; but please, wait until you've heard what I have to say before you summon the guard."

Curiously, critically, she regarded Aragon in unmoving silence. He had grown to be a tall, lean-muscled man hardened by the rigors of life outside the comforts of a castle. He was self-confident in a way some might mistake for arrogance. His face still possessed a youthful appearance, despite the bitter lines engraved upon its surface. Sensing no immediate danger and interested in how else Aragon had changed as well as in what message was important enough to have brought him back to this forbidden land, she took a seat and invited him into conversation.

"I suppose the guards can wait," she said.

"Thank you." Aragon sighed, placing two lank fingers to his temple as if his head ached. "The time has come. Torrin is on his way back to Gairloch and he is not alone. He has amassed a sizable following, a force of unprecedented composition. Somehow he has built an army of humans, dwarves—and elves. Their goal, his goal, is Gairloch; and I fear there is nothing he wouldn't do to take it from you. I no longer know what he is capable of, but I know he is a threat you should take very seriously. If he isn't stopped, the world will suffer."

Bryana studied Aragon for several moments without uttering a word. She looked somber and when it came, her answer was not what Aragon expected. "When Torrin was five years of age and yourself only seven, you came to me to report a vision you had received, a prophesy that Torrin would one day be my bane, the cause of my downfall. I likewise had experienced similar visions that I kept to myself until you forced my disclosure by your own. Although no clear details were ever forthcoming, we both saw that Torrin would be associated with, if not the source of, great misery and evil. My advisors counseled me in all earnest to do away with Torrin, that he was simply too great a risk to tolerate. But in one of the few times in my life, I was indecisive and unsure in how I should act. It was you, a child, who persuaded me to spare Torrin's life. You said that we did not know enough to risk action as rash as the killing of an as yet innocent child, that it may be the very outrage from such an act that would bring me down, tearing the kingdom apart and moving the land toward ruin. You said that by keeping Torrin near and raising him under my tutelage, I could better prevent disaster, that I would secure his loyalty and be able to anticipate problems in advance and thus be better equipped to respond to them. I was swayed by your arguments together with your mother's pleas to spare Torrin's life."

She paused and swallowed deeply to fight off the sour taste of remembered grief. "When he killed Devin, I thought that the prophecy had been realized. And I still do. The tragic death of my son caused me great pain and brought turmoil to Gairloch. If I hadn't controlled the situation it could have turned catastrophic. The rippling effects of that atrocity are still being felt. As you may know, other rumors of rebellion associated with Torrin have been brought to my attention. And a response to these rumors that got out of control resulted in the wanton destruction of a harmless village and a smear on my good name. I have even received reports of Torrin's death. So, what am I to believe? I believe your childhood prophecy has witnessed all the reality it was ever meant to see. The danger Torrin represented is gone and we have only to repair as best we can what damage his actions have already caused."

Prodded by Bryana's reminiscence, Aragon recalled another disturbing experience from his ungentle youth. The recollection was of Aragon's mother rocking his then three-year-old sibling to sleep. He remembered his mother telling Torrin, as mothers will, that he could be anything when he grew up, anything at all. But that seemingly innocent sentiment had terrified Aragon, left him shaken and afraid. Rather than the casual words of encouragement Marketa intended, Aragon heard a warning and from that point on, doubt of whom his brother might prove to be lurked in the back of Aragon's mind.

"No," asserted Aragon. "You're wrong, Bryana. Torrin is still alive and still a threat. I have seen him and the force he carries with him. Prepare yourself, Bryana, or Gairloch, if not the world itself, is doomed."

"Damn it, Aragon," she snapped, lurching to her feet. "Do I look like a fool that I would believe in the present day existence of elves or that dwarves would join forces with humans? Ridiculous! I don't know what your motives are but it is *your* plan that is doomed, not Gairloch. What is it that you want? Do you want me to search the land for Torrin, hunt him down and kill him? Isn't that inconsistent with your previous advice? What would you do? How confident are you that Torrin is a peril that must be thwarted? If he were here in this room with us now, would you kill him?"

Aragon shrugged his shoulders tiredly and answered, "I don't know."

"Of course you don't," complained Bryana as she moved to a window and gazed outside. "You never had the nerve to take action, much less responsibility, only to demand it of others. I don't trust you anymore, Aragon. How could I, after what you did? You had such promise when you were young. Yours was such strong magic. Because of the promise I saw in you, I was going to part with accepted custom and appoint you as my successor rather than my own child. But you ruined all my plans by betraying my trust and taking leave of your senses."

"I took leave of the wizard Prelature, not my senses. There is a difference," Aragon argued. "Besides, it was never meant for me to rule as king."

Bryana continued to stare at the starlit firmament, lost in thought. Coal-black clouds began to roll in from the west, slowly consuming the evening sky.

"So much went wrong," observed Bryana. "I wish you would have at least discussed it with me first. But no, you just announced your resignation before the full Prelature and walked out. It was never the same between us after that. You've given me no reason to trust you, Aragon. Even if he yet lives, I simply can't accept that Torrin, my son's weak and vile spawn, is any threat to Gairloch. If he is alive and he breaks the law, he will be punished. And if he or any other is foolish enough to attack Gairloch, rest assured that we can defend against it."

When no reply came from Aragon, she turned and found him gone. He had vanished without a sound, as if he had never been there at all.

Outside the castle, Aragon saw that Helicon had gone. Having fulfilled the duty he had required of the pegasus, there was no compelling need for Helicon to remain or even for him to bear Aragon back to the Barisan Mountains. Alone with his uneasy thoughts, Aragon walked the shoreline of the lake from which Castle Gairloch drew its name. The landscape lay wrapped in an unruffled calm; a pervasive hush permeated the cool night air, broken only by the soft measured sound of shallow waves breaking against the lakeshore, repeated over and over in an invariable rhythm and with a tranquilizing quality. The quiet was so complete, so strong, that it seemed almost indomitable, as if nothing could destroy the serenity of this moment. But Aragon's prescient vision pierced the night's deception, the illusion of unshakable serenity. He recognized the delicate fragility of this peace. At the core of his heart he knew chaos and destruction were charging toward this site like a crazed beast, violent and unreasoning.

Seated upon the shoreline's grassy slope, Aragon stared out across the lake, pondering the calamitous situation he believed was about to unfold.

Tenebrous, the black surface of the water appeared hard and flat like a vast expanse of slate. Threatened by approaching storm clouds, the moon hung full and heavy in the night sky, casting a broad band of pearly luminescence across the lake, a shimmering reflection of the moon's milky, lambent light.

Silver maple, cottonwood, box elder, and pin oak circled the lake, visible now only as huge shadows, like dark sentinels looming over him and whispering warnings of imminent danger. Amidst the tall grass and shrub, the shore lay littered with rocks and deadwood. At Aragon's left, a large shellbark hickory extended from the bank at an angle so that its limbs hovered above the lake, the leaflets of its drooping lower branches dipping beneath the water's surface. The lapping waves had partially eroded the shoreline at the base of the tree, leaving its roots exposed and reaching out like the gnarled fingers of a giant's hand. Darting between these submerged roots, like silver flashes in the shallow water, gizzard shad scrapped algae off rocks, with some of these fish falling prey to larger bass also feeding in the near-shore littoral area of the lake, a bustling center of biological activity. The ample food and habitat of this ecosystem supported an abundantly diverse community of animal life. A great blue heron lifted gracefully into the air, taking flight. Aragon watched as a muskrat left its haystack-like home built of vegetation and above the high water mark. Wet, its rich brown fur glistened in the moonlight as the rabbit-sized rodent swam, foraging for roots and tubers and leaving a gentle wake behind him in the otherwise quiet water.

Suddenly the calm was broken. From below, something burst from the water in a flash of yellow and red, snatching the muskrat and disappearing again beneath the lake's surface. Startling him to his feet, it happened too quickly for Aragon to determine what the hunter had been. For a few minutes more Aragon remained motionless, listening and surveying the area for some sight of the intruder, some clue to its current position. There seemed something unnatural, yet familiar, about this mysterious predator.

The water broke again, but this time the animal's head and upper torso remained visible, its cold amber eyes staring back into Aragon's. The power in Aragon's staff flared to life, casting light from the gem affixed at its top that radiated outward in an illuminating emerald glow. The light fell upon the animal. Its head, the size of a large man's, was that of a snake, with a cobra-like hood spread laterally from the sides. It opened its mouth, exposing long fangs slick with the muskrat's blood and flanked by rows of small, sharp, recurved teeth. Unlike a true snake, it possessed shoulders and a pair of arms. Each hand carried three large, fingered claws. From its nose to the tip of its tail, the snake-like creature measured at least nine feet in length, covered in glittering iridescent scales of red, green, and beige with a gold colored underbelly of larger, overlapping rectangular plates.

From his youth, Aragon recognized the serpent. They had been friends at one time, many, many years ago. "Massuaga!" Aragon said in surprised greeting to his former childhood friend. "What brings you back to Gairloch after all this time?"

"Same thing that brings you, Aragon," hissed Massuaga, his sibilant words expelled with the flickering crimson of a long, forked tongue. "I am here because of Torrin. I see no reason why I shouldn't benefit from the actions of others. You and I both know the world is about to change; to survive we need to be prepared, to flourish we need to be well positioned."

"How do you know what is happening?" demanded Aragon. "Are you working for Torrin; is he your master?"

"Stupid human, I am my own master. I see things. I can scent the changes in the air. That is why I'm here, so that I can be in a position to take advantage of the new order. Don't you feel it? Exciting times are at last returning to this drab world."

"Is that it?" asked Aragon. "Have you lived so long that you would welcome any novelty, even the kind of cruel revolution proposed by Torrin? How old are you, Massuaga, you never told us? You look unchanged, the same as you did when I was a child, ancient yet with an exuberance usually reserved for the young."

"Of course I haven't changed," answered Massuaga. "When one is perfect, there is no need for further evolution. I am old though, Aragon, very old indeed. In fact, I knew the elf who once wielded the staff you now possess. His name was Shikai, a very powerful wizard. He had other toys too, things that might serve us both well in this uncertain age, this dynamic point in your history. Care to bargain, care to form a partnership of sorts with me? I can be of help to you."

"What are you babbling about, Massuaga? Are you saying that you have things which once belonged to the elfin wizard Shikai, magic items that you propose to use against Torrin?"

"I don't have them, no," Massuaga hissed. "But I know where one is located, one very powerful toy—the Orb of Empathy. It was mine once, but she took it from me. Together, we could get it back. If you agree to help me, I'll let you use it on Torrin, however you wish."

"Wait just a minute, Massuaga. You're getting ahead of yourself. What exactly is this Orb of Empathy and who has it now?"

The lake water rippled as Massuaga splashed forward, slithering closer to Aragon and resting upon the rocks lining the shore. He looked carefully over each shoulder as if in fear of eavesdroppers, and in a hushed, sibilant whisper he spoke with the manner of a nervous conspirator. "The Orb of Empathy is very strong magic; wondrous, exciting, potent magic. With it, the user can feel the exact emotions of others; you feel what the other person feels. But there's more, oh much more. The Orb can be employed both ways. You can use the Orb to force the emotions of your choosing upon another, making them feel whatever the user wishes—love, fear, remorse, anything at all. Being able to control someone else's emotions has great potential; don't you agree? The Orb of Empathy was my favorite thing in the whole world, but that rotten, stinking sylph stole it from me. Oh, I hate her so much; but only if I'm out of range or only if she lets me. Damn her! She wants the Orb for herself; you can guess why.

"Aurelia is a sylph, a spirit of the air; although she can certainly manifest herself in a very solid, bodily form. I suppose you humans might consider her beautiful. But being a sylph, Aurelia has no heart. She's a magical creature who can assume a mortal form yet remains a soulless spirit. And because she is incapable of feeling any emotions of her own, she uses the Orb to live vicariously through others, sharing their emotions as if they were hers. She samples of them freely, surreptitiously, and without anyone's consent. She is a thief and a spy and a terrible woman. She has no right to the Orb; it is mine and I want it back. Help me get it and I'll let you use it against Torrin. Then you give it back to me and it's mine forever, just as it should be."

Although Aragon recalled a reference to this Orb of Empathy entered in one of Shikai's journals preserved on file at Shantung Crypt, he remained suspicious of Massuaga. "Why should I believe any of this? And why should I trust you? After all, I remember the reason you were driven out of Gairloch so long ago."

"That was not my fault," Massuaga spat furiously. "You and Torrin were more to blame than me for that unfortunate incident."

"You kidnapped an infant, stole a baby girl from her crib. She died," stated Aragon coldly.

"It wasn't my fault! You and Torrin stopped coming to see me; I missed the games we used to play. I never meant any harm to the baby. I only thought that if I took her and raised her, she would always be my playmate and never leave me. Not like you and Torrin, who forgot all about your old friend

Massuaga."

"Still, the baby was found dead inside your lair," said Aragon.

"Not my fault," he inveighed, hissing angrily. "You probably told them I did it, told them where my lair was located and had them route me from my home. Damn your treachery. I did not kill the babe. She was unmarked, was she not?"

"Your logic is a bit twisted," Aragon argued. "And there were other things equally disturbing uncovered in your lair as well. Your innocence is a hard pill to swallow."

Massuaga spat in quick-tempered disgust. "Enough of this stupid reminiscing. The past is past. Let's limit our discussion to the present, the future. Do we have a deal or not?"

Aragon labored over deciding what action he should take. Bryana seemed unwilling to heed his warning. *Should I attempt to stop Torrin?* he asked himself, finding the question ponderously difficult. Both Aragon and Torrin held philosophies centered around power, but they approached the central issue from radically different perspectives. Where Torrin lusted for power, viewing it as the supreme achievement, the greatest good, Aragon viewed power with trepidation, fearing that it would be misused.

I cannot say that I am without any doubt that my vague prophesies of doom will come to pass, thought Aragon. *And still I have love, as well as hope, for Torrin, albeit difficult to preserve. Would it be right to kill Torrin for a wrong he only appears to intend?*

Aragon felt reasonably confident that Torrin was about to wage war on Gairloch, about to perpetrate unspeakable atrocities in an insatiable pursuit of power. If he intervened, Aragon might be able to prevent the horror he believed was imminent. But would it be moral to punish Torrin for the mere contemplation of a crime? *What if I'm wrong?* Aragon asked himself. *What if Torrin elects to use his army only as a bargaining tool to parley with Bryana, working from a position of strength in negotiating the settlement of their feud? Or what if at the last minute, Torrin finds conscience enough to turn away from his destructive ambitions? But what a risk to take on that unlikely hope. Is one man's death, even that of my brother's, acceptable to safeguard the lives of many? If this Orb of Empathy does exist, perhaps it could be used to determine exactly what moves Torrin's heart, if virtue may yet reside there. Once I know Torrin's true emotional state and see how far gone he is, I'll know what I must do and how. But I will not use the Orb to take possession of him, not that, not by the Orb or any other means. If I'm forced to choose between killing him and possession, I'll kill because that would be the lesser of the two evils. To dominate his soul would be far worse than dominating his physical person even if such restraint were carried to the extreme, to the point of ending life. No matter what evil might be forestalled by using the Orb to oppose Torrin, I will not take possession of his soul. I cannot argue that the end would justify the means, for it would not. The fact that through possession rather than termination, Torrin would still be alive may make the former seem like an easier burden on my conscience, but that is wrong. His life would be a lie, Torrin's will would no longer be his own, and that would be a fate worse than death. His soul must be free to choose or he is not a man at all. I will use reason and even physical force against him if necessary, but never possession. To take his life would be a lesser harm than the destruction of his individuality, the spiritual freedom of his soul. That above all else is sacred.*

"I'm not making any deals, Massuaga," Aragon told him. "But I will go with you to check out your story concerning the Orb of Empathy and this sylph, Aurelia. Where can we find her?"

"What do you mean, no deal? You don't trust me, is that it?"

"I didn't say that," assured Aragon. "I just don't want to make any commitments without knowing more about what's involved. But we can do this together; tell me where Aurelia resides."

"No," insisted Massuaga. "I'll not tell you where. If I do that, you may start thinking that you don't need me anymore. I'll show you and I'll tell you what more you need to know only as you need to know it."

"Fine," conceded Aragon. "Let's get moving; we haven't much time in which to complete this investigation."

Massuaga at least admitted that their search would take them down river. To quicken their passage, Aragon untied a skiff from its moorings, its theft made acceptable by the urgency of his purpose. It was a long narrow rowboat with a small sail. Aragon was not particularly skilled with boats, but he confidently presumed that he could pilot the craft adequately and carry them with good speed. Massuaga pulled himself over the side rail and slithered into the skiff, his serpentine body coiling and twisting. Aragon pushed off from the dock and they were on their way down the Dunegall River.

The waning twilight melted into a cloud-covered dawn. Aragon busied himself with the responsibilities of the helmsman, steering the small boat upon a steady course. Neither trusted the other enough to hazard the luxury of sleep. So it was, without much further discussion, that the unlikely companions embarked upon their quest. They would not stop for rest nor other comfort during this journey; Aragon was determined and spurred onward by a pressing need for haste.

During their passage south, suspicion and fear began to nag at Massuaga. He desperately wanted the Orb back, desperate enough to ask for help. But now he worried that he would lose the Orb again, that Aragon would cheat him and keep the prize for himself. *I will have to kill Aragon once we recovered the Orb,* thought Massuaga, *there is no other choice. But can it be done? Aragon is a strong wizard; it will not be easy to subdue him. It will have to be by ambush, taking him by surprise. Maybe Aragon was not necessary after all,* Massuaga speculated, ruthlessly scheming the framework of a crime. *I cannot risk losing the Orb again. It is really much too dangerous for me to involve Aragon any further. But I must have it! Maybe, just maybe if I had Aragon's magic staff, I would not need his help. Then I could do it all myself and share the Orb with no one. Yes, I will take the staff and with it the Orb will once again be mine. He deserves it; I owe him nothing. After all, he first betrayed me. It is only fair that he now give me the staff in compensation.*

With villainous resolve, Massuaga's anxious thoughts quieted. He glanced eagerly at Aragon from time to time; greed glittered in his wicked amber eyes. Patiently, Massuaga waited for the right opportunity to strike. Licking the air in perverse expectation, his tongue darted between deadly teeth.

"The storm's getting bad," shouted Aragon, loudly so that his words would not be lost to the near gale force wind. The weather had turned frightfully foul; sheets of rain blew violently, drenching them and lashing at their sail. The boat pitched, rising and falling in the rough water. "Is it much further? Do we have to take shelter or can we make it if we keep going?"

They were caught in a flash flood. The river was cresting, its current racing in a treacherous velocity. The brown, sediment-laden water boiled and surged around the boat, attacking the stream banks and any obstacle in its rampant, turbulent course. Overwhelmed by the force of the raging water, the unstable stream banks began to fail in several places, causing large masses of bank material to slough into the river; dragging soil, shrub, and even trees into the torrential flow. Trees and other debris that had been undermined and swept into the river began to accumulate in the channel, making the current increasingly erratic and dangerous.

Like a flag of surrender, the boat's white sail flapped wildly before being ripped from the mast and carried off in the howling blast of wind. The boat was out of control. It spun and jounced like a plaything of the fearsome floodwaters. Every bump and jolt of its perilously rough current threatened to capsize the small craft.

Then, before there was time even to brace themselves for the impact, it happened. The river smashed their boat against the hard, granite flank of a large boulder that lay partially submerged in the watercourse, splintering the skiff's wooden frame. Mercilessly, the water continued to drive the boat into the unyielding boulder, sundering the craft into a mass of broken timbers. Both Massuaga and Aragon were thrown into the river. Aragon, still clutching tightly to his wizard's staff, fought the rushing current, trying desperately to gain the safety of the stream bank. But the river foiled his attempts, keeping him a prisoner of its helter-skelter fury. The wild, incessant rapids pulled at him and beat him with wave upon wave formed from the frothy brown water.

Massuaga, more adept at maneuvering within an aquatic environment, saw this misfortune as an opportunity to seize possession of Aragon's staff. Beneath the stormy surface of the river, Massuaga swam toward his target. Directly in front of Aragon, Massuaga burst from the water, his serpentine tail coiling around Aragon's waist and legs in an effort to further immobilize his prey. Like daggers, the sharp fangs of his gaping maw struck deeply into Aragon's unprotected shoulder. Fighting back, Aragon gripped Massuaga's hooded throat, holding the serpent's lunging jaws at arm's length while pounding at him with the staff. Massuaga battled against him, tearing at Aragon's arm and raking the long talons of his right claw across Aragon's face, opening deep wounds down his cheek.

Like a bizarre musical accompaniment to their violent dance, the river swept the adversaries forward in the shifting, bobbing movement of their watery passage, buoyed upon its fast-paced and fluid rhythm. Although the river played on, it brought their battle to an abrupt end. Charging on the momentum of the heavy current, the deadwood trunk of a fallen tree smashed into Aragon and Massuaga, breaking them apart like a battering ram. Stunned by the blow and numbed by the frigid water, Aragon's battered body was now tossed about all the more savagely by the rushing river. The current had taken nearly complete control of him. Still futilely struggling with the river, Aragon's head struck a rock. The collision was devastating. Aragon's eyes rolled back beneath closing lids, and the last element of consciousness of which he remained aware was a desperate gasp for air cut short by the strong, all encompassing embrace of the cold water.

Fortunately, Aragon did not drown. He was rescued, but by those with motives not exclusively confined to unselfish concern for his well-being. His rescuers took him to a water-filled cavern beneath Loch Eriboll, a refuge sheltered from the passing storm. The clear, green tinted water in which Aragon lay floating was blissfully calm and warm. Filled with a pacifying sense of safety, his body felt limp, his mind utterly relaxed.

Around him they swam, perhaps the most lovely creatures to inhabit the water—mermaids. They moved with an unequaled grace, gliding through the water effortlessly, each dive, roll, and frolicking undulation expressed as a dynamically evolving work of art, like sculpture set in motion. Their tails were pale gray in hue and dolphin-like in form, merged perfectly to their human torsos. All were distinctly feminine and full bosomed. There were nine in this group, cavorting with an exciting playfulness. Their faces were slender and marvelously beautiful, surrounded by wondrous drifting manes of long flowing hair, some blonde, some a deep auburn in color, and others of a brunette shading.

They circled and spun around Aragon, approaching him singularly or in pairs. But he did not feel threatened, experiencing instead a deep contentment and a sense of profound wonder which seemed to efface any hint of apprehension. They brushed and rubbed their sultry bodies against one another and against Aragon. The smooth, sensitive skin of the mermaids was indescribably soft and pleasant to the touch.

Two lingered by him, caressing him gently and holding him firmly in a sensual, fondling embrace. Charged with sexual overtures, their kisses were long and seemed to fill Aragon's lungs with the mermaid's warm exhaled breath, an intoxicating vapor. Words were whispered in his ear, but he could not discern what was said, hearing only that the sound was strangely soothing and seductive. It felt as if he were dissolving in their tender grip, but it was an agreeable sensation. The two slowly unwrapped themselves from Aragon, releasing him to the lovingly curious hands of another mermaid. She likewise held him nestled to her ample bosom; her sumptuous lips pressed purposefully over his.

Although mermaids are intensely social creatures, with many of their favorite activities based on physical contact, this erotic performance was more than a mere game. Beneath the tranquilizing effect of their touch, Aragon began to suspect that he was involved in something dangerous. Dangerous, but not a sinister nor malicious threat. It was not a danger to his life but to his way of life. And in their hearts, the mermaids saw no harm in what they did.

For his own inspection, Aragon held up his right hand, finding only that the skin was puckered from prolonged immersion in water. But his left hand had changed; the skin was smooth and the fingers now slightly webbed. His body was being altered, purposefully mutated! The shock of this discovery worked to liberate him from the soporific daze under which he lay entranced. The mermaids were engaged in the performance of an exotic ritual, executing a formula for the creation of a merman. By the mermaid's touch and with each breath they breathed into Aragon's lungs, he was being transformed. Only in this manner could a merman be produced. And once the metamorphosis was complete, it would be his duty to breed with the mermaids to provide for the natural birth of more females and the continuation of the species. The merman would be expected to stay with the group, continuing to perform his unique services as needed or for sport. It could be a very pleasant way of life and many men might have welcomed such an opportunity. But not Aragon. Although he perceived that they meant no ill will and good intentions motivated their desire of him, he could not accept this offer nor allow himself to be so possessed, not even temporarily.

There was still time to stop the transformation, for as yet only his left hand and the ability to breathe underwater had been altered. With a grudging reluctance and in an effort that required tremendous strength of will, Aragon disentangled himself from the mermaid's compelling embrace.

As he swam abruptly away, they beckoned to him, calling him back with persuasive pleas and tantalizing gestures. Concentrating on the problem of his brother, Aragon blocked from his mind the enticing lyrical call of the mermaids, the strong drawing power of their seductive allure. Although they could have easily caught Aragon, they let him go. One sweet-faced mermaid, mesmerizing in her physical charm, even returned Aragon's staff. With brilliant green eyes, she regarded him sorrowfully, saddened at his decision to leave. She kissed him lightly on the cheek, then waved in a final farewell. The maids of Loch Eriboll did not force human males to become what they desired; such action was generally unnecessary. Most men would willingly succumb to their enchanting magnetism. But then Aragon held little in common with most men.

Time is running out, thought Aragon, worried that it may already be too late. He had left Loch Eriboll and entered The Barrens to pursue one final, yet meager, hope. The Orb of Empathy would have to wait for another day. Massuaga had disappeared, and Aragon realized that it would take far too long to search out the Orb of Empathy on his own. So he took a different course, setting out on a quest for other aid. Exhausted and ill at ease, Aragon spent the past twenty-for hours since his departure from Loch Eriboll working his way over rugged terrain and penetrating deep within The Barrens.

Dry and empty, The Barrens is a vast rocky canyon, a gorge gigantic in width and depth but sparsely populated with life of any kind. It formed a formidable gateway to Mount Karakulrum, the dwelling place of the trolls. Trolls are an ancient race, seldom seen and often referred to as the Old Ones because of their immemorial lineage. The history of their existence stretches further back in time than that of any other civilization. Yet, so little is known about them. For theirs is a solitary race, refusing any contact with the outside world and having sufficient might to preserve their isolation. If detected, Aragon's presence here could easily provoke the hostility of the Old Ones. But he was on a mission worth the risk, one about to bear fruit.

He had heard legends describing its existence and it was the goal of his quest within The Barrens. But these preparations were inadequate, for nevertheless, Aragon was struck with awe by the exceptional magnitude of the temple, the Oracle of Gurrot. By trolls, it had been constructed in a wide opening of the canyon. In the center was a huge flat-topped pyramid. Several yards from each corner of the pyramid's square base, a massive obelisk had been erected, four vertical stone shafts with pyramidal apices carved from a single piece of granite. A fifth obelisk had been placed centered atop the pyramid, towering as the temple's highest point.

Humbled by its impressive size and grandeur, Aragon approached the stone temple with uncharacteristic timidity. Massive, it grew larger with each step taken toward it until he stood at the foot of the pyramid, dwarfed by its enormity. The stairs scaling up the pyramid's slanted, tapering wall had been designed to accommodate legs longer than his own, compounding the arduous nature of the climb.

His muscles cramped with strain and with lungs burning from the demanding physical exertion, Aragon reached the summit. Before him, at the toe of the crowning obelisk, was the Oracle of Gurrot. It was for this that Aragon had come.

The Oracle of Gurrot was alleged to be a medium through which knowledge of the past and future might be revealed, along with the secrets of one's soul. It had been made from stone in the form of a shallow basin filled with water and perched upon a thick pedestal. Like the pyramid and the obelisks, the Oracle's stone framework was flat and smooth, unadorned with markings of any kind. There was, however, one exception. On the Obelisk directly behind the Oracle, a single symbol had been carved upon its surface, the image of an eye and coincidentally the same icon branded into Aragon's palm.

Invoking the supernatural power of the Oracle, Aragon passed his hand over the basin. The air felt suddenly cooler and quiet, an unearthly stillness. The water in the basin began to swirl in a luminous whirlpool of color.

Aragon had little, if any, control over what the Oracle chose to divulge. It began by showing him deeply personal scenes from his past, painful and haunting images. The eerie display continued to evolve; changing in the where, when, and who of its presentation; shifting to other incidents, different people and places. The emotions elicited by these magical pictures were as potent as if Aragon were presently living the illustrated episodes. Joy, regret, love, shame, anguish—it was overpowering. For hours it held his gaze until at last its focus turned to Torrin's campaign against Gairloch.

Such horror, Aragon shook with the intensity of it. Never did he imagine Torrin to be capable of such evil. In vivid, horrifying detail, the Oracle verified Aragon's own vague prophesies of Torrin's corruption. All doubt was now erased. The sight was overwhelming, more than Aragon could bear to witness. But he could not turn away nor terminate the Oracle's damning revelation. Desperate to break its abhorrent hold on him, Aragon plunged his hands into the sacred water of the Oracle.

A heavy tremor rumbled through the pyramid in answer to Aragon's unconscious violation of this holy vessel. The water ignited into a wild, boiling, churning frenzy; turning a bright blood-red. Shapes formed in the crimson pool, the writhing figures of ghastly miniature demons. Then the smooth planed surfaces of the obelisks began to glow, revealing thousands upon thousands of carved symbols that before had been mysteriously concealed from view. Sheets of shimmering lavender light flared from each obelisk, connecting the four corner shafts to one another and then to the pinnacle of the central obelisk. The mystical light formed a prison in which Aragon was sealed in consequence of his sacrilegious act. Now certain of Torrin's wicked intentions, Aragon was incapable of acting on that knowledge.

Chapter 9
Home

It stormed that night. Lightning sundered the sky with brilliant flashes of arching light and the earth rumbled in echo of each thunderbolt. With howls of wild wrath, turbulent gusts of wind whipped the heavy rains with tremendous violence. But it did not stop him. Nothing could.

Through the tempestuous twilight, Torrin rode the griffon, focused on the distant castle lights and navigating toward them despite the buffeting storm. Behind him followed four other griffons, although one had lost its rider to the strong winds. The winged creature serving as Torrin's mount had a name, a name that he had given it. Torrin called the griffon Nemesis. Its dun-colored feathered wings defied gravity and the wind swept sky, beating powerfully against the rain above the chestnut flanks of its lion-like posterior. Its blue eyes and black, deeply dilated pupils sparked with a ghastly luster, mirrored flashes of the brilliant lightning. Torrin spurred Nemesis forward, raising his axe and shouting above the storm in a howl of excitement.

At last they reached Castle Gairloch, angling toward its highest tower, a tower patrolled by seven soldiers. Their cries covered by the storm, three of the seven were quickly disposed of by a trio of death-delivering bolts fired from well-aimed crossbows. Before the remaining soldiers could react, the griffons dove and hit their prey full on. They seized the soldiers with their massive talons, digging into their chests and ripping at their hearts. With a brutal grace, the griffons snapped their victims' necks in their razor sharp, eagle-like beaks, and tore open the soldiers' throats. Watching, Torrin considered it a beautiful, almost artistic, kill.

"You know what to do," Torrin commanded his fellow saboteurs. "Make certain the gates are ready when the army gets here. Now go! And death to anyone who fails me."

Torrin turned back toward the leader of the feasting griffons. The beast was rending and devouring large chunks of human meat. "Nemesis, you and your brothers are my servants now, now and forever. Finish your meal; then get out of sight. But come back to me, your home is here now. And there will be more work for you once the fighting begins."

Torrin descended the tower stairwell rapidly, his eyes ablaze with evil anticipation. It felt good to be home. Moving past the familiar stone block walls, it was as if with each step he regained more of Gairloch. Soon it would all be his. Gairloch, the jewel of the known land, was his home and from it he would never again be dispossessed. Memories, good and bad, welcomed Torrin back. They were his memories and he had a right to claim the structure in which they lay encased. He had spent most of his life here; that time and the intimacy in which it was expended made Gairloch his. There was power in Gairloch, power in its structure, occupation, and its familiarity. He would seize that power, hold that power, and from it extend his domination throughout the world.

Guards stood bored and idle at their post outside Bryana's door, guards Torrin remembered, guards he killed. It was easy, and Torrin gave their lives no more thought than he would give a cockroach squashed beneath his boot.

Silently, Torrin dragged the bodies through the double doors into the oak paneled anteroom of Bryana's chambers. Once inside, he closed and barred the doors. The rooms were quiet, dark, and still. Torrin had been in these private chambers only a few times in his life but he remembered every detail, its smell, its furnishings and their arrangement, and the mysterious allure of its forbidden nature. A soul stirring excitement washed over Torrin as he worked his way through the room in death-like silence.

He stepped into Bryana's bedchamber and, holding his own breath, Torrin could hear the faint and gentle rhythmic pulse of a sleeper's breathing. The remnants of an earlier fire burned within the hearth, casting a dim, orange glow about the room and filling it with strange shadows. A smile curved upon Torrin's lips as his eyes came to rest on Bryana.

She lay slumbering in a large four-poster bed ornately carved from dark rich mahogany. Cornered by the tall erect bed posts, Bryana slept peacefully, her body wrapped in a soft quilt and her long silver hair draped across mauve colored pillows thickly stuffed with down. Focused on Bryana, Torrin crept closer and in doing so carelessly brushed against a nightstand. The sound brought Bryana awake. Propped on her elbow, she searched the dark with squinting eyes for the source of the sound.

"Is someone there? Aragon, is that you?" she asked, still caught in the confusion of disturbed sleep.

Then she saw him, saw the glimmer of light reflected off the curved steel of Torrin's axe. Out of the shadows, he stood at her bedside, soaked with rainwater and dripping with malice.

"You!" Bryana gasped in horrified astonishment.

But she was crudely forced back into unconsciousness by the violent sweeping backhand of Torrin's clenched fist. The steel gauntlet around his hand impacted against the side of her head with monstrous brutality, cracking unprotected cheekbones and driving Bryana back down upon her mattress.

When after several minutes Bryana awoke again, her hands were bound, her mouth gagged, and her eyes blindfolded. Her body's sense of touch told Bryana that she was still upon the bed, positioned on her back and extremely vulnerable. Her mind remained dizzy from the blow delivered by Torrin and his punishing assault left her head throbbing with intense pain.

Torrin noted that despite her years and through the aid of magic, Bryana remained an attractive woman. She was a potent wizard and formidable warrior; the muscles of her athletic frame remained hard and her tan skin firm. In consideration of these virile attributes, Bryana's sleepwear seemed a strange incongruity, being distinctly delicate and feminine. She wore a white gown with a ruffled neckline, a hemline that came above the knee, and graceful lace insets that ran the full length of the long sleeves to the barrel cuffs at her wrists. It appeared curiously out of character for the strong leader, as if the High Queen should be expected to sleep in armor and her crown.

At the touch of Torrin's bare sweaty hand upon her cheek, she instinctively jerked away, making her pain-racked head swim against new waves of agony. Torrin slipped his fingers through her soft white hair, leaning in closer to his victim. Bryana cringed at the airy rub of Torrin's hot and heavy breath upon her face.

"It's me, Bryana," he whispered intimately into her ear. "Your grandson Torrin has come home to pay you a visit. I see that the years have been quite kind to you."

His heart swelled with sadistic venom, a hateful desire. Giddy with the anticipation of savage pleasure and of the acquisition of power, Torrin rubbed one hand along the exposed flesh of her calf, embrocating it with perspiration.

His touch was abhorrent, making Bryana's skin crawl with disgust. But when she tried to slide away from him in order to avoid the offensive stroke of his disturbing massage, Torrin clamped his groping hand over her leg, kneading painfully on her thigh and holding Bryana firmly in place.

"Don't move or I'll make it worse. Much worse," snarled Torrin. His voice held a scintillant eagerness. Torrin was excited, stimulated by her weak and helpless state or rather by his own mastery over the "great and mighty" Queen Bryana.

Rage and terror bubbled through Bryana's veins, but for the moment she stopped fighting him. A shudder of revulsion washed over her. She was revolted not only by Torrin but also by the sense of doom and defenselessness he instilled within her. Having always been proud, brave, and confident, the feelings of helplessness she was experiencing now were as repulsive to Bryana as Torrin's radiant malice. To be at Torrin's mercy was offensive as well as frightening. Reeling with pain and terror, she realized there was nowhere for her to run, no way of summoning help or to save herself.

"Why did you call out for Aragon when you woke?" Torrin asked his gagged victim. "Have you welcomed him back? Is he a common visitor to your bedchamber? It makes no difference to me; Aragon is no threat."

Smug in his dominance over Bryana, Torrin plucked a piece of fruit from a bowl on the nightstand by the bed. Hovering over Bryana, Torrin bit into the succulent peach. Juice from the overripe fruit rolled down his chin and dripped upon Bryana's cheek. She winced as if the juice were a more potent acid, capable of stinging and searing her flesh. Amused by the reaction, Torrin took another more extravagant bite, purposefully causing a heavier stream of juice and saliva to fall upon her face.

He tossed the remaining fruit aside. "What's the matter, Bryana; are you afraid of me? Well, you should be; you should be."

He placed his hand over her cheek, grinding the fluid of his fruit into her split and bruised flesh. The syrupy mixture blended with her blood under his hurtful pressure. Pressing hard against her cheek, he pushed the feverish pain blazing inside her skull to burn more intensely, bright like the wet reddish smudge smeared across her face. Pausing from the abuse, Torrin slid his sticky fingers from her cheek, placing his palm gently around her throat but applying only a hint of pressure, a mere suggestion of mortality.

"The years may have been kind," said Torrin, speaking softly and with a cruel edge honed upon each syllable, "but I won't be. Gairloch is mine. And so shall be the power of your magic. But before you die, I want you to feel your life fade, and your wizard power drain from your soul and into mine."

She struggled to swallow beneath his tightening grip. Fear and outrage throbbed at her pinched jugular, imparting warmth to Torrin's clammy hand held constricted mercilessly about her windpipe. His fingers dug deeply into her neck, crushing her throat. She tried to draw away from him by pushing her back harder against the bed, as if she could escape by burrowing inside the mattress. Wheezing and gurgling, she frantically fought for air, kicking and thrashing futilely beneath Torrin's debilitating embrace. Trembling in a convulsion of devastating horror, fighting beneath the hand of death, the contracting muscles of her body shuddered in a series of violent spasms. Her head began to spin into blackness, her awareness melting slowly into the approaching dark. Loosing the battle and her life with it, Bryana only won the vital breath of precious air, the inhalation necessary to save her once again from unconsciousness, after Torrin released his choking hold. Over her own gasping inhalations, she heard him chuckling softly as he pushed off the bed and stood looming ominously over her exposed, prone body.

"You're so quiet, Bryana," joked Torrin, full of arrogance and black humor. "In the old days, even a gag would be hard pressed to keep you from finding words of reprimand or uttering some scolding criticism. Or perhaps my new manners have finally won your favor and I am now free of your reproach. After all, you're the woman who protects, even loves, murderers and rapists. What say you, Bryana, do you now have love for me? No, well no matter; your power and your kingdom are all that I desire."

He turned and the sound of his footfalls moved from the bed to a trestle table on the other side of her room, a table on which a dagger lay, a dagger possessing a serrated edge and a handle of carved white bone. Through unaccustomed fear and a stupor induced by pain, her mind numb with trauma, her abilities constrained, all Bryana could think was that she could not let this happen. She absolutely could not allow Torrin to steal her control nor to gain possession of her power.

Overcoming the protests of her injured body, she thrust herself from the bed and to her feet. Carried on a gelid rush of adrenalin, she ran. But misremembering the room's design, she charged blindly into the hard stone surface of the tower's inner wall. Recovering from the collision, she heard Torrin laughing at her failure.

"Going somewhere?" Torrin scoffed, watching as Bryana continued to inch sideways with her back braced against the wall.

In answer to Torrin's query and on reaching an open window, Bryana stopped. Her frame straightened and she stood as if believing she were on the brink of victory. Like the brave before a death sentence, she fixed her posture with a rigid pride. Her white bed gown flowed in the soft current of the night breeze; it moved with an ethereal quality and stark before the black expanse framed behind the window.

Torrin took a step toward her, and in the space of a heartbeat Bryana cast herself out the open window. As she fell silently to her death hundreds of feet below, Torrin's jaw dropped with her in unbelieving shock.

"No!" A cry of astonishment burst from Torrin. His mind howled with rage as he rushed toward the window.

Down below in the queen's private garden, amid flowers and apple trees whose color the twilight left obscured, her body lay broken on the cobblestones. No one had seen or heard her fall, but that came as little comfort to Torrin. By killing herself, Bryana had robbed him of the opportunity to absorb her wizard power. She had cheated him and, like ashes, scattered her magic across the cosmos.

"No," groaned Torrin, striking the wall with his fist in a discharge of hysterical wrath. His body clenched in anger. His face contorted with a wild murderous urge, robbing his face of nearly all human quality. He pulled at his hair and stormed around the bedchamber in a fit of enraged hatred. But he had no time for it; there was work to do despite this devastating setback in the penultimate phase of Torrin's plan. The sun was on the rise and his army would soon be here.

Torrin changed his clothes, donning the robe of the archprelate. He then cast a spell of illusion, using magic to mask his appearance so that he resembled Bryana in body as well as mantle. In the adjoining room there was a pull cord to a bell that was used to call the Prelature to assemble. Torrin sounded the bell, its hollow ring breaking the early morning calm. Then he left for the hall of the Prelature, the only imperfection in his facade of Bryana being the axe clutched ready in his knotted grip. But even this needed little explanation, for Torrin's army could now be seen marching in the distance. And shortly after Torrin's ringing of the tower bell, the alarm went out summoning soldiers to their battle stations.

Torrin moved swiftly, purposefully, through the corridors that would lead him to the hall of the Prelature. With each step, his hateful, predatory need mounted in escalation toward a new peak, an evil pinnacle of unprecedented and unimaginable proportion. Anger raged through him, feeding on itself and growing exponentially so that Torrin could barely keep it from premature eruption. Holding back the discharge of the violent emotions twisting in his soul required enormous restraint on Torrin's behalf. The pressure continued to build, as did his lust for power. Control, demanding and intense, was also necessary to maintain the illusion composed by magic that allowed Torrin to masquerade as the High Queen. Tremendous effort went into preserving his guise, the outward appearance of Bryana assumed to conceal the cruel truth of Torrin's real identity.

So far, his passage through the castle brought him in contact with only a few people and no one seemed to notice any imperfection in his disguise. But in an otherwise empty corridor, shortly before reaching the Prelature, that changed. Running quickly from around a corner, a small child of six or seven years blindly collided against Torrin's imposing frame. The little girl's mother followed close behind, full of apologies.

"Your Majesty," blurted the mother, "I'm terribly sorry. We heard the alarm, that the castle is under attack. We're on our way to our rooms in accordance with the curfew order for non-military personnel. My daughter's afraid. She didn't look where she was going. Please forgive her."

Torrin said nothing. He only gave the woman a hard and unforgiving look.

"Mommy," said the little blonde-haired girl in a sweet, innocent voice while tugging at her mother's sleeve, "that's not High Queen Bryana."

"Of course it is dear," corrected the mother. "Hush now and let's be on our way. By your leave, your Majesty?"

"No Mommy, it's not the High Queen. I know it's not."

Angered by the child's challenge, Torrin locked his stormy gaze upon the girl's gentle blue eyes and held them as firmly as her mother held her hand. Frightened by the scowling, silent image of the queen, a wave of doubt rippled across the mother's face.

In answer to her suspicion, Torrin swung his axe, biting deeply into the mother's neck. Awash beneath a fountain of her own blood, the woman died as her body fell to the floor. Muted by shock and horror, the child stared at the mangled beauty of her slain mother. But even before her grief had time enough to settle in, the arching death of Torrin's blade sliced through the observant youth.

Beyond the passing thrill provided by their short lived fear, the kill meant little to Torrin. He pursued greater goals than these. The lives of others meant nothing to Torrin now unless they served to enhance his power. The Beast was on the prowl. With concentration and exuberant energy, Torrin invoked his magic to strengthen his mask of illusion, his disguise of Bryana.

He reached the queen's private entrance to the hall of the Prelature. An attendant stood waiting and held the door open for him. Torrin passed through the arched portal and to the center of the dais. A loud rustle met his ears as the full congregation of the Prelature rose to their feet to honor and receive who they thought to be the archprelate, Queen Bryana. *Back at last*, thought Torrin as his attention swept slowly across the blue robed panorama of the crowded hall, a hall in which virtually all the world's wizards were pooled. So much power, a lake in which to drink.

The thought sent his evil spirit soaring, filling his vile heart with expectant glee. Poised on the advent of atrocity, Torrin's hands began to tingle, his heart raced, the muscles of his face twitched, and his eyes sparked with vicious delight.

His arms spread wide like wings, Torrin spoke in a booming voice full of power and command. With this voice, he wove a spell around the unsuspecting wizards, a spell which entranced his audience, paralyzing the wizards and driving them collectively into a state of suspended animation. Prelates, master prelates, and acolytes lay strewn recklessly about the floor, still living but harmless and disabled.

Dropping the illusion which had masked his appearance, Torrin laughed at the ease of his victory. He left the dais to bar the doors, sealing himself inside the hall. The shouts and cries of the beginning battle could be heard; their faint brutal sounds muted by the imposing walls came as music to Torrin's ear. Towering above the unconscious form of a master prelate, Torrin stood admiring his axe. He gazed upon his prized weapon of destruction with a kind of perverse affection. Lovingly, he caressed the cool steel of its twin curved blades and the leaf-shaped spike at its tip, his other hand clutching firmly to the hard wooden spine of its handle.

Then he acted. Gripped tightly in both hands and carried by the full force of all his physical might, the axe swung up and slammed down upon the master prelate laying prone at his feet, burying its metal deep and killing the defenseless victim in a single blow. Torrin waited for the reward, and it came.

A glow of magic light swelled around the wizard's corpse. The power was being drawn out of the victim and concentrated in the air like a corona. Jagged and meandering fingers of light arched from the body and streamed out from the glow, wrapping its lightning-like coils along Torrin's axe. Once the searching, tentacle-like filaments of light touched Torrin's hand, the current was complete. The concentrated power of the fallen wizard burst forth, discharging across the axe and into Torrin in a blinding flood of magic.

The magic of the slain wizard hit Torrin like a tidal wave, a wave of pain, pleasure, and power. He absorbed it, letting the wave wash through him. The experience was fatiguing and exhilarating all at once. Caught up in the wicked rapture of the moment, Torrin howled in elation, overwhelmed by the thrill of this conquest, the intense joy, the ecstasy of newly acquired power. This new and unique experience was wildly fantastic but not enough. No, not nearly enough.

Propelled by extravagant enthusiasm, Torrin's axe ripped through the heart of a sandy-haired young acolyte. Again Torrin received the violent, wondrous surge of power. Again he killed, and again, and again. The torrent of stolen magic energy could not drown his appetite for more. The slaughter continued with an ugly euphoric fervor, each added victim amplifying the elation of Torrin's depraved spirit. Each time the axe reaped another soul, Torrin felt himself being raised to a higher level of power and mastery, exalted to a superior plane of human existence. He thought himself a god. His heart filled with a rapturous sense of fulsome vitality, a tumescent sensation of virtual omnipotence. Intoxicated with malevolent rage and a growing rush of power, Torrin could no longer even think in coherent thoughts. So he stopped thinking and just killed, creating an abattoir from the sacred hall of the Prelature, a slaughterhouse of murdered wizards. Blood and bile pooled upon the floor, encircling the mutilated bodies of Torrin's butchered victims.

Gradually, Torrin's shoulders grew numb from the repeated shocks delivered with each killing blow of his merciless axe. Body and mind ached from the strain of absorbing so much sorcerous power. But the vicious orgy of death continued. And as the Prelature died, a century of work was undone by the madness of a single man.

Through the approach of morning and in defiance of nature's opposition, Quinn led Torrin's unified army toward Gairloch with remarkable speed. In moving soldiers and supplies across a difficult landscape, Quinn had proved himself to be a man capable of working miracles to reach his objectives.

With the exception of Quinn's mount, the few horses they had were used to pull the siege engines and war machines. It had been difficult and backbreaking work to keep them from becoming mired in the mud of the heavily rain-soaked earth. But Quinn had managed to keep men and machines moving. And despite the miserable conditions of their march, the soldiers remained strong, their spirits still animated for battle.

Their pace grew even more rapid now that the rains had finally stopped. Beneath the rising sun, the gray-black thunderheads were breaking up and a brilliant blue filled the broadening gaps. The radiant yellow glow of the ascending sun blanketed the land with sunlight around shadows cast by the dissipating storm clouds. The air was fresh and sweet smelling, light sparkled off the water-slick grass, and birds greeted the day with song.

It was the dawning of a day Quinn might well have taken pleasure in had he not been charged with leading an army into battle. The soldiers at his back and Castle Gairloch looming closer before them weighed heavy on Quinn's heart. He did not want to be here; truly he did not. He did not want to shed so much as an ounce of anyone's blood. But he had responsibilities. He had promised Torrin he would win this war and the army was in his charge. If he should forsake his duty or approach it halfheartedly, he would be responsible for the death of soldiers under his command.

If he felt otherwise, Quinn at least held the appearance of a resolute military leader, a noble champion. A bull of a man, his large armored frame and hard, warped features projected an intimidating image of confidence and strength. He rode at the vanguard and mounted on a mighty destier, Torrin's white war-horse. The animal was armored in an impressive coat of thick black leather and blued metal. The horse's proud head was defended by a stiff leather shaffron, a crinet of joined steel plates shielded its neck, a crumper protected its hindquarters, and a black peytral guarded the horse's broad chest.

Behind Quinn marched an army of diverse composition unified by the banner of the griffon and their brutal intention, a purpose of war, an aim of victory. The foremost human infantrymen carried pavises, large rectangular shields to protect the elvin archers during the siege. Behind these and in more haphazard arrangement, soldiers held colorful convex heater-shields, round bucklers or targes, and elongated teardrop shaped shields. Standing in wait above the soldiers' heads were the points and blades of fierce staff weapons —gisarmes, spears, bills, glaives, and halberds. Sunlight glimmered in reflection off the elfin scale armor, armor made of small overlapping plates laced together to give a rigid yet flexible defense. The elves armed themselves with long bows and scimitars. The humans and dwarves wielded virtually every other type of weapon. There were even drummers in their ranks to help set the pace of the march. Drum. Drum. Drum, drum, drum. The rhythmic beat spurred them forward, the sequence repeated over and over.

The sky clear, the armies in place, the battle began. Quinn rode among the ranks, barking orders and deploying the troops. Mangonels catapulted massive stones against the castle's bulwark, impacting Gairloch's walls and ramparts in an effort to rupture its defense. A gale of arrows raged above the army's sheltering shields. Ladders went up and were pushed back down. Vats of boiling oil were dumped from the castle parapets, their scalding contents descending like a waterfall on those below. Torrin's army responded with fustibals, using staff-slings to throw heavy shot and to launch incendiaries. They also hurled clay vessels, or stinkpots as they were called, containing burning sulfur and quicklime into the castle. Fires caught and began to fill the air with noxious palls of billowing black smoke. From out of the boiling fumes, the griffons returned to join the combat, terrorizing the castle soldiers with ferocious attacks.

The sun began its descent into the western sky as the day burned away into late afternoon. The fighting continued and Quinn had still not breached Gairloch's virtually impregnable defense. By this time they had lost many soldiers and two of their catapults had been consumed by fire. Although repeated and costly attempts to batter down the gates had failed, Quinn managed to preserve the bulk of his fighting force. He began to worry that Torrin had failed, perhaps even been killed. The only sign of hope was that they had, as yet anyway, not been attacked by wizardry.

A siege is grisly, arduous work and it would have gone on for days, even weeks, had the saboteurs been unsuccessful. But finally, miraculously, the gate went up. The saboteurs had secured the gatehouse, raised the main barrier, and jammed the devise so that it could not be lowered.

Mounted, Quinn led the charge through the open portal, the army following behind him in a frenzied, massive swarm. Stormed, the castle became a vast arena of pell-mell killing. The illustrious military might of Gairloch was overwhelmed; it could not repel the invading army. Over the bodies of Gairloch's soldiers, the sights and sounds of warfare swept beyond the castle courtyard, filling the passages with carnage. Beyond their wildest expectations, most of Gairloch's citizenry could now sense defeat; and those that could, fled the castle in haste. Even some of her sworn defenders broke from their fellow soldiers and ran in fear for their lives. While the battle yet raged, many of Torrin's army prematurely took to sacking the conquered castle, plundering its riches and abusing its subjects.

Overcome with revulsion, Quinn was sickened by the senseless savagery of it all. The horror of this wanton death and destruction choked at his throat, threatening to strangle him with grief and shame. He wanted nothing more to do with it, wanted desperately to distance himself from the barbarity of it. He fought now to stay alive, no longer to win. No one could be counted a winner this day. And with each kill accrued by the powerful sweep of Quinn's long broadsword, he felt his heart break anew. Turning from the battle, he pushed his way through the castle in a reckless, hopeless search for Torrin and for peace.

When Quinn finally found Torrin, it was a sight hard to bear even for a man fresh from the battlefield. Quinn broke down the barricaded door to the hall of the Prelature. He was appalled at what he uncovered. Reeking of murder, the floor was littered with bodies, robed in blue and sodden with blood. Grotesque wounds lacerated the lifeless wizards. Butchered, decapitated, and disemboweled corpses lay scattered everywhere. Quinn's heart fell and his eyes filmed with nauseated despair. He coughed and choked, bringing his broad hand to his face and cupping it over his nose and mouth in an effort to filter the gruesome stench.

There was no one left alive within the hall, except one. Amid the heaps of his mutilated victims was Torrin. Enveloped in a bright, pulsating glow of aquamarine luminosity, Torrin lay with his back flat upon the floor. There was so much red fluid pooled upon the marble tile, it looked like a lake of blood on which Torrin appeared to float. Quinn moved toward him, working his way through the human detritus, the strewn mortal wreckage of mangled bodies, cleaved limbs, hacked bone, and gutted remains. Disgusted by the liquid's warm touch against his feet and ankles, Quinn plodded through the morass of blood and gore, each step precarious and leaving a splash of small waves in its wake.

Quinn found that, indeed, Torrin was alive. But he bore no similarity to the man Quinn had once called a friend. In fact, in his transformed state, it was difficult even to consider Torrin human. His eyes were open but they did not move, indicating that he was deep within a trance, unconscious if not unaware. But he was alive, his existence changed yet still evolving. As the plundered magic worked through him, Torrin's skin seemed to ripple and churn as if worms were burrowing beneath his skin. The mystical aura of colored light around Torrin served as protection, a barrier that prevented anything from touching him. Either intentionally or as a serendipitous product of devouring so much magic, the spectral illumination held Torrin in a kind of suspended animation, a shield of invulnerability which gave his body time to absorb and assimilate its newly won power. Quinn shuddered to think what Torrin would become once he emerged from this ill conceived cocoon of magic.

Beside Torrin lay his axe, the only weapon to be found in the room, a room filled with death. A faint blue glow surrounded the axe as well, and a strange hum of magic energy emanated from the weapon. The axe had become enchanted by serving as the conduit for the passage of so much magic from the dying wizards into Torrin. Residual magic lingered in the axe. Quinn could not guess the potential of its unknown power. But he assumed it could only be a wicked power, an evil tool. The axe, like its owner, radiated a foul quality. Quinn could do nothing about Torrin, but he was not about to let anyone use that axe ever again.

Not wanting the cursed blade to touch his bare skin, Quinn wrapped the axe in a thick coarse cloth. This would also conceal it from anyone who might take interest in the weapon's mysterious properties. After hiding the axe, Quinn left the hall on his way to leaving the castle. Riotous pandemonium still reigned in the aftermath of war. People seemed to be running in every direction beneath an umbrella of shouts and screams and amid the continuing clash of arms.

From the confusion permeating the castle courtyard, Quinn acquired a horse. He took a plain brown gelding with no distinguishing markings. Although a stronger beast, he absolutely did not want Torrin's white stallion, as it was far too conspicuous. At a slow pace, so as not to attract attention, Quinn rode his mount through the gate and away from the conquered castle.

He was on the run, running from the horror he had sadly helped create. And he was alone, utterly and miserably alone. Quinn's physical qualities made him easily recognizable and anyone he should happen to meet would consider him an enemy. By running, he would be a traitor to Torrin's army. To anyone else he would be seen as the man who led the war on Gairloch, a slayer of innocents. No matter how long he lived, the stigma of this retched day would live with him. He would be defined by it forever. Even if Quinn could find some way to eventually forgive himself for what he had done, no one else would. He was alone, forever. *At least that way I won't hurt anyone else*, he thought dismally.

He stayed away from the roads, but from time to time still passed refugees from Gairloch. Most were still in a state of shock, hopeless and frightened. Quinn kept his head low and rode quickly by them. An old woman cried out to him once. She had fled the castle without shoes and her feet were now torn and bloody from her flight, her hands and face scraped from repeated falls. Quinn stopped to help, but there were others around who recognized him and they began pelting him with stones. He could do nothing but save himself. So he rode on, his spirits dragging. On three separate occasions Quinn was accosted by angry men who tried to rob him of his horse. But Quinn was successful in fighting them off. He passed families too. They carried the remnants of what they once owned, the few items they had managed to grab while running for their lives. His heart continued to sink deeper into a morass of guilt-ridden sorrow.

Wanting to avoid any more encounters with the displaced inhabitants of Gairloch, he traveled further from their likely route. Most of them would be headed southeast to the other human kingdoms. So Quinn went west, bound back toward the Tissima Mountains.

After a couple of hours Quinn failed to come across anyone else. So when he saw her it was with some surprise. From a few yards behind, Quinn could see that she was a young woman walking alone and sobbing tearfully. He closed the distance and rode at her side, surprised again when he looked down and recognized her.

"Midori, what on earth are you doing out here?" asked Quinn with sincere curiosity.

She turned her face, a visage still fair despite its sorrowful expression, to focus her attention up at him. Her crying stopped. Then seeing it was Quinn, she looked suddenly scared, as if she might bolt.

Quinn saw the reaction and tried to calm her. "Don't be afraid. I won't hurt you. But tell me, why aren't you at Gairloch with the others?"

Without a word, she turned away from him and continued walking on her previous course, her small sandaled feet kicking up dust in a cloud of suspended sediment that sullied the luster of her plum colored gown and long raven black hair. She was neither dressed for nor suited to solitary wayfaring across a hostile land. But behind her delicate appearance and tear-streaked features, there seemed to reside a resolute determination, a noble form of courage.

"Midori, listen to me," said Quinn, walking his horse along side her. "It's not safe here, particularly not safe for you. You can't be walking out in the open like this. If anyone should see you, see that you're an elf, they'll hurt you or kill you. They will take out all their anger on you just because of who you are. Get back to Gairloch where you'll be safe."

"It's not safe for me there either," answered Midori.

"Why not?"

"Because I'm pregnant."

"What does that matter?" asked Quinn, confused by her answer.

"The baby is half human. The father is Lord Torrin," Midori explained with sad resolve as she continued walking. "Something went wrong. I don't know if my magic failed or if it was overpowered by the potency of his wizardry, but somehow I got pregnant when I shouldn't have. I could use magic to abort the child. That's what my people would tell me to do. It's what they would demand. I know other women who have done it, and for lesser cause, and for them it seemed the right thing to do. But I want this baby. So I had no other choice but to leave. All I care about now is the welfare of this child. And I won't be stopped by you or anyone else."

Stunned by her revelation, Quinn was slow to respond. A child—Torrin had sired a child. The fate of that child seemed bleak. Its mother was an elf and Quinn could see that the world was about to witness a renewed hatred for anything elfin. If they could not avoid humans, mother and babe would have a hard life, if not a short one. And pity them if anyone should learn that Torrin was the father. Some might try to use the child against Torrin as a hostage or as a contender to the throne. Through its return, others might attempt to use the child to win favor with Torrin. And only the World Spirit knows how Torrin himself would react to the existence of his scion, his heir. Midori wanted only to raise and to love the child. But that would not be easy.

"Let me help you," urged Quinn. "You're going to need it." He drew rein on the horse and swung down from the saddle. "Please, let me take you somewhere safe. I promise you can trust me."

He had had more than enough of the clenched fist. So Quinn reached out with an open hand, his palm extended to offer of aid. Apprehensive, Midori did not jump at the offer, but her fear pulled at her in both directions. There was danger both in taking and refusing his help. She was also tired, bone weary from all the traveling she had endured over the past several days, marching to and from Gairloch. The horse and Quinn's assistance were an invitation with a strong appeal. And something about Quinn spoke to her that he could be trusted, that he was a gentle man despite his appearance.

After Midori nodded her consent, Quinn lifted her petite frame and placed her gently astride the horse. He pulled himself up on the gelding's back behind Midori with his arms wrapped securely around her to keep her from falling. Responding to the "click, click" sound Quinn made with his tongue and the light touch of his heels to its flanks, the horse moved forward at a smooth pace. Midori leaned back against Quinn's chest and was within minutes fast asleep.

Disturbing questions, as much as the need to keep moving, kept Quinn awake. He wondered about Midori's unborn child, if it was destined to be corrupt because its father had become a man of such great evil. Was their some inherited trait that would force the child to follow in his father's footsteps? Why did Torrin change; what turned his soul so cruel? Was there anything he could have done to prevent it? Certainly Torrin had suffered. The loss of Lenore was a tragic blow and he had had a hard life. But who has not? Poverty and pain do not excuse crime. Nor could Quinn believe that evil is inherent. People are not born evil but accept it of their own free will. They become evil by their own making. The elements of evil are not branded upon a man's soul at birth. Nor can anyone else apply that brand upon another. It is a mark a man makes for himself. The love of friends and family does help to keep one's heart pure. Kindness received and given serves to improve the quality of one's soul. And if we do not acknowledge responsibility for our actions, we are free to abuse others and helpless to change. Having done things for which Quinn was ashamed, things that would haunt his nights forever, this came as a bitter truth. He had killed innocent people and aided in the execution of an atrocity. Quinn could not deny his responsibility in this. Others might have refused this hard truth through self-serving rationalizations or self-delusion, such as claiming that Torrin had tricked him. But ignorance is no excuse and being sorry seemed like an impotent gesture. Quinn could not expect forgiveness from anyone.

Night was closing in and it began to rain again. Quinn quickly unbridled and unsaddled the horse, looking for cover in the trees. But the rain grew heavier, penetrating the leaf covered branches overhead, and the pair were soon thoroughly drenched.

From sticks, branches, and the saddle blanket Quinn assembled a crude lean-to but it proved to be a poor shelter. The rain still harassed them and the wind bit coldly at their skin. Quinn wrapped his shirt and cloak around Midori, but she continued to shiver frightfully. The trembling in her arms grew worse until her whole body shook with it. He tried to warm her with his own body heat by holding her close. Still the tremors would not abate. Her skin was pallid and cold. It scared Quinn, frightened him to the marrow of his bones.

"This is no good." Quinn asserted, detaching from Midori and rising to his feet. "You're freezing. I've got to find us some place out of this rain, somewhere dry and warm. Wait here and I'll look around. Don't move. I'll be back after I find something."

"No. Don't leave me," pleaded Midori in a tremulous voice, barely strong enough to conquer the roar of falling rain. "Don't leave me here to die."

"I'm not. I swear I'll be back. Just hold on and stay put."

She looked so frightened, so fragile, it was hard to turn away from her, but harder still to stay and watch her life slowly drain away. Perhaps it was the common tendency of men to want to protect women or because of all the death he had already witnessed. Whatever the reason, Quinn was not about to let Midori freeze to death. Into the downpour, he slipped through the trees, a desperate man.

About an hour later, he returned and found Midori curled in a fetal position on her side. Her breathing was very shallow, her skin like ice, and the pulse in her neck weak and irregular. Despite his efforts, he could not revive her. Scooping her small, frail body up in his arms, Quinn charged through the rain and brush, running but careful not to fall.

Quinn took Midori to the large cave he had found earlier, getting her out of the rain. But that alone was not enough. He had to raise her body temperature. So he frantically set to building a fire at the mouth of the cave but could not force a spark to light upon the damp wood. His own hands began to tremble, as much from fear as from cold. In spite of all the problems they seemed to carry with them, Quinn now desperately wished for the company of a wizard, someone with magic enough to light this fire and save Midori. And upon that thought, as if it held a power of its own, the fire finally caught. It was weak and smoked badly. Water sizzled from the sodden wood, but he coaxed it to life, enkindled it with care. Once he was confident that the flames would not die from want of his attention, Quinn turned to Midori.

He stripped off her wet clothes so that the warmth of the fire would more readily reach her flesh. He positioned her close to the now strong and brightly burning fire, then stripped himself and spread their clothes on the rocks to dry by the blaze. He collected more wood, as dry as he could find, and kept checking on Midori's condition while tending the flames. She remained unconscious; but her skin, although still covered in gooseflesh, was warmer and again showing some color. In an effort to speed her recovery and improve her circulation, Quinn began vigorously rubbing her arms and legs.

Gradually Quinn rescued her from the icy grip of death and Midori passed quietly from unconsciousness into a healthy slumber. Quinn relaxed his ministrations and, once they were dry, he piled the clothes on Midori for added warmth. For himself, and for modesty's sake, he kept his pants. He settled down finally on the other side of the fire and watched Midori for a long time, surveying her breathing and making certain that she was safe.

When morning woke them, Quinn had perhaps obtained a total of two hours sleep. Dark circles ringed his heavily lidded eyes and his back was stiff from past exertion and from the discomfort of stone bedding. Quinn rubbed the exhaustion from his face and sat up. He looked over the lifeless, gray ashes of last night's fire, relieved to see Midori alive and well.

Under his concerned gaze and a penetrating quill of early sunlight, Midori stirred. Her lissome arms stretched and pushed back the burdening weight of her covers. After raking the fingers of her small hand through the tangles of her long shiny black hair, she rose eloquently to her feet. Nude, she stood before him entirely exposed. He had of course seen her that way last night but it seemed different now. Last night he was preoccupied with saving her life. Concerned only with her health, Quinn gave no thought to anything else, least of all her alluring womanly attributes. But he could not help but notice now, now that she was well and so openly revealed. She was a strikingly attractive woman with small delicate features, dark hued skin, and slender limbs. Her face was pretty, a pleasure to look upon. Her stomach was slightly swollen, an indication of early pregnancy, but even that was beautiful, particularly so.

Midori noticed him looking and smiled. Embarrassed, Quinn hastily averted his eyes, his face turning three shades of red. Picking up her clothes, she laughed quietly at Quinn's shy behavior. It was not something she was accustomed to seeing in men and to her surprise she found it strangely flattering. She knew he had not turned his gaze aside because he considered her unattractive but because he thought he was being considerate. Some human males did that. It was sweet, in a way.

"Are you all right?" inquired Quinn, his words catching at his throat in nervous chagrin.

"Yes," she answered. Her voice owned a lyric quality. "How did we get here?"

"You took a chill last night, pretty serious. I discovered this cave and carried you here to get you out of the rain. Did anything happen... I mean, is the baby all right? Can you tell?"

"Yes," Midori said, placing her palm gently upon her now clothed abdomen. "The baby is fine. Thank you."

"Good. I was worried," stated Quinn. He then rose to collect the remainder of his own clothes.

Midori touched his arm, looking at him as if she had something important to communicate. But when it came, the query belied the grave expression. "The baby needs nourishment. What are we going to eat?"

"That's a good question, one we'll have to answer on the trail. But first I need to see if I can find my horse. I left it out there when I brought you here last night. Come on, help me look."

Surprisingly enough, they found the brown gelding not far from the abandoned saddle where they had first taken shelter from the rain. The animal was a little scratched up and still skittish from the storm but sound. *Thank the World Spirit the horse had not run off or hurt any of its legs*, thought Quinn. Relieved at this small blessing, they resumed their positions on the horse and were again under way.

About a half hour into the day's ride, Midori asked. "Where are we going?"

"Well," answered Quinn, "where were you headed when I found you?"

"I don't really know. There's no one left at Kweiyang and even if there were they wouldn't accept me unless I aborted the child. I don't know what I'm going to do."

"Well, you won't be accepted in any of the human settlements either. So, I think it best if we take refuge in the Tissima Mountains."

"Not back to Prakrit," insisted Midori.

"No," Quinn assured her. "We aren't bound for Prakrit or to anywhere that people live. We are going to find a place where there is no one else around, somewhere secluded where you can have that baby safely. We'll worry about what happens after that when the time comes. We'll cross one bridge at a time."

"You mean you're going to stay with me until it's born?"

"I think I should," suggested Quinn. "I'm the closest thing you have to a friend right now and I think your going to need help over the next several months. Don't argue with me about this. Even if you don't want me around, you have to think about what's best for the baby."

She did not argue. In fact, she felt suddenly a great deal better than she had just minutes before. At least for a little while she would not be alone. Quinn was human, a stranger to her, and intimidating in his physique. But he seemed sincere as well as kind. She wanted to trust him. Already he had helped her when no one else would have. And he seemed to want nothing in exchange. He did not even expect, much less attempt to steal, what most men would have desired.

"It's getting late," observed Midori. "I really should eat something. There's a stream over there. Perhaps we could catch some fish?"

"No," said Quinn. "I'll go hunting for some small game. Rabbit, maybe."

"Fishing would be easier," suggested Midori. "Besides, I don't want to separate and you look like you could use some rest."

"I'm fine. And if you must know, I hate fish. I can't stand the taste of it. It's so...so fishy."

She laughed at that. "Don't be silly, fish is good for you. Come on, I'll show you. You'll like my fish."

After setting out a line, Midori began scouring the banks, gathering other items for their meal. She caught and cleaned the fish, refusing assistance from Quinn, saying that she wanted to make herself useful and that she was not helpless, only pregnant. She flavored the fish with herbs and spices and prepared a salad from watercress and leafy vegetation. She offered the fish to Quinn raw but he insisted that it be cooked. Even with that concession, he eyed the meal suspiciously. Midori smiled at his reluctance and held a bit of meat to his lips until he took it in his mouth. His face wrinkled in a sour expression as he chewed.

"You don't like it?" she asked with a tone of surprise and hurt feelings.

"No, no. It's not bad. I like it," lied Quinn as he tried to push his features into a cheery face so as to make his words appear more convincing.

"I told you; it's best when eaten raw. Here, have some of mine."

"That's all right," blurted Quinn, holding up his hands to ward off her sacrifice. "This is just fine. Really, it's quite good."

He forced another handful into his mouth and swallowed. While he ate, Midori stared at Quinn in silence. Her scrutiny made him uncomfortable. He thought she was looking at the misshapen contours of his face, thinking him ugly and deformed. The thought bothered him and he was not entirely sure why. It had been a long time since Quinn had been self-conscious about his appearance; why should it affect him now, with her? Perhaps her own beauty made him more acutely aware of his lack of it. The thought that she considered him repulsive made him angry, then angry at himself for feeling that way. He was so wrapped up in these thoughts that when Midori spoke, her question shocked him.

"Why are you here? Why aren't you at Gairloch with Lord Torrin?"

"Because it was wrong," Quinn answered. "Because I don't like what Torrin has become. We should never have attacked Gairloch. Hatred and greed were the only motive behind that war. I didn't see that until it was too late. I couldn't stand to be a part of it any longer."

"But why are you here? Why are you helping me?"

"I'm doing it because you need help," explained Quinn, "because that baby deserves a chance at life. Despite all the cruelty the world may possess, that baby deserves a chance to sample the joy that life can also offer. And after everything else I've done, I don't think I could live with myself if I turned my back on you now."

"That's it? Is there something you want from me or from my baby?" she asked seriously.

255

"No. I don't want anything."

"Not even companionship?" Midori pried.

The question hit him so hard he almost wept. It was true. Kindness was not his only intent and Quinn could not deny his selfish motives for helping her. Midori was probably the only person in the whole world he could trust, the only one that would not attack him or who wouldn't at least shun him. She may be only a stranger, but without her he would be utterly alone.

"Let's get moving," grumbled Quinn, coldly avoiding her question and terminating the discussion. "We need to put as much distance as we possibly can between us and Gairloch. The sooner we get to the southern tip of the Tissima Mountains, the better. The weather's starting to turn. Won't be long till winter's here and we have a lot to get done before its arrival."

"Rovers," whispered Quinn in answer to Midori's question.

Squinting against the crimson radiance of the setting sun, she followed his line of vision. Screened by the trees and boulders of a wooded hillock, they watched the Rovers pull their wagons into a ring, making camp for the night. The Rovers, on the other hand, made no attempt to conceal their presence, filling the air with friendly shouts and hardy laughter. Bright, almost vulgar, multi-colored canvas awnings were unfurled from the wagons. Fires were kindled, throwing up large plumes of smoke and light.

It was a large group; with nearly two dozen horses, some hitched to the wagons, others ridden independently, and a few merely tethered behind. There were even a couple of head of cattle in the caravan, and several dogs. Before long, the beckoning aroma of hot food reached out to Quinn and Midori, carried with the competing melodies of a mandolin, tambourine, and mouth harp. Children could be seen playing around the campfires in that all too brief period between chores and bedtime.

Quinn and Midori moved back from the edge of the trees where they could talk with less fear of being detected. Over a week had elapsed since the overthrow of Gairloch and in that time they had seen few people, careful to avoid those they had come across.

"We can't risk a fire tonight," Quinn asserted. "I'm not sure if they would take any interest in us but it's best if we don't take any chances."

"Who are they?" Midori asked for the second time, wanting Quinn to offer more clarification than his earlier declaration had afforded.

"Most people call them Rovers, but I've heard they refer to themselves as

'The Family.' I haven't seen them in a long time, not since I was a kid. I don't know where they've been all these years and I can't imagine what's brought them back now. They're a group of people who shun settled life and refuse to embrace the lifestyles of established civilizations, the social character of kingdoms and villages. Instead, they assimilate others into their cultural pattern. They have their own customs, their own beliefs. Their tribes are composed of members drawn from virtually all over and include many different races. Rover's are not allowed to marry outside 'The Family' and I've heard that once you're accepted as a member you can never leave."

Punctuating the sudden arrival of a new idea, Quinn snapped his fingers, interrupting his previous thought. "That's it! That's what you could do. There aren't any elves among the Rovers, but I see no reason why they should object to one. They have no loyalty to Gairloch or affiliation with any kingdom for that matter, human or otherwise. So even though the rest of the world may now hate elves with a renewed bitterness, I can't believe the Rovers would possess such bigotry. It simply isn't their way. You could join 'The Family.' They would take care of you and your baby. It wouldn't be the life you're used to, but at least you'd be with other people."

"What about you?" asked Midori tentatively. "Will you join them too?"

"No. I'm not suited to that kind of life. I like to wake up in the same place day after day. I want a place that I can call home, a place where I can belong, something fixed and permanent. Besides, where you as a female elf should pose no great danger to them, I would. People will remember me as the man who led the attack on Gairloch. And when people remember, they will want revenge; and I don't think the Rovers could protect me. Nor would I want to force them into such a perilous situation."

"Then I don't want to join them either," insisted Midori with a conviction that confounded Quinn. "I want to stay with you."

"But you can't. You need more than I can give; you need to be around other people. Your future would be a lot safer with them, and the future of your child. Once accepted, they'd help you and it isn't a bad life they offer. They're just nomadic; they travel constantly, choosing to roam from one place to another and make their living as they go. But you could get used to the itinerant way of life. They would take care of you and you might even find their ways exciting. They don't farm or herd livestock. They're mainly musicians, horse dealers, peddlers, metal workers, artists, and basket makers. Sure, some of them are also pick pockets, swindlers, fortune-tellers, and thieves. But they're not dangerous. Other than their need to roam, they're nothing like raiders.

Rovers aren't bloodthirsty outlaws who take what they want by force and kill for sport."

"Maybe not. Maybe the Rovers are decent people. But I don't care," argued Midori. "Please don't leave me with them. Please! You're the only thing I know in this land. You're the only person I can trust. I'm too frightened of everything right now, too scared to start a life so strange and new with people I know nothing about. Please, at least until the baby's born, let me stay with you."

Against his better judgment, Quinn agreed. "All right, you can stay with me; but I think you're making a mistake. And I don't think we can wash our hands of the Rovers yet either. If we're going to live on our own over the course of your pregnancy, there are things we'll need and neither of us can risk being seen to buy them even if we had the money. So that leaves the Rovers."

Quinn began bundling up his armor in a stiff canvas cloth, stuffing it with leaves in order to muffle the sound of clinking metal. He then tied the bundle to his long broadsword. Midori watched, perplexed by the activity.

"What are you doing," she asked.

"Giving them something in return for what I take."

"You're going to trade your armor to them?"

"Not exactly," explained Quinn. "I'm not going to bargain with them directly; hopefully they won't even know I was there until tomorrow. If I talked to them in an attempt to negotiate a trade, they'd try to swindle me or maybe just rob me outright. So I'm going to sneak into their camp, take what I can, and leave this in exchange. It's not much, but it will help to ease my conscience."

"But why?" questioned Midori, her brow wrinkled in confusion. "If they're thieves, why worry about stealing from them? Why should you leave them anything? And shouldn't you keep your armor? At least your sword; you might need it?"

"Just because they're thieves doesn't make thieving from them right." Quinn argued. "It's wrong; but at the moment it's also a necessity. And I hope never to need armor or sword again. I'd much prefer other tools, implements of peace. But if it will make you feel more secure, I'll keep the sword. Now stay here, and stay out of sight."

He turned and plunged into the black night, creeping silently down the hillock to the Rover camp below. With trepidation, Midori watched him leave until the darkness stole him from her. He was in the camp before he knew it, perhaps because he feared it, feared discovery and the disrupting consequences it would bring. He did not want to be forced to fight his way free, did not want to kill or injure any of these people. Not that, not ever again.

His heart pounded so hard he irrationally thought the sound would divulge his presence. Darting from shadow to shadow cast by the campfires, he searched for the wagon containing what he desired. From the hillock, Quinn had seen the wagon which was used for preparing meals. He would stop there before leaving to acquire pots, pans, and cutlery, but he needed more than this, things like a saw, hammer, chisel, and axe.

Detection was narrowly avoided several times before Quinn discovered the right wagon. Most of the Rovers were still gathered at the fire, sharing each other's company. But the children had been put to bed and three lay sleeping in this wagon. Undaunted, and with all the stealth in his possession, Quinn crawled into the wagon, determined to gain what he required. His movements were painfully slow with caution as he gathered the essential items and each creaking board filled his heart with panic. Finally, he had what he needed and turned to go. Then it happened.

A child stirred and waking sat up, blocking the wagon's exit. It was a young girl, somewhere between eight and ten years of age. She rubbed her sleepy eyes, then in the dim light, she focused them on Quinn. He froze in mid step.

In a quiet, sedate voice, she asked. "Who are you?"

"I'm a friend," whispered Quinn. "Your daddy told me to get these things for him," he lied. "But I wasn't supposed to wake you. So go back to sleep."

"No you're not. I've never seen you before; you're not a Rover," she stated. Despite her pronouncement, her words were still hushed and calm. But it was enough to wake the other children, who also sat eyeing Quinn suspiciously. "You're trying to rob us."

"No," argued Quinn. "Here, look. I was going to leave my armor in exchange for these rusty old tools. See, that's fair isn't it? Please don't tell on me. Ok?"

"What good is that dumb old armor?" said the girl. "It's way too big for us." The other children nodded in agreement. "I know, tell us a story. Tell us a really good story and we'll let you go."

"With the tools?" asked Quinn.

"Sure. What do we care? But it has to be a good story," stated the girl.

"And not a short one either," said another child.

"It's a deal," conceded Quinn.

He sat down by the young children, trying to think of a suitable story. For several moments inspiration eluded him and the youngsters grew impatience.

So Quinn started blindly into it, using the children themselves for the main characters. From that humble beginning and in a theatrical yet practical undertone, he produced a tale of fantastic places and wild adventure. The children were enthralled, but so excited by the narrative that Quinn had to hush them several times. The story ended happily and everyone seemed pleased.

"Well, I've delivered," said Quinn. "And now I'll be on my way. Remember your promise to keep quiet and not to tell anyone I was here."

The little girl grabbed his hand, stopping him. "Wait! Tell us another one. Please."

"No, no. Our deal was for one story. I've got to get going; the sun will be up soon. Maybe I will come back again sometime and tell you another story. But now I've got to leave."

"Ok," whispered the girl. "Take care of yourself and we'll see you when we see you, story man. Bye, bye."

Quinn left the wagon in careful haste, bound for the one which housed the cooking implements. He took what he needed and could still carry, then slipped back into the night. Although weighed down by his stolen loot, his spirits felt strangely uplifted. He found the delight of children to be contagious.

"Thank Navar you're back," said Midori. "I was about ready to go looking for you. What happened? What took you so long?"

Quinn recounted the peculiar episode of his theft. Midori listened, captivated and equally amused. Reliving the precarious, yet precious adventure, the two laughed with muffled volume. After the nervous catharsis, they remounted their horse and resumed their journey.

Two weeks later, Quinn found a mountain and a site on its slope which he liked, one which they felt they could call home. The area leveled out into a flat region, a plateau high within the mountain range. There was a natural clearing ringed by a thick forest of trees and through which a large, limpid stream flowed like a silver ribbon. In the center of the clearing, the stream slowed so that its sparkling waters pooled in a deep, wide cavity. Birds called overhead as they winged past towering rocky peaks capped in snow. The air was warm with the bright autumn sun and beneath it basked a land of lush greenery, rich in texture and variation.

The deep blue sky was pierced and slit by the jagged stone spine which formed the peaks of the Tissima Mountains. It was a pretty scene but prettier still because now it would be home. The unique beauty of this place was not an inert assemblage of the terrain's biological and physical constituents. Instead, its special quality, its peculiar attraction, was in the way it interacted with Quinn's soul, the way it seemed to animate the sensitive elements of his being, the poetic emotions of his heart. He felt his soul being lifted upon a current of sublime tranquility, an easy exuberance. It was a sensation that had eluded Quinn for so long that he received it with keen surprise and with a deep hope that the buoyant peacefulness would not soon leave him. It was a place in which they felt safe, alone but not lonely.

Quinn and Midori had grown closer over the two-week period and were now more comfortable with each other. An early friendship was developing but as yet no more than that. As a result of their situation and her changing body, Midori suffered periods of debilitating melancholy. Quinn fretted over her and did his best to keep her spirits up.

The first challenge to be met was the construction of a temporary shelter and then one of a more permanent and sturdy design. Before long they had a respectable one-room log cabin complete with fireplace and furnishings. Midori had helped as much as Quinn would allow, which as her pregnancy progressed was less and less.

Busy quilting a blanket for the baby, she sat rocking in a chair Quinn had built and of which he was quite proud. By the hearth Quinn reclined on a fur rug spread atop the wooden floor. Exhausted from a day of hard labor, he was tired but not yet asleep. He listened contentedly as Midori sang some elfin tune, the words mysterious to him but still lovely.

"Quinn," she said, interrupting the serene melody, "we really need to build a bath house with winter coming and all; don't you think?"

"I thought you wanted me to build a room for the baby?"

"Well I do," answered Midori. "We need both."

"And a root cellar too, I suppose?" Grinning, Quinn complained facetiously.

"Wouldn't hurt," she said, smiling back and sharing Quinn's almost constant good humor. "And don't forget about finishing the baby's crib, and we're going to need more shelves, and I'm sure there's a hundred other things we haven't thought of yet."

"Oh don't worry, I'm sure they'll come to you," groaned Quinn.

"Hey, I'd help more if I could. Remember, I'm the one who has to give birth. That's not so easy either, you know."

"I know; I'm just joking around. I still want to make some more toys for the baby too. But no more tonight. Please, let me rest tonight; I beg you."

Midori's nesting instinct was reaching full bloom, which meant she had an endless supply of projects to be completed and all before the big day. Quinn did not truly mind. He enjoyed it actually, enjoyed working, enjoyed spending time with Midori and making her happy, enjoyed thinking about and planning for the baby.

"So, have you decided on a name yet?" Quinn inquired.

"No. Is there one you would like?"

"Well," began Quinn thoughtfully. "If it's a girl, you might want to consider the name Lenore. I knew a woman by that name once and she was a very kind soul. Now, if it's a boy…"

"I know what the baby's sex is," interrupted Midori.

Quinn sat straight up, excited by this news. "You do? How do you know that? Oh yes, I know. Magic, right? Well, don't tell me. I don't what to know; I want to be surprised. You promise me you won't tell me? Don't even let it slip by calling the baby a he or a she. Ok? You promise?"

"If that's the way you want it," said Midori, amused by Quinn and touched by his intensifying interest in both her and the baby. She found herself growing very, very fond of him.

After a few quiet moments, Quinn leapt to his feet. "I can't wait! I have to know too. Is it a boy or a girl? Oh my gosh, it's not twins is it? Come on, tell me! Forget what I said about wanting it to be a surprise. Either will be great. Is it a girl? Little girls are so sweet. I'll bet she'll look just like you, a real little beauty. Come on, tell me."

"No. You told me not to. You'll be mad if I tell you," she teased.

"Oh, I was just being stupid. I swear I really want to know. There's no point in waiting and I'll go crazy if you don't tell me. Please, please, please."

"It's a boy," she announced.

Quinn jumped into the air, letting loose a whoop of unbridled joy. "That's great! A boy, I can't believe it. What do you think about the name Keenan? Can we call him Keenan? It's a good name, don't you think?"

"Keenan," Midori tested the name, pondering the quality of the moniker, excited by Quinn's enthusiasm. "Keenan. Yes, that's a fine name. I like the sound of it."

"Wonderful!" shouted Quinn.

Buoyant with emotion, Quinn kissed Midori on her forehead, the first physical expression of affection that had passed between the two. It seemed to shock them both back into reality. Quinn remembered what he sometimes forgot, that this was not his child. Not only was he not the father, he was not even Midori's husband nor had she given him any indication that she perceived him as such. The realization that they would be expected to part once the baby was born frightened him. He did not want to be alone again. But more than that, he did not want to leave Midori. He genuinely cared for her.

"You know," Quinn said with new soberness to his voice. "After the baby is born, you'll still need someone to look after you, at least for a little while."

"Yes," agreed Midori. "I was hoping you would stay, like you said, at least for a little while."

"Well, let's get some sleep. I've got a bath house to start work on tomorrow," Quinn said behind an insecure smile as he went to his corner of the room to bed down and Midori went to the other. "Good night, Midori. Good night, Keenan," called Quinn across the distance of the darkening room.

The months passed and winter settled over the land. By the first snow, Quinn had managed to complete not only the bath house and nursery but also the root cellar and to stock it with food for the cold months ahead. They spent most of their time indoors now but the cabin was comfortable, with plenty of wood to keep them warm. And the company they shared was pleasing.

The bond between Midori and Quinn had flourished, growing much stronger in those months, but still it seemed to be only a bond of friendship. He also felt closer to the baby every day. It seemed more real now, like more of a person now that it had both a male identity and a name. And Keenan's presence became more obvious and substantial as Midori's belly continued to grow larger and larger.

The miracle of birth has been going on for as long as anyone can remember. So as a result of hundreds of years of repeat performances, it might be expected that people would cease to consider it miraculous and view it instead as a mundane occurrence. But for Quinn nothing could be further from the truth. He found the whole idea amazing, wondrous in a purely unique way. In a very personal sense, it was all brand-spanking-new to Quinn, a marvel of unprecedented proportion. Each new change Midori experienced was wildly exciting for him and he found her changing body radiantly beautiful. Every day with her was a celebration of life and beauty.

She likewise viewed the pregnancy with wonder and anxious anticipation but also with less romanticism than did Quinn. Rightly so, as she was the one who along with the child bore the burden of abdominal discomfort produced by stretching ligaments, occasional nausea, leg cramps, fatigue, sleeplessness, frequent urination, shortness of breath, and the prospect of a painful delivery.

Quinn did what he could to help her get over these hurtles. In answer to her complaints, he would gently massage her aching lower back, legs, and feet for hours until his own strong arm muscles moaned with the effort. She was not accustomed to being pampered by a man but found that she very much liked it at times, particularly the pampering of this tenderhearted man. Although impossible to satisfy entirely, Quinn responded to her mood swings with notable effectiveness. As the circumstances dictated, he was enthusiastic, kind, stern, or sympathetic as she worked through the cycle of joy, misgivings, fear, irritability, and elation. When she fretted about feeling ugly because of the unavoidable weight gain, the slight swelling in her extremities, or the thin varicose veins rising on the backs of her legs, Quinn was there to shower her with compliments on her beauty. And he meant every word, not a one was spoken in false praise. She was beautiful in spirit as well as form.

Toward the end of her fifth month of pregnancy, things changed between Midori and Quinn. It was late into the evening. The cabin's interior was bathed in the yellow-red wavering glow cast by the fire sheltered within the hearth. Close by, Midori lay upon the fur rug carpeting the floor, her back propped by several large pillows. Her gown was pulled open, exposing the bare flesh of her swollen belly. Quinn sat beside her. They had been there for hours, talking easily with one another. But they were quiet now. Entranced, Quinn stared in fascinated awe at the rippling skin and shifting contours of Midori's pregnant abdomen. Watching the evidence of fetal movement, he was amazed, filled with wonder. Midori took Quinn's large calloused hand and placed it over her stomach, smiling as she watched his face light up in reaction to the new sensation beneath his fingers.

"That's incredible," observed Quinn after several minutes.

"I know," agreed Midori. "But just wait, it'll get a lot stronger in the next couple months." It happened to be one of those occasions in which the pregnancy caused Midori to experience temporary nasal congestion. So her voice sounded funny, as if she were speaking with a cold.

Quinn was drunk with jubilant good-humor. Feeling playful, he pinched his nose with thumb and forefinger so that he could mimic Midori's nasally voice. "It will? No, I can't believe this little boy can kick any harder than that," he whined facetiously, grinning from ear to ear.

"Stop it," insisted Midori with mock seriousness while holding back a laugh. "I can't help it. My head feels all stuffed up. Don't tease me."

Quinn turned his attention back to her stomach, leaning in close to her abdomen to talk to the child. "Hello in there. Can you hear me? Can you believe how weird your mom talks, Keenan? You better have me teach you how to talk; you don't want to pick up her speech problems." Quinn joked, taking no notice of the irony his former stutter gave his statement. He continued his cheerful discussion with her belly in a blend of gibberish and genuine dialogue. As he did, Midori smoothed her hand over Quinn's blond hair and idly traced her fingertips around his cheek. Quinn felt happier at that moment than at any other time in his life. His heart threatened to burst with the joy he felt building inside. His emotions refused to be contained any longer. He looked up suddenly and locked eyes with her.

"I love you, Midori," he blurted without thinking.

The revelation seemed to shock them both for neither uttered a word for several uncomfortable seconds. Quinn pulled back a little. Caustic tears welled behind his eyelids, threatening to breach his resolve. They continued to stare wordlessly at one another across the distance separating them.

Struggling to suppress his nervousness and embarrassment, his hopes and fears, Quinn broke the awkward silence. "You don't have to say anything. You don't have to lie about how you feel in order to spare my feelings. I don't expect you to love me; I just had to tell you. I wanted you to know. I knew I shouldn't. Now this will mess up everything we had. Damn it; let's just pretend this never happened. You don't have to love me, but please don't shut me out because of this."

"Quinn. Quinn," interrupted Midori, leaning toward him and placing two fingers over his rambling lips. Once their movement stilled, she slid her hand gently to his cheek, lightly caressing his face and neck. "I do love you. I have for a long time now. I didn't say anything because I didn't want you to think I was trying to trap you, that I was only looking for a father for my child. I love you for who you are and for how you make me feel. My relationship with you has made my life richer than ever I have known, or ever I had hoped. I love you; I really do."

She bent closer still and pressed her mouth to his in a kiss warm with affection and spiced with passion. It led to more, and for the first time Midori and Quinn made love to one another. At last the emotions that had matured in the months behind them were allowed a release. Finally, they embraced, accepting the knowledge that there was a bond between them beyond that of the child's welfare.

In the months that followed, the bond between the two, and the three, strengthened even more. Midori grew larger and they both grew happier. As Midori promised, the fetal movement intensified, becoming more forceful and more frequent. The sight continued to thrill Quinn. Both were adapting well to their new lifestyle, giving up elements of their past cultural customs. Midori was even able to persuade Quinn to eat more fish and he encouraged her to add more red meat to her diet. They were devoted to each other. The world beyond their mountain ceased to exist. They had no contact with the outside world and gradually the harsh memories of their past lives faded, making room for the happiness of the new life they forged together.

With Midori's help, Quinn stopped tormenting himself with guilt over his crimes committed at Gairloch and put that part of his life behind him. Time is a powerful healer but its medicine is not nearly as potent as the company of those you care about and of those who care for you. Now Quinn saw himself through Midori's eyes and he felt whole, complete, reborn. Despite his misshapen features and imposing muscular bulk, she saw him as the most handsome man in the world. He told her it was because she had been too long on this mountain and forgot what the rest of the world looked like. She assured him she had not.

Although Quinn found himself in a nearly overwhelming state of joy, he was not without worries. To avoid transferring his tensions and anxieties to Midori, he tried to confine his worries to nighttime when Midori was asleep. He considered himself the father now, but worried that he would be a poor one. The welfare of Midori and of the baby weighed heavy on his mind. He worried that something would go wrong, something he could not fix. *What if the baby's head is too big?* he wondered anxiously. *What if the cord gets wrapped around the baby's neck, what if it's born breech, what if it's sick?*

He tossed and turned at night, telling himself that all would be well. He repeated the assurance over and over, trying to convince himself. Eventually, usually on one of her frequent nocturnal visits to the outhouse, Midori would see that he was awake, understand why, and repeat his words to him, telling him that everything would be all right. She had the power to make him believe that prophesy. But doubt always discovered a way to worm past his defenses and back into his heart. Quinn even found himself becoming more religious. Midori instructed him in the teachings of Navar. Many nights as he stared at the dark ceiling, Quinn prayed fervently to the World Spirit or Navar or to whatever name the great deity chose for himself. He prayed to keep mother and baby safe. He prayed with such intensity that sweat beaded on his careworn brow. "Please don't let anything bad happen to Midori. Please keep her safe and help her to get through the delivery quickly, painlessly, and unharmed. And please make the baby be born healthy, normal, intelligent, and beautiful. Please," he begged the lightless air.

During the day, however, Quinn was lost in a haze of exuberant cheer and expectant joy. So much so that the slightest amusement was received as riotously comical. He smiled or laughed like an dimwitted idiot each time Midori asked him to pull her awkward body up from a chair. Adding fool to his repertoire of skills, he made a buffoon of himself in trying to make certain that her spirits never dipped. He danced for her, pretended to rock an imaginary child, talked to the empty nursery as if it were a child, and even stuffed a pillow in his shirt so that she would feel less alone in her pregnancy. Anytime a frown touched Midori's sweet lips, he was there with a joke or a song or a story or some other witty diversion designed to keep her spirits high. It annoyed her at times but she loved him for it. They did everything together, even bathing together sometimes. She would lay back against his barrel-chested breast, cradled in his arms while they discussed plans for the future.

Time passed quickly and they soon found themselves in the final month of Midori's pregnancy. The false contractions came more often and with greater intensity. Both Quinn and Midori were ready for the big day, wanting to get it over with and finally have the baby. Quinn continued to nag Midori about eating right, getting plenty of rest, and to not sleep on her back.

After several more days of expectation and disappointment, it started. Midori woke Quinn in the middle of the night, complaining that the contractions were coming more frequently and stronger, much stronger. Quinn helped her up from bed and told her to walk around. To get her mind off the pain and fear, he talked to her. Now he assured her that all would be well, that he knew what to do because he had seen cattle and pigs give birth. It was a comparison she did not appreciate in the least. But having him there helped despite his inept chatter.

The contractions continued to escalate and a few hours later, the membranes ruptured and the bag of waters broke. After that, Quinn made Midori stay in bed but encouraged her to change positions regularly. Although internally Quinn was going crazy, he endeavored to project a calming influence, doing what he could to help her relax. Labor is work, demanding work and she had a lot of it ahead of her.

The hours dragged on, one into the next and it seemed like it would never end. Quinn made certain Midori did not hyperventilate or dehydrate. He showered her with praise, applied and reapplied a cool, damp cloth to her face and hands, and rubbed her back in a gentle, unhurried massage. He did anything he thought might help. Sometimes she liked it, other times not. But he took no offence when she ordered him to shut up or not to touch her. She was the one in charge and he followed her changing demands without question or grievance.

Weeks earlier, Quinn had built a bar over the bed in anticipation of the delivery. Midori used it for support, crouching in a semi-sitting position. The intent was to take full advantage of what help gravity would provide. She pushed and pushed, to no avail. Exhaustion threatened to overwhelm her. She was becoming disoriented and discouraged.

"I can't do it!" Midori panted heavily, weak with fatigue. "I can't push any more. It's never coming out. Let me sleep. Please let me sleep."

"Come on, don't give up," encouraged Quinn. "You're almost there. Look how much progress you've made. You can't give up now. Besides, I don't think it works that way; I don't think Keenan will let you quit. Come on, honey, one more time. Push!"

She did, again and again. During the delivery and like a leaf blown through the air by a strong breeze, Quinn was carried on a wild ride of erratic emotion, spinning and turning out of control. At times his heart ached with sympathy that Midori had to work so hard and that it seemed to hurt so badly. Then pity would suddenly escalate into terror that Midori might die or be seriously injured during childbirth. Other times when things appeared to be progressing well, Quinn felt intensely proud to be a part, albeit a relatively minor part, of this glorious miracle. And he was so very proud of Midori, impressed by the strength she had to have to persevere in the face of such great pain. Pointlessly, he wished that he could take her pain upon himself, and wondered if he would be able to tolerate it as well as she. Hope and love welled within him as he looked forward to all the joys that parenthood would bring and to the happy prospect of sharing them with Midori.

Again and again, Midori continued to push. Then, the pressure became tremendous, carrying with it a powerful stretching, stinging, and burning sensation. Quinn saw the baby's head crown.

"There's the head! I can see the top of its head," exclaimed Quinn. "The hard part's nearly over. Keep pushing. You're almost done."

Energized by the prospect of completion, Midori continued to push with renewed vigor. The head finally emerged and Quinn quickly cleared the mucus from its nose and mouth. He then helped ease the baby out, deftly maneuvering the small shoulders through the cavity.

Now, as the baby made its entry into the world, the heaviest rush of emotion hit Quinn. His heart lifted with unbridled amazement at witnessing the emergence of a new life. The sight of the baby, healthy and strong, produced a buoyant current of elation on which Quinn's spirits rose to unprecedented heights. He was gripped with such astounding emotion, feelings he thought lost forever or he never knew existed within him. It was all so beautiful and overwhelming; so much so that he began to cry. There was beauty not only in the purity and optimism of this new life but also in the way in which Midori delivered him, her strength and courage, and the love between them all.

The cord was cut. Midori fell back upon the bed, weary but ecstatic. And Quinn held a new and wondrous life cupped within his palms.

Gazing down upon the child, Quinn felt his heart swell ten times its normal size. As one grows older, life tends to harden the heart a little bit every day, numbing it with pain and disappointment, leaving the individual cynical and callous to some degree. Even a good man like Quinn loses some of the optimism and gentleness of youth. The effect of this loss was instantly undone as Quinn's heart was reborn with the birth of the child. A lifetime of disillusionment was washed away the moment he was certain both Midori and Keenan were all right. Cleansed, he was swept into a sea of sentimental bliss, feeling the purity of good, wholesome emotions with greater depth and intensity than he had since he himself was a child.

Their lives were irrevocably changed from that point on. But after about a month, they settled comfortably into their new routine. Midori and baby Keenan recovered nicely from the ordeal. All were happy, and love flourished on their mountainside. What might be happening at Gairloch or in the rest of the world was a mystery to them, a mystery they chose to ignore. They had each other and that was enough. It was all they wanted.

The End

Epilogue

In Gairloch, a peril to the world had taken seed and was growing larger by the day. Torrin was awake, hungry, and so much mightier now that the sorcerous hibernation was over. He had emerged from his slumber, having completely assimilated the accumulated magic of the slain Prelature.

Reveling in his new unequalled strength as a wizard, Torrin lounged upon the throne that was once reserved for the archprelate. He was alone. The hall was empty of all other life. Already his stolen axe had been recovered and returned to Torrin. Leaning against the throne beside him, the axe hummed with latent power; its metal blades gleamed with the promise of death.

Lazily, he stared at a huge marble pillar, one magnificently sculpted in the image of a human male. With an almost effortless concentration, Torrin used his inflated magic to alter the pillar's shape. The marble wavered and moved, changing its form into that of a grotesque gargoyle. Torrin smiled at the ease of it, thinking how in time he would just as easily change the face of the world to suit his whim and to serve his will. Torrin's heart burned with a desire for power, darker and more intense than any other emotion he had ever known. He convinced himself that the world and all its people were created solely for his amusement, produced only for him to dominate.

"I hate the world, and yet I want to take possession of it all," Torrin thought out loud. "The acquisition and exercise of power is the greatest pleasure. Power is the one and only thing of value in all the universe. There is only one form of success. Power. Only it provides pleasure or makes pleasure possible. It is real and productive, not debilitating fantasy, like love or friendship.

Quinn—you deserter, I have not forgotten you. I will find and punish you for your cowardly, mutinous act. Only complete obedience will be rewarded; anything less will suffer my wrath. And Aragon, I know you're out there somewhere. You're plotting against me, no doubt. I will find you too. Your life shall serve to further empower me.

"I shall not allow Gairloch to become a cage for me. I shall reign free over all the world," he avowed. A furious passion and a cruel reason fueled Torrin's malevolent plan to surpass and subdue the world. "My hatred serves as motivation toward the gratification of my desire, my desire for power. And power is nothing if not used to dominate. Through the domination of others, I will be exalted. We take the strength of what we defeat. Power is the fulfillment of life's potential; domination is perfection. And power built purely on self-interest will last forever.

"Let them despise me," continued Torrin. "Let them think me immoral. As long as fools cling to their misguided ideals of justice and morality, they will be weak and defenseless. There is no such thing as justice, here or in the afterworld. Weakness is evil, as is all that it produces. Power makes right and by power, I shall be made a god. The wealth of a man's soul is measured in his power and his ability to use it. There is nothing divine except he who effectively and selfishly wields power to dominate. Blessed is the influence I exert in acquiring strength by defeating others.

"The only man that is wise enough to have power is he who is willing to take it and to use it," explained Torrin to an empty room. "To possess others is to live freely and nobly. Great is the soul that is free, with freedom won through the exercise of power. And the only freedom worth promoting is my own. Life is a constant state of conflict, a perpetual struggle to dominate; and to be moderate in this struggle would be the act of a fool. War. War is the crowning achievement of wisdom, the highest, best use of one's intellect. One's strength grows out of conquest. I shall have total control, absolute power, true omnipotence. I am the Beast, and I am hungry. Tremble at my warning, for I see the world and I want it all!"

Printed in the United States
38461LVS00003B/32

9 781413 773002